THE
MIND'S
EYE

THE MIND'S EYE

Christopher G. Nuttall

Elsewhen Press

The Mind's Eye
First published in Great Britain by Elsewhen Press, 2014
An imprint of Alnpete Limited

Elsewhen Press, PO Box 757, Dartford, Kent DA2 7TQ
elsewhen.press

British Library Cataloguing in Publication Data.
A catalogue record for this book is available from the British Library.

ISBN 978-1-908168-47-4 Print edition
ISBN 978-1-908168-57-3 eBook edition

Designed and formatted by Elsewhen Press

To my sisters, Elspeth and Catherine

Chapter One

...In pursuit of Operation Soaring Eagle, US Marines are apparently carrying out operations in an unspecified country. They're not giving anything away tonight, folks.

-AP News Report, 2015

"It's quiet," Gunnery Sergeant David Bass muttered. "It's too quiet."

Lieutenant Art Russell swallowed several responses that came to mind, none of which were very helpful. The twenty-four Force Recon Marines had spent the last few hours walking from the Forward Operating Base to the small complex up ahead, hoping that the insurgents – Taliban, terrorists or simply drug runners – wouldn't notice the advancing American force. The locals were thoroughly cowed by the enemy and, despite the presence of most of the 1st Marine Division, weren't inclined to offer aid and comfort to the Americans. Art couldn't blame them. The day the Marines had moved into the area, a local headman and his family had been beheaded by the Taliban – the women had been raped first, according to the locals – as a warning to others who might be considering assisting the enemy. The Marines couldn't count on any help and, if a local who had a cell phone saw them, he might just call them in to the enemy.

He rubbed his forehead, cursing the headache that had appeared several hours after they'd departed the base and made their way towards the small cluster of buildings. A person who had never seen Afghanistan would not believe that it could get so hot, but Art – who had served two terms in Iraq – had rarely been in a hotter country. The heat beat down on the Marines, sending rivers of sweat running down their backs, despite the latest cooling battledress. His aching head was just another problem. He should have called it in, he knew, and allowed someone else to take his place, but he was no quitter. Besides, calling for a helicopter to evacuate him back to the FOB would have blown their cover. The NATO forces in the area had been quietly placed on alert to support the Marines if they needed it, yet they'd been told to stay away from the complex. The last thing they needed was to alert the High Value Target – HVT – who was supposed to be based there.

"No argument," Art muttered back. The small complex – nine small buildings and one large warehouse, clearly built during the Soviet occupation of Afghanistan – appeared deserted, at least from the outside. But then, it was dangerous to assume that proved anything. The Taliban had a reasonable idea of just how good the American surveillance and communications systems actually were and knew better than to show their faces without good cause. A seemingly deserted building might hold an entire enemy unit, hidden away under cover. Or maybe the locals had abandoned the area after the Russians had pulled out and left it alone. Afghanistan was a land of contradictions, where timeless beauty went hand-in-hand with mindless brutality and enough barbarity to make a Roman Emperor sick. "Spread out and check the area. My spider-sense is tingling."

Bass nodded wordlessly and used his hands to signal to the other Marines, who slowly started to creep out around the buildings. If they were seen, a fire-fight would break out almost at once, but the Force Recon troops were expert in operating without being seen. They'd trained against opposition forces with night-vision gear and the latest in remote sensing equipment, although they'd also trained in low-tech environments. The Marine Corps had been in the forefront of counter-insurgency campaigns for a long time and knew that a low-tech environment could be just as dangerous as a high-tech environment, perhaps more so. There were too many people in the rear who would refuse to believe in the existence of an enemy force if it wasn't radiating radio or cell phone transmissions, but the Marines on the ground knew better. The enemy could be anywhere, or anyone.

The headache refused to fade as the reports came back through his earpiece. The Marines used a subvocal communications system to allow them to talk to one another without being overheard, or detected by any means the Taliban were known to possess. Art had never taken that for granted; the Russians or the Chinese might well have sold them some advanced detection gear, perhaps calculating that the longer the Americans stayed bogged down in Afghanistan, the greater the opportunity they'd have to reshape their regions to their own best advantage. The Russians hated the Taliban, but if they were willing to get into bed with the Nazis, they'd probably be willing to get into bed with the Taliban as well. His lips quirked into an amused smile as he contemplated the mental image for a long moment and then shook his head, dismissing the thought. Headache or no headache, he had a job to do.

"The snipers are in position," Bass said, as he crawled back to where Art was waiting. He gave the Lieutenant a concerned look as he settled up next to him. The NCO had over twenty-five years of experience in the Marine Corps – he'd taken out plenty of green lieutenants before and saved them from making stupid and career-ending mistakes – and he could probably sense that something was wrong. "There's still no sign of…"

"*Contact*," one of the snipers hissed. Art froze at once, feeling his body and mind jerk into overdrive. The absence of gunshots probably meant that they hadn't been spotted, but the enemy could be playing it cute. "I have four jingly trucks on their way up to the complex, each one carrying at least twelve bearded men."

Art and Bass shared a glance. The Taliban, among the other bizarre rules they had fought to impose on Afghanistan, insisted that every man should have a beard – and jailed everyone who refused to grow one. The presence of beards meant nothing in and of itself, but there were no Afghanistan National Army or Afghanistan National Police units in the area. Anyone coming to the complex was almost certainly hostile. The presence of so many men suggested that they had something else in mind than a social visit. Did they intend to escort the HVT out of the area?

He frowned as he pulled his terminal out of his belt and accessed the direct feed from the orbiting UAV, so high up that no one, even Bass, could see that it was there. The trucks had been tracked as soon as they'd entered the area, coming out of no man's land to the south, towards Pakistan. It was another strike against them. Anything crossing from

Pakistan to Afghanistan should have been declared at the border, but then no one would bother unless they were stopped at gunpoint. Art found it hard to blame them. Years ago, someone in the West had drawn arbitrary lines on a map and separated Afghanistan from Pakistan – it had been part of India at the time – and torn tribes and families in half. The tribesmen refused to accept the border as possessing any influence on their lives and crossed it freely, creating lines of communication that could be used by the Taliban and their supporters. Afghanistan was a witches' brew of factions, each one determined to see that they came out on top, with NATO in the middle.

Bass tapped his side. "Sir," he muttered, as the trucks came into view. "Look!"

Art followed his gaze. The large building at the centre of the complex had suddenly come to life. Seven men had appeared at one side of the building, one of them very familiar. Mullah Mohammed, as he called himself, had a sizable price on his head for terrorism and other crimes against humanity. He was, at least as far as NATO intelligence could put together, the Taliban's district commander, with control over terrorist groups and cells in the entire region. He'd been marked for capture or death as soon as NATO had identified him, but no one had tracked him down, until now. He watched as men leapt off the trucks and embraced their comrades. The Marines were heavily outnumbered, yet Art found it hard to care. They had the greatest weapon of all on their side. No one suspected their presence.

He keyed his radio, taking care to keep his voice below hearing level. The tiny mike on his throat would pick up the words and transmit it to the waiting Marines. "Get ready to move," he ordered, scanning the remaining enemy fighters as they clambered out of the truck. They moved rather unprofessionally, part of his mind noted; they clearly weren't expecting trouble. His headache seemed to grow worse every time he looked at one of the enemy fighters, so he tried to look away from them. He verified his equipment with one hand as the Marines checked in, the snipers leading the way. The enemy, nicely bunched up as they were, would provide easy targets for the sharpshooters. Even the Taliban had learned to fear the NATO snipers. "I'm calling the contact in now."

Art tapped his terminal, sending the call to arms back to the Marine FOB ten miles to the north, and then checked his weapon one final time. The attack helicopters would be spinning up their rotors now, preparing to come out and join the fun; the transport helicopters, carrying additional Marines, would be right after them. The fighters and bombers NATO kept orbiting over the area – a mixture of American, British, French, German and Dutch aircraft – would be receiving the alert seconds later. A thunderstorm was gathering and it was about to pour itself down onto the unsuspecting terrorists. They had no idea what was coming their way.

He keyed his radio again. "Go," he ordered. His headache sparked and he winced in pain. Bass frowned, but said nothing. "Open fire."

The snipers opened fire at once. They were used to firing from much greater ranges than they were faced with and the enemy fighters didn't stand a chance. One by one, the terrorists started to topple over before they realised that they were under attack, the ones who had been identified as commanders going first. A handful started to blaze back towards the snipers with AK-47 rifles, but their bursts went wide of the mark. The Marine Corps trained its snipers well and armed them with the best; there was literally no flash for the enemy to use as a target. The smarter enemy fighters – including the Mullah, Art noted absently – had ducked back into the complex, trusting in its Russian-built walls to protect them from enemy fire. They were probably right. The Russians might have deliberately built ugly and soulless buildings – the true nature of communism could be seen in the buildings the communists had gifted their unwilling allies – but they were strong and certainly resistant to sniper fire. A single air-dropped bomb would smash the building, of course, yet there would be no chance of taking the HVT alive.

Art swallowed a curse as enemy fighters began firing from the buildings. Their shooting wasn't particularly accurate, thankfully, but it was making life interesting for the snipers and the other men, who were crawling closer and closer to their targets. His radio buzzed with a report of four men who had attempted to escape from the other side of the building, only to run into fire from the three Marines who were advancing on the enemy rear. The four men were dead and the Marines had the remaining enemy forces trapped. A smart enemy commander would have offered to surrender, but the Taliban rarely surrendered, even when their enemy wouldn't simply kill them out of hand. Afghanistan's warrior mentality bred tough fighters. The ones who learned to think like true soldiers were formidable opponents.

He picked himself up and half-ran down towards the complex, while the snipers provided covering fire from their positions. Now that every enemy soldier in the open was dead, the snipers had started to fire into the buildings, aiming their shots through portholes that had been used as enemy firing positions. The snipers who saw their opponents could shoot them, perhaps even kill them, even when they were firing from cover. The ones who couldn't see their targets directly could still discourage the enemy from firing by shooting a handful of shots through the portholes. Who knew – perhaps the ricochets would take out an enemy fighter or two.

A deafening explosion echoed across the compound as one of the trucks blew up. Art's radio buzzed a second later, filling him in; the enemy had attempted to use one of them as a firing position, so a Marine had tossed a grenade into the vehicle. The force of the explosion suggested that the truck had been transporting explosives and ammunition to the Taliban in the area, ammunition that would be turned against the Marines and the remainder of the NATO forces. The Marine who had tossed the grenade was uninjured, but stunned, so Art ordered him to stay back until he had recovered. His headache was growing worse…

He pressed himself against the side of one of the smaller buildings, certain – somehow – that there were still enemy forces inside. There was only one way into the building – through the door – and he cursed under his breath. The enemy would have to know that, because no one larger than a child could fit through the portholes that passed for windows. The Taliban had been known to use children as suicide bombers – sometimes knowingly, sometimes without telling them what was at stake – and Art kept one eye on the window, even as he pulled a grenade off his belt. Bass caught his arm and shook his head, motioning for two of the junior Marines to lead the way. Art wanted to swear at him – if something happened to Art, Bass was perfectly capable of running the entire force on his own – but there was no time for an argument. The lead Marine held up five fingers and counted down, while the others prepared their grenades. At zero, they tossed their grenades through the window and explosions shattered the door. A moment later, the Marines were through the remains of the door, weapons raised and looking for trouble. There were seven enemy bodies in the room and one living enemy fighter, who Art suspected rather wished he was dead. His legs had been blown off and he was bleeding badly from a gash in his left arm.

His radio buzzed as the Marines reported in. The smaller buildings had been cleared of the enemy – at a cost; two Marines had been injured as they struggled to escape the trap – but the large building was still occupied. Art scowled as the Marines reformed outside the building, readying themselves for the final assault. There was no time to waste. The Mullah might, like several other Taliban leaders had done, take his own life when he realised that there was no way to escape. Art hated the Taliban for what they did in order to fight their way, yet even he had to respect such an act. It didn't change the problem, however; the Marines needed to take him alive, if possible.

Bass glanced at him and then used hand-signals to get the Marines ready for an assault. The longer the enemy had to get ready to fight, the harder it was going to be to clear the building. The snipers could keep the enemy away from the windows, but they'd have plenty of room inside to manoeuvre, particularly if they'd prepared the building for an attack. The Marines had looked for any details they could find on the interior of the building, but they'd found nothing. The Russians had claimed that the files had been lost. Who knew – they might even be telling the truth.

Art gritted his teeth against the headache and nodded, signalling for the assault to begin. One Marine used shaped charges to blow down the door; two more threw grenades into the opening, attempting to kill the enemy before they could pick off the incoming Marines. There was a brief burst of machine gun fire, a pair of explosions and the fire dropped off sharply. The Marines slipped through the door, weapons raised, and opened fire when they saw four more enemy fighters lifting their own guns. A hail of fire from above pinned down two Marines before a third fired a long burst up the stairs and silenced the enemy gunner. Art, Bass and two other Marines advanced to a door, threw in three grenades and followed them into the room: it was deserted.

The interior of the building was a dark nightmarish maze. Art pressed onwards, feeling his headache pounding inside his skull. From time to time, an enemy fighter would pop out of hiding, scream *Allah Ackbar* and open fire, forcing the Marines to gun him down before he could find his bearings. The enemy didn't seem to have scattered IEDs through the building, thankfully, but they were successfully delaying the Marines. God alone knew where the Mullah and his inner circle had gone. Art had kept his bearings, yet he had no idea how one part of the massive building related to the others.

A burst of firing up ahead concentrated his mind on staying alive. The enemy had taken up a strong position in the semi-darkness, using a Russian machine gun to force the Marines to stay back, by firing from time to time. Art struggled to locate them, straining every sense he had as he listened for sounds of movement in-between the bursts of fire and…

…Something *snapped* in his head. A torrent of noise, of screaming and shouting, poured into his mind. He barely heard Bass calling his name as the pain worsened and the noise grew louder. His head seemed to explode as he screamed, feeling blood trickling down from his nose and ears…

…And then he collapsed into blackness.

Chapter Two

...Marine forces today captured an unnamed High Value Target and several of his principal supporters in a daring raid on an enemy compound. A spokesman for the USMC commended Lieutenant Russell and Sergeant Bass for their actions during the raid. Lieutenant Russell was injured during the fighting and was transferred to a NATO base in Afghanistan.

-AP News Report, 2015

His mind hurt.

Art wasn't sure if he was awake or asleep, alive or dead. There was a dull roaring at the back of his mind, a nightmarish roar of static, with words he thought he could hear if he listened closely, yet the mere act of trying to listen only made the pain worse. He thought he could hear Bass's voice, and that of a young female doctor, yet there was no way he could pull out individual words. It crossed his mind that he might be in Hell and, somehow, that thought gave him the ability to open his eyes. A bright light was pouring down from high overhead and he cried out as it stabbed deep into his mind. A second later, the light was switched off and he almost gasped in relief. It had simply been too much to bear.

"It's all right," a voice said. Art was suddenly certain that it was *not* all right. "Can you understand me?"

Art recoiled. The voice had been young and female – and therefore interesting, because he hadn't seen a woman he'd been allowed to talk to since going on deployment – but there were waves of communication in her words. His head was buzzing with pain, yet he could pick out that the woman had lied to him. Everything was very definitely not all right.

"Yes," he said, finally. It took several tries to get the word out and then it sounded rather dull and atonal in his ears. Her voice was laden with meaning; his was just...his voice. "What happened to me?"

Knowledge crashed into his skull and he almost cried out again. He'd *fainted* in combat, simply collapsed while advancing on an enemy position. His memories were blurred, but he recalled the headache and the final moments when he'd been struggling to locate and identify the enemy…and then there had been nothing, apart from darkness. It had almost been a relief. Bass had taken command, called in the medics from the helicopters that had swooped down to provide fire support for the Force Recon troops and arranged for him to be evacuated all the way back to the Heathe Craig Joint Theater Hospital, at Bagram Airfield.

"You've been evacuated back here," the nurse said. He twisted his head until he could look up at her. She was very pretty, with dark hair tied up into a bun and a nice – if worried – smile. Art would have tried to chat her up if he'd come under other business, but something told him that she wouldn't be interested. Just looking at her seemed to make the noises in his mind grow louder. It dawned on him, suddenly, that he knew what had happened, even though she hadn't told him anything significant. "You're fine, really."

Art grunted as he tried to sit up. A burst of pain seemed to blast through his skull and he fell back onto the sheets. The nurse – her name was Marian, he realised, somehow – reached out and touched his arm. Art almost screamed again. Her touch wasn't unpleasant – far from it; it was the first touch of a woman's hand in months – but the roar in his head grew louder. Marian recoiled herself, surprised at how she'd affected him. The instant she took her hand off him, the pain in his head receded.

"I think I'd better get the doctor," Marian said. Art shook his head. "No; you gave us a nasty fright when we brought you in and we don't want to lose you to something unexplained…"

"Marian…please don't call the doctor," Art said, before he could stop himself. "I'm fine, really I am."

Marian stared at him. "How do you know my name?"

Art stared back at her. How *had* he known her name? She wasn't wearing a nametag or anything else that could be used to identify her; he'd just somehow reached out and pulled her name from somewhere. The roar in his head seemed to fade away into whispering voices as he concentrated, voices that spoke of worry and pain and fear. Somehow, Art knew that he didn't dare say that out loud.

"I had a friend who went into care here," he said, lying. "He told me that the prettiest nurse in the centre was called Marian."

Marian flushed. "And so you decided to call me Marian," she said. She thought of him as a jerk, he knew, somehow. He couldn't blame her for that, even though the roar in his head was growing louder again. "Once you get better, I am going to slap you silly."

A few days ago, Art would have laughed, or joked about being a masochist, or maybe even being so desperate for a woman's touch that he didn't mind being slapped. Now…now he just wanted time on his own, time to think and work out what had happened to him. He couldn't have pulled it right out of her mind, could he?

"I look forward to it," Art said. He smiled at her, as best as he could. "I'll give you a call if it gets any worse, I promise."

Marian gave him one final doubting look and walked off, going to tend to the other patients in the centre. Art settled back on his bed and started to think. She hadn't told him her name, or anything particularly useful, but he'd known the moment he posed the question. The dull roar in his head, like having a radio set programmed to switch between random channels, seemed to be fading away, yet somehow he knew that it would always be there. Sleep seemed impossible, not with the fascinating mystery confronting him, but somehow he dozed off. When he awakened, it was the middle of the night and a different nurse was on duty. She was tending to one of the other patients, yet the moment he looked at her, he knew that she was called Dolly and that she was in love with an officer from the other side of the airfield.

Art concentrated hard, remembering meditation tricks his sister had told him about, back when she'd been dating a Buddhist Monk. The more he concentrated and calmed his mind, the clearer the voices in his head became. He looked over at Dolly and suddenly the voices grew much louder and clearer. She was thinking about her lover, and about how she used her mouth on his penis to make him come and … Art recoiled, horrified. There no longer seemed any room for doubt. He was reading her mind. She shouldn't be thinking about her boyfriend while she was at work. He pulled a name out of her head – Peter – and smiled to himself. It would be fairly simple to test his theory. He waved at Dolly and she came over to him, checking the computer placed by his bed.

"Dolly," he said. It was hard to look at her now that he knew one of her most intimate secrets. "Would you like to go to dinner when I get out of this pit?"

Dolly shook her head. "I'm dating a lovely young man called Peter," she said, with a wink. Her forthright attitude made him smile. "He's popped the question and...well, I am keeping him waiting for a few days, as my mother advised."

Art nodded to himself. Her words seemed to shimmer in his head, carrying impressions of her innermost thoughts. She was telling the truth; she truly loved the young man and wanted to marry him, even though she was delaying things just to prolong his agony. Her memories started to shade back towards their last few days together and he looked away, but somehow they kept pouring into his head. He was starting to realise that being a mind-reader – and it seemed impossible that he could be anything else now – wasn't all it was cracked up to be.

"Good for you," he said. He was tempted to ask her more questions, but manfully resisted the temptation. "What happened to me?"

Dolly, unlike her predecessor, didn't seem inclined to hide anything from him. "You collapsed while in combat," she said, flatly. "The preliminary tests suggested that you had fainted, but the doctors noticed that you had some unusual brain activity and decided to transfer you here while you were thoroughly out of it. They were talking about sending you back to the States when you woke up."

Art blinked. "What kind of unusual brain activity?"

"I guess a jarhead like you wouldn't know what it meant to be actually thinking," Dolly said. It was the first falsehood she'd told. Her superiors were concerned about Art's condition, more concerned than they were prepared to admit, at least to him. It was just like doctors, in his experience; they cared more about their superiors than about their patient's concerns. "How are you feeling now?"

Art considered the question seriously. Now he knew what was happening, the pain was fading away, although the static in his head refused to vanish completely. When he closed his eyes, Dolly was a nexus of thoughts and feelings standing in front of him, viewed through the mind's eye. He could tell the doctors what had happened…and then, he suspected, he'd end up being treated like a lab rat, dissected to see what made him tick. He'd certainly never be able to return to his unit.

"Much better, thank you," he said, finally. It was the truth, in a way; he knew what was going on and could deal with it. "I'll see about getting back to my unit in the morning."

Dolly wasn't pretending to be shocked. "You're staying here for at least a week," she said, firmly. There was no give in her at all. "You collapsed while in combat. You need to be checked properly before you're allowed back into the line of fire."

Art nodded, rolled over and pretended to go back to sleep. Dolly walked off, her thoughts fading away the further she walked, and Art allowed himself a moment of relief. He knew, without looking, that there were four other patients in the room, all rather more seriously injured than him. One of the four was a British Para, who'd been wounded while chasing a group of Taliban fighters through their hideout; the others were asleep, dreaming unpleasant dreams. They were broadcasting mental waves towards him, he decided; they were the source of the static in his mind.

"Damn it," he muttered to himself. "What do I do now?"

A thought occurred to him and he returned to meditation. A trick he'd picked up back when he'd been a recruit back at Parris Island had been to snatch sleep whenever he had a spare moment. By combining the two … sleep overwhelmed him and he fell into darkness. The night wasn't a pleasant one – he realised at some level that he was tapping into other people's nightmares as well as his own – but at least he managed to sleep. In the morning, there was a third nurse, a young black girl. Art had half-hoped that it had been a dream, but he could read her thoughts as clearly as he could read those of the other nurses. A thought occurred to him and he tried to beam his thoughts into her mind, yet nothing happened. It was, he decided, probably for the best.

The first three days of his imprisonment – as he soon came to think of it – passed slowly. The doctors came and visited him, putting him through all kinds of tests, which turned up nothing. The unusual brain activity they'd told Dolly about was still present, but they didn't have any idea what it actually meant and – perhaps luckily – they didn't ask Art if *he* knew what it meant. It turned out that, by slipping into meditation, Art could effectively turn off the telepathy for the tests, reducing the brain activity to almost nothing. One of the doctors suspected that he was doing it on purpose, but the others refused to take his thoughts seriously. Art kept his mouth shut and waited impatiently for them to clear him for duty. His unit was engaged against the Taliban – the capture of the wanted Mullah had clearly stirred up a hornet's nest – and he wanted to rejoin them. It was his duty.

On the fourth day, he received a visitor.

"I understand that you've been lollygagging around in bed, you lazy bastard," Lieutenant Chad Dexter said. Art felt his mouth fall open with a mixture of amusement and outrage. Dexter had been an old friend from Parris Island, but after they'd qualified as Marines Dexter had gone in for Marine Combat Training before qualifying as an Explosive Ordnance Disposal technician and being deployed to Iraq, and then Afghanistan. It wasn't a duty Art envied him. Bomb disposal was the most dangerous task in the war. "Get out of bed and we'll go get some chow."

"Thank the Lord," Art said. "What are you doing here anyway, you retard from Hell?"

Dexter opened his mouth, but before he could speak the answer flowed into Art's mind. He'd been assigned to clearing IEDs from the nearby area, and then deployed in support of Ranger operations to the west. Art shivered and fought hard to control his mind. It hadn't occurred to him – and it should have done – that he'd be able to read the minds of his friends as well as his enemies and random encounters. It felt as if he had violated Dexter somehow and the fact that his friend would never know the truth didn't change it. He'd been treating it as a game, poking into the minds surrounding him, but now…the full nature of what he'd done hit him.

"Art?" Dexter sounded worried, as if his voice was coming from a far distance. "Art – are you all right?"

"Yes," Art growled, cursing himself for the display of weakness. It would probably convince the doctors to keep him in bed for another few weeks. "I'm fine and I'm coming..."

He pulled himself out of bed, reached for his uniform and donned it quickly, before checking his sidearm out of habit. The airbase had been attacked before he'd been deployed to Afghanistan and everyone on the base was supposed to pack heat, even when off duty. Art privately suspected that some of the REMFs on the base were more dangerous to their own side than to the enemy, but it hardly mattered. If the Taliban risked an attack in force, it would be touted as a victory by the enemy, even if they were wiped out to the last man.

The hot air struck him as soon as they stepped outside the hospital and he recoiled, gathering himself before he could continue onwards towards the chow hall. The airbase was the size of a small town, complete with American restaurants and other entertainments. The chances were good, Dexter informed him with an evil wink, that some of the female personnel on the base were running a prostitution ring, although that was strictly against regulations and they'd be punished severely if they were found out. Art found it hard to care. It had been too long since he'd been with a woman and they had strict orders not to even think about trying to chat up the local women. Besides, he had always found the heavily-veiled Afghani women to be more than a little creepy.

"We'll go to KFC," Dexter said. Art didn't bother to argue. "They do meal deals for soldiers from the front lines."

"How respectful of them," Art said, as they stepped into the building. "You'd better order and..."

He broke off. Coming into the KFC had been a mistake. There were over fifty people in the room, all broadcasting their thoughts and feelings into the air. Art's head spun and, for a moment, he was on the verge of blacking out again. Dexter didn't seem to notice, but Art knew...and fought hard to control his mind. It seemed impossible to prevent the thoughts slicing into his mind and tearing his world apart. If he couldn't learn how to control the ability, he realised bitterly, he would have to live a secluded life. It was the only way he could have any peace.

And then he sensed it. It was another nexus of thoughts and feelings, but one brimming with hatred and deadly intent. His head snapped up and he started to look around, trying to locate the source of the hatred. His eyes settled on a local contractor, one wearing a suspiciously large local robe, who was pressing his way into the middle of the crowd. The anticipation in his mind sparked higher and Art realised, with a shudder of terrifying horror, what was about to happen. He drew his weapon with lightning-quick reflexes and pointed it directly at the contractor.

"Hands in the air," he shouted. The contractor's eyes opened wide with anger and then his hands snapped down towards his belt. Art didn't hesitate. He fired twice, putting two shots right through the man's head. As his body collapsed to the ground, the robe tore, revealing a suicide belt. Dexter dropped the chicken nuggets on the ground and dived for the bomb, disarming it before it could explode. Art, his mind reeling from the sense of death, stumbled and fell towards the ground.

The MPs arrived and took control of the scene. Art wanted nothing more than to stumble away and think, but he found himself collared by one of the MPs. He was a bluff aggressive man; someone – Art guessed – who had been rejected by the front-line forces. The moment his skin touched Art's, there was another burst of thoughts and feelings, but they were too jumbled up to make any sense.

"Good work, Marine," the MP said. "How did you know?"

Art took a breath and confessed. "I read his mind."

Chapter Three

*...An attempted suicide bombing at Bagram Airfield
was foiled by the quick reactions of a Marine
Lieutenant who had been repatriated to the airfield to
recuperate after being injured while on active duty.
The bomber was a man who bribed his way onto the
base's workforce and smuggled a suicide belt into the
base over the preceding week. The bomber was killed
and no one else was hurt.*

-AP News Report, 2015

He wasn't formally under arrest, but it felt very much like prison.

Art looked around the small apartment for what felt like the thousandth time and tried to relax. The MPs hadn't believed him, of course, so he'd demonstrated his ability to their leader. Their leader had taken him to the base CO, who *also* hadn't believed him, but had handed him over to the local CIA officer once Art had finally managed to convince him. The CIA officer, whose mind had lit up with a curious mixture of anticipation and fear, had ordered Art transported home by the shortest possible route. That had turned out to be one of the CIA's classified rendition flights, which had also been transporting several prisoners the Marines had taken in their recent raids. Art had stayed away from the prisoners – the hatred radiating from their minds had poisoned the atmosphere around them – and tried to sleep. It hadn't come easily.

He rubbed his rear as he picked up the book and tried to concentrate on it. After arriving in the United States, he'd been transported further inland, towards what he was starting to suspect was a secret CIA installation. In hindsight, it seemed very likely that the CIA would want to make use of a telepath, if they actually managed to get their hands on him. He had found himself seriously considering trying to break out and escape – the CIA might just want to dissect him, just to find out what made his telepathy work – but a quick check had revealed that the door was not only locked, but secure. There was no other way out of the apartment.

The one blessing, as far as he was concerned, was that he was alone. He'd tried hard, but he hadn't been able to shut down his telepathy; the best he could do was reduce the static that blared through his mind every time someone came close to him. There was no background noise now, thankfully; he couldn't even sense someone on the other side of the door. He suspected that he was being observed through hidden cameras – he'd searched the apartment on general principles, but found nothing – and he was tempted to do something unspeakably rude just to upset the watchers. Instead, he forced himself to read another chapter of his book. The CIA officer back at the airfield had given him a box of paperbacks a publisher had sent out for the troops, although Art wasn't sure if they were a gift or a loan. He shook his head at the thought. The books had been sent out to the troops in the field and he'd send them back to the Marines when he had a chance.

They'd taken his watch when he'd entered the compound, along with his cell phone and holstered pistol, but Art had always had a good time sense. He'd been in the apartment for over four hours, just waiting for the CIA to decide what to do with him. Irritated, he looked over at the bed and shower, something that struck him as almost sinfully luxurious after the harsh conditions of Afghanistan. Perhaps he'd take a nap – all soldiers learned to sleep when they had a chance – and wait for something to happen. He wasn't in any physical danger, or so he told himself. Unfortunately, the paranoid part of his mind refused to believe him.

***

Alice Spencer looked down at the file in front of her and then up at the computer screen, which was showing the live feed from the hidden camera in the observation suite. Lieutenant Russell could hardly be described as handsome, she decided after a moment, not after his face had been rearranged during a bout at Parris Island. On the other hand, there was a certain rugged charm in his features and her last boyfriend, an over-paid pretty boy, had cheated on her twice and then run off with one of her girlfriends. There was something to be said for a man who wasn't full of himself.

She looked back down at the file and shook her head slowly. Alice had no direct military experience – she'd only graduated from training a year ago and had been assigned to Project Looking Glass because she'd come in near the bottom of the class – but the file was very impressive. Lieutenant Russell had joined the Marines as an enlisted man – whatever that meant – and had been at the top of his class at Parris Island. Deployed to Iraq as part of the Surge, he'd been commended for heroism in the face of the enemy three times and reprimanded for being insubordinate once. The Marine Corps hadn't worried about the latter; he'd been encouraged to become a commissioned officer after taking command of a mixed platoon when the senior officer had been badly wounded during a battle in downtown Baghdad. The Marine Corps would be sorry to lose him.

It probably wouldn't matter anyway, she knew. The really interesting part, at least as far as she was concerned, was that Lieutenant Russell had scored highly on the Zeller Test, a test that was administered to everyone who joined the United States Armed Forces, regardless of the branch. He should have been recruited for Project Looking Glass instead of being allowed to deploy, but apparently he'd turned down the offer of stateside duty and his superiors had backed him up. And now he'd turned into a telepath. Alice felt the first stirrings of genuine excitement as she read through the report that the officer in Afghanistan had hastily cobbled together. The CIA had always had its doubts about the Zeller Test, yet it couldn't be a coincidence that a person who'd scored highly on the test had turned into a telepath. The test had been designed to measure psychic powers, after all.

"Psychic potential," her superiors had said, when she'd been assigned to Project Looking Glass. Looking Glass was a tiny operation within the CIA, not least because Congress refused to fund it openly, fearing that they would be turned into a laughing stock. Some results had been interesting and terrifying; more often, the project seemed to be permanently on the verge of failure. "A person who scores highly on the test may never develop anything we can actually use."

Alice sucked in her breath as she stood up, knowing that she was procrastinating. Her superiors had been quite clear as to why it was her, rather than someone more experienced, who would be conducting the first interviews. Alice was new and her only CIA duties had been with Looking Glass. She knew nothing a telepath could extract from her mind. The thought was unpleasant. Like all CIA employees, Alice had been through the verification process – she'd been hooked up to a lie detector and shot full of truth drugs, leaving her sick for hours afterwards – but this was different. Lieutenant Russell could look into her mind. She might have known nothing of interest to an enemy intelligence service, yet she had plenty of embarrassing secrets ...

Taking a breath, she strode towards the door before she lost her nerve completely.

***

Art looked up sharply as the door clicked open, revealing a young woman wearing a casual suit. She had long blonde hair, tied back in a ponytail, and a face that was pretty, rather than beautiful. He didn't need any telepathy to sense her apprehension; in some ways, she was acting rather like a newcomer to a unit rather than an experienced professional. He couldn't help but notice how she'd pulled her shirt tighter than it really needed to be, revealing high firm breasts and wide hips. It struck him, a moment later, why she'd dressed in such a manner. She wanted to be both business-like and attractive. His telepathy reached out towards her, but he held it back. He didn't want to go crawling through her mind.

"Good afternoon," the girl said. She had a warm voice, one that would have been seductive if she hadn't sounded so nervous. Art found himself liking her on sight, even though she looked almost as if she was still growing into womanhood. "I'm the CIA officer assigned to your case."

The emotions underlying her words were complex, too complex for Art to pick apart quickly. "Pleased to meet you," he said. He held out a hand and she took it. He was instantly *aware* of her, of the flickering emotions running through her mind. Her handshake was firm, but she didn't keep the contact open any longer than she had to. "What are you going to do now?"

"Answer me a question first," the girl said. "What is my name?"

Art blinked, and then understood the test. He reached out with his mind and sensed a name bubbling on top of her mind. It felt *right*. "Alice," he said. Her face seemed to freeze with shock. "Your name is Alice Spencer."

Alice swallowed, hard. "Yes," she said, finally. "Welcome to Looking Glass, Lieutenant."

"Hold on a minute," Art said, quickly. Her emotions were shifting too quickly for him to follow easily, but she seemed to be frightened. "I haven't agreed to do anything."

"We...ah, the Company, the CIA, have had a research program into ESP ever since the start of the Cold War," Alice said. Her emotions seemed to be quietening down as she spoke with increased confidence. "Looking Glass is merely the latest version of that project. As a telepath, we have arranged your transfer to detached duty with us..."

Art felt as if he had been punched in the gut. He should have expected it, he knew, yet it was still a shock. Somehow, he'd thought that there would be a few experiments, perhaps a few medical tests, and then he could head back to his unit and reassume command of the platoon. As a young enlisted man, he knew what he would have thought of any officer who deserted his men...and he felt as if he were deserting them, even though it hadn't been his choice. Alice was watching him sympathetically, but Art ignored her. How could she understand what they'd done to him?

"Right," he said, finally. "And how long do I have to wait until I return to my unit?"

He knew the answer before Alice could speak. "You cannot return to your unit," Alice said, finally. There was genuine sympathy in her mind. "At the moment, Lieutenant, you represent a priceless asset – you *are* a priceless asset. We cannot simply throw you away and send you back to combat. You might be *killed*!"

"Occupational hazard," Art said, dryly. "What makes me so special? Surely, if you have a research program into telepathy, you have more than one telepath."

Alice started to answer and then stopped herself. "Read my mind," she said, finally. Art, who could sense the feeling of violation flickering through her mind, shuddered inwardly. Her mind was raging up a storm again, a mixture of a desperate desire to test him thoroughly and fear of what he might find in her mind. "Why don't you find the answer to your question yourself?"

Art looked at her for a long moment and then extended his mind again. This time, he found himself running into memories of attending a concert – he recognised Midgard Metal, a band that had been quite popular with some of the younger soldiers – as he slipped into her mind. Alice, he realised suddenly, was deliberately thinking of other memories and thoughts, trying to distract him and force him to pull out of her mind. That realisation allowed him to understand that thoughts alone weren't enough; the emotional shading covering the thoughts was just as important. It seemed impossible to rifle through her mind as easily as one could use an internet search engine. Even a very young person would have hundreds of memories to use to distract him.

Her mind seemed to flare around him and he found himself sitting in a small classroom, where a tutor was lecturing a tiny group of students – no, prospective CIA officers for Looking Glass. As if the mere thought of the project's classification was enough to draw the memories to his attention, he found himself suddenly swimming through her memories. Her tutor – staring at a man though a woman's eyes was surprisingly disconcerting – hadn't pulled any punches. The CIA had only a handful of people with ESP potential and none of them had been telepaths, at least not in the same sense that he was a telepath. The most advanced had been remote viewers, who tended to burn out quickly.

Art pulled out of his mind and sat back, surprised. "You don't have any other telepaths?"

Alice looked equally surprised. "I couldn't feel anything," she admitted. Her words were shaded with undeniable truth. "I knew that you were peeking" – another flicker of violation blazed through her mind, sending a wave of guilt running through Art's own mind – "but I couldn't sense anything. What did you find out?"

"You like Midgard Metal," Art said, with a wink. Alice laughed. "I know soldiers who'd be prepared to date you just for that."

"I like to think that I bring other attributes to a relationship," Alice said primly...and then burst into giggles. Art found himself chuckling; the sound of her giggles seemed to blow away all the uncomfortable tension in the room. "My girlfriends and I went to the concert a few years ago, where I met a boy who fucked me right in the stands while we were dancing..."

Art lifted an eyebrow. Her words had been shaded with falsehood. It wasn't outright malice, as far as he could tell, but she was definitely lying and clearly testing him again. "You're lying," he said, with a wink. He couldn't see the truth without looking into her mind, but he knew that she was lying. "What actually happened there?"

Alice grinned back. "You tell me," she challenged. "What really happened there?"

Art gathered himself and peeked. A moment later, he felt a shocking rush of emotion as her memories opened up in front of him. For a moment, he teetered on the brink of blacking out, as memories that were uniquely female rose up and roared through his mind. Her first boyfriend had been a daring young man and had danced behind her, slipping up her skirt in the semi-darkness and slipping into her, all the while concealing his activity from everyone else. He was suddenly aware that his penis had swelled and grown hard...

"Art," Alice was saying. His mind was swimming and it was hard to pull his mind back together. "Art...Lieutenant...are you all right?"

"Just dazed," he said, shaking his head. At least it didn't hurt. For a few seconds, he had been female, at least in his mind. The intensity of the emotions had overwhelmed him. "You went with your boyfriend and..."

He found himself smiling at the memory. "Brave bastard," he said, finally. "What happened to him?"

"He wanted to have a foursome with me, one of my girlfriends and a boy he knew," Alice said, reluctantly. "I said no and he dumped me." She shrugged. "I was on the verge of leaving him anyway. He had too many weird demands."

Art flushed at the emotions that echoed in her words. The young Marines had shared tales about women they'd known openly, including some very strange stories; he'd always suspected that most of them were lies. He'd bullshitted a few times himself back in the barracks, telling stories that sounded as if they came out of *Penthouse Letters* or *Playboy*. Perhaps some of the stories had been true after all.

Alice cleared her throat and changed the subject. "What else can you do?" she asked. "Can you pick something up with the power of your mind?"

It had honestly never occurred to Art to try. He pulled a pen out of his pocket, placed it on the table and stared at it, willing it to rise. His eyes felt as if they were going to pop out of his head with the effort, but the pen adamantly refused to move. He concentrated hard, and then tried to defuse his concentration, yet nothing happened. Finally, he gave up and returned the pen to his pocket.

"No," he said, finally.

Alice nodded. "There were some odd results back in the past," she said, finally. There was something in her voice that warned him not to push the issue, at least not at once. He could have pulled it out of her mind, yet...that would have left him feeling like a peeping tom. "The Russians claimed to have made staggering advances in mental science. We never managed to acquire any hard data."

She swallowed again. "Let's try something else," she said. "I want you to try and make me do something."

Art stared. "Are you serious?"

"Yes," Alice said. She held up a hand before he could speak. "No, don't tell me what it is; try and make me do something. Try and make me do anything."

"All right," Art said, finally. He stared at her, concentrating on trying to make her lift up her shirt and show him her breasts. It was the first thing that came to mind. He concentrated hard, but her hands refused to move. He could see her mind, he realised, and read her thoughts, but he couldn't alter them. "No luck."

"You wanted to see my chest," Alice announced. Art blinked at her. How the hell had she known? She laughed at his expression. "It's the first thing a man would think of, dummy. *Men*! Telepaths or not, you're all pigs."
Art shook his head in disbelief.

Chapter Four

...In a speech today at the New York Paranormal Institute, Professor Zeller, the former director of the CIA's Project Star Gate, claimed that the human race was approaching a breakthrough into a new age, when humans would be able to access and manipulate cosmic forces with the power of mind alone. The sceptics in the audience noted that Professor Zeller had never provided any concrete proof of his increasingly grandiose claims...

-AP News Report, 2015

"You know," Art said, several days later, "anyone would think that you didn't believe me."

The man facing him refused to smile. "Extraordinary claims require extraordinary evidence," he said, flatly. "We have to test you as thoroughly as we can."

Alice, sitting next to Art, smiled at him. "It's nothing personal," she assured him. "You would be astonished to discover how many frauds there are who try to get themselves onto the Company's payroll ... or, for that matter, how many *real* remote viewers simply have a bad day from time to time and cannot produce anything. We test them heavily to see if they score above the mean on the Zeller Scale, more than the law of averages would allow for."

Art scowled. Alice had, at his request, provided him with files on the CIA's research into the paranormal, but most of the files didn't seem to apply to him. The CIA's small group of remote viewers – men and women who could send their perception out of their bodies and start roaming across the world – weren't telepaths. The testing system the CIA had devised wasn't intended for telepaths and it showed. Art had tried his hand at remote viewing, at Alice's suggestion, only to discover that whatever abilities he had, he didn't have *that* one. He couldn't see through walls, or clothing, let alone send his mind roaming away from his body.

"Fine," he said, dryly. "Let's get on with it, shall we?"

The man facing him – he had refused to give his name, silently daring Art to peek into his mind – produced a sealed pack of cards from a pocket, tore it open and shuffled them with the ease of long practice. Art guessed that he was a poker player when he was off duty, which suggested all sorts of new and interesting uses for his powers – if anyone on the base could be convinced to play poker with him. The ability to know if a person was bluffing or not, let alone to see what cards they held, would be very useful.

"The odds, in case you are interested, are one in fifty-two against you," the man said. He produced a card and held it face-down on the table. "What card have I produced from the pack?"

Art shook his head in irritation. Apparently, some of the CIA's paranormal operatives were able to predict the cards without having someone else look at them. That, too, was an ability Art didn't seem to have developed. The man looked at him, shrugged, and held up the card so that he could see it, but Art couldn't. Art looked into his mind and blinked. The man was concentrating hard on the same thought – *jack of hearts, jack of hearts* – yet his thoughts were shaded with falsehood. He had a more organised mind than Alice and it took Art longer to realise that the card was actually the six of diamonds.

"Six of diamonds," he said, finally. He couldn't resist adding a snide comment. "And you were thinking of the jack of hearts."

The man seemed, just for a second, to blink in surprise. "Not bad," he said, grudgingly. "That was very clever, Hans."

Art rolled his eyes at the bad joke. Clever Hans had been a horse who, according to the story, had learned to count and answer questions. It had turned out, after investigation, that the horse's owner was subconsciously cuing the horse to give the right answers. The CIA seemed to be aware of the possibility that someone on the base was giving cues to him, hence the several different formats, the different questioners and the stranger questions. Alice hadn't been the only person to challenge him to dive into their minds and pull out the answers.

The base, Art had discovered after asking the right questions, had originally been a command and control centre for military operations in the event of a bomb taking out the White House and NORAD. The base had been exposed by an inquisitive reporter – the lowest form of life, in Art's opinion – and the CIA had obtained it after the government had spent billions of taxpayers' money on building a new complex in a secret location. Project Looking Glass was merely the latest in a long line of CIA projects to use the base, forcing the CIA to scramble to outfit the base for Art and any other telepaths that might be discovered. Art privately hoped that they would have the sense to remain undiscovered. People just didn't react properly around a telepath.

Alice, at least, seemed to accept that he could read her mind, but others – the ones who believed him, at least – were far less inclined to take it peacefully. No matter how many times Art swore that he wasn't peeking through their minds without permission, they seemed unwilling to believe him and avoided him where possible. The sceptics, on the other hand, refused to believe that he could do anything special until he showed them the truth, at which point they joined the other group. He hadn't understood, at first, why the CIA had kept sceptics on the base, but Alice had explained that they helped keep the researchers honest. Project Looking Glass was always starved of funds and a handful of researchers had tried to fake up results a few years ago, just to get the funding they needed. It hadn't struck Art as particularly honest.

"No worries," Art said. They ran through several more cards before the man nodded and stood up. "What are you going to do now?"

The question, as always, provoked a deluge of thoughts from the person's mind. He was going to go back to his quarters, get very drunk and then report back to his shadowy superiors at Langley. They probably wouldn't believe him when he reported that Art was a genuine telepath, but then...he hadn't believed either, not until he'd seen the proof. He was oddly worried about what telepaths meant for the future of the human race.

"Nothing in particular," the man said. If he knew that Art knew he was lying, he refused to show any sign of awareness. "Thank you for your time."

Art watched him go and then looked up at Alice. "Don't they believe it yet?"

Alice gave a pretty shrug. "You have to understand," she said. "The ones who backed Project Looking Glass are doubtful because you don't fall into any of the expected categories. The ones who wanted the project shut down don't want to believe in you because that would mean that the project shouldn't be shut down. The ones who think that a telepath could solve all their problems are also the ones who think that funding will be redirected from their particular projects..."

"Oh," Art said. "And to think I used to think that the CIA knew everything."

"A cunning tissue of deceit spread by our devious political superiors," Alice said. "It's good to know that something works."

Art frowned. He hadn't asked – because he didn't want to know the answer – but he had a nasty suspicion that he was working solely for the CIA now. It wasn't a pleasant thought. In the military, the CIA and the State Department competed for the position of least-liked government bureaucracy; the former because the information they provided was often wrong, the latter because they gave away gains the military had won at huge expense. Art had been a young enlisted man in Iraq during the Surge and he believed, firmly, that the State Department and the CIA had, between them, prolonged the war. It might well have been an unfair belief, but it was his. And now he might well be working for the CIA. He would have to hang his head in shame when he returned to his unit, if he was ever allowed to return to his unit.

Alice, clearly unaware of his thoughts, grinned sourly. "Everyone thinks that we have the ability to see everything, control everything and shape the world the way we want it to be," she said, dryly. "They don't understand that there are inherent limits in intelligence-gathering, just as there are in everything else, and that – at best – we see through a glass darkly. Or maybe we don't have to any longer; you don't have to guess at what someone is thinking."

Art was still thinking about it an hour later, when they reported to the base's medical facility. As befitted a bunker intended for top military and civilian leaders, the medical facility was first-rate, although the CIA had apparently had to fly in some of the more advanced medical scanners from private hospitals and research facilities. Art had honestly never considered just how many ways the human race had to monitor brainwave activity, cr how little the human race understood about the brain. It had made him wonder if he'd somehow learned to use a part of his brain that hadn't been working beforehand, but the doctors had set him straight. The human race used most of its brain, at least in theory.

"Your test results are very interesting," Doctor Peter Sampson said. He'd explained that he'd worked with the remote viewers before moving on to carry out research into mind-machine interaction at a classified CIA-operated research facility. Sampson had been delighted to hear that the CIA had finally discovered an actual telepath and, according to Alice, had needed no prompting to sign an updated set of security agreements and join the project. "If you'll take a look at that..."

Art smiled. The doctor was a tall lanky man with a shock of brown hair and a slightly-manic attitude to life. His thoughts, Art had discovered, seemed to run and jump in strange channels, moving from place to place faster than Art could follow. He was unquestionably a genius, yet Art privately wondered about his grip on reality. He didn't want to be too close to a madman. With telepathy involved, the madness might rub off.

The wall-mounted display was showing his brainwaves, as they'd been recorded over several days. The Marine Corps had never recorded his brainwaves, Art had been told, which was apparently unfortunate as they didn't have any baseline to identify any changes. Even so, comparing his brainwaves to the average person's revealed some odd spikes in his mind, even when he wasn't actually trying to use his telepathy.

"That spike there, I think," the doctor said, "is your actual telepathic activity. Just for a few seconds, your brainwaves..."

Art interrupted quickly. "Layman's terms, doctor, please," he said. The first time they'd met, Sampson had sprouted off an impenetrable wall of jargon that hadn't made any sense at all, even to a mind-reader. "I'm just a dumb jarhead and I need plain English."

"Very well," Sampson said. "Basically, human brainwaves are electrical activity caused by the firing of neurons within the brain. The level of brainwave activity changes depending on what you're actually doing ... ah, when you are asleep, your levels of activity are profoundly different to when you are awake. Certain people can actually control their brainwaves to some extent, allowing them to work towards merging their minds into computers ..."

He broke off, perhaps remembering that he wasn't supposed to talk about that particular program. "The important point is that we used Electroencephalography – what you laymen call EEG – to monitor your brainwave patterns while you used your telepathy," he said, tapping the small controller on his wrist. "That spike within your brain represents telepathy."

Art frowned. For someone who hadn't seen a real telepath before Art had arrived, the doctor seemed surprisingly confident. "When you use your telepathy deliberately, the spike skyrockets," the doctor added. "Even when you are at rest, however, the spike remains active; I suspect that you will never manage to block your mind completely. You seem to have become a receptor rather than a transmitter, although I imagine that, given time, other telepathic powers will develop."

"Oh," Art said. He rubbed the back of his head, feeling the static swelling within his mind. "How certain are you of this?"

"That spike isn't very common, even as a once-off," the doctor said. "It is the only unusual thing about your mind. The really interesting point is that we can use this to check out other telepaths. There is a good chance that some of the people in mental hospitals are actually telepaths who never learned to control their telepathy."

Art considered it. He had to admit that it sounded logical. "And what will you do with the results now?"

"Continue to study, of course," the doctor said. He didn't quite say *stupid*, but it took no telepathy to hear it within his voice. "You must understand that this represents a priceless opportunity for research. Why, just by studying you, I have conceived a dozen new theories to account for the unexplained manifestations of brainwave patterns within human minds and..."

Art held up a hand. "I understand, doctor," he said, firmly. He didn't want to carry on with the tests, but there was no choice. "Can I suggest that we get on with it?"

***

Later that evening, Alice returned to her quarters, locked the door with her handprint and keyed the small secure laptop she'd brought with her. The computer was designed for operations in hostile terrain and bringing it with her seemed unnecessary, but her superiors had insisted. It hadn't occurred to her until much later – when she'd finally realised that telepathy was actually real and it wasn't another attempt to waste time and funding on a scientist's pet experiment – that the advantage in using the secure computer was that it needed her handprints to work, rather than just a password. Lieutenant Russell wouldn't be able to hack into her machine, even if he pulled all of her knowledge out of her mind.

It was a truism that the CIA never slept. The Directorate of Science and Technology – which, among other classified programs, funded research into ESP and the paranormal – needed to remain at the forefront of research, whatever it took. Alice had heard, when she'd been briefed for the first time, that the Directorate's Director – her ultimate superior – was very interested in telepathy. He'd fought with Congress for a larger black budget and scrabbled with the other directorates to ensure that the remote viewing project received all the resources it needed. When he'd heard that a genuine telepath had been discovered, he'd ensured that Lieutenant Russell was transferred into the CIA. Alice sat back and relaxed as his face appeared on the laptop's screen.

"Officer Spencer," Director O'Donnell said. He looked tired, Alice noted; she suspected that he was, once again, working late at the office. She'd been told that working for the company tended to put a lot of strain on marriages and even relationships, not least because CIA officers couldn't talk about what they did with their partners. Alice's own relationships had floundered on the same principle and dating fellow officers was frowned upon. "I don't have much time, so this will have to be quick."

"Yes, sir," Alice said. Director O'Donnell would have been reading all of the reports that had been forwarded from the base, but he preferred to keep hands on contact with his officers, believing that the person on the spot knew what was going on better than home office. It was a rare attitude in the CIA. She ran through a brief outline of what had happened since they'd last spoken – very little, apart from additional tests – and concluded with a comment about Doctor Sampson's proposed research program to look for additional telepaths. "We're reaching the limits of what we can do here, sir."

"So I understand," Director O'Donnell said. He sounded distracted, which was odd. Normally, even when talking to a relatively junior officer, he was polite and formal. "What are your impressions of Lieutenant Russell?"

Alice flushed, lightly. "He seems a nice person," she admitted, finally. That, at least, was true, although she knew that it was far from enough. Some of the most embarrassing disasters in the CIA's long history came from 'nice' people. "I think he's growing bored with the procedures here. He isn't a lab rat, sir."

"And most of the remote viewers volunteered for service," the director agreed. He tented his fingers and frowned. "There are...other parties within the National Intelligence Community who have gotten wind of what's fallen into our lap. They want a share in the excitement."

Alice frowned. "What do they want, sir?"

"For the moment, nothing, but that is about to change," the director said. "I want you to warn Captain Russell – we've bumped him up a rank or two – that he may be deployed outside the base within the week, perhaps sooner. Matters are coming to a head."

"Yes, sir," Alice said, puzzled. *What* matters were coming to a head? Who else wanted to use a telepath? "Should I pass on any other message?"

The director shook his head. "Not to the Captain, Officer Spencer," he said. "We're very pleased with your progress so far. Hopefully, in the next few days, you should have a chance to operate alongside other...elements."

Abruptly, he straightened up. "We'll be in touch, Officer Spencer," he said, flatly. His voice hardened suddenly. "Until then, carry on as directed. We'll see you soon."

His image vanished from the screen. "Yeah," Alice muttered to no one in particular. She'd been given odd orders before, but the ones she'd just been given were the oddest. "Be seeing you too."

Chapter Five

The FBI today issued an alert warning for possible terrorist activity within the City of New York. This marks the seventh alert within the last four months, all of which failed to materialise. Speaking in New York, NYPD Commissioner Amy Angotti said that all alerts had to be taken seriously and asked for the public to trust the NYPD and the other emergency services to do their jobs. Sources within the Administration of Mayor Hundred, however, claim that the alert is not being taken seriously after so many false alarms.

-AP News Report, 2015

Art had been delighted to hear, from Alice, that he would actually be going on deployment again, but the excitement hadn't lasted. For the first day, he'd cooperated enthusiastically with all of the tests, yet as the days wore on, he became more and more claustrophobic, even to the point of returning to his half-baked plan of escape. The Marines had trained him in both escape and evasion techniques and he was sure that he could remain undetected, once he was out of the complex. By the end of the fifth day, he had decided that someone had lied to Alice about him leaving the complex and, when the call came, he was mildly surprised.

"We're leaving tomorrow," Alice said. She hadn't been told any more than he had – a security measure, he realised sourly, designed to protect the information from him – but she was just as glad as he was at the thought of leaving the complex. "You've been ordered to prepare for a short visit to a city."

"Shore leave," Art said, dryly. He ran through the items in his quarters and swiftly decided that the only thing worth taking was the pistol he'd brought with him back to the States. The unmarked uniforms he'd been issued were hardly worth wearing, not if they wouldn't allow him to wear his Marine battle dress. At least they'd given him some civilian clothes so he could pass unremarked. "And they didn't tell you why?"

Wondering about what it could be kept him up for far too long, but he had managed to get a good night's sleep before being woken up at seven in the morning. His body clock was a little disoriented from sleeping in the sunless complex, yet he felt surprisingly good as he washed and then ate a hearty breakfast with Alice. She wasn't a morning person, but she was good company; if they'd met under different circumstances, Art knew, he would have made a pass at her. As it was, with everything he did observed 24/7, he knew that there was no such thing as privacy in the base. Once they'd finished their meal, they were escorted outside and into an unmarked black car that had materialised on the edge of the base. The government-issue plates on the vehicle, Art suspected, allowed them to break the speed limit without worrying about local cops. A quick check revealed that the vehicle was also armoured, suggesting that it was normally used for VIPs, and the driver was clearly a trained bodyguard. His emotional sheen didn't alter when he saw Art, convincing him that the driver hadn't been told about the telepath in the back of his vehicle.

Art hadn't had the time to see the outsides of the compound when they'd brought him inside and so he took the opportunity to look around while enjoying the feeling of fresh sunshine on his face. The bunker had been built under what was clearly a guest inn, one of the many motels and suchlike built alongside the roads for tired and weary drivers. He wondered how *real* drivers were discouraged from calling in and trying to book rooms, but then it occurred to him that – with a little care – guests could be prevented from seeing anything classified, leaving them to drive away unaware that they'd been sleeping over a nuclear bunker.

"Come on," Alice said, firmly. "It's time to go."

Art allowed her to pull him into the car and close the door behind him. The vehicle was almost sinfully luxurious, with a complete set of communications equipment, a small drinks machine with coffee and alcohol and some of the most comfortable seats Art had ever experienced. It was an eye-opening insight, he decided, into what was really done with taxpayers' money. He wouldn't have been surprised to discover that a new Stryker vehicle could have been purchased for the cost of the limo. The driver started the engine and it hummed to life, quieter than in a civilian vehicle. Art rolled his eyes. Lifestyles of the rich, famous and unaccountable indeed!

"Tell me something," he said, as he settled back into his seat. Alice offered to pour him a drink and he shook his head. He had no idea how alcohol would react with his telepathy. If he lost control...it might explain why so many people acted badly when drunk. They might be unable to access their telepathic powers without being drunk, but then they were unable to control them, subjecting themselves to maddening bursts of unstoppable noise in their heads. He shook his head at the thought, smiling to himself. If telepathy ever entered the public sphere of awareness, that excuse was likely to become popular. "Where exactly are we going?"

It was the driver who answered. "New York, sir," he said. He sounded vaguely surprised that Art didn't know. "We'll have you there in forty minutes, unless we run into really heavy traffic."

Art shared a glance with Alice and then settled back to enjoy the ride. As the car slipped out of the side road and onto the interstate, he was suddenly aware of the fleeting thoughts of other drivers in their vehicles. The contacts were brief and very faint, but they were always at the edge of his awareness, like the buzzing of an unwanted insect that had made its way into the car. Some drivers, he noted with a thrill of alarm, were bored; others were nervous, or merely intent on getting to their work on time. As the traffic started to thicken on the way into New York, the mental murmur grew louder. He found himself closing his eyes in the hopes that it would help shut out the noise. It didn't help.

Alice reached out and touched his hand with her gloved hand. "Are you all right?"

"No," Art managed. He drew on reserves he hadn't thought he had and built a mental shield around his mind. The shield lasted as long as it took for him to take his attention off it and then it collapsed into a wave of splintered thought. Swallowing curses, Art focused his mind and tried again, imagining building a wall out of the building bricks he had played with as a child. The barrier didn't seem to hold for long. A second's eye contact with one of the other drivers was enough to bring it crashing down. "There are so many *thoughts* out there."

Alice frowned. "Do you want to go back to the base?"

She meant well, Art knew, which was all that kept him from snapping at her. He couldn't – he wouldn't – abandon his duty just because he felt unwell. His determination had been what had kept him going towards the Taliban base even though he was nurturing a headache, a headache that might well have been the precursor to developing telepathy. He knew that he could back out, that he could go back to the base and hide for the rest of his life, yet he couldn't do it. If he stuck with it, he might manage to learn how to develop perfect control.

"No, thank you," he said, as she started to prepare a mug of coffee for him. "I'll be fine."

The background noise seemed to rise higher as they entered the City of New York. It was strange; Art couldn't pick out any individual thoughts, but he could sense the collective mind of thousands – perhaps millions – of human beings. Sparks of life flittered through his awareness, granting him brief insights before fading away, leaving him feeling like a voyeur peeking into the lives of unknowing men and women. Back when he'd been at school, one of the nerds had managed to establish a concealed camera in the girls' changing room and Art, when he'd been let in on the secret, had been disgusted. Now, with his almost uncontrollable telepathy, he was left to wonder about the difference between him and the nerd who'd spied on girls who would never have given him the time of day. It occurred to him, bitterly, that there was no difference.

Somewhere in the city, a man was beating his wife; Art felt her pain as if the man was beating him. A girl was kissing her father before he went off to work. An older boy was running to school in the hopes of meeting his girlfriend for a quick kiss before they were called into class. A priest was kneeling in prayer; nearby, a cleaner was thinking impure thoughts about her local priest. Art flushed and pulled his mind back, trying to control it. His mind refused to behave.

"Here we are," the driver sang out, as they pulled into a sealed compound. Art had never been to New York before, leaving him completely lost until he saw the FBI sign on the door. "You're expected in Room 101 in ten minutes."

Art looked at Alice, who looked back equally puzzled. "Come on," Alice said, as the driver opened the door. "We may as well go in and find out what they want with you."

The interior of the FBI building was a bustling madhouse. A tired-looking man checked their ID cards against a central database, without really paying attention. Art resolved to write a sharp letter of complaint after he'd found out what they wanted with him; sloppy security generally meant that the enemy was about to launch a nasty surprise. Perhaps it wasn't such a concern back in the States – the transition from a war zone to a peaceful city was always shocking – but it still bothered him. If he'd found one of the Marines under his command being so careless, he would have chewed him out and then sent him to clean out the latrines, or worse. A careless guard was just inviting the enemy to stick the knife in one's back.

After they passed through security, a young Chinese FBI agent escorted them up the elevators and onto the thirteenth floor. The young man clearly knew something about Art's abilities, because he kept glancing sharply at Art and then looking away, while his thoughts were a blaze of maddened confusion. Art had no intention of peeking into his mind, but somehow he doubted that the young man would believe him if he had told him. The agent couldn't wait to get away from him.

"This is the briefing room," the agent said, finally. He waved them both into a small room with a set of chairs and tables. Art noted the presence of water jugs on the table and a coffee machine at the side of the room, along with a small basket of cookies. Someone, it was clear, expected the meeting to go on for a few hours. "The agents will be with you shortly."

Art barely had time to watch the young man fleeing out of the door when the three agents filed in, two men and one woman. They were wearing black suits that practically branded them as federal agents, complete with holsters and cell phones. Art, who had developed a fine eye for spotting concealed weapons in Afghanistan, suspected that the weapons wouldn't be so obvious to the untrained eye. The agents waved Art and Alice to chairs and took their own seats facing them. It felt rather like an interrogation.

"Thank you for coming," one of the male agents said. "I am Agent Coombs, from the Joint Terrorism Watch Centre. This" – he indicated the woman – "is Agent Evens of the FBI's local counter-terrorism unit and Agent Manning of the National Security Agency. We know who you are."

Art nodded. Agent Evens was tall and blonde, with strong cheekbones and an oddly vulnerable face. Agent Coombs was shorter, with dark skin and a surprisingly wide smile; Art liked him on sight. Agent Manning was older, with short grey hair and a heavyset body. All three of them had ordered minds – Art could tell that without trying to read surface thoughts – but Agent Evens was deeply worried about something. He suspected that it was probably to do with the reason they'd been called to New York.

"Thank you," Art said, dryly. "Why are we here?"

"I'll allow Agent Evens to handle the briefing," Coombs said. "She's the ranking officer for this operation."

Agent Evens nodded. "This" – she tapped a remote control, triggering the display – "is Yusuf Mohammad Patel, of New York."

"Ah," Art said. The face on the display was that of a dark-skinned man with a neatly-trimmed beard and dark eyes, not unlike some of the fighters he'd faced in Afghanistan. Evens tapped the control again and the image changed, showing Patel in western clothes and then in East Asian outfits. The expression on the face didn't change. "And who is he when he is at home?"

Evens assumed a lecturing tone as she spoke. "Patel is the child of second-generation immigrants from Pakistan," she said. "His grandfather was a canny old buzzard and invested carefully; his father took his inheritance and invested it again, earning a considerable fortune importing Pakistani goods into the United States. His distant relatives in Pakistan handle the purchase over there and Patel's siblings handle the distribution here. In short, his father and grandfather realised the American dream. Unfortunately, it seems that Patel has become involved in less than savoury activities over here.

"We first became aware of him largely by accident, after we raided a terrorist training camp in Pakistan," she continued. "We had known that Patel had made several trips to Pakistan as part of the grooming process for taking over part of the family business, but it looks as if he may have picked up Islamic extremism instead. The records we recovered suggested that he had been treated separately from the other recruits and perhaps assigned to remain in deep cover rather than going to join the fight against NATO forces in Afghanistan."

Art nodded. The Taliban and other Islamic groups were capable of attracting recruits even from the West, luring them out to Afghanistan to fight the American and NATO troops in the country. Some of them had been unwilling recruits who had come out to see the camps – and then been told that they couldn't go home – while others had been just as fanatical as their Taliban mentors. Art privately viewed them with disgust. America – and Europe – gave the young men good homes and far more freedoms than they would enjoy if the Taliban took over, yet they were prepared to spit on those freedoms and go fight for evil. If it had been up to him, the 'useful idiots' would all have been put in front of a wall and shot for treason.

"Be that as it may, he returned to the United States and, since then, remained undercover," Evens said. "He did nothing to trip any warning signals; we only became aware of him after raiding the terrorist camp. We know, now, that someone stole a considerable amount of money from his family business and passed it onwards, but – if the truth be told – we don't even know if it was him. It may be just a coincidence."

"I see," Art said, thoughtfully. "Why haven't you just scooped him up and interrogated him?"

"We decided, when we became aware of his existence, to watch him in the hope that he would lead us to another deep-cover ring operating on our soil," Coombs said. "Sadly, we do not have sufficient proof to arrest him and what we do have would be thrown out by a competent lawyer without much trouble. His family has donated considerable sums of money to the Mayor and various political figures in the country. We cannot simply arrest him without far more evidence."

"But now things have changed," Manning said, speaking for the first time. "We have detected signs that another big terrorist offensive may be imminent and that a major figure in the global terrorist network has come to our soil. Patel may well have been contacted by his controllers and warned to prepare himself for action. We need to head this operation off at the pass."

"Yes," Art said. "So why don't you arrest him *now* and grill him?"

"Two reasons," Evens said. "First, the terrorists may change their plans if Patel is pulled in for questioning. They know that everyone breaks eventually. Second, Patel will scream for a lawyer and refuse to say anything. Once he is released – and we won't be able to hold him – his daddy will sue the FBI, NYPD and anyone else linked to the arrest, while Patel holds a press conference claiming that he was brutally tortured while in custody. The media groupies will pick up on it and do vast amounts of damage to our public image. We have enough problems operating effectively against terrorists without the government slapping another layer of safeguards and bureaucracy on us."

Art nodded. All of a sudden, everything was starting to make sense.

"And that's why you want me here," he said, thoughtfully. The conclusion was inescapable. "You want me to read his mind and tell you what he knows."

"Yes," Evens said. For the first time, her mind felt a shiver of fear, fear of a man who could peek into her mind. "We have no other choice."

"If the Emir is truly on American soil," Coombs added, "the entire country could be in danger."

Chapter Six

...Reports that a major figure in the terrorist underworld had come to America were issued by the Joint Terrorism Watch Centre, but internal sources at the White House claim that the alert was issued in error. The alert is seemingly unconnected to the alert issued earlier in the week in New York...

-AP News Report, 2015

"Tell me something," Art said, slowly. "Is reading someone's mind even *legal*?"

"There is no law against reading a person's mind," Manning said, carefully. "There are laws that state that we are not allowed to pick up people off the streets at random, nor are we allowed to start brutalising suspects into signing confessions, but there is no law against employing telepaths in government service."

Art considered it. He disliked being a telepath at the best of times. As he'd discovered walking through the FBI building, he was always *aware* of people surrounding him, even if they weren't aware of what he was. The ones who did know what he was had a tendency to cringe away from him. If nothing else, reading a person's mind – even a suspected terrorist's mind – was of dubious morality. He didn't like the thought.

On the other hand, he didn't want to discover – afterwards – that Patel *had* been involved in something nasty and that his refusal to read Patel's mind had allowed him to carry out the terrorist attack. If he read the man's mind and discovered that he was innocent, he would be able to tell the agents that they'd found the wrong man. Put like that, he decided, his duty was to read Patel's mind ... *without* allowing Patel to know that his mind had been read. That, at least, shouldn't be difficult. They could arrange things so that Patel could be held without even knowing that Art was anywhere nearby.

"I have a question," Alice said, from where she was sitting next to him. Her voice broke the logjam in Art's mind. "Who is the Emir?"

"We don't know," Coombs admitted. He frowned. "From what we do know, the Emir is a senior personage within AQ Prime – the core of the terrorist movement that attacked New York years ago – but we have no idea, even, what he looks like. That's not actually uncommon in counter-terrorism work. The chances are good that we do have a file on him, yet we haven't managed to link the two together. Apparently, with AQ Prime being scattered by the war, the Emir assumed command of a number of sleeper cells and started working on a new spectacular to show global believers that the war is far from lost."

"I see," Art said. He decided to test the limits a little. "I'll want to see his file, of course, and that of our friend Patel."

"Of course," Evens said.

"I have a second question," Alice announced. "How do you intend to bring Patel into this building?"

Evens grinned. "It seems that our friend Patel has a small number of unpaid parking tickets to his name," she said. "A pair of uniformed officers from the NYPD will pick him up and transport him here as a common prisoner. When he's here, Captain Russell can read his mind while he's cooling his heels and then we can decide what to do with him. Ideally, we'd want to release him so he can perhaps lead us to the Emir."

"Very well," Art said. He thought about demanding that they allowed him to join the team hunting the Emir, but he decided not to push his luck too far. That could come later. "You arrange for him to be arrested and we will wait for him here."

As it turned out, it took nearly two hours before a handcuffed and loudly-protesting Yusuf Mohammad Patel was pushed into the office. The officers who'd arrested him had had to face his angry protests, threats to sue and finally an attempt at bribery before they'd finally managed to take him into the van and transport him to the FBI office. The van had parked in an underground garage, something – Art hoped – that would prevent Patel from knowing where he was being held. Perversely, even though it was a minor charge and no one expected someone with such a wealthy family to be held for long, Patel was still demanding a lawyer when Art was shown into the viewing room. The one-way mirror would allow him to see Patel while Patel couldn't see him. Back during training, Art and his comrades had joked around with their mock interrogators, but Patel seemed to be sitting uncomfortably still. It took no telepathy to realise that he was uneasy about something.

"Everyone else out," Art said, shortly. He was willing to put up with Alice being in the room, but not the three agents or their subordinates. Patel had been left in the room to cool his heels, or so he had been told, something that might put him in a far more cooperative frame of mind when the police returned to the room. Or maybe he would have the presence of mind to continue demanding his lawyer. "I'll see what I can find out."

He sat down on the uncomfortable chair and peered at Patel. Telepathy didn't seem to work according to logical rules, but it did seem to follow some rules of its own. One of them was that it was possible to read the mind of someone at a considerable distance, provided that he could actually *see* the person in question. The one-way mirror was so clean that it provided the illusion that they were sharing the same room. Art hoped that his mind would be deceived as he slowly reached out towards the tight nexus of thoughts that made up Patel's mind. He didn't need interference or interruption.

The blaze of thoughts that confronted him made him recoil in shock. Patel's mind kept chanting, over and over again; wave after wave of questions and fears and torments. He had no idea why he'd been picked up, but his mind kept returning to a single point; he had failed his tutors and the Emir. As if merely thinking that name was enough to convince his mind to go elsewhere, Patel's memories flared in front of him, revealing a handsome middle-aged man who had taken a young boy in hand and taught him how to be a man. Patel was, Art realised, a roaring tempest of hatred and resentment. The Emir had given him a focus for that resentment and a cause to live – and die – for.

Art found himself gripping his seat as he probed deeper. Patel's mind was surprisingly undisciplined for someone who had been entrusted with such a vital mission, but then – the terrorists probably hadn't expected to have such levels of access at all and had had to take the person who had offered it to them. As the youngest son of nine, Patel hadn't been entrusted with anything like the level of responsibility of his siblings...a wave of childish resentment blazed through his mind, almost stunning Art as he fell back and regrouped. Patel was acting as if he was trying to strike back at his father and fellow siblings. Absently, a part of Art's mind wondered if he had been so resentful before he'd gone to Pakistan and fallen into the hands of the Emir. He'd seen it before. A young man, unsure of his place in the world, who fell into the hands of someone who knew how to mould and shape him into an ideal form...the whole process was sickening, but it happened far too often. A young man who could have been a loyal citizen had been transformed into a fanatic.

Odd, he thought, as he started to probe again. *The bastard would have made a good Marine.*

The thought seemed blasphemous, yet there was a certain undeniable logic. Patel had remained faithful to his cause for several years, robbing his father to set up terrorist accounts for the incoming fighters and never weakening, never questioning himself to the point where he might have started to wonder if he was doing the right thing. Under other circumstances, Art would have been impressed; even now, part of him *was* impressed. The rest of him was sickened. Patel's thoughts swirled around him, a stunning mixture of emotions and memories, all blurring together into a single mass.

Art found himself wishing for a search engine as he probed deeper, forgetting his scruples as the horrors Patel had envisaged floated into his mind. It was easy to read Patel's surface thoughts – the man was in a hurry to leave, which suggested that they might have picked him up just in time – but the deeper thoughts and feelings were harder to find. Art concentrated as another memory burst over him – receiving the first message from the Emir in years - and followed it back to its source. The terrorist plan suddenly lay revealed in front of him and Art, horrified, fell out of Patel's mind.

***

Alice felt a cold shiver creeping down her spine as she watched Russell and Patel. No matter how she tried, she couldn't sense anything of the mental combat being waged, even if one of the combatants didn't even know that he was under attack. Hardly daring to move, she looked over at Patel and shivered again. The young man was twisting and pulling against his handcuffs, yet seemingly unaware of what was going on. It was uncanny and, even though she had embraced the concept of using telepaths for police and counter-terrorist work, Alice couldn't help feeling terrified. The world was changing right in front of her.

Once, years ago, she had watched a movie about a world where some of the population had been telepaths. The remainder of the population had had to know that their thoughts were being read whenever a telepath felt like reading them, but they hadn't been able to do anything about it. The telepaths ruled the world and served as the police force, reading minds and using the evidence as proof of guilt. Their telepathy allowed them to declare that even *thinking* about committing a crime counted as guilt. Alice believed that that was nonsense, yet if Project Looking Glass ever went public, how would the public react?

One of the most fundamental rights in the United States was the right to remain silent. A criminal could confess, if he or she decided to admit the truth, but they couldn't be forced to talk. Even terrorists, captured on American soil, received some rights. A telepath, on the other hand, could simply reach into their minds and remove information – any information. She remembered the games she'd played with Captain Russell, back when she hadn't really believed that he was a telepath, and shivered again. Everyone had private thoughts and feelings they wouldn't want the rest of the world to know, but a telepath could bring them out into the open.

She looked over at Captain Russell and scowled. He, at least, had a sense of ethics, but what would happen if other telepaths did not? Would some of them decide to read minds for fun and profit; would kids in school develop the ability to read the minds of their peers; would criminals seek to use telepaths for criminal activities? Part of Alice had been scared when she'd realised that his powers weren't a joke, but now ... she wondered if she shouldn't just draw her pistol and put a bullet through his head. No, she told herself; it wouldn't work. The CIA knew how to find other telepaths now.

Damn it, she thought. Perhaps it was living in close quarters to him, perhaps it was something else, but she was finding him increasingly attractive. And, of course, he could read that in her mind if he went peeking. And he'd know that she had considered killing him.

"Ouch," Captain Russell said. He looked badly shaken and she had to catch him when he tried to stand up. His body was heavier than she had expected, but somehow she managed to hold him upright long enough for his legs to recover, aided by a mug of coffee brought in by one of the FBI agents. "That...that was not a pleasant experience."

The three agents entered soundlessly. "You spent nearly thirty minutes staring at him," Manning grated. Alice didn't need telepathy to know that he was questioning the wisdom of allowing Captain Russell to use telepathy, or even if telepathy really existed. "What did you find out?"

"You were right," Captain Russell said. He sipped his coffee gratefully. "That young man is in bed with the terrorists and the Emir is in New York."

Evens looked up sharply. "Do you know where he is now?"

"Not at the moment," Captain Russell admitted. He grinned, weakly. "Apparently our friend over there" – he waved at Patel through the one-way mirror – "isn't trusted enough to know where the Emir sleeps at night. On their first meeting, he gave the Emir several thousand dollars in cash and left him to find his own resting place. I'm afraid that he and his allies in Pakistan have been quite bad boys."

He rubbed the side of his head before continuing. "We should have seen it at once," he said, dryly. "Patel's father owns interests in several freighters. The unwanted son – that guy has major father issues – has been using them to bring in the components of a very special bomb from Pakistan. The Coast Guard cannot find them where they were hidden, so they get to New York and are transferred to an old warehouse, where the bomb is being assembled. Once the bomb is finished" – he made a motion with his fingers – "BOOM."

Coombs couldn't turn pale, but Alice had the sense that he'd nearly fainted. "What kind of bomb is it?" he demanded. Alice knew what he was thinking without telepathy. "Did they somehow get their hands on a nuke?"

"A dirty bomb, apparently," Captain Russell said. He scowled, gritting his teeth against the pain. Alice, who'd seen him fighting headaches before, opened her purse and produced an injector, which she offered to him. The painkiller was strong enough to dampen the pain of almost any injury, but Captain Russell refused it. It also caused drowsiness. "In a few days, the Mayor is going to address New York and announce that he intends to run for re-election. The dirty bomb will be triggered in Times Square or as near to it as they can get."

"And hundreds of people will be killed," Evens said. "We have to warn them and snatch the bomb before they can trigger it."

"And that would risk revealing that we have picked up Patel," Coombs pointed out. "We need to be sneaky."

Captain Russell looked up, angrily. "Are you saying that you are not going to act on the information I have provided?"

"Captain," Manning said, slowly, "telepathic evidence is not admissible in court. Even California doesn't recognise psychic evidence, no matter how many people swear blind that they saw their dead grandmother in a séance and she really wants them to have the jewels that were left to the other sister."

"I am not a fucking medium," Captain Russell snapped. "We know where the bomb is, we know where they are assembling it and we know what they intend to do with it. What should we do? Wait around for that asshole over there to confess of his free will? He's still screaming for a fucking lawyer and the moment you release him, he'll go running right to the Emir and warn him that they might have been detected."

"Or they might start moving up their plans because Patel was arrested," Evens said. She frowned. "It wouldn't be the first time we've picked someone up on a trumped-up charge in the hopes they would spill their guts. They're probably wise to that trick by now."

Alice blinked in surprise. "Then we have to move now," she said. "If we capture a dirty bomb – we're not talking about an illegal handgun or an assault rifle, but a weapon of mass destruction – we'll be heroes. Any small irregularities will be forgotten or forgiven."

Evens snorted. "You haven't been in this business long, have you?"

"Enough," Coombs said. He thumped the table to make his point. "Petty bickering doesn't help us. We have received warrants because of communications intercepts before and classified them all under the Patriot Act. The discovery of the dirty bomb will prove their guilt far more than any...telepathic evidence."

Captain Russell nodded. "I'll give you the address in a moment," he said. "How are you going to hit it?"

"Carefully," Coombs said. "The NYPD SWAT team has been on alert for the last week; we'll get them online and pointed at the target. The terrorists might have completed the bomb and have someone sitting on the trigger, just in case. If there is any doubt, we'll shoot first and ask questions later. Doubtless, we'll keep a few hundred lawyers gainfully employed arguing about it for the next ten years."

He chuckled, humourlessly. "Good work, Captain," he said. He didn't sound too happy, but Alice guessed that he wouldn't be happy until the dirty bomb was recovered. "New York owes you a debt."

"I'm coming with you," Captain Russell said, firmly. Alice opened her mouth to argue, but he spoke over her. "You're going to need a telepath to make sure that none of them try to lie to you – and we have to track down the Emir as quickly as possible."

"That isn't wise," Alice protested. She wanted to say something stronger, but nothing came to mind. She had known, intellectually, that Captain Russell missed combat, yet this meant risking a valuable asset ... and he was right. The SWAT team would need a telepath. "You can't put yourself in danger ..."

"It's not debatable," Captain Russell said. "I'm going."

Chapter Seven

An unconfirmed report from a source within the NYPD claimed that the SWAT team, which had been placed on alert, was deployed ten minutes ago to an unknown destination.

-AP News Report, 2015

"Marine or not, you're not going in with the first team," Sergeant David Crawford said, firmly. "My orders are to keep you out of harm's way."

Art scowled at him, but knew that further arguing would be futile, even without telepathy. He couldn't really blame Crawford for his attitude. If he'd been running a raid with a platoon of Marines, he wouldn't want outsiders crawling all over the operation and getting in the way himself. He'd taken a moment to read Crawford's file and he'd been impressed. The NYPD SWAT team had a good record for dealing with terrorists, snipers and other threats to public safety. Behind the SWAT team members, who were donning body armour and checking their weapons, he could see the small NEST team that had been hastily summoned. The Nuclear Emergency Support Team had worked closely with the SWAT team in the past, after there had been reports – false, apparently – that a nuclear weapon had been smuggled into the city.

"Fine," he said, gracelessly. He should have known better than to think anyone would have let him close to the action. It sounded petulant, he acknowledged a second later, but it was *galling* to be needed for an attribute he didn't want and would throw away if he could. The background murmur of the city seemed to be growing louder in his mind. "I'll be coming in as soon as you have secured the warehouse."

Crawford didn't bother to argue that point. Instead, he strode away to his team and began barking orders. Art had to admit that he had a good voice, although the Marine in him found the SWAT team to be alarmingly unprofessional. But then, the Marines operated in war zones, while the SWAT team had to operate in a civilian environment. If they shot an American citizen by accident, all hell would break loose. He glanced over at Alice, who was looking down at the charts of the warehouse that someone had pulled out of City Hall, and then wandered over to join her. Being so close to a dirty bomb – even though dirty bombs were not quite as dangerous as the media made them sound – was bothering her. Art didn't blame her. It was bothering him too.

Patel's father, according to the records, had bought the warehouse before the first economic shockwaves had started to shake the entire financial system. He'd found himself with a white elephant, a warehouse that had to be maintained, but with very little to actually store in it. Matters weren't helped by the fact that the warehouse was in a very rough area of New York City and that local gangs kept breaking into the building in search of drugs or money. He was surprised that Patel had chosen to risk using it as a base, but he had to admit that the terrorists would probably be capable of dealing with any intrusion from the gangs and no one in authority would give the building a second glance. The chances were good that his father or his relatives would never look at the building until it was far too late.

The SWAT team had sent a set of covert observers into the area as soon as they'd received the warning and they had slipped close to the building, their tiny cameras sending back a live feed to the SWAT team at the assembly point. The building itself had only three entrances; a small door at the front, an oversized loading bay and a fire escape at the rear. According to the plans, there was a small office at the front of the building and the remainder was storage space, but Crawford had warned them that they couldn't rely completely on the plans. There were plenty of tricks the terrorists could have pulled to make life hard for the team, just to buy them time to detonate the bomb and score a victory, of sorts. A dirty bomb going off anywhere in New York City would be a victory for the terrorists.

"All right, listen up," Crawford said, as the team assembled. They'd already been briefed extensively, but he was clearly the type of person who insisted on going over the high points before each operation began. "You know what's reported to be in that warehouse. You know there are people alive in there. We will take them alive, if possible, but if they move towards the bomb, or draw weapons, shoot to kill. You may not get a second chance."

Art scowled to himself. The NEST team had run a covert scanner – disguised as a bird, of all things – near the warehouse, but they'd been unable to pick up any traces of radiation. The bomb, assuming that it was still in the warehouse, could be anywhere. Patel's mind had sworn blind that the terrorists were packing it into a white van, one that wouldn't earn a second glance from anyone who might have been able to stop them before it was too late, but they could have lied to him. If a person who was lying – without knowing that he was lying – could fool a lie detector, he could fool a telepath as well. Patel's mind had been a seething cauldron of resentment and hatred, but underlying it all had been an uneasy concern about his allies. Were they setting him up for a fall?

"Good," Crawford said. "Let's go."

Art had been curious to see how the operation was conducted and watched with interest as the SWAT team moved into position. It had been decided not to attempt to evacuate the surrounding area – a gutsy call on Crawford's part, Art knew – as that ran the risk of alerting the terrorists. Instead, several unmarked police vans would convey the SWAT team to their destination and then standby to provide support if necessary. Additional forces – and the NEST team – were already on alert. They'd be moved into position as soon as the SWAT team launched their offensive.

"They'll be cutting power to the warehouse just before they go into view of the security cameras," the watch officer commented. Art could sense a knot of concern in his mind, a fear that something would go badly wrong. "Ah...there they go."

On the screens, Art saw a group of men in black outfits running forward to the two small doors and smashing them down, charging in with weapons raised and shouting orders for the terrorists to throw down their weapons and raise their hands. A handful of gunshots rang out in the confined space, seconds before the NEST team was called into the building. The SWAT team searched the building from end to end before calling back to the base and reporting that it was secure. Art just hoped they they'd remembered to tell the enemy that the building was secure. While clearing houses in Afghanistan, the Marines had often been surprised by enemy fighters who had hidden within the buildings or crept back to reoccupy a cleared house.

"All clear," Crawford's voice said, finally. "Come on in; the water's fine."

Art concealed a smile as he was escorted into a police van and driven the five blocks to the terrorist-held warehouse. From the outside, it wasn't any more impressive than the pictures had made it seem, although the presence of police vehicles – marked, this time – suggested that something bad was going on inside the building. The uniformed police officers were already setting up lines and warning a handful of curious onlookers to keep their distance; it wouldn't be long before the media arrived. The chances were good that someone with a cell phone had already called the media and – if they had a camera on their phone – had taken footage that would probably be uploaded to the internet. It was very hard to do anything in total secrecy, Art knew, even in the intelligence community.

The interior of the warehouse was almost empty. A single white transit van sat in the centre of the cavernous interior, with the NEST team poring over it. Art realised, with a shiver, that the Emir might have intended to launch the attack ahead of time, perhaps because Patel had been arrested or because he had never trusted his ally. His mind sensed the terrorists before he saw them; seven men, lying on the hard floor with their hands cuffed behind their backs. Two more terrorists lay dead on the ground. Art checked the bodies out of habit and discovered that they'd been put down swiftly and professionally. He guessed that they'd made the mistake of attempting to fire on the SWAT team and had been gunned down.

"We have a problem," Crawford said. "Come and look at this."

Art followed him over to the van. The terrorists had pulled out the van's normal fittings and piled in a crate, attached to a simple remote timer and keypad. The timer was clearly counting down to something, but the display had been scrambled, making it impossible to tell how long they had left before the bomb detonated. The NEST team's bomb disposal officer looked up and shook his head. The weapon, Art realised from his mind, had been carefully constructed to make defusing it impossible.

"I push into this and it will explode," the officer said, flatly. Art sensed the cold professionalism underlying his words and shivered. Bomb disposal officers were the bravest of the brave. "We need their disarming code."

Art nodded. "Lucky I came along, then," he said. Crawford scowled. He'd been briefed on Art's abilities, but he hadn't believed a word of it. It wouldn't be the first time officers and men had been fed an absurd story to see how much of it they believed before common sense asserted itself. Art had always hated the practice, even though he understood it. It would be a disaster if a team of Force Recon Marines blindly followed orders that ended with the assassination of the President, or worse. "Which one of the assholes is in charge?"

Crawford stepped out of the van and pointed to one of the terrorists. "That was the one giving orders when we broke in," he said. His droll tone couldn't conceal the urgency spreading through his mind, the fear that the bomb might go off after all and kill his team. "You'll have to ask him personally."

Art nodded and stepped over to the terrorist. Up close, cuffed and helpless, he didn't look that impressive, but then they never did. The cowardly shits who were happy to beat up women and children – and force them to follow an ideology that was alien to them – rarely turned out to be impressive warriors. He'd discovered that while the Taliban were tough and determined fighters, the same couldn't be said for the allies they recruited from the West. Many of them had second thoughts when it was too late to back out.

"We can do this the easy way or the hard way," Art said, flatly. "I want the code for disarming the bomb. If you don't give it to me willingly, I will take it from you by force."

"Burn in hell," the man said, finally. He had an accent that reminded Art of a joint operation the Marines had conducted with the Pakistani Army, back along the border between

Pakistan and Afghanistan. "I accept death for my cause and…"

"Enough," Art said. He drew back his foot, as if he was going to kick the helpless terrorist in the ribs. "Believe me; I *will* get it out of you."

"You're not allowed to torture me," the terrorist sneered. "And even if you did, I can hold out long enough to make it useless. The bomb is going to go off very soon."

Art shrugged and reached out with his mind. "What is the code to disarm the bomb?"

"176363," the terrorist said, out loud. Art knew he was lying; the falsehood blazed through his words. The code would actually trigger the bomb ahead of time. Ignoring it, he reached into the terrorist's mind as he repeated his question. This time, the answer floated on the top of the terrorist's mind.

"273939," Art said. The terrorist was staring at him in disbelief – the entire room was staring at him in disbelief. Even the terrorist who seemed to be on the verge of breaking into tears was staring at him. "Put the code in and disarm the bomb before it is too late."

The NEST bomb disposal officer scrambled back into the van and started to input the code. Art braced himself for an explosion and sudden death – the bomb was partly made up of C4, used for scattering radioactive material everywhere – but nothing happened. The team could dismantle the bomb and remove the radioactive material without any further problems. The terrorist was still staring at him, sheer terror flickering through his mind. Art smiled at him and the terrorist recoiled. Somehow, deep within his mind, the terrorist had guessed what had happened. Art knew, beyond all doubt, that he was terrified. What did it mean for Global Jihad if minds could be read at will?

"You can answer me one other question," he said, flatly. "Where is the Emir?"

The terrorist tried to stammer out an untruthful answer, but the real answer was bubbling away on the top of his mind. The Emir, after a brief visit to Ground Zero, had gone undercover – hidden even from his own most trusted adherents – until the time came to use the bomb. He was actually expected at the warehouse that evening, after the bomb had been completed and everything else prepared for action. Details of the full scope of the terrorist plot – details concealed from Patel, for whatever reason – flared through his mind. The terrorists had obtained assault rifles from a crooked arms dealer and intended to attack the emergency services when they responded to the dirty bomb. The carnage would have been unbelievable and horrific. Art allowed himself a moment of relief. The chances were good that they'd headed the terrorist plot off at the pass completely.

"He's coming here this evening," Art said. It was odd. If the terrorists had intended to launch their attack so soon, where had they intended to target? The Mayor hadn't brought his speech forward for their convenience, after all. He posed the question to the terrorists and found nothing. The Emir hadn't bothered to tell them the target. "We'll be here, waiting for him."

"He won't come," one of the terrorists spat out. "He'll see you here and vanish before you can catch him."

Crawford nodded. "The bastard is probably right," he said, as the follow-up teams arrived. The terrorists were picked up, their legs were chained to make running impossible and they were marched out towards the prison van. They'd be transported to a secure prison and held until charges could be filed. The dirty bomb would provide all the evidence the FBI needed to charge them with terrorism. The forensic teams might pick up enough evidence to make additional charges stick on Patel, rolling up the entire terrorist network. "The media have already been alerted and reporters are on their way. My superiors want to make a public statement."

Art rolled his eyes. "Just remember to say nothing about how the information was obtained," he said. He knew that it was probably useless. The entire warehouse had seen telepathy in action. Someone – he wondered who – would spill the beans to someone else and the word would be out. Even a rumour would be disquieting to the world ... on the other hand, there had been conspiracy theories about secret groups of telepaths running the world for years and society hadn't broken down into anarchy. "What about ...?"

"You saw the Emir in their minds," Alice said, suddenly. "You could do a composite picture of him so we'd know who to look for and then ..."

"Good idea," Agent Evens said. She'd remained behind with her two friends and colleagues. Art had been privately grateful, as – he knew – had Crawford. The last thing either of them needed was superior officers blundering around and issuing impossible orders. "Once we have the picture, we'll upload it into facial recognition programs and issue a public warning. Someone may well come forward and tell us where he is. It's certainly worked before."

Art nodded. "All right," he said, shortly. The background hum of the city was growing louder, distracting him. "Let's go back to base and we can work on the image there."

***

As it happened, once the FBI's best artist had helped Art come up with an image of the Emir as his men had seen him, the Emir was arrested within four hours. His face had been picked up by a set of security cameras as he made his way in and out of an expensive hotel – where he'd stayed while his men slept on hard floors in the warehouse – and stored until the image had been uploaded into the NYPD's database. As soon as the cameras had reported his presence, the SWAT team had mobilised, secured the hotel and arrested him. They'd expected a fight, or a suicide attempt, but instead the Emir surrendered at once. Art wasn't too surprised. Terrorism was the weapon of a coward and the men who sent people out to die in his name were rarely the bravest of the brave.

"You did well today," Alice said, once they'd been allowed to move into their sleeping quarters and get some rest. The FBI seemed reluctant to let them out of its building and had already arranged for Art to be present when the Emir was interrogated. "You've changed the world."

Art grinned. "I have, haven't I?"

Chapter Eight

A terrorist cell was broken up and arrested in New York this evening, sparking concerned remarks from City Councillors about the lax response of the Mayor to the terrorist alert issued by the JTWC. Furthermore, a vague report has reached this reporter that non-standard interrogation methods were used by the arresting police forces…

-AP News Report, 2015

"You do realise that you could have been exposed?"

Art found himself counting to ten under his breath. It wasn't the first time he'd been chewed out by a superior officer, but at least those superior officers had had the courage to face him while they were expressing their opinion of his misdeeds, his general level of competence and his parentage. Director O'Donnell – who had been introduced to him as the Director of the CIA Directorate of Science and Technology, which meant nothing to Art – was talking to him from a video screen. It took no telepathy to realise that the Director was concerned that Art might read his mind.

"It was a necessary risk," Art said, firmly. He'd always disliked being second-guessed out in the field. "If I hadn't been there, the dirty bomb would have detonated, and the results would have been unpleasant and devastating."

They would have been far worse, Art knew, than any prior terrorist attack on American soil. The terrorists had somehow obtained enough radioactive material to poison most of New York and the C4 to ensure that the radioactive material was spread far and wide. Even if the bomb had gone off in the warehouse, rather than in Times Square, the results would have been disastrous. The city's population would have panicked and fled, causing a massive economic crisis. And the terrorist movements across the world would have taken heart at their great success.

"It was my call," he added, sharply. "I trust that there have been no unpleasant repercussions?"

There was an uneasy pause. He might not be able to read the Director's mind through the viewscreen, but he could feel the alarm flickering through Alice's mind at the way he was speaking to her superior officer. It was amusing to discover that the CIA – the so-called secret power behind the world – was far more risk-averse than the Marine Corps, but then the CIA had much more to lose. The Marines were beloved by most of the American population; the CIA was generally seen as a wasteful government office populated by dangerous incompetents.

"No," the Director said, finally. "We have more than enough evidence to try Patel for terrorism without bringing telepathic evidence into the mix. Your support was most welcome and you have the thanks of many powerful departments."

Art smiled. The week they'd been in New York had been spent watching as the terrorists were interrogated and noting the truthful answers as they tried to lie to their interrogators. The terrorists hadn't really grasped it, even though some of them suspected the truth, and the Emir had proven an intelligence windfall. Terrorist cells in Britain, France and Germany had been broken up by the local security forces, while safe houses and training camps in Pakistan had been exposed. No matter how one looked at it, it was a great victory for peace and civilisation.

"However," the director continued, "there is a more important concern. We need to locate other telepaths."

Art scowled. The CIA's research had proven the existence of a telepathic spike in a person's brain, but it had been alarmingly clear – even before they'd taken a jaunt to New York – that not everyone with the spike was able to use it. In fact, they'd been planning to bring in the people with the most potential and hope that they could somehow trigger their telepathy, something Art doubted would work. He'd been stressed and desperate when his telepathy had been triggered and it wouldn't be easy to reproduce the effect. The recruits had been arriving at the base since he'd gone to New York and none of them, it seemed, were very happy with the situation. He didn't blame them.

"We're going to be working on that this afternoon," Art assured the director. There was no point in pushing the issue any further. "If there are any other questions...?"

"No," the director said. He paused. "And thank you for your services, Captain. You made a very real difference this week."

Art was still smiling when he walked into the small lecture hall, four hours later. The bunker hadn't been designed with a lecture hall in mind, but one of the massive storerooms had been cleared out and a number of chairs and tables – and a pair of computers – had been slotted into the room. It had a vaguely ramshackle look that Art liked more than the more formal conference rooms he'd had to endure in New York. The fourteen men and women in the room stood to attention when he entered. Two of them outranked him, but it had been made clear that he was in charge.

"Thank you for coming," Art said. He could sense their impatience and irritation without needing to probe very deeply. Ten of them had been pulled out of the front lines; the remaining four had been pulled out of various operational and intelligence centres and probably suspected that they were in deep trouble. None of them had any idea what they'd been summoned for, or what their superiors wanted with them. "Please be seated."

He ran his eyes over the crowd and smiled. Six of them were Marines or regular army; five came from the Air Force and the remainder came from the intelligence community. They'd had a chance to compare notes and had probably realised that they had only one thing in common. They were all over-achievers, the men and women who were just very good at their jobs. It made him wonder if telepathy, even if used without any awareness of what they were doing, was involved somehow.

The research staff had advised him to break it to them gently. Art knew his fellow Marines, at least, well enough to know that they wouldn't tolerate any bullshit. He intended to break it to them as bluntly as possible. He wondered, suddenly, if any of the Marines knew him personally, but he didn't recognise any of them. It might have made it easier for them to believe him.

"Recently," Art said, "I developed telepathic abilities while on deployment."

He didn't need to be a telepath to sense the waves of disbelief rolling towards him, emanating from the seated men and women. It took everything he had not to recoil in pain as their emotions poured into his head, but somehow he remained upright and focused. Briefly, as quickly as he could, he ran through a brief explanation and then an outline of what had happened in New York. That received some surprised looks; there had been rumours that something odd had happened in New York and telepathy would explain it nicely. Or so they thought.

"If that is true," a short man wearing an Army Ranger tab said, "please would you tell me what I am thinking of right now."

Art had to smile at the challenge in his tone. He liked the Ranger on sight, even if he *was* a Ranger and therefore not quite as good as Force Recon. Art concentrated, reached out towards the Ranger's mind and had to smile. The Ranger was thinking about having sex with Bugs Bunny.

"You have a filthy mind," Art said, and told everyone. The Ranger gaped at him. Simon Hawking had deliberately thought of something no one would consider believable. Art sensed the sudden flurry of fear – fear that he might be peeking into their thoughts – that ran through the group. The look on Hawking's face was unmistakable. "Why did you think about Bugs Bunny?"

Hawking leered. "My girlfriend and I once dressed up as Bugs Bunny and Daffy Duck for charity," he explained. "Afterwards, we were so tired that we couldn't be bothered getting undressed before we had sex and…"

"Oh," Art said. He carefully held back the other comment that rose to mind and cleared his throat loudly. "The important part of the story is that I have a telepathic spike in my brain…and you have it too. You are, at least potentially, telepaths like me. What we intend to do here is to unlock your powers and put you to work serving your country."

There was a long uncomfortable pause. "Sir," one of the women said, finally, "what do we have to do to get out of this chicken-shit outfit?"

Art gave it to her straight. "If it doesn't work," he assured her, "you will be returned to your unit with a letter of commendation. If it does, you may discover that working with us is more rewarding. I helped catch a set of very dangerous terrorists and save New York City. You may end up doing the same."

There was a second pause. Art knew what they were thinking, even without reading their minds. None of them wanted to attempt to become telepaths, although he was sure that at least a few of them were tempted by the prospect. They wanted to continue to serve in their units, instead of abandoning them on the whim of a crazy officer's scheme. He wondered if their reluctance to accept that telepaths were real – or that they had telepathic powers themselves – was driven by fear that they would never be able to live a normal life again.

The thought made him smile inwardly. Somehow, after the operation in New York, he'd accepted it without quite admitting it to himself. A Marine Lieutenant – even a Force Recon Marine Lieutenant – was replaceable. Sergeant Bass was probably breaking in yet another green lieutenant right now. A telepath – so far, as far as they knew, the only telepath – was unique. If it meant that he could no longer be a Marine, at least he'd found a worthy cause.

But the others would not accept it so quickly.

"If we agree to go through with this," the woman said, even though Art knew that she knew that there was no choice, "what will happen to us?"

"You will be tested," Art said, and refused to be drawn any further. The researchers had drawn up a whole list of experiments – Art had vetoed two of them on the grounds that they were too dangerous – and were looking forward to trying them out. It made Art think of the blind leading the blind, or carrying out delicate surgery by touch alone, without any prior training or experience. God alone knew what was going to happen. He wasn't even sure if it was legal. "Unless you have any further questions, we'll make a start at once."

"I have one," Hawking said. "Is this telepathic power good for picking up hot chicks?"

"You're not allowed to talk anymore," Art said, firmly.

***

Alice watched from behind a one-way mirror as the potential telepaths started to undergo the procedure that should – in theory – allow them to develop their telepathic powers. Doctor Sampson had explained it to her, but Alice had only been able to follow about one word in ten of a very complicated explanation. The gist of it – as she'd been able to establish after he'd finally finished the main explanation – was that the doctors intended to use electrodes to stimulate parts of the brain and hopefully allow the patients to develop telepathy.

She watched as one of the female patients, stripped down to her underwear, was placed on a surgical chair. The doctor attached the electrodes to her forehead and took the baseline readings, checking that she was thinking properly before the experiments began. The woman looked nervous and Alice didn't blame her. She'd been briefed that the CIA had developed a way to stimulate emotions in a person's mind, yet she also knew that the process was not one hundred percent reliable. An oversight committee had cancelled the process on ethical grounds after an experimental subject somehow became overwhelmed with bliss and ended up trapped in a permanent high.

When she'd been young, she'd read about experiments carried out by doctors – if they deserved the name – in Nazi Germany. It had surprised her to discover that the CIA carried out its own experiments, although she had to admit that the CIA was a great deal more moral about the whole process. The experiments were carried out on volunteers or, in a handful of rare cases, on Death Row prisoners. Some of the fruits of the covert research programs had found their way into the public domain. Even so, the whole process disturbed her on a visceral level.

She liked Captain Russell – not least because he hadn't made a pass at her when they'd wound up sharing the same room – but she didn't know the other potential telepaths. If the experiments worked, they'd end up with fifteen telepaths in all, who would probably be distributed among the various intelligence and counter-terrorism agencies. And what would happen then? Alice knew, even if Captain Russell didn't, that they'd gotten lucky with Patel. If the SWAT team hadn't been able to find enough evidence to implicate him, a great many hard questions would have been asked, starting with the obvious one of how they'd known to pick him up.

An alert tone rang through the observation room and she turned back to watch the woman. The doctors had strapped her to the table and the experiment was about to begin. Alice didn't want to watch, but she felt as if she had no choice. It was her duty.

***

The emotions running through the room were loud enough to make him want to flee and head back to his quarters, but Art forced himself to remain in the room as the first experiment began. The woman on the table had had the highest rating on the scale and so the doctors had chosen to start with her, using both the induced emotions and a tailored group of drugs to bring out the telepathic ability. Art could sense her fear – almost panic – as they placed the skullcap on her head and started tapping the computers. The timer was counting down …

Art cringed as a blast of absolute terror blazed through the room. He staggered and then found himself on the floor, his head reeling in pain and horror. Before he could get up, another blast of terror flashed though the room, followed rapidly by a third and then a fourth. He opened his mouth to demand that the experiment was halted, but it was already too late. There was a fifth burst of absolute terror … and then the woman's mind opened wide. Art pulled himself to his feet and yanked the doctor away from the controls. The woman's telepathy had flowered suddenly and violently, just like his had back in Afghanistan. She was reading, without any preparation, the mind of everyone in the room, Art included. A moment later, before he could do anything, she fainted.

"Take her to the recovery room and clean her up," the doctor ordered, calmly. Art wrinkled his nose. The woman had been so terrified that she'd lost control of her bowels and bladder. "We'll move operations to the next room until this one can be cleared."

Art stalked away, angrily. The experiment had worked … and he felt ashamed of what he'd done, or started, just by developing his abilities. Who knew where it would all end?

***

The experiments were a success with twelve of the potential telepaths, in the end. One of the men resolutely refused to develop any telepathic powers; one of the women went into a coma and nothing they could do would bring her out of it. Art cursed the doctors aloud, but they and his new superiors were unmoved. A legion – or even a platoon – of telepaths was worth any risk. He suspected – the superiors had refused to meet with him or the other telepaths – that they'd already decided that some potential telepaths were expendable, as long as they developed a small number of telepaths under their control.

Once the new telepaths recovered, however, they made progress by leaps and bounds. It was easy to tell when one telepath was probing another's mind and they held competitions to develop ways of shielding their thoughts from other mind-readers. The embarrassments that Art and most of the others had anticipated didn't materialise, although the non-telepaths in the base tended to give them all a wide berth when contact wasn't absolutely necessary. At least it was becoming easier to block out the thoughts of others, telepaths or not, now they could practice on each other. Art suspected that it wouldn't be long before several of them were deployed to work in other covert interrogation teams, but for the moment they could act least practice. It was much easier when he had someone to talk to who genuinely understood what telepathy was like.

The other discovery was that, with effort, they could actually send telepathic messages from mind to mind. They couldn't reach a non-telepath, sadly, but they could contact each other at a quite considerable distance. Once they'd mastered it, the telepaths had started using it to talk in private, knowing that the watchers – the entire base was still under scrutiny – couldn't listen to them. Art had a private suspicion that the effects of *that* were still undiscovered. Who knew where it would all end?

The day afterwards, four of the telepaths received marching orders to join various intelligence agencies. Art waved them off, knowing that they would still be in touch mentally. As far as they could tell, telepathic messages didn't seem to have any range limitations, although they'd never been that far apart since blossoming into telepathy.

And, somehow, they'd never gotten around to describing that ability to the researchers. It would only have upset them.

Interlude One

From: Project Looking Glass Analysis Team
To: Looking Glass Distribution List
Classification: Looking Glass Cleared Individuals Only

As per the directive from Langley, we have been carrying out experiments into the alleged mental powers demonstrated by Subject Alpha. The results of the tests have proved that Subject Alpha possesses genuine mental powers. A series of tests were devised and conducted – see attached document – with the intention of qualifying the nature and limitations of these powers, as well as devising a test in the hopes of locating others with comparable abilities.

Subject Alpha is essentially capable of reading minds. Going from his testimony, it is extremely difficult to control the ability, let alone neutralise it. (Closing the mind's eye appears to be impossible.) The ability does not appear to follow logical rules, at least as we understand them. Subject Alpha is incapable of reading the mind of a person five meters away when he is unable to see the person; but is capable of reading the mind of a person ten meters away, provided that he is able to see the person.

There appear to be several levels to the ability. First and foremost, Subject Alpha is capable of reading the emotions of a person speaking to him, even at quite a considerable distance. This ability turns him into an organic lie detector. He claims that he can always tell when a person is knowingly lying to him; their words are shaded with falsehood. It seems impossible to fool him.

Second, Subject Alpha is capable of reading the surface thoughts of another human being. To use a specific example, he asks a question and then reads the answer out of the target's mind. The truth apparently floats to the top of the mind – his words – even if the target chooses to lie verbally.

Thirdly, Subject Alpha is capable of digging into a person's deeper thoughts and memories. This process is apparently unreliable as the target can distract him by thinking about other thoughts and memories. To some extent, this process requires physical contact; the wags on the base have already termed it the 'Vulcan Mind Meld.'

Subject Alpha does not appear to be capable of influencing or controlling other human minds. Despite some experiments, he is also unable to use telekinetic abilities or remote viewing.

As Subject Alpha scored highly on the ESP test administered to all new recruits into the military – his specific test was administered at Parris Island – other high-scorers were tested and pushed into developing telepathic abilities. It is recommended that others who scored highly be also tested for telepathic ability. However, as Subject Alpha's abilities appeared under stress, it is likely that others (i.e. not people involved with Looking Glass) will develop telepathic powers on their own, without medical intervention or support (see attached file). All field commands should be alerted to watch for signs of stress that might lead to a telepathic breakthrough.

It should not need to be stated that this is both an opportunity and a considerable security threat. A telepath with comparable abilities could pull classified data out of the mind of a security-cleared person, who would not know that their mind had been read and that the data was loose. (A handful of people on the base were able to sense Subject Alpha's mental touch; interestingly, they also scored high on the ESP test administered at intake.) If other telepaths appear, we may be forced to face rapid and unpleasant social changes when the details become public.

In line with that, I have several possible recommendations…

Chapter Nine

Yusuf Mohammad Patel, arrested four weeks ago on charges of terrorism, claimed in a court hearing that his mind was read by government agents without his consent. This marks the third such claim surrounding the New York City Dirty Bombers, a claim that has been roundly dismissed by the government. In a statement issued to the media, the NSA stated that while some evidence had to remain secret for reasons of national security, the evidence discovered with the bombers was enough to convict them.

-AP News Report, 2015

"So tell me," Professor Benjamin Zeller said, "how are we today?"

Elizabeth Tyler scowled at him. Zeller looked rather like a genial – and mobile – version of President Roosevelt, but his smile concealed a razor-sharp mind and an obsession with the paranormal that led him to spend his own money on his private quest. Elizabeth knew that she shouldn't mind too much – after all, his money was helping her get through college – yet he could be irritating, all the more so when she had a date with her boyfriend lined up in a few hours.

Two years ago, when she had moved to college to study for her degree, she had underestimated how much it cost to maintain a respectable student lifestyle. She'd blown through her funds alarmingly quickly and had been reduced to begging her parents for money, a source that had started to dry up after the third time she'd gone home, hat in hand. It was hard to get good jobs while being a student and some of the jobs were downright sleazy. As a young brunette with a perfect figure – or so she considered herself – she was a magnet for all kinds of indecent proposals. One recruiter had even offered her dollars for posing naked on a website. She had been seriously considering the offer – she had been that desperate – when a friend had pointed her to Professor Zeller's program. Elizabeth hadn't expected much, but the reward had been surprisingly high. They'd been offered fifty dollars just for completing a test.

Elizabeth had been surprised to be called back a few days later by the Professor himself, who had explained that her tests scores had been very high and offered to work with her to develop her psychic abilities. Elizabeth had been stunned. It wasn't uncommon for college students to be given all kinds of tests and she honestly hadn't realised that the test she'd undergone had been intended to measure ESP. She'd thought it was just an odd survey for psychological research. It had crossed her mind that it was a joke – or another attempt by a lecturer of dubious integrity to get her into bed – but she'd been offered a hundred dollars for each successive test. That, she'd decided, was too much for a joke.

"Tired and headachy," she said, finally. The headache had been pounding in her temples all day, despite swallowing twice the recommended level of painkillers. "Do you think that we could get on with it? I have to be home early tonight."

"Of course, of course," Zeller said. He smiled as he passed her the first set of cards. "Shall we play a game or two first to lighten the mood, or should we get straight on with the program?"

Elizabeth hesitated, and then nodded. She hadn't played Snap since she'd been a little girl, but playing with Professor Zeller was surprisingly fun – and challenging. The professor had no sense of chivalry when it came to playing games and never let her win. It was an attitude she wished, sometimes, that her boyfriend shared. Ron would take her bowling, or playing pool, and then throw the game, allowing her to win easily. It just wasn't challenging.

The Professor dealt out the cards and chattered away about nothing as he sorted them out into two piles. He'd actually altered the rules of the game slightly, providing no less than four different ways of calling *snap*, although Elizabeth wasn't sure if it added anything to the game. She tried to push the headache to the back of her mind as she bent over her cards, watching as he placed his first card down gently, but it refused to fade. It only grew stronger as she put down her own cards, watching carefully for the first matched set. The shout, when it finally came, was loud enough to send new shivers of pain through her head.

"I win," Professor Zeller said. Elizabeth was tempted to remind him that she had a headache and therefore couldn't be expected to win, yet such excuses never worked with Zeller. He'd pointed out, to one of his other students, that life not only wasn't fair, but also never gave second chances. One couldn't expect to come back from the grave just because one had had a headache when crossing the road and therefore missed the bus barrelling towards a fatal impact. "Shall we move on to the other tests now?"

Elizabeth rubbed her forehead, hoping that the pain would fade soon. "All right," she said. A sudden stab of pain through her head made her feel as if she was going to be sick, all of a sudden. "Let's get on with it."

Professor Zeller brought out the big table and waved for her to sit in one of the chairs. There was no way to see what his hands were doing on the other side, or the cards he was studying, forcing her to try to guess at what card was in his hand. The test confused her at times, but then...it was his money and it sure beat flipping burgers for a living, or selling her body on the streets.

"So tell me," he said, after a moment. "What card am I holding?"

Elizabeth took a wild guess. "The four of hearts," she said. She allowed some of her anger and pain to slip into her voice. "What card are you holding?"

Professor Zeller didn't answer, but then he never did. They ran through all fifty-two cards, the Professor keeping score on a sheet of paper, and then repeated the process, by which time Elizabeth's headache had grown to alarming proportions. She found herself slurring the words, her vision fading in and out ... and he barely caught her before she slid off her chair and hit the floor. For a moment, she was sure that she had blacked out, as she awoke lying on the couch, a nervous face peering down at her.

"You fainted for a moment," the Professor said. Somehow, she didn't doubt his words. "How are you feeling now?"

Elizabeth stared up at him. The pain in her head had faded away, but it had been replaced by an odd background noise, like millions of voices murmuring away just quietly enough to be heard yet too low for her to pick out individual words.

She tried to stand up and discovered that her legs were threatening to fail her. It took two tries before she managed to stand upright and push away his helping hand.

"Tired," she said, honestly. She hadn't felt so tired since she'd run a marathon for charity back at school, back when she hadn't been able to wait to go to college. How long ago that seemed now. "Can I...would you mind if we finished the tests another day?"

Zeller gave her a calculating look, and then nodded once, shortly. "I dare say that we can pick up again next week," he said. He frowned to himself. "You can always come again tomorrow to complete the tests, or..."

He shook his head. "Never mind," he said. "You'll get the payment for this set of tests anyway, without worrying about the rest of the tests we should have conducted. You have a nice evening and don't worry about a thing."

"Thanks," Elizabeth said, giving him a quick hug. The Professor was nicer than he had to be, but then he could afford it. If she'd been working in a burger bar, she would probably have been sacked for daring to suggest that she needed time off work, if only to recover from a headache. "I'll see you soon, all right?"

She was smiling as she ran down the stairs and out into the open air. It was summer and so there were hundreds of students enjoying the warm air. Harvard University – her father kept muttering about the People's Republic of Massachusetts whenever she asked for an additional loan – wasn't a bad place to study, but it did have its problems. One of them was the fact that it cost far too much – her parents were paying most of it – and that degrees counted for less and less these days. At least Harvard had a good reputation still; several of her friends from school had had to go to inferior colleges and wouldn't be able to find a high-paying job when they graduated.

The walk back to her student housing took only a few minutes normally, but this time it took longer, much longer. The noise in her head had grown louder the moment she stepped outside, as if it was ringing in her ears. She scratched at her ears in the hope that the sound would fade away, but it remained there, mocking her. Her legs kept shaking and it took an effort of will to keep walking back to her flat, one shared with four other students. It wasn't a bad arrangement, even if they were living in each other's pockets. She envied the students whose parents obtained houses and even single flats for their use. They were the luckiest people on campus.

Her head was spinning when she reached the flat and it took several tries to remember her PIN code to get through the security gate and enter the lobby. Oddly, the sound at the back of her head faded away the moment the gate was closed behind her, falling back to a background murmur. She was alone. Puzzled, but grateful, Elizabeth took the stairs two at a time and ran into her flat. As she had hoped, her roommates were all out, allowing her to make herself a cup of coffee and settle down in front of the television. She had intended to take a short nap before her boyfriend arrived, but she ended up being shaken awake by one of her roommates.

"Your boyfriend is here," Lilly said. Elizabeth almost fainted again. Lilly's words were calm and dispassionate, but she sensed an outpouring of emotion behind them. She had known that Lilly didn't like Ron, yet she hadn't realised just how much scorn lay behind her feelings. The background noise seemed to be growing louder. "Can I kick him out or should I send him in to see you?"

Elizabeth felt her head spinning. "Please show him in," she said, grandly. Lilly made a face at her and headed back to the door. By agreement, the roommates weren't allowed to show anyone in without the permission of the person they'd come to visit. It was a safety issue more than anything else. A university campus wasn't always the safest place in the world. "I may not look my best, but..."

She'd liked Ron from the moment she'd seen him on the football field. He was tall, beefy and handsome, even though Lilly had told her that there was nothing between his ears. She suspected that Lilly had dated Ron at one point and the relationship had ended badly. It wasn't something she could hold against either of them. It wasn't as if she hadn't had any relationships before she'd started dating Ron. She looked up, smiled at his red hair, met his eyes...and knew. Elizabeth couldn't have said how she knew, or what told her the truth, but she knew to the deepest fibre of her being that he was cheating on her. She stared at his face, looking for the lipstick she was sure was there, yet she saw nothing. It was all she could do not to scream in rage and frustration. She'd been looking forward to their night out, damn it!

"Ron," she said. Her voice was shaking and she had to swallow hard before she could speak again. It was more of an effort than she had expected and she wondered, dimly, if she had suffered a stroke. "Why did you cheat on me?"

He was staring at her in complete disbelief, but answers roared into her head, somehow. She saw a dark-skinned girl with brown eyes and large breasts, someone who was willing to do something for him that she had refused to consider. Memories – Ron's memories – flared through her mind. The girl and he had kissed, and made love, and done everything together ... while she'd thought that he was in love with her. Elizabeth felt hot anger boiling through her mind and tried to stand up, intent on murder. How *dare* he treat her in such a manner? She wanted to kill him.

"I didn't cheat on you," Ron said. It would have been convincing if every word hadn't dripped with insincerity. His thoughts were spinning madly through her head. He was thinking that he could charm her back into his bed, perhaps for just one more time, perhaps forever ... and she'd forget about the other girl. "Who's been telling lies to you?"

"They're not lies," Elizabeth ground out. The boiling rage in her mind was making it hard to think. "Who is she?"

A name flashed through her mind. *Janelle*. Ron's memories of her were tinged with lust and admiration; lovely breasts, long dark legs and skilful lips. Elizabeth shuddered as the memories played out in her mind. Her mother had told her that all men were animals. She hadn't realised that her mother had meant it literally.

"But there is no other girl," Ron pleaded. Elizabeth knew, beyond a shadow of a doubt, that he was lying. He reached out a hand for her and she pushed him back. "Elizabeth, I love you..."

He reached out for her again and this time bare skin touched bare skin. Elizabeth screamed as more memories roared into her mind, each one stronger than the last. She was barely aware of Lilly running back into the room, followed by Gayle – another flatmate – and *her* boyfriend. Ron's life was pouring into her. She saw his earliest memories, his first kiss, his first sexual experience ... everything. Lilly had been right. Ron was a bastard who had hurt too many people for his own amusement.

But what was happening to her?

"Get out," she said, as Ron let go of her. Impossible as it seemed, the more people there were in the room, the louder the noise in her head. What was happening to her? "Just get out! I never want to see you again, you..."

Ron looked as if he wanted to say something sharp and cutting – she heard it in her head before he could speak – but Gayle's boyfriend took him by the arm and pushed him towards the door. Ron was a bigger boy, yet he offered no resistance. He seemed to be in shock. Elizabeth shouted after him, in anger, that she would speak to Janelle and then he would have neither of them, feeling his shock blasting through her mind. She could see the question – how the hell had she known – blaring through his mind...

Understanding clicked. She *had* read his mind.

Lilly touched her skin gently and Elizabeth recoiled as Lilly's memories flared through her mind. She had never realised how desperately lonely her friend was, although she was amused to realise that Lilly had never dated Ron. She had thought that she'd seen Lilly in Ron's memories...what was happening to her? What had she become that she was willing to probe her friend's mind? A thought occurred to her and she smiled. She could ask the lectures what questions they intended to use in the exams and study for them, once she'd read the answers out of their minds. And, perhaps, she could check any future boyfriend to avoid dating another cheating asshole.

"Elizabeth," Lilly was saying. In Elizabeth's dazed state, it was hard to separate what her friend was saying from what she was thinking. She fought to overcome the confusion in her mind, but every time she managed to control it the background noise rose up and overwhelmed her. It dawned on her that the background noise was the massed thoughts of everyone within range. "Do you need a doctor?"

"No," Elizabeth said, flatly. She knew who she had to take it to, the only person who might believe her and be able to help. She'd wondered why Professor Zeller had chosen her for his experiments – none of the explanations seemed to fit – but now she understood why. "I need you to help me get back to Professor Zeller."

Lilly frowned. "You really ought to rest," she said. She didn't understand what was going on, for which Elizabeth was eternally grateful. She knew how *she* would have reacted if Lilly had told her that she could read her mind and she suspected that her friend would react in the same way. Her little brother's friend had once peeked on her while she was changing and she'd kicked the little asshole so hard that he'd gone home bruised. Her mother had understood even if her father had given her a lecture on holding her temper under control. "I can get you a drink and..."

"No," Elizabeth said, again. Now that Ron was gone, it was easier – somehow – to stand up. Perhaps with practice she would be able to block out the feeling – the thoughts of everyone within range – completely. Professor Zeller had been teaching her mental exercises and one of them, at least, came in handy for the situation. It was weird. Had he known, in advance, what was going to happen? "Please ... help me get back to the Professor."

Chapter Ten

The reports that telepaths have been used in military and intelligence operations have been impossible to prove and have therefore been relegated to the same level as UFOs and ghostly encounters...
-AP News Report, 2015

Roger Erickson silently cursed his superiors under his breath as he made his way up the stairs to Professor Zeller's study. Sending him here was probably their idea of a joke. It wasn't his fault that the last interview he'd undertaken had turned out so disastrously; after all, no one had warned him that the interviewee was so difficult to interview. He'd been told – after the fact – that he should have watched her prior interviews, but then it had been far too late. The disaster had turned him into the laughing stock of the newsroom and while the union had kept his superiors from firing him, they hadn't been able to help him to maintain his position. Instead, he got all of the shit jobs, including interviewing a professor whose only real claim to fame was once having worked for the CIA.

It wasn't, in Roger's view, a particularly good item to have on one's CV. He'd checked, of course, with Head Officer and he'd been assured that Professor Zeller's ex-CIA qualifications were impeccable, even if he had left the CIA ten years ago. The details hadn't been clear on just how willingly he'd left the organisation, but – this time – Roger had taken the precaution of skimming through three of the professor's published books and he was starting to think that Zeller had been sacked for delusions of grandeur. Or perhaps he'd developed them after he'd retired. He would hardly be the first ex-CIA officer to publish largely fictitious memoirs and retire on the proceeds.

Harvard University clearly didn't think that much of Zeller either. There was no clear explanation as to why Zeller was allowed to live and work at the university, although there was a vague suggestion that he'd actually donated a sizable part of the family legacy to the college It would have explained quite a few things about him, not least the fact that he didn't seem to have any official duties or responsibilities. The most strenuous thing he'd done for his official employers had been to give a lecture on the CIA from time to time. He had no secretary, no young intern or even a modern office. They'd given him an office that probably served as his apartment as well.

He knocked on the door and it opened, revealing a comfortable lounge with a pair of sofas and a single comfortable chair – and a roaring fire in the grate. It was a warm day outside so he was surprised to see the fire, unless it was meant to make him feel comfortable. There were three people in the room; an elderly gentleman he assumed was Professor Zeller, a younger Indian man and a brown-haired student. He gave her a quick once-over, wondering absently what she would be like in bed, and was surprised when she flushed dark red. Her clothing was surprisingly conservative for a university student.

"Thank you for coming," Professor Zeller said. "This is Kareem Ganchi, my legal representative and Elizabeth Tyler, one of my students."

Roger eyed Ganchi with new respect. Ganchi had been involved in several legal trials that Roger had covered, back before his fall from grace, and had won them all. He tended to take on cases involving civil liberties and was a known opponent of the Patriot Act, even taking on cases without pay if he felt that human rights were being violated. It hadn't made him popular in all places, but it was an impressive history. He was also known for winning vast damages from various corporations for all kinds of misconduct.

"Charmed," Roger said, slowly. He'd assumed that Zeller had intended to waste his time – or his superiors had intended to send him on a wild goose chase – but he doubted it if a lawyer was involved. "Might I ask what is going on here?"

Zeller smiled. "What do you think is going on here?"

Roger scowled at him. His tolerance for games was limited. He saw the girl – Elizabeth – cringe back as he looked at her, something that puzzled him. Unless ... had she been raped and they intended to blame it on him? No, that couldn't be the answer. Proving his innocence would be simple enough and then three careers would be ruined. His uncertainty made him disinclined to try to guess.

"I don't know," he said, finally. "What is going on here?"

Zeller indicated the girl with a wave of his hand. "After ten years of trying, my experiments have finally produced a result," he said. "Yesterday, Elizabeth developed telepathic powers. You're looking at the first human telepath to come into existence."

Roger's first inclination was to laugh. Back when he'd been a very junior reporter, he'd been sent to report on mediums and magicians and all kinds of confidence tricksters – people who, by and large, had fooled people who wanted to be fooled. It didn't take much effort to come up with a convincing trick, one that might even stand up to careful scrutiny. But then...what if?

There had been vague reports filtering through the internet that the government *had* developed a new tool for hunting down and capturing terrorists. Roger had never been sure how seriously to take them, not least because many of the regular sources had dried up or refused to talk about it. Leaking information to the media was part of the political game, yet very few whispers had made it out to the hundreds of waiting ears. But ... the New York Dirty Bombers had released official statements claiming that their minds *had* been read, something that – on the face of it – was absurd.

Roger wasn't blind to the weaknesses of his profession. He knew that reporters often picked up enemy statements and reported them as fact, even though they should have known better. It happened because such statements were often *possible* – even though they were far from accurate – and therefore *believable*. It was easy to believe that a CIA agent had authorised the torturing of suspects, even if it was against regulations; it was harder to believe that they had been reading minds. Why would a group of terrorists put forward a lie that everyone knew was a lie? The answer was obvious. They wouldn't; they'd just make themselves sound like idiots.

And that suggested, he realised, that there was some truth to the story after all.

He shook his head. It couldn't be possible.

"So you're a telepath," he said, turning to Elizabeth. It would be easiest to deal with her first and see if she was actually what they claimed her to be. If they were lying ... well, he could go back to the office and bitch to his superiors about wasting his time. "I'd like you to prove it."

Elizabeth's voice was very faint. "When you entered the room," she said slowly, "you wondered how I would look naked and how I would be in bed with you."

Professor Zeller coughed loudly as Roger flushed himself. She was right. He *had* wondered that, yet ... any normal male would wonder that when confronted by an attractive female. A homosexual would have similar thoughts about another handsome male. And, come to think of it, she *had* flushed when he had wondered about it. A chill ran down his spine. It could be real ... or it could be a coincidence. Further testing was needed, clearly.

"Very well," he said. He considered for a long moment and then concentrated, summoning a mental image of a unicorn being ridden by a version of his ex-wife. The woman had been sweet when they'd married, but when they'd spent two months together she had turned into a complete harridan. "What am I thinking of now?"

Elizabeth told him.

And Roger's world turned completely upside down. There was no way that that could be a coincidence. She could read his mind. A thousand memories flashed in front of his eyes, memories that he had considered to be private, ones he would never have shared with anyone. He knew that she could see them in his mind, or perhaps she could dig them out of his deeper memories and share them with the world. The thought was horrifying.

"You have to tell the world," Professor Zeller said, finally. Roger was still shocked, but he was nodding slowly. If Elizabeth had telepathic abilities, it was possible that the rumour about military telepaths was true after all. And that meant that *he* would have the scoop of a lifetime. And *that* meant that he would have to be reinstated as a top reporter. "The longer you delay, the greater the chance that someone from the government will succeed in classifying this and hiding it from the public."

"I understand," Roger said. He took one last look at the girl and smiled. "Why don't you brief me in private so I can file a proper article? And then there are some forms for you to fill in, just in case of legal trouble."

"There will be none," Ganchi assured him. "The law does not cover telepaths."

***

The day went slowly for Elizabeth. Surprisingly, somehow, Professor Zeller had almost no mental presence at all. Everyone else she met over the course of the day was a tight knot of emotions, thoughts and feelings, but Professor Zeller was a complete blank. It made her wonder if the CIA's experiments had produced more results than they'd realised at the time or if Professor Zeller had made a breakthrough and then concealed it from his superiors. His mere presence was reassuring, if only because she wasn't picking up any background noise from him. On the other hand, he was looking at her as if she was his meal ticket.

She scowled as she settled back into the sofa after proving herself – again – to the latest set of visitors. Professor Zeller had been calling in scientists from all over the city, making it harder and harder for anyone to cover it up. No one believed them at first, not until Elizabeth read their minds to prove it. It wasn't the most relaxing experience. Their disbelief had given way to shock and then to fear. One of the men who had visited her had had a very dark mind. She wasn't sure how to tell the difference between real memories and fantasies, but his involved children and horrific sexual acts. She'd told Professor Zeller's attorney – whose mind tended to focus more on the attractive young men who came to check the story – and he'd promised to look into it. It seemed that telepathic evidence wasn't legally admissible in court.

The thought bothered her. One of the thoughts that had run through the lawyer's mind – he hadn't said it out loud – was that she could be arrested and charged with intruding into a person's privacy. It had scared her, not least because she had no idea how she could prove that she *hadn't* been into someone's mind. She had been arrested once – at a protest march a year ago, for a cause that had seemed a good idea at the time – and that hadn't been a pleasant experience. What would it be like if she was arrested for real?

She looked over at the untidy stacks of books and smiled to herself. Professor Zeller had encouraged her to read his books and papers and so she had, although not all of them had made sense. He believed that human evolution was still underway – although it had been slowed by the development of tools and procedures to cheat Darwin – and that the next logical step in human evolution was the development of telepathic powers. The CIA had been happy to recruit him to help with their remote viewing project, but much less keen on his ideas about human development. Elizabeth privately suspected that they had a point. She had a friend who was confined to a wheelchair and *she* wouldn't have liked it if anyone had suggested that nature should be allowed to take its course, killing her friend and anyone else who happened to be crippled. Besides, someone who had been crippled as a child would not have being a cripple in their genes.

Professor Zeller came back into the room and grinned at her. "Success, of a sort," he announced, cheerfully. "The entire university is chattering about you, my dear."

"Oh," Elizabeth said. It dawned on her, suddenly, that her life was about to change completely. No, it *had* changed completely. She could no longer hope to keep what she was a secret. Her friends – and Ron, her ex-boyfriend – would know that she could read their mind. The fear and suspicion she'd faced from the people who had come to see her – to gawk at her – would be multiplied in the minds of her former friends. They would never know if she was reading their minds or not and it would destroy them. "What happens now?"

Professor Zeller beamed. "Why, we tell the world and ..."

He broke off as someone knocked on the door. When it opened, it revealed Charlie Lain, one of the other members of Professor Zeller's research program. Blood was gushing out of his nose and ears, for no apparent reason. Elizabeth reached out with her mind and recoiled in surprise, as his mind was reaching out towards hers. She *knew* him then, far more intimately than she had ever known anyone else, and he knew her. The words didn't have to be spoken aloud. Charlie had developed telepathic powers of his own.

Zeller didn't seem surprised when she told him, although he was surprised by the violence of Charlie's awakening. He'd had a headache during his own tests, but nothing had happened until he'd gone to watch a football match with some of his friends. His awakening – and Elizabeth winced at the feelings emanating from his mind – had been in the midst of thousands of people. He had been incredibly lucky to survive the experience.

"You should have stayed in the hospital," Zeller said, firmly. Charlie glared at him, his emotion blazing out like a beacon. "You're not well and..."

"I want you to make it stop," Charlie snapped. He didn't seem willing to compromise. "You're the one who insisted that we do your tests, you're the one who monitored our brainwaves and suggested that we try different exercises ... I want you to make it stop!"

Zeller seemed surprised for the first time. "Why would you want it to stop?"

Charlie jerked forward, caught the professor by his collar and pushed him against the wall. "I can hear them," he hissed. "I can hear them all! I can hear everyone in the world thinking and thinking and thinking and ..."

His voice trailed away. "I can't think for myself," he said, in a quieter tone. "I cannot think at all."

Elizabeth caught her breath. Charlie didn't know it, but he was bombarding her with his thoughts and feelings – and those of everyone within range. Or perhaps he did know and he just didn't care. She suspected that he would know if she tried to look into his mind to find out the answer, or ...

"Calm down," she said, quietly. She wanted to touch him, but she didn't dare. Physical touch seemed to make the contact stronger. "Listen ..."

"You calm down," Charlie shouted. "Stop shouting; just stop *shouting* ..."

"I'm not shouting," Elizabeth said. She recalled one of the basic mental exercises and concentrated on it. It was easier so close to another telepath. "I want you to think about building blocks, ok?" Charlie nodded, letting go of Zeller and rubbing his head. "I want you to think about building a wall of blocks around your mind. I want you to concentrate on the blocks, one by one, as you slot them into place. Your thoughts are inside the barrier; everything else is outside, kept away from your mind by the walls ..."

Charlie's mind seemed to quieten down as he concentrated, although – as he built his mental walls step by step – it was growing harder to read him. The walls didn't seem to conform to natural laws, but then they were really nothing more than mental constructs. Her own blocks seemed to topple the moment she questioned their value to her.

"All right," she said quietly, once Charlie's blocks were in place. "I think we'd better check on the others. What if they developed telepathy at the same time?"

"I'll see to that," Zeller said. "You two can remain here and relax. Keep working on your mental blocks ..."

"Professor," Elizabeth said suddenly, "why are you so hard to pick up mentally?"

Zeller smiled. "Long story," he said. "I'll tell you it one day."

***

Roger finished writing his story and scowled down at it, knowing that his superiors would question it before allowing it to be published ... and also knowing that failing to publish it would result in someone else beating him to the punch. He'd confirmed everything as far as he could, with no less than four academics willing to add their names to a statement that corroborated what had happened. He'd even kept speculation as limited as possible.

Staring down at the computer, he tapped a key and uploaded the story to the publishers. The story was out now, whatever else happened. If his superiors didn't want it published, he would upload it onto the journalists' internet network and his scoop would be preserved when the story finally broke – and his superiors would end up with egg on their faces. The computer pinged a second later and he read the message with a flicker of surprise. The story was going to be published.

Grinning, he walked out of the building and went for a celebratory drink. Whatever happened now, the story would be impossible for anyone to kill. The human race was about to discover the existence of telepaths and the world would never be the same again. And it was his story. His name would go down alongside Woodward and Bernstein.

Chapter Eleven

Scientists at Harvard University today confirmed the first known development of telepathy in human beings, producing no less than seven people with mind-reading powers of varying strengths. Professor Zeller, the developer of the research programs that produced the telepaths, stated that it was the dawn of a new era for the human race. The federal government refused to comment, both on the development of the telepaths and the suggestion that telepaths were used to catch the New York Dirty Bombers...

-AP News Report, 2015

"So," Art said, as the government car pulled into Harvard, "who is Professor Zeller anyway?"

They had been caught completely by surprise. Despite the NSA's hugely expensive system for intercepting and monitoring phone calls and the internet, Professor Zeller's bombshell was already hitting the news by the time Looking Glass was alerted. It had been sheer luck that Art had been even remotely close to Harvard and by the time they could reach the building, the news was spreading all over the United States. The coverage had a detectable tone of 'have they gone mad' but it was spreading. The testimonials from both staff and students were helping to push it along.

Art rubbed the back of his head as the car parked next to cars belonging to a dozen media outlets and other interested parties. If Professor Zeller had been CIA at one point, he should have known better than to trigger off a media feeding frenzy. The CIA had recruited several think-tanks to attempt to puzzle out what would happen if an awareness of telepaths entered the general public mentality and few of the results had been good. The worst case had suggested that telepaths would be rounded up and sterilised by the government, if not shoved into gas chambers and left to die. It hadn't made pleasant reading.

It was easy to see the writer's point. In the six months between discovering other telepaths and Professor Zeller's brainstorm, Art and his comrades had been used in a role that made him uneasy. The CIA routinely did security tests on its staff, including lie detector tests and drug interrogations, but this time things had been different. Art had been concealed behind a one-way mirror, watching and reading minds as questions had been thrown at the test subjects. They'd uncovered four Russian moles, six Chinese spies and several officers who had been slipping information to the media from time to time. The CIA had a nasty reputation for leaking like a sieve, yet Art had never realised the scale of the problem. Lie detectors and security vetting were far from completely reliable. Even so, it was setting a worrying precedent.

The CIA's recruits had known that they would be expected to undergo various security checks, but none of them had signed up to have their minds read by telepaths. They didn't *know* that their minds had been violated and when they found out ... Art wouldn't be too surprised if they were angry. Even with light peeks – the term had entered general use – he'd picked up too many secrets. Quite a few officers were homosexual, or cheating on their partners, or worried about their expenses and paperwork. He'd said nothing about that to his supervisors. They didn't need to know.

Alice frowned. "Why don't you read my mind?"

"I'm lazy," Art said. Pulling individual facts out of a person's mind was possible; it was a great deal harder to obtain a complete story, particularly when it wasn't of great significance to the source. "Why don't you tell me everything and I'll tell you if you're telling the truth?"

"I thought Marines weren't allowed to be lazy," Alice countered, although her words carried a worried emotional state. She, too, was concerned about the effects of the leak. "Let's see ... he actually left the Company before I joined, so I never met him in person ..."

She ticked off points on her fingers as she spoke. "Professor Zeller was the youngest son of very old money, one of the richest people ever to join the CIA," she said, thoughtfully. "He could have wasted his life without ever touching the seed money, but instead he developed an interest in the paranormal from a very young age. The CIA was throwing money at ESP in those days and they decided that a scientist who was obsessed with proving the existence of telepathy would make a suitable recruit. The Russians were supposed to be making advances in turning ESP into a weapon and the CIA thought it needed a counter."

Art smiled, although in truth he felt no humour. It had crossed his mind that *he* might not be the first telepath after all. It was possible that the Russians had developed telepaths of their own and that they continued to operate in secret, without alerting the Americans or anyone else to their existence. So far, most of the reports he'd read that had come out of the Russian ESP program had been vague in the extreme – or written to be sensational – but it was possible that there was a hard core of truth somewhere within the reports. But it was equally possible, as Alice had reminded him, that they were all nonsense. The CIA had been desperate for funding in those days.

"Professor Zeller developed the Zeller Test and many of the other tools we use to measure psychic potential," Alice continued. "He pioneered some of the research into remote viewing – Project Star Gate – and made several strides forward. Unluckily for him, most of the research wasn't particularly impressive and some of his enemies claimed that he was faking the results, despite the most secure tests we could conduct. Remote viewing simply doesn't seem to work according to the laws of science as we understand them. Unlike ... say, a gun, it doesn't always seem to work. Zeller eventually quit in disgust and went private, writing several articles on his life with the CIA. We didn't even consider calling him back to see you."

"Oh," Art said. "And since then he's been carrying out his own research?"

"So it would seem," Alice admitted. "The Company didn't bother to keep a close eye on him afterwards. Far too much of the details surrounding Project Star Gate had already leaked out into the public and generally been dismissed. Zeller was allowed to continue his research in private and ... well, we may have misjudged him. He's produced civilian telepaths."

"Yes," Art agreed. Ahead of them, the background noise was sparking with shock and fear. More and more people, he realised, were becoming convinced of the truth. They had come to Harvard intending to prove that there was no such thing as telepathy, but instead they were realising that telepaths were real. The thought made him wince. There was no way to shut down the media circus now. "What on Earth was he thinking?"

A thought occurred to him and he frowned. He'd developed his telepathy through stress while on a combat mission and the other telepaths had been developed through being forced to feel stress and fear. How had Zeller developed *his* telepaths? Somehow, Art doubted that any student would stand for allowing a professor to conduct pain experiments on their bodies. Or, as one of the researchers back at Looking Glass had speculated, had the presence of a handful of telepaths started to speed up the development of additional telepaths, *without* the need for induced stress? There was no way to know.

"I called ahead," Alice said, as she opened the door and stepped out onto the streets. The noise of people milling about ahead of them grew louder. "The Professor has agreed to meet us in private, rather than subjecting us to a press conference."

"Right," Art said. "And what exactly are we supposed to do?"

"Find out just what the real situation is," Alice said, briskly. "And then report back to Looking Glass. I heard that the President himself is being briefed now."

Her voice was normal, but her mental tone was worried. If there were other telepaths up ahead – and Art was sure that he could sense at least one telepath in the general area, although his mind could just be playing tricks on him – all of her CIA secrets would be exposed. Her superiors had sent her to Art because she knew relatively little, but that was no longer true...and none of the non-telepaths had succeeded in producing a mental shield to protect their thoughts.

Art had to smile. It hadn't occurred to him – until it had been pointed out by one of his briefers – that the President himself hadn't been told the details of Project Looking Glass. It didn't sit well with him; he might have had some problems with some of the people who had sat in the Oval Office while he was alive, yet the President was still the Commander-in-

Chief of the United States Military and therefore Art's ultimate superior. He suspected that the President, no matter how relieved he was because of the success in New York, would be unhappy about not having been told in advance. As it was, Professor Zeller's success would fall upon a President who was mentally unprepared for the shock.

Alice seemed to know her way around Harvard and led them away from the crowds, towards a rear entrance that was guarded by a pair of campus policemen. Art checked them out as they approached and smiled at their reactions to the card Alice held up for them to see. Harvard University had provided more than a few recruits for the CIA and the rest of the federal government over the years, yet they were still a resolutely liberal college. They would not be comfortable with intelligence agents prowling around on campus. Art shrugged, dismissing their concern. It hadn't been that long ago that several terrorist recruiters had been arrested at various campuses across the United States, an operation made harder by the reluctance of the college authorities to allow the FBI to operate on their territory.

"Professor Zeller will be with you shortly," a harassed-looking secretary said. Her mind was a maelstrom of shock and disbelief, shading rapidly towards horror. Art guessed that she hadn't believed in telepaths until she had found herself confronted by several, all college students. He hated to think what they would do with telepathy, particularly if they hadn't been identified as telepaths. The opportunities for blackmail were staggering.

A moment later, a door at the far end of the room burst open and Professor Zeller swaggered through, followed by a mousey-looking brown-haired girl and a green-haired boy. Art kept his face blank with an effort. He had never considered dying his hair and couldn't understand why anyone would choose to do so while they were studying. Of course, while the staff might think that the students were there to study, the students might have different ideas.

"I'm sorry about the delay, my dear," Professor Zeller said to Alice. His voice was larger-than-life, a booming sound that made Art detest him instantly. "I had to check up on Charlie. I'm afraid we had to sedate him and transport him to an isolated medical centre owned by my family. His telepathy was torn wide open and he was unable to maintain mental blocks for long."

Art frowned and reached out mentally towards Professor Zeller ... and recoiled. The Professor seemed to be a complete blank. Even another telepath, one who was capable of shielding himself, could still be detected, even if it was impossible to pull information out of his mind. The Professor ... didn't seem to be there at all. Art felt a shiver running down the back of his neck. Not for the first time, he had been confronted by the inexplicable. Had Zeller been experimenting on himself as well?

"Thank you for seeing us," Alice said, formally. "You know who we represent."

"The Company can go piss up a rope," Zeller boomed. Art had to smile, even though he was still unable to probe Zeller's thoughts. "I could have developed telepaths for them, but no – they insisted on developing cell phone intercepts and satellite observation ... BAH! What use is it if the Company knows what someone is doing when they do not know what they are thinking? I told those half-witted morons years ago that they could develop telepaths and they rejected me ..."

"... Mocked you, cast you out," Art said, dryly. Zeller glared at him. "Professor ..."

He stopped as he felt the intrusive tickle of a person trying to worm their way into his mind. He turned to look at the girl and blinked; she was one of Zeller's telepaths. Art frowned, tightened his own shields and looked back. Her mental blocks were impressive for one who had only developed telepathy two days ago – they had to be, or she would have gone insane from being so close to so many people – but Art had drilled with other telepaths and knew how to break down blocks.

"You're telepathic," the girl said, in shock. "I thought I was the first."

"That would be him," Alice said, dryly. Professor Zeller, for the first time, had been struck speechless. "Professor, we need to talk about the future."

"There's nothing to talk about," Professor Zeller said. Art had no difficulty in realising that the Professor's obsession was blinding his mind to reality. "The entire world will know about my success and you can't cover it up."

"Yes," Alice sighed. "Congratulations. You've single-handedly changed the world. Well done."

Her voice hardened. "Every single person you tested – if they're telepathic or not – will have been marked down by now," she said. "The human animal is a suspicious beast. How long is it going to be before mobs arrive at Harvard to storm the gates and burn your telepaths for poking into their minds? How long will it be before people who have nothing to do with you get accused of being telepaths and attacked? You should have brought this to us!"

"So you could cover it up for the next thousand years, like all of the research you laughed at?" Zeller demanded. "It was my success and ..."

"No one is disputing that you made a remarkable breakthrough," Alice said, patiently. "You have to understand that ..."

"No," Zeller said, flatly. "I will not cooperate with the Company. They had their chance and now the world will see what I can do."

Art smiled. "You can't do anything," he said. At the back of his mind, he wondered if that was actually true. Why *was* Professor Zeller a mental blank? "You're not a telepath yourself."

He looked over at the two telepaths, the scared girl and the green-haired boy. Somehow, Art had no difficulty in believing that the lad would enjoy using his telepathy to peek into other minds, without regard for any ethical qualms. When he'd been a young man, it would have probably seemed a cool idea to him too. He could have answered the age-old question of what women actually wanted, picked up girls who were interested in him ... the possibilities were endless.

"Tell me," he said. "What do you want to do?"

***

Elizabeth didn't know what to think. Professor Zeller had explained that the two people they were going to be meeting were from the CIA, but she hadn't expected a rugged-looking man and a pretty girl only a few years older than Elizabeth herself. On the other hand, the man was a telepath and the woman had calm and disciplined thoughts, although she also had the underlying edge of fear that was becoming alarmingly common. Elizabeth didn't probe too closely. She didn't want to alert the CIA telepath.

"I don't know what I want to do," she admitted. It had been cool proving that telepaths existed, but after that ... the growing air of fear and worry was wearing away at her. Worse, Charlie's mental blocks hadn't held at all, despite her support. She hoped that being sedated would make life easier for him, even though there was no way to know for sure. She had taken a brief nap herself and discovered that the thoughts and feelings of everyone around her seemed to bleed into her sleep. "I used to think that I was going to become a lawyer."

The CIA girl – Alice – smiled. "You may well be in danger here," she said. "You and your fellow telepaths may find yourself targeted by all kinds of people. We can take you and the rest of you into protective custody where you will be able to sleep safely."

"And then they won't be able to leave," Professor Zeller said, sharply. "You'll just cover them all up and ..."

The CIA telepath smiled. "Do you think that they will be able to resume a normal life?"

Elizabeth placed both hands on her ears, as if by doing so she could blot out their words. She didn't even want to think about it, yet there was no choice. If she went with the CIA, they might be able to help her, but it would mean letting Professor Zeller down badly. He needed her to prove that telepaths existed and ...

"You need to see this," the secretary said, bursting in. She tapped the television at the end of the room and switched to Fox News. "I just got an update from a mailing list ..."

The television showed the face of a well-known presenter. "... have just come in," the presenter said. "A man has been arrested in Kansas after shooting his neighbour, who he accused of being a telepath and reading his mind at their poker games. The claim is a reference to the announcement made a day ago that actual human telepaths had been discovered and are capable of reading minds ..."

"Well," Alice said, as Professor Zeller turned off the television. "I don't know if that man was a telepath or not, but I do know that you are likely to be in danger. Please ..."

"No," Elizabeth said, flatly. She couldn't let Professor Zeller down, not now. And besides, if the CIA had telepaths, who knew what they could do – had been doing - with them? "Thank you for the offer, but no."

Chapter Twelve

In an update to the Kansas Telepath Shooting, State Police have confirmed that the shooter was a 'deeply disturbed' man who had a long history of violence, alcohol abuse and several prior convictions for disturbing the peace. There is no proof that his victim was, in fact, a telepath. Even so, chatter on the internet is running in support of the right to shoot telepaths for mental intrusion; the term used most often is mental rape.

-AP News Report, 2015

The President of the United States knew he could not allow himself to appear surprised by anything. When he had entered office, he had believed that he would be able to shape the future of America, steering the country towards a grander future. Instead, there had been crisis after crisis after crisis, leaving him feeling as if the country was rudderless and heading towards absolute disaster. His predecessor had warned him that as long as he was in office, he would be the least popular President of the United States ever, at least until his successor took up the office and the public discovered that they missed the previous President. It was easy to see why. The President was both the most powerful man in the world and the most constrained. A single wrong move could spell disaster.

He kept his face blank with an effort as he looked up at the CIA Director. The file that had been put on his table – he'd had to clear the afternoon to deal with the crisis, something that had become regrettably common ever since he'd been inaugurated – sounded like something out of a bad novel. Telepaths – mind-readers – existed. It seemed impossible, yet the file was quite clear that it worked and that the CIA had moved to take advantage of them, at least as long as the secret remained a secret. And now the secret was out. The President's country was awakening to the fact that the world had changed. There had been no advance warning for him, leaving him stunned and scrambling to catch up. Heads would roll if he had time to deal with it personally.

"And all of this is real," he said, sharply. The CIA Director nodded flatly. "How long have you known about this without telling me?"

"The first telepath appeared six months ago," the CIA Director said. They were not friends and would never be friends, as the CIA Director had been appointed by his predecessor. "We had no idea that Professor Zeller was running a private research program until it was too late."

The President nodded towards the silenced television at one end of the room. Professor Zeller was giving yet another news conference, telling the world about telepaths – including telepaths in government service. The President swallowed a curse before it had properly formulated itself in his mind. The last thing his government needed was an accusation that it had been reading the minds of ordinary innocent civilians. And yet, he didn't see any way to prevent such accusations from being made. The world had just turned upside down.

"Fine," the President said, rubbing his forehead. The presidential inbox was already filling with secure emails from various congressmen and senators, asking what – if anything – the President intended to do about the crisis. The President had no idea what to do. He knew how to handle a terrorist strike, he knew how to handle a natural disaster or an act of war, but telepaths weren't in the presidential playbook. The suggestions he was receiving ranged from ignoring the issue, which was impossible, or declaring martial law, which was also impossible. "What do you suggest that we do about it?"

"I suggest that you speak to the nation," the CIA Director suggested. "You could tell them how telepaths have helped make the country more secure and how some of them saved the city of New York from a dirty bomb explosion. You could tell them that ..."

The President scowled. "You do know, I assume, that the lawyers acting for the terrorists have claimed that their minds were read by the police?" The CIA Director shrugged. "Two days ago, that sounded absurd; now everyone is going to believe it. And does telepathic evidence count in a court of law?"

"There is no law forbidding the introduction of telepathic evidence," the CIA Director said. "Besides, even without the use of telepathic evidence, there is more than enough to convict them and send the bastards to Death Row."

The President, who had been a lawyer before turning to politics, shook his head. "It could tie the case up for years," he said, sharply. "If the police only raided their base because of telepathic evidence, a lawyer could argue that *all* of the evidence was obtained illegally and should therefore be thrown out."

"That makes no sense," the CIA Director protested. "We *know* they're guilty."

"That will only be the start," the President predicted, with a droll smile. He was privately enjoying the CIA Director's unease – except how did one know that thoughts were private any longer? No one could know if their thoughts were private or not. Not now. "How many other cases have enjoyed the help and support of your telepaths?"

He didn't wait for the answer. "And how can we prove," he asked, "that telepathy has never been involved? How many cases will have to be reopened just because defence lawyers claim that their clients had their minds read?"

The President sobered. "And all of that doesn't change the fact that the public awareness of telepaths is going to change the world," he added. "What do we do if a telepath reads someone's mind without their permission?"

"I have a proposal," the CIA Director said. He frowned. The President, who was fairly good at reading people, knew that he was nervous. "We draft telepaths into government service and..."

The President cut him off. "No one has been drafted against their will for years," he said. "Legally, I doubt that we could draft anyone without a special act of congress and then lawyers could tie it up for years."

"Mr President," the CIA Director said, "we are standing on the brink of absolute catastrophe."

The President frowned and quirked an eyebrow in disbelief. "Every time there is a new development, the world changes," the CIA Director said. "Back when internet file sharing became popular, the public started to share MP3 files and suchlike and it was very hard to legally stop them. The music industry went berserk and tried to stop it, which only made file-sharers more determined to continue sharing files. People who didn't give a damn about the issue one way or another became involved in trying to regulate it and they largely failed. It wasn't an easy field to regulate.

"Telepathy offers us the same problem," he added. "How do we know what a telepath is capable of doing? We don't have laws covering telepathy on the statute books, so reading minds is not – technically – illegal. We may be able to catch a telepath on charges of invasion of privacy, but it would be hard to make it stick. Even so, there is a moral issue when it comes to mind reading. I doubt that anyone who has their mind read will be willing to accept legal hair-splitting."

The President rubbed his forehead. "Get to the point," he ordered. "What does file sharing have to do with telepathy?"

"We are all brought up to regard our minds as inviolate," the CIA Director said, quickly. "What will happen to our society when we discover that our minds are not inviolate? The music industry tried to hit back against the file-sharers by pushing for all kinds of bad laws, all of which were very difficult to enforce. If we draft telepaths, we may be able to control them without risking major social change..."

"I see," the President said. "How many telepaths do we know about?"

"Around forty," the CIA Director said. "The chances are good, however, that more will be coming out of the woodwork in the next few weeks and months. What happens if even one percent of the American population is telepathic?"

The President nodded. "I see," he said. "I'll think about it."

***

Three hours later, the President rose to his feet in welcome as Senator Tom Brookline was shown into the Oval Office. Brookline was one of his oldest friends and political rivals; a man whose sincere belief in the Republican Party was as strong as the President's belief in the Democratic Party, yet he was someone the President could talk to without it turning into a political catfight.   Politically, they were deadly enemies, but that didn't stop them being friends outside politics.

"Mr President," Brookline said. They shook hands firmly. "What can I do for you?"

The President smiled as the maid brought them both coffee and then faded away. "What's the word in the GOP about the telepaths?"

"Very little as yet," Brookline said. "Half of the senior leadership are still convinced that it's a joke and they'd end up with egg on their faces if they jumped too quickly." He looked up sharply. "It's not a joke, is it?"

"I wish I could say that it was and laugh at you," the President said. He picked up the file the CIA Director had left behind and passed it to Brookline. "Read this and tell me what you think."

Brookline skimmed through the file quickly and thoroughly. "I see," he said, finally. "It looks as if at least one telepath deserves a medal."

The President shrugged. "So it would seem," he agreed. "The fact remains that the secret is out and spreading – and that new telepaths, civilian telepaths, are beginning to pop up. What does this mean for the future?"

Brookline did him the honour of considering the issue carefully. "Well ... I suppose it depends on just how many telepaths there are," he said. "What happens if we all become telepathic over the next year or two? I think that we'd all be much happier if we knew what everyone else was thinking all the time. Or what if only a tenth of the population becomes telepathic? Or half the population ... it could be a nightmare."

"Yes," the President agreed.

"There will be demands for immediate regulation, of course," Brookline continued. He grinned. "I suspect you may be urged to create a Psi Corps at once." The President snorted. "You'll have to change the name, of course, or the government will be sued, but I think that that is what they will want you to do. Telepaths to be licensed; branded and put to work for the government – and kept under control.

That won't please civil liberties groups or the telepaths themselves. Why should they be kept under an insulting level of control?"

He scowled. "The problem with humanity, of course, is that we keep dividing people into groups. Protestants against Catholics; Sunni against Shia; Muslims against Jews; Americans against Russians ... it never really ends. We have conflict between people whose only real difference is skin colour, discrimination against women because they are women, discrimination against gays and lesbians ... I could quite easily see people discriminating against telepaths.

"Why do straight men generally dislike homosexuals? Is it because a homosexual man might see a straight man as a sex object? That he might do unto him as *he* would do unto a pretty girl? You remember the old joke about how guys spend all of their time thinking about sex? The joke gets less funny when you realise that gay men are just the same – they just think about men rather than women. And it hits straight men right where they live. They want to do the fucking, not be fucked themselves."

The President nodded. Unlike the CIA Director, Brookline was actually making sense.

"It will only get worse when telepaths are involved," Brookline added. "A telepath can look into your mind and see all of your secrets. All the thoughts and feelings that you keep bottled up for the sake of your own sanity and safety. It will seem to everyone that a telepath could be reading their mind every last second of the day – it will strike them right where they live. How many dirty secrets does the average person have? Do you lust after your married workmate? Do you secretly wonder what it would be like to make love to a person of the same gender? Do you have a habit of helping yourself to leftover food at the place you work? Do you steal paperwork and office supplies? Do you feel guilty because...?"

The President held up a hand. "I get the idea," he said, flatly. He remembered the shooting in Kansas and scowled. The latest reports were clear that the victim had never been a telepath.

"And there is another problem," Brookline said. He tapped the report with one long finger. "This report says that four known telepaths are effectively incapable of functioning within normal society – and that several other telepaths have been pulled out of mental care centres, where they have been driven insane by their own powers. You may need to separate telepaths from normal society as much as possible, if only for their own good. Find a nicely isolated patch of land somewhere in flyover country and set up a home for them there."

The President nodded. "So ... what do you suggest I do?"

Brookline considered it. "The best I can suggest is setting up some kind of regulatory agency," he said, finally. The President blinked in surprise. He wouldn't have expected a statist solution from Brookline. "You see ... the difference between a working and civilised state and a failed state is the rule of law. People have to believe that the law will be fair and even-handed. If not, they tend to take the law into their own hands. You need a way of identifying and punishing telepathic criminals, if only to prevent lynch mobs from forming every time a telepath may be involved in a crime."

"This problem isn't going to go away, is it?" The President asked, bitterly. "The telepaths aren't going to just vanish ..."

"Probably not," Brookline said. He pinched himself and grinned. "I didn't wake up."

"Thanks for your help," the President said, sincerely. "I just have to run a few ideas past my cabinet and then ..."

"There's something else you need to know," Brookline said. He hesitated. "You're a good man, even if you are a Democrat. You have to understand this."

He paused. The President realised that he didn't want to continue. "Where I live, Mr President, back home, I have a neighbouring family who has a beautiful daughter. I see her every day as she goes out running through the gardens, including mine, and she waves to me. She wears short skirts, so short that sometimes they flip up and I see her panties, or very tight shorts. I know that I shouldn't, but I watch her and sometimes I wonder what it would be like to reach out for her, pull her towards me and take that fantastic ass in my hands. There are times, when I am in bed with my wife, that I think of the neighbour's daughter instead."

"I don't understand," the President said, confused. "You would hardly be the first man to lust after a pretty girl."

"She's *fourteen*, Mr. President," Brookline said.

The President stared at him in horror. "Fourteen?"

"She's fourteen years old and looks seventeen," Brookline said. Once he had started talking, he seemed to be unable to stop, despite the President's shock. "I have never touched her and never will, no matter how tempting it becomes – even though I know that she will grow older. Touching her now would be statutory rape. I might have thought about it, but I would never actually do it.

"Now tell me; what would happen when a telepath read my mind and found that?"

The President frowned. "They'd accuse you of lusting after her," he said, flatly. "But merely thinking about it isn't a crime..."

"Before telepaths came into existence, no one could prove that someone was thinking about doing something," Brookline said, sharply. "Even when we discovered bombs and weapons stored in a terrorist hidey-hole or two, it was still hard to press charges against them and a good lawyer could argue that they weren't *thinking* of blowing up a building or two in the United States. Now ... now you can *prove* that someone was thinking about doing something unpleasant."

He spoke on before the President could interrupt. "Have you never wanted to strangle an irritating reporter who insists on misreporting everything you say? Have you never wanted to send the Marines into some foreign country to kill the leader who keeps irritating Americans and keeping his own people in bondage? Have you never wished that you could pull a Nixon and act outside the law?"

Brookline smiled. "How many secrets do you think are in Congress and the Senate? How many Congressmen do you think are fucking their interns like President Clinton? How many Senators have dirty little secrets that they won't want revealed, whatever the cost? Everyone is *scared*, Mr

President, and you're going to have to reassure them, somehow."

The President snorted. "What was I thinking when I ran for this post?"

"I dread to imagine," Brookline said. "That's why I never threw my own hat in the ring."

He stood up. "I've taken up enough of your time, Mr President, so all I can really do now is wish you good luck," he said. "Good luck."

"Thanks," the President said, dryly.

Once Brookline had gone, he settled back into his chair and stared down at a sheet of blank paper. He preferred to write down his thoughts where possible, knowing that hackers had hacked into the White House's computers before. Now ... now a telepath could pluck his thoughts out of his mind. He understood what Brookline had said. There would be no such thing as privacy any longer. And that would scare people. The arguments and protests over telephone tapping and email interception would be nothing compared to the coming storm.

Carefully, thinking hard, he started to draw out the future on paper.

Chapter Thirteen

With reports spreading through the country, that government-supported telepaths have been probing the minds of suspected criminals and terrorists a number of civil liberties organisations have already started demanding injunctions against any further telepathic probes being carried out by the government without a legal warrant. This comes on the heels of a protest lodged by two of the lawyers of the New York Dirty Bombers – and the sacking of a third lawyer when he refused to lodge a comparable protest. The New York Attorney General called the protests a grotesque attempt to delay justice – New York is seeking the maximum penalty for the terrorists.

-AP News Report, 2015

"Mind-readers OUT, Mind-readers OUT, Mind-readers OUT..."

Roger winced as the sound assailed his ears. It looked as if all of Harvard and most of the surrounding city had come out to join the protests against telepaths. In the two weeks since Professor Zeller had introduced his pet telepaths to the world, the reaction had moved from awe to anger and fear. Matters weren't helped by several eye-witness testimonials of what had happened when telepathic talent had blossomed into life. One man, a former boyfriend of one of the telepaths, had even filed a formal complaint against his ex for mental rape, claiming that she'd exposed his cheating through reading his mind.

"You'd better be careful in there," the policeman said, as Roger tried to slip closer. "So far, it's quite orderly, but it's going to get a lot worse very quickly."

Roger nodded, trying to ignore the lines of policemen that were rapidly forming up and preparing themselves to contain and disperse a riot. He'd seen student protests that turned into riots before, back when he'd been a cub reporter and the G20 Protests were underway, but this had an altogether nastier tone. He saw yet another police van arrive, followed by a pair of ambulances, and realised with a shiver that the police were expecting wounded. The last news report he'd picked up on Twitter had claimed that the Governor was calling up the National Guard to assist the police if the riot got completely out of hand.

The noise was only growing louder as he made his way along the edge of the crowd. He'd seen plenty of basically good-natured protests where he'd felt fairly safe but this was different. There was a hard edge to the protest, not helped by the presence of hundreds – perhaps thousands – of professional protesters and troublemakers that had arrived to join the excitement. A source in the Campus PD had told him that the internet had been used to advertise the protest – billed as a march for mental privacy – and thousands more were expected to arrive any moment. The police, apparently, were setting up roadblocks and shutting down public transport in the hopes of preventing more protesters from arriving at the campus. They'd probably end up taking part in an impromptu march against telepaths elsewhere. Riots had a life of their own once they got really started.

He caught sight of a speaker, standing on a table someone had hauled out of a classroom, and paused to listen. "... They can read our thoughts and feelings," the young woman was saying, her words booming out over the crowd. Roger could feel it responding to her chosen words, a shifting wave of anger and fear that seemed to spur them onwards. "What sort of privacy will we have in a world where our thoughts can be read?"

Another speaker stood up as the girl stood down. "We have to make them see that they cannot expect us to stand still and have our minds read," he thundered, using the microphone to amplify his words. "We have to demand that telepaths be barred from the public and forbidden to read minds! The government will not listen to us unless we make our point clear! March with us for mental privacy!"

Roger turned and headed onwards, towards the protest office. The protest was still getting organised, with several stewards trying to point the crowd in the right direction. With so many eager volunteers standing up and speaking to the crowd, matters were already getting out of hand. He could feel the energy washing through the crowd, the sensation of thousands of humans all united towards a single purpose. It was seductive; he could have lost himself within the sensation. No wonder that so many protests got out of hand. The madness of crowds was overpowering, pushing people to do things they would never do on their own. He wondered, vaguely, what a telepath would make of it, before realising that a telepath would never be able to endure the presence of so many people. It was common knowledge that several telepaths had had to be removed to a deserted part of Alaska before their minds gave out completely. They hadn't been able to block out anyone, or control their powers.

The protest organisers looked harassed when he arrived. He knew that they were not completely in control. Some of the people who had started to publicise and encourage people to come to the protests had kept their identities hidden, refusing to meet with the other organisers or provide stewards for the protest. That almost certainly meant that radicals from a dozen different groups were present within the protest, looking for a chance to cause trouble. He caught sight of a pair of teenage girls, carrying heavy bags and, oddly, a stuffed bunny and winced. They were out to cause trouble, he was sure. Very few people would carry a bag to a protest, not when pickpockets and other thieves saw it as a chance to operate without detection.

"I'm Roger," he said, taking it for granted that they would know who he was. His scoop had made him incredibly famous and earned him death threats from all over America. It seemed that he'd managed to annoy both conservatives and liberals; the conservatives thought that he'd betrayed American military secrets, while the liberals thought that he'd been encouraging telepaths to come forward and admit to reading minds. It was odd to see the two sides of American political discourse united on anything, but both conservatives and liberals, for different reasons, disapproved of public telepaths. Or maybe it was just a basic human reaction. Both sides would have secrets they wouldn't want to make public.

"Yes, we know," the leader said. He was tall and beefy, with red hair and a smile that didn't quite conceal his own nervousness. They had thought that they were in charge until they discovered just how many people had come to the protest. If they didn't please the crowd, it could turn on them as easily as it could march against telepaths, or the police. "I don't think that we have much time for interviews..."

"There's always time," Roger said, making a show of consulting his watch. There was still half an hour until the protest was actually scheduled to begin. He glanced up as a police helicopter flew overhead, and then looked back at the leader. "To start with, then, what is your interest in being here?"

The leader frowned. "My girlfriend read my mind," he said, shortly. Roger nodded in sudden understanding. He'd interviewed Elizabeth Tyler and she'd mentioned Ron, her boyfriend, during the interview. She hadn't been too impressed with him, he gathered, although that might just have been hindsight talking. He wouldn't have been too impressed if a girl had cheated on him, both with her for cheating and with him for taking her seriously. "I want to make sure that that doesn't happen again."

One of the other leaders caught his arm. "We're here to make sure that there are new laws passed against telepathy," she said, firmly. She had a faint smile that would have been charming, if some of her teeth had been smaller. As it was, her smile made her look like a happy rabbit. "We want to make sure that our mental privacy is respected."

It wasn't Roger's place to debate with them, but he needed answers. "But how do you intend to prove or disprove that mind-reading did in fact take place?"

"We want all telepaths isolated from the rest of us," Ron said, firmly. He sounded hurt, although Roger couldn't find it in him to be sympathetic. He'd cheated on his girlfriend, after all, and had to have known that she would find out one day. "They have to be rooted out and transferred to somewhere else ..."

"That's what they used to say about niggers," Roger said. He used the pejorative for shock value. "And then Hitler used to say the same about the Jews. They didn't *ask* to be telepaths ..."

"And we didn't ask to have our minds read," the girl snapped. "Don't you dare pull a Godwin on this conversation!"

"He's a reporter," a third leader said. "What do you expect? Besides, Godwin's Law is really Godwin's Folly."

Roger would have said something else, but then a new wave of shouting burst out over the crowd. A young boy – he couldn't have been much older than fifteen – had fallen to the ground, blood flowing from his nose and ears. The crowd had gathered around him and were slowly kicking him to death, screaming "telepath, telepath" out loud. Roger watched in horror, unable to move, unable even to summon the police to intervene. The small camera mounted on his lapel caught it all as the boy was battered to death. The crowd roared, as if it were a living thing, and surged forward towards the campus – and Professor Zeller's telepaths.

He was suddenly able to move again, but it was far too late to help the boy. His body was lying on the ground, trampled under thousands of pairs of feet as the crowd kept moving. A wave of bile rose up in his throat and he vomited in disgust, unable to believe his eyes. He heard sounds from the police lines, and the pop-pop-pop of tear gas canisters, but somehow he knew that it would be far too late to save the boy. The entire crowd had gone mad.

***

"You shouldn't be here," Leo said, as Elizabeth stood at the window, watching the surging crowd down below. It seemed to be a living thing, thousands of minds blurring into one single supernatural creature. She could barely look at it without feeling a growing pounding inside her mind, yet she kept forcing herself to look. She needed to develop her mental shields, whatever it took. "They want us dead."

Elizabeth nodded. She'd felt at least one person die within the crowd, a sensation akin to feeling a rubber band snap in her mind. She didn't want to know what would happen if someone died while she was within their mind, although she had a suspicion that the shock would kill her or drive her insane. Professor Zeller had wanted to reach out and test the inhabitants of the closest mental hospital for telepathy, but the moment they'd reached the building they'd been repelled by the waves of maddened thought reaching out towards them.

"I have to be here," she admitted. Part of her believed that it was all her fault. Ron was down there, whipping up the crowd against telepaths; Ron, her former boyfriend. She suspected, from his mood, that Janelle had dumped him as well. "I have to see it happen in person ..."

"They're morons," Leo said, simply. Unlike Charlie, or Elizabeth for that matter, Leo had *always* had a superiority complex. He was fiendishly smart – and knew it, and made sure that everyone else knew it – and telepathy had only added to his arrogance. He'd proposed, quite seriously, that the telepaths should breed together to produce telepathic children who would be stronger than their parents. Professor Zeller had been inclined to support the idea, but all of the female telepaths had flatly refused. "They're lashing out in hatred and fear at something they don't understand and will never have for themselves."

Elizabeth scowled. In two weeks, she had come to realise that every time a normal person – a mundane, to use Leo's term, which he'd stolen from *Babylon 5* – met a telepath, there was a brief flash of fear and shame, fear at the thought that their mind would be read and shame at the thought of someone else knowing their darkest secrets. She found it depressing and a little demeaning – she was more than just her telepathy – but some of the other telepaths, Leo in particular, got off on that sick little feeling.

"They're scared of us," she said. She hadn't dared go back to her flat, not even to pick up her possessions. Professor Zeller had cleared the building for the telepaths and set up a camp bed for her in one of the abandoned offices. It was uncomfortable, but at least she wasn't surrounded by babbling minds. "Wouldn't you be scared if your innermost thoughts were known to the entire world?"

"Perhaps," Leo said, easily. He slipped into the telepathic waveband, transmitting his thoughts to her directly. "But then, my thousands of intimate thoughts are *not* known to the entire world."

Elizabeth was preparing a cutting reply when the door burst open, revealing a campus policeman. "You have to get out of here now," he said, sharply. "The crowd has gone berserk and is heading here ..."

"Doubtless with pitchforks and torches," Leo said, calmly. Elizabeth couldn't detect any concern in his words, which suggested either foolishness or bravado. "The modern-day witch-hunters are coming to kill us all."

Elizabeth turned and looked back out of the window ... and stood, transfixed by the roar of emotion that was reaching out towards them. Thousands of people were advancing on the building, their minds baying for blood – telepath blood. She couldn't move as their screaming minds bore down into hers. She was only vaguely aware of the other two until someone slapped her face, hard. Elizabeth staggered and fell towards the floor; Leo caught her just before she could hit the ground.

"They're coming," Leo said. For the first time, he sounded shaken ... and yet the fear in his mind was rapidly becoming replaced by anger. "They're coming for us."

"You're not superhuman, you dimwit," Elizabeth swore at him. She allowed her contempt to flow into her voice as the noise outside grew louder. "You have to move, now."

Her legs were still wobbly and she had to hang on to Leo's arm as they stumbled off towards the rear of the building. "We're evacuating the surrounding area," the policeman said. His words were reassuring, but his mental tone was grim and worried. And, she realised with a shiver, part of him was wondering if the crowd wasn't right after all. It had simply never occurred to her, before, that policemen were human too and would worry about mental intrusion. "Once we get outside, we should be met by others who will escort you to a safe area and ..."

The entire building shook. Elizabeth felt, more than heard, rioters pouring in. She could hear the police demanding, through megaphones, that the crowd stand still or disperse, but it didn't seem to be working. The crowd had turned into a maddened animal, its thoughts pervading the telepathic waveband and demanding blood. It would be impossible to stop the crowd until the madness faded away. Perhaps the police could use knock-out gas on them, or...did the police even *have* knock-out gas? They hadn't used it at the last protest she'd attended ...

She winced. If she had realised just how terrified the targets of those protests had had to be, she wouldn't have gone and added her voice to the crowd. She had been all fired up with youthful outrage and she hadn't thought about their victims. Now ... now, if she could take it all back, she would. The policeman grabbed her arm and pulled her back, too late. The protesters had, deliberately or otherwise, blocked their line of escape. Elizabeth stared in horror as they advanced, their faces twisted with madness, as they had recognised her. Professor Zeller had identified her to the world and now she was their target. Their thoughts and feelings bombarded her, hatred so deep that it was far beyond logic and reason, the same kind of hatred that she felt for rapists and molesters. In lashing out at her, they were lashing out at all telepaths, hating them all. Shame turned her legs to jelly and she collapsed, knowing that her life was about to come to an end. The campus policeman was drawing his pistol, clearly intending to go down fighting, yet there was no hope of escape. The crowd was closing in, the ones at the back pushing the ones at the front forward ...

Leo caught her arm. *GO AWAY*, he thought. It took Elizabeth a second to realise that he was broadcasting to the crowd, a desperate measure. They'd never been able to communicate telepathically with mundane humans. *GO AWAY, GO AWAY, GO AWAY ...*

Fear for her life gave her thoughts power and she pushed as hard as she could, adding her mental voice to Leo's. *GO AWAY, GO AWAY, GO AWAY ...* the crowd recoiled, as if it had run into an unbreakable barrier. *GO AWAY, GO AWAY, GO AWAY ...*

***

Roger had been trying to run, to get away from the crowd and the advancing policemen, when the thoughts slammed into his brain. The power and compulsion was impossible to resist. He ran, unable to stop himself, fleeing for his life as unholy terror washed through his mind. He saw a police helicopter fall out of the sky as the pilot jumped out – without a parachute – and saw the police lines breaking up into chaos. The protesters had turned on one another and were fighting and kicking to get the hell out of dodge. He couldn't help himself; he just kept running until the compulsion faded away. Stumbling, he fell to the ground and gasped for breath, one thought running through his head.

What the hell had just happened?

Chapter Fourteen

An emergency report from the riot at Harvard claims that upwards of four hundred people have been killed in the crush and over a thousand others have been injured. Police sources are saying nothing about the riot, but the governor stated that martial law had been declared in the area and that the National Guard had been deployed to assist with the clean-up. The President is expected to address the nation at some point this day.

-AP News Report, 2015

"It looks like a freaking war zone."

Art said nothing, but he couldn't disagree with Alice. It had been barely two hours since the telepathic blast had stopped the riot and the local police, National Guardsmen and emergency services had barely been able to make a dent in the damage. The official estimate was that five hundred protesters, policemen and innocent bystanders had been killed in the riot. Art suspected that the actual number was far higher. He'd never seen anything like it in Iraq or Afghanistan.

There were bodies – dead or merely stunned – everywhere, too many for the emergency services to handle at once. Many of them were policemen who had been caught up in the telepathic blast or crushed by the protesters in their unreasoning flight from danger. Others had just been caught up in the disaster, or jumped out of windows when the telepathic blast had roared into their heads. Art had sensed it from several hundred miles away; in fact, he was sure that telepaths had felt it all over the world. It was lucky that non-telepaths outside a mile or so from the epicentre of the blast had felt nothing, or the disaster would have been far worse. Even so, there were crashed cars on the roads and hundreds more dead and wounded when they'd suddenly found themselves consumed with an urgent desire to run away. It would take weeks to sort out the damage and months to reassure the public that it wouldn't happen again – except it might just happen again. Art knew that there was no way to predict such an event or prevent it from happening. He wasn't even sure what had happened at Harvard.

He looked over towards the line of prisoners and scowled. He had never had much time for protesters in his life, yet watching lines of young men and women being cuffed, searched and loaded into police vans was chilling. They'd probably all be released unless something could be pinned on them; according to the police, quite a few protesters had arrived with weapons and bad intentions. The fire raging on the other side of the campus was proof of that, apparently; the protesters had brought Molotov cocktails and tried to use them on the telepaths. God alone knew how many had really been injured.

The wounded, at least, were being treated decently. If there was one good thing to come out of the crisis, it was that the protest had been stopped dead in its tracks, allowing the wounded to be evacuated without further delay. Art didn't know how many of the wounded could be saved. The city's doctors had all been alerted, but were they prepared for so many casualties? Years ago, he'd taken part in an exercise that had rehearsed what the Marines would do if a nuclear bomb was deployed against an American city and the results had not been encouraging. Local medical centres had either been destroyed or overwhelmed. It had proven hard to get the wounded to centres that were further away.

"Yes," he agreed. "It does look like a war zone."

The media coverage they'd picked up as they'd been raced from Washington to Massachusetts hadn't been too detailed. It looked as if the protest had somehow gotten out of hand and then ... something had triggered a telepathic blast. The talking heads on the various networks hadn't known anything more than that, which hadn't stopped them pontificating on the implications and on what they thought the government ought to do about it. Some of them were suggesting, loudly, that the government should lock up every telepath at once to prevent a second disaster, without caring one whit for human rights. A couple were even claiming that this proved that the more absurd claims against telepaths – including one where a woman claimed that a man had telepathically forced her into bed – were actually true and therefore criminal offences.

Art shook his head. The Looking Glass project hadn't produced anything other than mind or emotion readers, but this ... he caught sight of a pair of dead bodies, their features twisted by absolute terror, and shivered. The world had just changed again. He knew, from the feeling of the mental blast as it slammed into his skull, that the telepaths who'd broadcast it had been absolutely terrified, yet somehow he doubted that it would matter. If the government could consider new gun control acts because someone – terrified – had shot the wrong person, he had no doubt that they would consider new telepathic control laws. Worse, those laws would be extremely difficult to enforce, which would weaken them. He had no idea where the world was going, yet he doubted that he would enjoy the destination when he found out.

And to think that, several months ago, he'd been in Afghanistan. Everything had been so much simpler then.

The police had moved the telepaths – and their representatives – to the Houghton Library. The Houghton Library, he'd been told, held many of the university's special collections, at least under normal circumstances. Now, it had been cleared and was being used as a clearing house for the lightly-wounded and, separately, the telepaths. No one knew if the telepaths could or would produce a second telepathic blast, but they didn't want to take chances. The policemen at the door saw their ID cards and looked – and felt – relieved. They didn't want to handle their dangerous prisoners any longer. Art found it hard to blame them.

"Thank you for coming," Professor Zeller said. The man was still as much a blank as ever, but his self-confidence didn't seem diminished by the disaster. "We need you to help escort these two out of the police lines."

Art pressed his lips together, angrily. The two telepaths – Elizabeth Tyler and Leo Davidson – looked rather shell-shocked by what had happened. He found it impossible to blame them. Their lives had turned upside down when they'd developed telepathy and then turned upside down again when they had developed new powers under stress. Art scowled. Back at the Looking Glass headquarters, Doctor Sampson was doubtless already devising experiments to stress telepaths further, in hopes of developing stronger and more remarkable powers.

"I'm afraid that they will have to remain in custody for the moment," Alice said, firmly. "Far too many people have been killed for any other ..."

"You cannot, legally, hold them," the lawyer said. Mr Ganchi had an odd mental tone, Art realised; he was nervous being so close to the telepaths, yet he was determined to defend their rights. "They acted in self-defence. I could get a judge to order their release quickly ..."

"I doubt it," Alice said, angrily. "Do you know how many people died out there?"

"They were trying to kill us," Leo snapped. He looked up angrily, his eyes glaring daggers at Alice. Art sensed the thoughts accompanying the words and scowled. Just what they needed – a self-righteous prick who thought that he was God. He'd met too many young officers who had had the same attitude and they, of course, had lacked telepathic abilities. Leo sounded as if he was on the verge of hysteria. "They were trying to *kill* us!"

"Call it protective custody," Alice said, patiently. "The fact remains that whatever happened here, whoever was right or wrong, is going to have alarming effects right across the world. The public needs to know that matters are under control or worse things may happen ..."

"Why should we do anything for them?" Leo demanded. "They tried to kill us!"

Art scowled, unsure of how to proceed. The hell of it was that Leo was right, in one sense; they had acted in self-defence. And, in addition, they hadn't known what they were capable of doing until they had been stressed and forced to develop new abilities. They could not be held responsible for what they had done, any more than a child who found a gun could be held responsible if he or she accidentally shot someone. And many of the people who had died were trying to kill the telepaths when the telepathic blast sent them running for their lives.

On the other hand, many of their victims hadn't been protesters. Policemen who had been trying to save their lives had been killed, either directly or indirectly by the telepathic blast, and dozens of drivers had been killed or wounded well away from the protest itself. The telepaths weren't homeowners who had shot intruders without bothering to ask questions first; they had more in common with homeowners who had opened fire with machine guns and sprayed bullets over the neighbourhood. They could be charged with negligent homicide, he suspected – law wasn't his strong suit – except they hadn't known what they could do. The lawyers were going to have a field day.

"Because people are scared," he said, finally. "You're telepathic, just like me. You ought to know that."

Leo stared at him, angrily. "And do you agree to keep your talent under control because it would upset people if you didn't?"

Art swallowed the urge to smack some sense into the young man. "You seem to have missed the point that people are scared," he repeated, calmly. He'd endured drill sergeants and recruits who should have been kicked out of Parris Island in disgrace. He could handle one young man with an inflated sense of entitlement. "What happened here – and your blast killed or harmed people who were not trying to kill you as well as people who were trying to kill you – is going to send shockwaves across the globe. You need to help us put a lid on it before it gets far more out of hand."

"I am not responsible for their stupidity," Leo said. His thoughts were coldly superior, but Art could sense an underlying layer of fear. Leo didn't dare back down. "They tried to kill us and I will not submit to mistreatment because of their stupid fear ..."

"Perhaps I could propose a compromise," Professor Zeller said. "My family owns a sizeable mansion some distance from local population centres. I intend to transfer the telepaths who have agreed to work with me there, where they will be away from the people who fear and hate them ..."

"They'll be calling him Professor Z soon," Leo said.

"... And they won't be picking up stray thoughts from the general population," Professor Zeller added, ignoring Leo's snide remark. "They will be able to learn how to shield their minds and avoid reading other people's thoughts, at which point they will be able to re-enter the world as responsible telepaths."

Alice frowned. "Telepaths who have agreed to work with you?"

Professor Zeller beamed. "We have inaugurated the world's first institute of telepathic research," he said. "We will be working both to teach telepaths how to master their powers and to study telepathy in the hopes of learning how to control, develop and perhaps even create the powers within mundane human minds. I intended to make the formal announcement in a week's time, but we already have hundreds of scientists signed up to join the research into telepathy and other mental powers."

He beamed in delight. "We should make a whole series of wonderful breakthroughs into the innermost workings of the mind," he added, seriously. "How can anyone stop such a project?"

Art scowled. If Professor Zeller had so many people already signed up to work with his institute, it would be difficult – politically speaking – to shut it down. Furthermore, the idea did have a certain inherent logic – and it *would* keep telepaths from non-telepaths and minimise the dangers of additional riots. It would even provide an alternative to drafting telepaths into Looking Glass, as some political figures were already suggesting.

"You know," Alice said, flatly. "The reason the Company chose to fire you was because you never thought about the consequences of your actions."

Professor Zeller glared at her. "I was making breakthroughs that scared the Company," he hissed, angrily. "They refused me additional funding because they feared that I would change their tiny minds and deny them their chance to win vast amounts of funding for spy satellites and ..."

"No," Alice said. Art sensed the anger she was fighting to keep under control. "You wanted to make breakthroughs without ever asking what might happen if you succeeded, or what it might do to the world. You wanted to push ahead and didn't understand why everyone else wanted to advance slowly. You were so obsessed with your project that you never thought about how it would affect the outside world."

She met his eyes, refusing to budge. "There are all kinds of ... *things* concealed within the vaults at Langley that have been deliberately concealed from Joe Public," she said. "There are advances that would change the world for the worse if they got out and truths that would merely give new life to old causes. There are secrets about attempts to smuggle backpack nukes into the United States and biological weapons that were – barely – captured before they could be destroyed. Releasing any of those little details – how close we came to collapse – would shock and terrify the nation. And telepaths are just another little detail, one more powerful and dangerous than most."

Alice stepped back and waved a hand towards the chaos outside. "The world just changed," she said. "People believe, now, that telepaths exist and can do things to them ... and that there is no defence. The world is going to change again and again and it's going to become much darker. Did it not occur to you that we might have good reasons to cover everything up as long as possible? Instead ... it's going to get a lot worse before it gets better, *Professor*. Think about that when the State Prosecutor starts trying to assign blame for the riot."

"The riot," Leo said, "was caused by a group of stupid idiots who believe that we would spend our entire day reading their minds."

"You are applying logic and reason," Art said sharply, "to something that is not governed by logic and reason. People are scared. How long do you think it will be before political leaders start demanding that telepaths be rounded up, tattooed and sent to Alaska where they will be away from the mundane population? I'm telling you, right now, that your actions today have brought that day closer."

"We didn't mean to hurt anyone," Elizabeth said, from where she was seated. She hadn't spoken a word since they'd entered the room. "We didn't know ..."

"I know," Art said, more gently. "I know you didn't know. Do you think that that will make any difference to the public reaction?"

Alice looked at him, and then nodded. "We will provide transport and escort to your mansion," she said, to Professor

Zeller. "These two telepaths, at least, are to remain within the mansion until the whole ungodly mess is sorted out."

Leo looked up, sharply. "But ..."

"The other choice is going into protective custody until the lawyers manage to reach a consensus on who is responsible for what," Alice snapped. "I suggest, very strongly, that you accept being under house arrest for the moment and don't push your luck any further. If you go on live TV and start calling people stupid idiots – just because they're afraid of you – you'll just provoke additional riots. The choice is yours."

They locked eyes for a long moment.

"We're going to the mansion," Elizabeth said, flatly. Leo looked surprised, but nodded. Art could sense his relief and frustration, relieved because he knew he should back down and didn't quite dare, frustrated because he wanted to push back against the world. "We didn't mean to do any of this ..."

"I know," Art said. "But I'm afraid that you will have to deal with the consequences. We all will."

***

Roger showed his press pass to one of the National Guardsmen and was surprised when the guardsman waved him through, after warning him to stay out of the way of the emergency services. The scene was a nightmare and it seemed impossible to believe that everything could have gone so bad so quickly. His head still ached from where the telepathic command had slammed into his skull, forcing him to run ... dear God, if they could do that, what else could they make people do?

I did this, he thought, and shivered. He'd been pushed into visiting Professor Zeller, convinced that he was wasting his time, when instead he had stumbled over the scoop of the century. He'd gleefully shouted the news to the world, convinced that he would win the Pulitzer for his efforts and instead ... he'd helped provoke a riot. Perhaps several riots; there were reports of unrest down south and several more suspected telepaths being lynched across the United States.

He'd always approached his profession with a cynical air. The modern-day reporting environment was based around speed, not accuracy. A half-correct report that beat a correct report to air was a victory ... and, with the speed of the news cycle, an inaccurate report could be swept away and forgotten, not retracted. Reporters had become careless with the facts over the years, allowing half-truths and even outright lies – and enemy propaganda – to enter the news sphere. How many other riots had been triggered by reporters, he wondered; how many lives had been lost, or ruined, because a reporter had no time to do his homework?

And how much of the riot that had destroyed the campus was his fault?

Roger looked into his soul and wondered, for the first time, if he had done the right thing.

Chapter Fifteen

Las Vegas became the first city to unilaterally ban telepaths from entering for any reason, particularly gambling, after intensive lobbying by casino owners in the city. The measure was challenged by a number of civil liberties organisations, but after the events at Harvard it is expected to stand. The news came too late to prevent a telepath – who went under the name of Henry Sugar – from breaking the bank at two different casinos within the city. A second telepath was apparently caught in the act and arrested by security guards ...

-AP News Report, 2015

Joe Robertson had learned to listen, from a very early age, to the voices in his head. They told him, sometimes, what people were thinking and what they intended to do in the near future. It had honestly never occurred to him that there was anything unusual in having voices in his head. As a child, it had been a defence mechanism against a drunken and abusive father and uncaring mother; as an adult, it was his gift for survival. And gambling; if Joe hadn't had a drug and drink habit that far surpassed his father's addictions, he would have become one of the richest men in Atlantic City. As it was, he earned money at the tables and then lost it to the pushers and bars in the city.

He looked down at his cards while listening to the voices in his head. There were five players at the table, all – technically – playing illegally. Atlantic City was second only to Las Vegas when it came to gambling, with dozens of official casinos, but the men and women who played at private games disliked having to give anything to the casino authorities. Joe had his own reasons for avoiding playing in the official casinos; a player who was too lucky, or too good, might find himself suspected of cheating, or quietly barred from the casinos. That, too, was technically illegal, but who gave a damn? Money talked in Atlantic City and the casino owners preferred to rake in the dough, rather than hand it out to lucky little players. Joe had never given a sucker an even break, if only because no one had ever given *him* a break.

The voices whispered their words into his mental ears. Two of the players – both women attractive enough to make him wish that they were playing strip poker – had good hands, although nothing spectacular. The other two had poor hands and would probably fold rather than raising the stakes, although one of them – a gambling addict rather like Joe himself – was thinking about bluffing and raising the stakes. Joe knew – thanks to the voices in his head – that the man's wife was bedridden with cancer and that he had chosen to gamble in order to raise the money for her care, but the addiction had long since overwhelmed him. If he had managed to break the bank, he would have lost it all within hours at the tables.

Joe sat back and studied his companions. One of the women was determined to keep raising the ante and see what happened, confident in her hand and playing skills. Her face was impressively controlled, but she couldn't hide anything from the voices in his head. They told her that she regarded him with disgust and he felt a wave of anger, anger that he knew would never be allowed physical expression. The other woman was nervous, unsure of what to do or how to act. Joe wasn't sure what she was even doing at the private game; she acted more like an innocent young debutante who had been tossed into a pool full of sharks. The chances were good, he decided, that that was exactly what she was. Atlantic City drew losers like her like flies to honey, hundreds of thousands of young hopefuls called by the siren song of easy money. In the end, they either broke the addiction or found themselves trapped for the rest of their lives.

The game went on for two rounds before the confident woman scooped up the pot. Joe shrugged, accepted his own losses, and joined the second game. This time, his cards were better and he knew that his opponent was bluffing. The pot fell into his lap and he pocketed the cash – there was no need for gambling chips at private games – before joining the third game. It wasn't going to be a lucrative night, he realised, as the third and fourth games were both busts, but at least it was interesting. He leered at the confident woman and smiled inwardly at the disgust she refused to show on her face.

Pulling himself to his feet – several thousand dollars richer – Joe waved goodbye to his playmates and headed out of the small apartment block. The grimy surroundings of the poorer regions of Atlantic City were home to him and the thousands of others like him, although none of them possessed the voices in their minds. Shaking his head, he walked into the nearest bar and ordered a beer for himself, settling back in a dark corner to drink it and enjoy the show. If he had enough to drink himself into a stupor ... he didn't care. Only then, when he was swimming in enough alcohol to pickle a hog, could he get some peace from the voices.

He looked up as the music changed and the dancers came out on stage. They were all young and attractive – and two of them, he suspected, were below legal age – but they all shared the same trait: desperation. They were the dispossessed; the young women who had found themselves on the streets, helpless and alone. They had been easy meat for the pimps and suchlike who watched for such women, worked them into an early grave and then moved on to the next one. There were hundreds of thousands of such women in Atlantic City, their flesh and blood used until there was nothing left, their bodies eventually dumped and left to rot. The dark underside of the city rarely gave up its victims.

The voices in his head hissed as he looked at a young blonde girl, her naked body showing the tell-tale signs of cocaine addiction. He could have had her, he knew, simply by offering her some of the dollar notes in his pocket. In her situation, she couldn't afford to be picky – or pricey. He could meet her outside, give her a few dollars, and then make her suck him off in a side street, or take her back to his apartment for the night. And then he might find that she had taken revenge. The chances were good that she, like many street whores, carried a sexual disease that would cause him some pain and hardship, at the very least. Or she might carry AIDS and infect him ... he shook his head. If he wanted pussy, he would go to one of the high-class joints in the more upmarket areas of the city.

Staggering to his feet, he left a small handful of dollar bills on the table and headed out, walking back to his flat. Darkness had fallen over the city while he'd been playing and drinking, but the party never stopped in Atlantic City. He heard the sounds of police cars driving to the scene of one crime or another and shook his head in disgust. Atlantic City didn't want to admit it, even to itself, but it had a real problem with corrupt police. Joe had been in a dozen private games that had been raided, a problem that had been solved by handing the cops a few thousand dollars apiece.

He shook his head as a street whore stumbled out of the shadows and offered him whatever he wanted, in exchange for a few dollars. The whore, at the end of her lifespan, shrugged. Her emaciated body suggested that she would die soon and she knew it. Her pimp had long since abandoned her for someone younger and prettier. She wouldn't see another summer. Joe had no time for sympathy. Instead, he walked into his flat and turned on the light.

"Just in time," a voice said. The voices in his head screamed a warning, too late. He wasn't alone. "Just think – we were starting to wonder if you had been waylaid by a pretty face with a handful of gold."

Joe recoiled. The man facing him, sitting on *his* chair, was a very familiar face, even if they had never spoken before. He was completely bald – rumour had it that one of his enemies had shaved him and then done something to prevent his hair from growing back – and covered in silver rings that had been inserted into his skin. When he opened his mouth to speak, Joe could see the glint of implanted golden rings in his tongue. He presented a chilling appearance, but then it was hardly needed. Everyone knew that the Capper – he'd picked up that name after he'd kneecapped four of his rivals in a single night – owned a third of Atlantic City's criminal activities and that he wanted the other two-thirds. Joe had hoped never to come to his attention.

"I'll get right to the point," the Capper said. He had an accent that suggested New England, although the truth was that no one knew where he had come from, or even if he had family elsewhere. It gave him a certain strength that many of the other gangsters lacked. "I wished to talk to you in private."

Joe shivered. The last person who had talked to the Capper in private had been skinned alive. And they weren't truly alone either; the voices in his head were warning him that there were two men behind him, their stares boring into the back of his skull. If he dared to raise a hand to the Capper – fear kept him from moving in any direction – they would be on him before he could land a blow.

"I've been watching you for some time," the Capper continued. The voices in his head were unusually silent. Joe found himself floundering without his secret advantage and knew that he was completely at the Capper's mercy. "I always look for people who seem to … shall we say be bucking the odds? I run the games that you and your fellow vermin play and I don't like cheaters. The pattern surrounding you is odd."

The Capper smiled. It was the most fearsome expression Joe had ever seen. "You don't always win and you don't always have good hands," the Capper said. "You certainly aren't dealing from the bottom of the pack … on the other hand, you don't ever lose very much and at times you seem to lose nothing more than the first stake. I think that you somehow know what cards your opponents are holding."

His gaze sharpened. "I think you're one of those telepaths."

Joe couldn't move. He'd heard the voice in his head screaming *GO AWAY*, but he'd assumed that it was just another voice, another helpful whisper within his mind. He hadn't paid much attention to the news, but the voices in his head, suddenly focusing on the guards behind him, whispered that telepaths – perhaps *other* telepaths – had been discovered. And he, a man who had always been on the verge of madness, might be one too.

"Ah," the Capper said. "We do understand one another, don't we?"

Joe couldn't move as the Capper stood up and advanced towards him. All the stories about how he treated his enemies – the things he did for his own sadistic amusement, the fate of the trusted lieutenant who had tried to betray him and set up his own criminal ring – raced through his head. What would happen to him? Joe knew, without the voices in his head, that the Capper was angry. He could do anything, to Joe or to his friends and family, and no one would dare try to stop him.

"I have an offer for you," the Capper said. The pleasant tone didn't fool Joe for a second. "You come and work for me as my pet telepath. You tell me what my rivals are thinking and which of my allies is plotting to betray me. You'll find that the rewards are quite … pleasant. You could move from this dingy little brownstone to a luxury apartment in my home, with servants and even whores at your service."

He learned closer, close enough that Joe could smell his breath. "Or you wind up in the river with your throat cut," he added. "The choice is yours."

Joe was sobering up fast. He knew that he couldn't trust the Capper, but … refusing him meant certain death. And besides, being allied to the Capper would give him some protection, protection he had never enjoyed in his life. His apartment had been robbed before by thieves who thought that he had more money than sense.

"I'll join you," he said, finally.

"Excellent," the Capper said. He managed a grin that was the most disconcerting expression he had performed so far. "This is the start of a beautiful friendship."

***

David Campbell had been thinking of his wife and two children as he walked home from work in San Francisco. He was worried about them, not least because they lived alarmingly close to where the first anti-telepath riot had erupted two days ago. The police had managed to break up the riot before it could wreck the neighbourhood, but he was still unsure of their safety. He'd tried to convince his wife to take herself and their daughters to her uncle, who lived on a farm in Kansas, yet his wife had refused. She had never gotten on with her uncle. David was so distracted by his thoughts that he didn't notice the figure behind him until it was far too late. A cosh came down on the back of his neck and he crumpled to the ground.

A pair of strong hands rolled him over and he saw a masked face staring down at him. David's vision was blurred and he couldn't move, or fight back as the mugger searched him and removed his wallet, house keys and a handful of papers he'd brought home from work. He tried to make his body move, but it seemed as if he couldn't move a muscle, even his eyes refused to blink on command. It crossed his mind that he might be paralysed for life and he almost panicked. The mugger, who had somehow managed to open his briefcase, took some of the papers from the interior and dumped the rest of them onto the street.

"Answer me one question," the mugger said. David, who was unable to speak or even moan, would have laughed if his body hadn't hurt so much. "What is the PIN number for your bank card?"

David said nothing, but the mugger nodded, slapped him across the face and ran off. David's mind blurred, sinking into darkness; it seemed that, a moment later, he was in hospital. His wife was sitting by his side, watching him nervously. David tried to move and discovered that while his body hurt like never before, he could move again. He took her hand – he hadn't realised just how much he loved her until he had thought that he might never see her again – and squeezed it tightly.

"Oh, David," she said. He saw the tears in her eyes and refused to let go of her hand. "They took everything out of the bank."

David stared at her in disbelief. The bank card should have been secure. He hadn't told the mugger his PIN. He was still in shock when a pair of policemen arrived and questioned him, pushing him to recall each and every last detail about the mugger. David couldn't be much help. His memory was blurred and the mugger had been masked. The one question echoing through his mind was how could the mugger have obtained his PIN code?

"We believe that he was a telepath, sir," one of the policemen said, finally. "You're not the only victim; thankfully, the bastard doesn't seem to have that much imagination. A person with telepathy and no scruples could do a hell of a lot of damage."

***

Senator Walker liked to open his mail himself, once the security staff in DC had checked it to make sure that no one was sending him bombs or small letters filled with anthrax. It struck him as just the sort of think a populist senator should do, and besides it made sure that certain private letters were never seen by anyone else. Like many political figures, Walker had secrets, secrets that would destroy his career if they ever got out into public view – and enemies that wouldn't hesitate to use them to attack him.

The envelope was plain and unadorned, the writing inside was clearly typed out on a computer, but the message almost made him faint. Years ago, he'd had an affair with a young woman shortly after entering the Senate. She'd become pregnant, borne him a son and insisted on raising him as a single mother. Walker had set up a trust fund, knowing that he could never acknowledge the child as his own, but over the years he had watched his son grow into a young man from a distance. He was proud of his son, yet no one else apart from him and the child's mother knew the truth of his parentage.

Until now, he realised numbly.

The note was clear enough. It included the address of the mother and his teenage son and offered him a simple choice. He could pay the demanded price – with no guarantee that it would be only one demand – or his career could be destroyed. Walker stared down at the note, feeling bitter tears pricking his eyes. Only one kind of person could have ferreted out his secret. Only a telepath could have learned the truth.

Chapter Sixteen

Speaking to packed crowds today, Senator Thomas Wallis, a front-runner for Republican Party candidate for President in the 2016 elections, demanded that the government place immediate controls on telepaths to prevent a repeat of the Harvard Stampede and other disasters. This comes on the heels of a growing series of telepath and telepathy-related criminal offences against non-telepaths. Wallis stated that if he were elected, all telepaths would be registered, their powers would be brought under control and they would be transferred to a place well away from non-telepaths.

In further news, the Reverend Joshua Peterson, the founder of the controversial Church of the Rapturous Awakening, claimed today that telepaths were hearing the voices and temptations of the devil and were therefore sinners. He called on all good Christians to refuse to have anything to do with telepaths. The Church, which is infamous for its refusal to accept feminism, homosexuality and multiculturalism, demanded that the government ban telepaths from operating on American soil.

-AP News Report, 2015

The President looked down at the folder in his hand and scowled. The Presidency conveyed many blessing as well as curses, but everyone took the President so damn seriously. In his first week in the White House, he had requested – and then forgotten about – information on an obscure topic relating to military readiness. A week later, he had been presented with a massive report on the subject and discovered, much to his alarm, that the entire Pentagon was waiting on tenterhooks to discover what the new President thought of their report. He had learned, quickly, not to make any requests that others would take seriously, at least unless he actually wanted the data.

He scowled as he opened the report. After the first public announcement of telepathy, he'd ordered the Attorney

General and the Department of Justice to research telepathy and produce a legal framework for using – or rejecting – telepathy in criminal cases. Their report now lay in front of him and the President found himself unwilling to read it, even though he'd cleared a couple of hours to go through it and then compose a statement for the nation. If the truth be told, he didn't want to know.

The thought wasn't reassuring. Outside his office, a telepath had been added to the Secret Service officers guarding his life. The telepath – one of the first to be discovered – had orders to check that no one intended to do him harm, but the President knew that the other Secret Service personnel were uneasy with having a telepath near them. Anyone who complained about 'need to know' and how they had been deemed as not 'needing to know' was either ignorant about OPSEC or a self-obsessed and therefore untrustworthy idiot, yet having a telepath made a joke out of mental privacy. Did the President have a right to order a person's mental privacy violated because they *might* pose a threat to his person? He could imagine no more alienating activity. People who had been completely trustworthy might become untrustworthy because their mental privacy had been violated.

Shaking his head, he opened the report and turned at once to the executive summary. President Reagan had once remarked that he wanted all reports and proposals put before him to be no larger than a single sheet of paper and his successors had tried to do the same, although as the government had expanded even further, it was hard to convince the various departments not to produce reams of paper – or its electronic equivalent – every year. If the President made a point of reading all of the reports, he would never have any time to actually do his job.

The writer – an up-and-coming young lawyer on the Attorney General's staff – knew his stuff, at least. Telepathic evidence was unlikely to be admissible under the current rules even though it was not specifically banned. The writer had noted – and the President smiled at the evidence of a wry sense of humour – that it was not banned because no one had considered it possible, not unlike having God come down from heaven and decree a suspect innocent of all charges. The authors of the rules of evidence had never considered it as a possibility.

Furthermore, telepathic evidence could reasonably be construed as hearsay. A court would not be keen on accepting evidence based on hearsay – a person who heard something from someone, rather than directly witnessing it themselves – and a telepath might be unable to prove that he was speaking the truth. The President turned to the expanded section of the report, which noted that there were several ways to make the system workable, but he doubted that the courts would be eager to accept it. The court system tended to be highly conservative. The writer did mention that Spectral Evidence – evidence based around dreams and visions – would never stand up in a modern courtroom. The last time it had been generally accepted was back during the Salem Witch Trials. The President remembered the preacher who had castigated telepaths as witches and shuddered.

Turning back to the executive summary, it quickly became apparent that telepathic evidence ran into a number of other problems. The Constitution itself could be read as banning telepathic evidence. The Fourth Amendment – which banned unreasonable searches and seizures – could be cited; a good lawyer could probably argue that peeking into a person's mind was an unreasonable search. The Fifth Amendment – which prohibited self-incrimination, among other things – could be cited, as could the Sixth Amendment, which allowed the accused to confront his accuser. Judges, the writer had started, could draw a parallel between coerced evidence – such as evidence obtained through torture – and telepathic evidence, which could be used to throw the telepathic evidence out of court. The President suspected that it could shatter the traditional lines between liberals and conservatives.

It was possible, of course, to rewrite the rules to allow telepathic evidence to be considered in court, but that would open up a whole new can of worms. The President knew that very few people would be keen on the idea of giving telepaths free rein, which would leave their testimony as nothing more than hearsay – except that, without telepathy,

New York would be experiencing the after effects of a dirty bomb explosion. Certainly, telepathic evidence could be used to point the police towards a terrorist, but a competent lawyer could turn that upside down.

The writer had cited a case from Massachusetts to prove his point. The police had been directed to a suspected criminal by a member of the public and they'd obtained a warrant to search his house on those grounds. They'd found evidence suitable to convict the suspect, but his lawyer had argued that the search was carried out on poor grounds and had been able to get most of the evidence thrown out of court. The President flipped to the back and read the latest update on the New York Dirty Bomber trial. Their lawyers were stalling for all that they were worth, knowing that the case would eventually go to the Supreme Court.

And then there was the issue of telepathic crime.

The writer had admitted that while reading someone's mind wasn't a crime – again, because it had simply never been an issue before – it could certainly be counted as invasion of privacy and charges could be brought on those grounds. However, how could someone *prove* that their mind had been read? The mere belief that something had happened proved nothing. Another telepath could, presumably, look into the first's mind and discover the truth, but that raised other questions. And then there was the minor issue that stronger telepaths, when their talent blossomed into life, ended up reading the minds of everyone around them by accident. Could they reasonably be held accountable for that?

And then there was the issue of mind control.

The incident at Harvard – if one could call a riot that had killed around seven hundred people and injured well over a thousand an 'incident' – had been an accident, but what if there were telepaths who developed the ability to influence or control minds? Could 'a telepath made me do it' serve as a defence? The writer noted that it was possible to draw parallels between involuntary intoxication – where a victim was drugged without his knowledge or consent – and telepathic mind control. The victim would not be held accountable for what he or she did … except, of course, one would have to prove that they were the victim of mind control, which raised the old issue of hearsay evidence again. Although, of course, a telepathic scan could reveal the truth, if a victim was willing to be scanned by another telepath.

On the other hand, mind-controlling someone into doing one's bidding could easily be defined as a crime. A person who made someone act under duress – either though naked force or more subtle intimidation – was already committing a criminal offence. If it could be proven that someone had used mind control techniques, charging them with a crime would be easy.

"Enough," the President said, finally. The writer had gone into too much detail and his head was hurting. "What do we do now?"

He put the report to one side and picked up a different report. As a young candidate, he had hired the services of Boyd and Marshall, one of the most reputable and capable polling firms in the United States. Their firm grasp of the public pulse had helped push him to victory, although he was honest enough to admit that luck – and a damaging sexual scandal that had blown his opponent's career out of the water – had played a major role. He had continued to retain their services while in office. He wasn't entirely sure he trusted the polling figures produced by the Washington bureaucracy.

Boyd and Marshall, after conducting a hastily-organised and extensive survey, had concluded that public feeling was turning rapidly against telepaths. It had never been favourable – the news about the New York bombers, they'd added, should have been put out quicker – but what had happened at Harvard had scared most of the population shitless. They noted that over sixty percent of the population favoured laws intended to deal with telepaths, while a small minority actually wanted to exterminate telepaths or segregate them from the mainstream of public life. It was already having an effect on public policy. Las Vegas's ban on telepaths was of questionable legality – it smacked of discrimination based on an inherent trait, like gender or skin colour – but it was unlikely that it would be overturned by the State Court. The Supreme Court would probably wind up tying itself in legal knots ... and, of course, it was perfectly legal for shops and stores to ban known shoplifters. The casinos in Las Vegas could probably get away with banning known telepaths.

The report went on to say that political figures who loudly demanded action against telepaths were already seeing an upswing in their poll numbers – but then, the President had never needed a polling agency to tell him *that*. Political figures who jumped on the public bandwagon, for any issue, always saw a rise in their popularity, at least until they got into office and discovered that the real world defied quick and easy solutions. Making speeches was easy; actually crafting political steps and putting them into action was hard. The President had learned that in his first week on the job.

He looked up at the painting he'd placed on one wall. It was traditional that the incoming President had to redecorate the Oval Office and he'd added a painting of all of the American Presidents from Washington to his predecessor, as if they'd remained alive so that they could share their advice and impressions with their successors. There was George Washington, who was dressed in traditional clothes, rubbing shoulders with Abe Lincoln and Richard Nixon, while John Kennedy stood next to Franklin Roosevelt and George Bush II. They had all been great men, in their way, and how they had conducted themselves had reflected on America. How would any of them have dealt with telepathy?

President Franklin Roosevelt's beaming face seemed to mock him. In the darkest days following Pearl Harbour, the United States had rounded up and interned hundreds of thousands of ethnic Japanese civilians, for fear of what they might do. It had been a shameful act, one of the worst in American history, yet many people wanted to do the same to telepaths. The President hated the thought, but at the same time he knew that telepaths had to be brought under control. If the public lost faith in the government's ability to administer justice, they would start taking matters into their own hands.

He ran his hands through his hair as he stood up and closed the report. There was work to be done.

***

It had taken several telephone calls to assemble both his Cabinet and a number of prominent figures from the other party. The President wasn't fond of bipartisanship – it had always struck him as a way for the other party to force concessions or to stall long enough for the idea to be scrapped – but this was important. Besides, with the public eye fixed so firmly upon Washington, no political figure could afford to stall for long. It would reflect badly upon them at the polls and at the coming elections.

"Gentlemen, thank you for coming," the President said. He had taken the liberty of distributing copies of both reports to his guests and insisting that they read them prior to the meeting. "Our country stands on the brink of anarchy. History will judge us on how we react to this crisis."

No one spoke as his words echoed in the air. They knew that he was right. The riot in Harvard had been the worst, but there had been other riots and over a hundred people had been lynched – often people who were not and probably never would have been telepathic. Matters weren't helped by growing fears about what other countries might be doing with *their* telepaths. Iran and Saudi Arabia had publicly proclaimed that telepaths were the spawn of the devil and therefore to be stoned to death, but Russia and China were maintaining a cold silence on the subject. The CIA had stated, in a report meant for the President's eyes only, that both countries were looking for telepaths who might have been awakened by the Harvard Blast.

It seemed that telepaths were flowering into existence everywhere. The Looking Glass Project had found seventeen telepaths before the Harvard Blast; Professor Zeller's civilian project had found only fifteen. Now there seemed to be hundreds of telepaths appearing out of nowhere, their telepathy shocked into existence. The crisis was rapidly growing out of hand. The extremists – the ones who believed that telepaths were a colossal threat – were growing louder. The President knew that violence – more violence – could not be far behind.

"We have to act now," the President said. "This is what I propose.

"We will start a Telepath Corps that will have jurisdiction over telepaths and telepathic crimes committed within our borders. This corps will have the telepathic resources that were scattered out over the different agencies, with a mandate for registering telepaths and dealing with telepathic criminals. Telepaths who work legally – in the courts, for example – will have to go through a training session and accept an ethical framework."

He smiled inwardly at their reactions. They knew that the political firepower assembled in the room could push it through Congress and the Senate, but the various agencies wouldn't want to give up any control, particularly to a new organisation. The unwillingness of intelligence agencies to cooperate had led to 9/11, the President knew, and neither Bush nor Obama had been able to do much to improve it. No one wanted to give up any power or influence.

"We will *insist* that all telepaths register themselves with the government, just as we insist on young men registering themselves for possible drafting," he continued. "Being an unregistered telepath will be treated as a federal offence, with a mandatory prison sentence, as will harbouring an unregistered telepath. We will open up accommodation in Alaska for registered telepaths who wish to live apart from non-telepaths. Registered telepaths who wish to work *as* telepaths will be allowed to do so – telepaths who do not want to work as telepaths will be forbidden to use their powers in public life and doing so will be an offence.

"We will continue research into telepathy, particularly into finding a way to block telepathy and to suppress telepathic powers. If telepaths are unable to control their powers, we may be able to find a way to prevent their powers from driving them insane – or prevent criminals from using them for criminal activities."

He paused. "There will be considerable debate over these measures," he added. It was the understatement of the century. "There will be those who will claim that we are discriminating against telepaths – and yes, to some extent, that is exactly what we will be doing. We cannot avoid it. We must remember, however, that human rights are important and must be honoured, even for – perhaps especially for – telepaths as well as non-telepaths. If the only thing we have to fear is fear itself, we have to draw out and neutralise the fear. I ask you all to support me in this."

There was a long chilling pause. He knew what he was asking them to support and knew that, for some of them, it would cost them votes, perhaps even their positions. None of them had risen so high without an ability to keep their finger on the public pulse and they *knew* that the public would be behind them … as long as their actions didn't lead to a disaster. They all knew that Harvard might be only the beginning…

One by one, they all pledged their assent. The President felt sick. He was under no illusions as to what they were doing, or where it would all lead. He just knew that there was no other choice. Telepaths had to be controlled.

The only alternative was anarchy.

Interlude Two

From: Project Looking Glass Analysis Team
To: Looking Glass Distribution List
Classification: Looking Glass Cleared Individuals Only

Following the Harvard Blast, it has rapidly become clear that the blast awakened hundreds – perhaps thousands – of telepaths across the world. Several telepaths within forces deployed in South Korea or Afghanistan were awakened, which suggests that telepaths may have become a global phenomenon. There is relatively little information on telepaths within unfriendly states, but we must accept that our enemies will attempt to use telepaths against us as soon as possible.

Researchers within the Looking Glass Project/Telepath Corps have been attempting to define and collate telepathic potential and power. Professor Zeller has, in addition, been attempting to define his own scale. The researchers have classified telepathic power on a rating from one to ten; ESP1 signifies relatively little power, perhaps only an ability to sense emotions, while ESP10 signifies the top of the scale.

It is difficult, however, to pin down what a telepath is actually capable of doing. A relatively weak telepath may be largely indistinguishable from the general population, while a strong telepath with sufficient mental discipline might be able to operate within the general population without being driven insane by their thoughts. Furthermore, it is becoming increasingly obvious that very low-level telepathic abilities have been present in humanity for years, with people being capable of reading emotions and developing an intuitive sense without being aware that they were tapping into telepathic power.

We therefore recommend the following:
- There is no point in tracking and arresting a person who possesses a rating of ESP2 or below. They are literally unable to invade thoughts, let alone influence them. Indeed, they may never register because they may never realise that they *are* telepaths.
- That all telepaths of ESP7 to ESP10 be urged to not only register with the government, but to work *with* the government, rather than with Professor Zeller or another civilian research program.
- That the project to create 'Telepath Town' in Alaska be expanded, in the hope that we can give most of the telepaths a reasonably normal life, separate from non-telepaths.

Regarding telepathic criminals, we have the following to report…

Chapter Seventeen

Federal watchdogs have warned that the so-called Mind-Lock, an amulet produced by GTROF LTD, that claims to provide protection against mind reading is in fact completely ineffective against telepathic probes. Even so, sales of both Mind-Lock and various drugs that claim to either provide telepathic ability or block it have skyrocketed since the first announcements. Sales of tinfoil hats – which are apparently equally ineffective – have also skyrocketed.

-AP News Report, 2015

"I can hear them," a man was shouting. "I can hear the angels in my mind!"

Alice watched, as dispassionately as she could, as the man was wheeled into the medical centre. The newly-formed Telepath Corps had taken him out of the Portland Mental Institute after the disaster in Texas City two weeks ago. A mental patient – committed to an asylum since birth – had had his natural telepathy boosted by the Harvard Blast and he'd developed the ability to reach into other minds and toy with them. His madness had run rampant in the institution, driving the staff and the remaining patients completely out of their minds. The emergency responders, when they'd finally realised that something was wrong, had walked into a scene from hell. Only seven people had survived the incident and most of them would be institutionalised for the rest of their lives.

"This won't be a pretty sight," Doctor Sampson warned. He sounded as if – for once – he was finally taking his duties seriously. The Telepath Corps now hosted over seventy telepaths and over four hundred were registered with the government, provoking a crisis over housing and compensation. The towns in Alaska that had been intended for telepaths still only existed as nothing more than building plans. The government had reactivated a number of former military bases to serve as temporary accommodation, but that hadn't gone down well with the civilian telepaths. "There's no way of knowing if the drug will work or not."

Alice nodded. The Telepath Corps – and every pharmaceutical company in the world – had launched a crash project to find a drug that would dampen or reduce telepathic abilities. So far, they'd found nothing and nearly killed three of their test subjects. Alice had known, intellectually, that mental shields tended to drop when the subject was tired, but no one had realised that sedating a telepath would cause them to lose all control over their shields. A sane man had gone to sleep and woken up mentally disturbed, unable to filter his own thoughts out of the general morass that had poured into his brain while he was asleep.

Strictly speaking, there was no need for her to be anywhere near the medical centre, but she owed it to herself – and to her new position as a senior officer within the Telepath Corps – to watch the experiments. It wasn't a pleasant experience. It made her wonder, bitterly, if the scientists who'd served Hitler had talked themselves into believing that their experiments on helpless subjects were justified as well. But then, the Nazis had actually launched a breeding program to try and develop telepathy – as well as carrying out hundreds of thousands of inhuman experiments, just to see what they could do when they were released from the shackles of human morality. The United States desperately needed a tool – a weapon – to use against telepathic criminals...and to give telepaths some hope of a normal life.

"I can hear you, hide how you may," the man shouted. He looked rather like an Old Testament Prophet, a man who had communed with God and come away with some rather disturbing answers. "I can hear you scuttling in the walls and hiding from the sight of the Lord..."

Alice looked away, unable to watch. The man – she'd carefully never looked up his name – had been clinically insane from a young age, so how had he picked up religion? The moment she posed the question in her own mind, the answer was obvious. He'd been peeking – which was becoming the generally-accepted slang for telepathic probes – from an early age, without ever knowing what he was. Alice suspected that the human race was lucky that Captain Russell had been the first telepath to come to public attention.

Someone with fewer scruples might have been able to cause havoc before he was stopped, if he ever was.

"The latest drug should work," Sampson said, flatly. He was watching the live feed from the sensors hooked up to the man's forehead. The EEG pattern on the display – with the tell-tale telepathic spike – seemed to flare madly as the man shouted louder. Alice wondered, feeling a tickling at the back of her skull, if he was looking into her mind, yet there was no way to tell. The subject himself probably couldn't tell the difference between her thoughts, the orderlies striving to hold him down and his own.

Alice shrugged. The latest research hadn't been able to identify any telepathic gene that turned a mundane human into a telepath, although the researchers were sure that locating such a gene was just a matter of time. There had to be something separating telepaths from normal humans or the Harvard Blast would have woken up the entire human race. Alice had read reports from Japan and Australia confirming that telepaths had emerged there, which meant that the blast had been global. She was still thinking – and worrying – about the implications of that.

"A cheater doth never prosper," bellowed the subject, as he was finally secured by the orderlies. "Why not, my lords, I ask? If a cheater should prosper, my lords – why none dare call it cheating!"

He broke down into cackling laughs that seemed to echo in Alice's skull. One of the orderlies, a strong-looking woman, looked flushed. Alice realised, with a sudden sense of bitter amusement, that she was having an affair and the mental patient had just shouted it out to the entire room. At least no one seemed to be taking note, although the poor woman might have to make some embarrassing explanations later – or maybe not. The ranting of a certified lunatic was hardly something to take seriously.

"Here we go," Doctor Sampson said. He nodded to her and slipped through the connecting door into the medical chamber. The injector gun with the drug – imaginatively, the developers had called it a sleeper – was already waiting for him, lying within a locked drawer. The mental patient, for once, was quiet as the doctor approached, looking down at him carefully. "Hold still..."

Wonder of wonders, the subject cooperated as the doctor pressed the gun against his arm, but let out a stream of curses as the drug was shot into his system. Alice winced at the expression on his face, half-terrified and half-threatening. It crossed her mind to wonder what his thoughts would look like, from the point of view of a telepath, but there was no way to know for sure. Captain Russell had been polite about it, as had the other telepaths in the Telepath Corps, yet it had been impossible to describe mind-reading to her. It was like explaining colour to a man born blind.

The thought made her shiver. The doctors, in their desire to push the limits as much as possible, had claimed that it would eventually be possible to create a drug that would give telepathic abilities to every man, woman and child. Alice hadn't been able to follow the technical explanation – something to do with recombining DNA strands, or so she had gathered – but the implications were alarming. What would become of the human race if everyone could communicate telepathically?

"The patient has been injected," Doctor Sampson said. "Continue to monitor his brainwaves. We need to know if they start to falter and..."

"Understood, doctor," one of the other researchers said, dryly. Alice smiled. There had been no need for Sampson to remind them of their tasks, but he was clearly nervous about the experiment. Sampson had a gung-ho attitude to medical experiments that rather alarmed her and most of his patients, yet he knew as well as she did that there were a great many hopes resting on their success. "The brainwaves remain active..."

Alice scowled as the researcher dropped into medical jargon that confused more than it educated. A human brain, she'd gathered, showed different levels of mental activity depending on what the person was doing. A deep dreamless sleep showed less mental activity than a person suffering from a nightmare, or even a pleasant sexual dream. A telepath, however, continued to have highly-active brainwaves even when sleeping, which doctors suspected accounted for the poor sleep habits and nightmares telepaths regularly suffered.

"So his telepathy remains undaunted," Sampson said, slowly. "The drug isn't affecting his telepathy at all..."

The subject looked up and smiled a very faint smile. "The angels are no longer talking," he whispered. He gave Sampson a childlike smile. "Are they talking to you instead, doctor?"

"Mother of...it's working," Sampson said, in astonishment. He looked up at the EEG display behind the patient's head. Alice was only a layman, yet it didn't look any different to her. Sampson looked back at the patient and frowned. "Your telepathy isn't working any longer?"

Alice shook her head in disgust. Perhaps the drug had worked, perhaps not, but there was no way to know for sure. Even without the mental voices of everyone within range blasting into his head, the mental patient was still insane, still inclined to couch whatever had happened to him in religious terms. His words verged more and more towards gibberish, almost as if he were a drunken preacher. They'd have to test the drug on a sane telepath, just to know if it worked properly.

"Interesting," Sampson said, finally. "The drug seems to have some effect, but the EEG shows that the subject's telepathy is still active. Further research and experimentation is clearly required."

"The angels are silent," the patient said. Alice rolled her eyes at the childlike fear in his voice. "God is silent in His Heaven and the forces of darkness have fallen still."

"Give me a full report as soon as possible," Alice said, as she turned to leave the room. She couldn't bear it any longer. "I want to know exactly what happened, and why."

***

"So the experiment was a success?"

"It would seem so, sir," Alice said. The videoconference might have linked her to her old boss, Director O'Donnell, but she doubted that it stopped with him. Director O'Donnell wasn't specifically within the chain of command for the

Telepath Corps, a situation that pleased no one. Congress was apparently baulking at some of the appointments the President wanted to create, as well as divesting all of the other intelligence agencies of their role in monitoring telepaths. The debates in Congress were growing steadily more acrimonious. "The doctors tested the drug on a second telepath, a minor criminal with a telepathic talent and not much else. The results were uniformly positive."

She smiled at the thought. Colin McGovern was a poor advertisement for telepathic honesty and integrity. He'd mugged hundreds of people, peeked into their brains for PIN codes and other security details and then robbed them blind. If he'd had the intelligence to equal his telepathic skills, he would have gone far, but as it was he had left plenty of forensic evidence at each of the muggings. The local police had drawn up a case and when he'd picked on the wrong target – a harmless-looking man who just happened to be a National Guard unarmed combat champion – it had been easy for them to link him to the hundreds of other cases. Alice suspected, from the report, that he'd grown overconfident, or he would have peeked first and discovered that he was about to attack the wrong man.

The Telepath Corps had claimed jurisdiction, much to the relief of the local police – he had attempted to escape twice, using telepathic illusions to hide himself – and McGovern had been transported to the secure facility. The doctors had told him that if he agreed to be used as a test subject, his service would be taken into consideration when he was finally put on trial. He'd agreed, reluctantly, and now stood as only the second telepath to lose his powers. She doubted that it was how he wanted to go down in history, but then he *was* a pathetic little man.

"So we have a workable weapon against telepathic criminals," O'Donnell mused. "I don't have to tell you – with Wallis making life hot for the President and the Republican National Congress – that that is very promising news. It should calm the fears of a few hundred frightened political figures."

Alice nodded, impatiently. Politics wasn't her forte, but then she was still only a very young officer. The CIA would have kept her at junior levels for years; only the transfer to the Telepath Corps had given her additional responsibility before her time. She wasn't sure if the promotion was a sign that people higher up the food chain had faith in her, or if it was a way of divesting themselves of a political hot potato...or, for that matter, if they expected her to fail spectacularly, discrediting the Telepath Corps.

"Still, we need to get more telepaths out on the streets in a policing role," O'Donnell added. "I'm afraid that not all telepaths are outstanding citizens of our country, or of other countries, for that matter. Did you hear the news from North Korea?"

"Yes," Alice said. The Japanese intelligence service had passed it on to the United States. The North Koreans had apparently captured and butchered at least thirteen telepaths, along with their families and – in several cases – their entire villages. There were vague reports that other North Korean telepaths had been forced into the service of the regime, or had tried to flee to South Korea or China, although nothing had been confirmed. The Chinese, at least, weren't talking. Alice suspected, from reading between the lines, that all Chinese telepaths were being drafted into service to the state. "I fail to see what that has to do with us."

"The North Korean mindset is one that is rabidly xenophobic," O'Donnell explained. "They – the leadership, at least – hate and fear the South, and us for that matter. They even hate the Chinese, despite the fact that only the links to China keep the state together. The common people are ground down and force-fed political indoctrination on a massive scale. Big Brother is alive and well in North Korea. And, if that wasn't enough, they have nukes and the missiles to deliver them to the south – and, perhaps, to here.

"What happens when they start accusing us of bringing telepaths to negotiating sessions?"

Alice blinked. The President had actually asked the Telepath Corps to provide additional telepaths for the State Department and the Pentagon. Even a low-level telepath could tell if someone was lying – at least if they were *knowingly* lying – and a more capable one could read surface thoughts and reveal the truth. The advantage of having a telepath in the background had been irresistible, even though it raised all kinds of questions about professional and political ethics. She doubted that any of America's allies, let alone the country's enemies, would take it calmly. All negotiations would probably end up being conducted through videoconferencing.

"The regime is touchy and when such a regime gets touchy, blood tends to be spilt," O'Donnell continued, unaware of her inner thoughts. "We don't want to risk creating a diplomatic incident when the world is in such an ... uncertain state."

"No," Alice agreed.

"I'll put your report before the Congressional Committee on Telepathic Abilities this afternoon," O'Donnell said, changing the subject. "That should hopefully stiffen a few spines..."

"I would ask you to consider the warnings," Alice added. She would never have dared speak to someone so senior in such a manner before. Part of her was amazed at her own daring. "The drug loses its effectiveness quickly and..."

"So increase the dosage," O'Donnell said, sharply. "The more of the drug in their bloodstream..."

"The greater the chance of an adverse reaction," Alice said. Even *she* knew that much. "Drugging someone permanently risks poisoning them, or allowing them to build up immunity to the drug. If we increase the dose, we might well kill them, or otherwise impair their ability to live in normal society. The doctors are clear that more research is necessary."

"We may not have the time to wait," O'Donnell said, grimly. "You know as well as I do that Harvard was only the tip of the iceberg. Telepath-related crimes are on the increase, both crimes committed by telepaths and crimes committed against telepaths – how long will it be before we have even more social upheaval?"

Alice frowned. "How much trouble will we have if we insist that telepaths take drugs that poison them?"

"Tell the doctors to work fast," O'Donnell advised. He shrugged. "On a different note, Senator Walker has requested a private interview with you and your top operative – I believe that that is Captain Russell. You won't be getting an official request; he wanted me to pass on the message personally."

Alice narrowed her eyes. "Is there any reason for that?"

"I don't know," O'Donnell admitted. He smiled, thinly. "But he is a United States Senator, with vast political power, so it would be wise to do as he wants. He may just want a private briefing from you personally. It wouldn't be the first time."

"Very well," Alice said. The Telepath Corps reported to the shadowy Telepathic Commission, established by the President, but she was effectively the operations director. She knew that that wouldn't last – someone more senior would be appointed to the post within weeks – yet she meant to use it while she had it. "We'll be there as soon as we can."

"Thank you," O'Donnell said. "And good luck."

Chapter Eighteen

The first use of a registered telepath in a court case provoked protests and demonstrations outside the courtroom by both pro- and anti-telepath factions. The telepath in question, a junior operative of the Telepath Corps, performed a quick peek on the defendant and bore witness that the man was innocent of the charges brought against him. Regardless, the prosecutor was able to delay the case by claiming that the telepath was, in effect, a friendly witness and therefore could only provide hearsay.

In further news, the enquiry into the events at Harvard University three months ago, which was expected to announce its conclusions today, has apparently been extended. No reason has been given for this change.

-AP News Report, 2015

The lawyer was uneasy in the presence of two telepaths, but then that was growing depressingly common.

"As you know," he said, trying hard not to betray his nervousness, "there has been some question over your status..."

"We know," Leo assured him. "Mr Tsing, we have been cooped up in this mansion for the last three months like good little boys and girls. We have cooperated with unreasonable requests from fearful men and women who weren't there at the time and have presumed to judge us based upon second-hand reports. I see no reason to beat around the bush."

Elizabeth scowled at him, although she had to admit that he had a point. Professor Zeller's mansion was a magnificent sight, a building that looked as if it had stepped out of a romantic film based in an idealised Victorian England, but it might as well have been a prison. The other telepaths in the group could come and go as they pleased – if they were prepared to endure life on the outside, near mundane humans – yet Leo and Elizabeth were stuck. They were under house arrest, to all intents and purposes, and it rankled. Leo hadn't stopped complaining about it ever since they'd been transported to the mansion and warned not to leave.

"On one hand, there is the undoubted factor that your actions were in direct self-defence," Mr Tsing said. He looked ethnic Chinese, although Elizabeth could tell that he was American through and through. Even without touching his mind, she could sense his pride in his heritage – his true heritage – as an American. "You had no choice, but to defend yourselves, and then you had no idea what you could do. The deaths of the rioters were unfortunate, yet there is a general consensus that it was not your fault.

"On the other hand, your actions killed at least a hundred people and wounded hundreds more who had nothing to do with the riot," the lawyer added. "Their heirs want you tried for murder and the fact that it was a terrible accident cuts no ice with them. Some of them are planning to sue Professor Zeller and the Institute of Mental Research for aiding and abetting the deaths of their relatives. What you did got out of hand quite badly."

"We had no choice," Leo protested angrily. "Don't any of you understand it? We were about to be killed!"

"I know that," Tsing said, patiently. Elizabeth could tell that he wanted nothing more than to leave, knowing that all of his guilty secrets might have been stolen by now. She knew better. In her experience, most people's secrets were boring or amusing. "The fact remains that this is a whole new can of worms as far as the law is concerned. Some parties are inclined to view it as an accident and an act of self-defence; other parties want to charge you both with mass murder."

Elizabeth leaned forward before Leo could explode again. "All right," she said, tiredly. It was odd how she was permanently tired these days. Her expanded mind made it harder to sleep than it had been before the riot...and telepathy had made sleeping difficult anyway. There were times when she was so tired that she seriously considered trying to obtain a strong sedative and putting herself to sleep by force. "What exactly is going to happen to us?"

"We don't know," the lawyer admitted. "The issue has become political and when it becomes political..."

Elizabeth pushed aside her moral reservations and peeked into his mind. His surface thoughts were sparking with nervous tension and memories of Harvard – no, she realised; memories of videos and photographs. He hadn't been there when the shit hit the fan, something that made her feel relieved. Underneath...she had known that they were in serious trouble, but she hadn't realised how much trouble. The entire case had been hijacked by political factions, some of which wanted to demand that both of them be put to death for mass murder. They were scared, scared of her...the thought almost made her laugh. The most powerful men and women in the land were scared of two teenage students, who just happened to be telepathic...

And then she understood why. The merits of the case were important, but public feeling was far more important, certainly to men and women who depended upon public goodwill to maintain their positions. If they let Elizabeth and Leo escape without punishment – no matter how undeserved the punishment was – the public would crucify them. Elizabeth had watched talk shows and browsed the internet. For every person who thought that they were innocent, there were ten who wanted the pair of them strung up from the nearest apple tree.

Unbidden, memories floated to the surface of her mind. When she'd been at school, there had been a pack of jocks that had delighted in tormenting everyone else. They should have been punished for their bullying, but the teachers had liked them – they were good at games – and so they'd been let off, because they were popular. Telepaths were *not* popular. They might have been innocent – she, at least, certainly hadn't intended to kill so many people – but that wouldn't matter. The court of public opinion had already convicted them and sentenced them to death.

"Right," Leo said. Elizabeth guessed that he had peeked as well. "So we have to sit here until the issue goes away? What do we have to do to escape?"

"Precisely," the lawyer said. He didn't seem inclined to hide his true feelings any longer. Just on impulse, Elizabeth peeked into his mind and found his guilty secret. A year ago, while his wife had been pregnant with their second child, he had made out with an attractive female workmate. Compared to some other secrets she had read in a person's mind, it was tame, but he was ashamed of it. He loved his wife, despite everything. "You have to remain here and keep your noses clean."

He stood up. "My office will be in touch," he added. "Goodbye."

Elizabeth walked him to the side door and out into the car park. The mansion might look great – it had a garden and everything, including a duck pond and a grassy field she would have loved as a child – but it was definitely a prison. The walls were surrounded by armed guards. The only way in or out was through a checkpoint at the bottom of the drive. They claimed that it was to protect the telepaths from outside threats. Elizabeth was sure that if she walked down and asked to be let out they would refuse. They were, after all, under house arrest.

She turned and walked back into the mansion. It had once played host to one of the great political dynasties and its interior design reflected their affluence, although quite a few paintings and other artworks had been pulled out and sold when the family lost most of its wealth. An internet millionaire had stepped in and purchased the mansion, only to lose it himself when the latest dot-com bubble collapsed. Professor Zeller's family fortune had more than sufficed to purchase it off the creditors and turn it into his Institute. The old man was happy. He'd finally accomplished his lifelong dream.

Elizabeth walked into her bedroom and closed the door, clicking it shut behind her. It was hard to maintain mental privacy in a building full of telepaths, but at least she could preserve something of her physical privacy. The room struck her as ridiculously large, even for a teenage girl, yet she hadn't been allowed to argue. Professor Zeller was proud of her. She'd had a hand in killing hundreds of people and she faced the possibility of a trial for mass murder, but he was proud of her. Shaking her head, she reached for her laptop, pulled it onto the bed and turned it on. Her old email address was useless now – it had been hacked barely a day after the

Harvard Blast – but Professor Zeller had given her a new one. Only her parents and a handful of friends had it.

She skimmed through the four emails quickly. Her parents were concerned about her, although thankfully they had managed to go into hiding before the media caught up with them. They'd offered to come and visit her, but Elizabeth had refused, warning them that they might be driving into danger. She could feel – when her defences were down – the presence of the protesters on the other side of the wall. Who knew what they would do if they knew that they had the parents of one of the Harvard Murderers in their hands?

A voice echoed in her head. *You may wish to come downstairs*, Angela said. The younger telepath looked up to Elizabeth, although Elizabeth had no idea why. Angela was only twelve, yet she was already saddled with telepathy and perhaps other gifts as well. *Leo is ranting up a storm.*

Elizabeth smiled at the mental image that accompanied the message – they'd established that one telepath couldn't eavesdrop on private telepathic messages between two other telepaths – and wearily pulled herself to her feet. Leo seemed to have some appeal to the other telepaths and that worried her. After today, she knew that it worried her less than it should.

The Smoking Room had, apparently, once been used by the men of the house after dinner. They'd retired there to talk about politics, while the women – who were assumed not to be interested in such matters - engaged in mindless chitchat in another room. One of the male telepaths had joked about it and one of the female telepaths had jabbed at his mind, giving him a headache that had lasted for two days. Elizabeth suspected that he would have preferred to have been slapped.

"...Don't have to put up with it," Leo was saying, as she entered. "Why do we have to carry the blame for *their* actions?"

Elizabeth winced inwardly and tightened her mental shields. Leo had shared his memories of what he'd seen in the lawyer's mind with the rest of the group, a process that made it impossible to lie, at least directly. It wasn't a pleasant experience – embarrassing or private memories tended to bubble to the surface for all to see – and using it showed just how determined Leo was to make his point.

"We are superior to the mundane humans," he continued. "We read their thoughts. We can, to some extent, manipulate them, perhaps even control their minds. We can kill them though the power of our mental force. Why, then, are we allowing them to dictate to us?"

There was an uneasy pause. Leo had expressed the same sentiments almost every day, but there was a new edge to it now. Elizabeth looked over to the man sitting behind Leo, watching their every move. Cyrus Valentine was a newcomer to the group, a man whose telepathy had emerged in the wake of the Harvard Blast...or so he claimed. His mental shields were very tight and Elizabeth rarely sensed anything leaking out from his mind. Professor Zeller was a mental blank, yet Valentine was also completely unreadable, unless he chose to be read. Elizabeth had not been allowed to read his mind.

"They're scared of us," Leo said. "And so they should be. We are, after all, their replacements on Earth. We're the next step in human evolution, which makes them the dinosaurs, doomed to die out and leave the world for us. We will take their place...

"And they know it. They're already trying to find ways to block our powers and take away the gifts that evolution has given us. They're looking for ways to adapt to us and eventually destroy us. Why else would they start exiling telepaths to the frozen wastelands of Alaska?"

Elizabeth winced. The Telepath Corps had been setting up temporary accommodation, but the media had managed to smuggle in a camera or two and portray the temporary camps as permanent accommodation. They'd somehow managed to draw a link between former military barracks and concentration camps from Nazi Germany, leaving many other telepaths reluctant to head to Alaska. And besides, why should telepaths have to move, just because mundane humans were reluctant to have their minds read?

"Think about it," Leo said. "They will gather us all in Alaska and then they will kill us. Our bloodline will come to an end. The race of telepaths – the superior form of humanity – will die. I ask you – is that fair?"

Elizabeth frowned. "If we are the replacements for the human race," she pointed out, "surely killing us will not stop the next generation of telepaths from coming into existence."

Leo scowled at her. "We carry the telepathic gene," he reminded her, flatly. "What will happen if that gene is eliminated from the human gene pool?"

He turned back to his adoring public before Elizabeth could work it out. Simple logic dictated that telepathy had to be spread far and wide. America was hardly the only country to have telepaths; Professor Zeller had been talking about opening up new chapters of the institute in Europe and Australia. The Russians and Chinese were drafting telepaths into their own version of the Telepath Corps. But then, on the other hand, the news had reported that telepaths were being killed in other parts of the world. There had been a particularly nasty story about a telepath being stoned to death in Afghanistan. If Leo was right – and she doubted it – how many other countries would attempt to exterminate telepathy?

"We cannot remain here, then," Valentine said. His voice, oozing charm, seemed to echo in the air. Elizabeth had wondered if he'd possessed a minor telepathic gift before the Harvard Blast, which would have kicked his telepathy into overdrive. There was no way to know for sure. "We might as well have a massive bull's-eye drawn on our backs."

Leo nodded, enthusiastically. "I don't intend to remain here much longer," he said. "I think it's time that we started to fight for our rights."

Elizabeth felt a wave of alarm. "Leo...we don't have to fight..."

"*Yes* we do," Leo said. His words were almost overshadowed by the anger and conviction that boiled through them and slid into her mind. "The Telepath Corps is already registering telepaths – all telepaths have to be registered. You don't see them insisting that all mundane humans have to be registered! They're planning to insist that all telepaths move to crappy little concentration camps in the middle of Alaska, away from everything they have ever known. What next? Will they be drafting us into their wars or will we be told that we have to be sterilised to ensure that no more telepaths are born?

"We didn't ask to be telepaths! We didn't intend to join a criminal caste purely by being born. None of us meant to become telepaths..."

Valentine spoke into the sudden silence. "The problem with human rights," he said, "is that they can be taken away. The Declaration of Independence lied to us. There is no such thing as an *inalienable* right. They will take our rights from us because we are unpopular – a hated and feared minority. Might does not make right, but it damn well ensures who comes out ahead. If we refuse to stand up for our rights, there will be nothing standing between us and the people who wish to strip us of those rights and turn us into chattel – or dead telepaths. You've heard the rumours, you've seen the reaction to what happened at Harvard...now tell me – if the government could get rid of us easily...what do you think they'd do?"

Elizabeth blinked. "You don't know they'd do that," she protested. "They could have killed us all by now."

"They're scared," Leo said. She hoped that she wasn't the only one who could taste the ugly feeling running through his words. "They saw what happened at Harvard and they blinked. How long will it be before they get over that feeling and decide to do something about us?"

"Quite a few years ago," Valentine added, "there was a case where land-developers wanted to take some Indian land. The Native Americans objected to the white man raping their land any further, so they took the developers to court and won. The court agreed that the Native Americans were in the right. What do you think happened? The developers went ahead anyway and the Native Americans had to move, again."

Elizabeth stared at him. His words had been sincere, truthful, yet how had she missed hearing about it? It should have made the news. There was a media circus whenever someone thought that their rights were being violated – except for telepaths, of course. Both Left and Right seemed to be backing the Telepath Corps and the laws intended to bring telepaths under control.

"So," Leo said. "I guess that we will all have to make a choice soon. What side are you on?"

"Leo," Elizabeth said slowly. "what do you *want*?"

Leo shrugged. "I want what everyone else wants," he said. "I want freedom and the right to live my life as I please. What else should I want?"

And he smiled.

Chapter Nineteen

A statement released today by the Church of the Rapturous Awakening claimed that the Telepath Corps was the first step in establishing a Thought Police that would invade the mental privacy of every American and expose their secrets to the world. The Church's leader warned that violence would be the inevitable result of invading American minds – a statement given ominous weight by the death of Officer Homchoudhury, a Telepath Corps operative who was shot down by a sniper in New York two days ago...

-AP News Report, 2015

"Well," Art said, as the exercise came to an end. "That was an interesting disaster, wasn't it?"

He gazed at the other eight telepaths, none of whom could meet his eye. Their emotions, leaking through their shields, were contrite; they all knew that they'd gone onto the field expecting victory and had been thoroughly screwed by the opposing force. Even telepathy couldn't turn warriors into superhumans. Art's team had been wiped out by the enemy.

The training ground belonged to the Marine Corps and Art had asked to borrow it for the day, once the Telepath Corps had finally been given the go-ahead to create a telepathic platoon of soldiers. Telepaths created whole new military issues and the United States intended to be ahead of the game. Art had picked eight telepaths with military training and experience, taken them onto the field and attempted to beat the opposition. The result had been a disaster.

He scowled. The telepaths might have been able to share thoughts and feelings, but none of them had worked together before, even in pre-telepathic training. It didn't help that six of them came from units that had a tradition of rivalry and that the remaining two had spent most of their time behind various desks. None of them had been able to conceal their opinions of the others – if anyone had actually tried – and Art had had to defuse several confrontations before they turned into fist fights. The opposing force, on the other hand, was a Force Recon platoon that had worked and trained together for several years...and had refused to be bullied into making mistakes by fear of the telepaths. They'd kept their distance, fought using snipers and mortar fire, and unceremoniously wiped out the telepaths. Art allowed some of his own irritation to leak out into the mental field. The Telepath Corps needed to take the lead in developing military telepathy, if only to prevent another country from gaining a strategic telepathic superiority.

"It could have been worse, sir," a former Delta soldier said, finally. Art managed to bite off a curse with an effort, but it was a waste of time. Everyone in the platoon would have sensed the mixture of shock and horror that had flashed through his mind. "At least we forced them to keep their distance."

"Yes," Art said. "And what are we going to do when the Chinese or the Russians start bombarding us with rockets or shellfire – weapons, I might add, that don't have human minds for us to influence?"

"Die, sir," the Delta Force soldier said. "On the other hand, we won't be engaging enemy soldiers in the field. They're not likely to put a platoon of telepaths in a place where they can be shot down by the enemy."

"One would hope so," Art agreed. He looked up as he saw Alice making her way towards the tired and smelly group. "Take five, guys; get showers and something to eat, then we'll hash out what we did wrong later in the day."

He had to smile as Alice wrinkled her nose when she caught a whiff of him. Four hours out on the training ground, rolling in the mud and attempting to hide from incoming fire, left one covered in mud, grime and sweat. He didn't want to think about what might have been hiding within the mud, although the smell gave him an unwanted clue. Alice looked clean and crisp and completely out of place on the training field.

"You," Alice said dryly, "stink!"

"Occupational hazard," Art countered, with a wink. "Just think; you're alive and free because rough men are getting muddy so you don't have to."

Alice smiled. "Senator Walker has invited us to a consultation," she explained. "He wants to see the pair of us as soon as possible."

"And so you came to pick me up," Art said. "You could have called ahead."

"I didn't want to stay in the compound any longer," Alice admitted. "Can you...ah, take a shower and join me in the car?"

"Sure," Art said, without enthusiasm. A meeting with Senator Walker – offhand, he couldn't remember much about the Senator, apart from the fact that he was on the Telepath Corps Oversight Board – would consume most of the afternoon. "Just give me ten minutes to get changed and issue a few orders and I'll be with you."

After spending time in Afghanistan, the showers at the base seemed like the height of luxury, but Art didn't delay. He washed himself, spoke quickly to his second in command and then donned his fatigues. The telepath corps didn't have a proper uniform yet – and if some had their way, it never would – so he wore basic Marine overalls. He left off his medals. The Senator would not be impressed and there was no one else to show them off to, except perhaps Alice. She probably wouldn't be impressed by his small collection.

The car was waiting outside when he strode out of the building, the engine already humming away. The MPs would have inspected the car when it came into the base – after a series of car bombings at military facilities in America, security had been tightened up considerably – and somehow he wasn't surprised to see them admiring the car as he climbed into the rear seat. The CIA-issue cars had been designed so that the driver couldn't hear a word of what went on in the back seats. Art's tired mind suggested a number of uses for that that the CIA would probably not approve of, if they ever found out.

"The Senator didn't say why he wants to talk to us," Alice explained, as the car powered its way out of the base and onto the interstate. Art had already guessed that. The wealthy and powerful were not in the habit of explaining themselves to their peers. "It could be something urgent, or it could be just a request for a private briefing. In either case, be polite; Senator Walker is sitting on a good chunk of our federal funding and offending him could have disastrous consequences."

"I hate him already," Art said. Alice made a show of rolling her eyes. "You don't have any idea what he wants?"

"Not even a guess," Alice assured him. She opened the secure case at her feet and brought out a set of files. "I did bring you some reading material to pass the time."

Art had to laugh as he took the first file and opened it, placing it on his lap. Despite himself, his mind was more on Alice than on the file. She was an attractive young woman and it had been a long time since Art had been with anyone. Part of him wanted to make a pass at her and the rest of him kept insisting that it was a terrible idea. They had to work together, somehow. It was lucky, he reflected as he pretended to read the first part of the file, that it wasn't *her* who was the telepath.

He lost himself in the files, refusing to even look at her, until the driver buzzed through from the driving compartment. "We're nearly there," he said, as they turned onto a private lane. Art had been curious as to what sort of residence a fairly-wealthy senator would own and he had to bite down a laugh when he saw the house. It was not only big, but ugly, as if the designer had deliberately tried to combine as many styles and cultures as possible. On the other hand, he decided after a moment's study, it would be easy to defend, at least against infantry who wanted to take the building intact. Perhaps the senator or the person who had designed the house had expected to be fighting off hordes of angry taxpayers. "Please have your papers ready for examination."

The car stopped at a car park below the house, forcing them to climb out and walk down the path on their own. Two armed bodyguards – Art sensed several more hanging back, probably covering them with hidden weapons – intercepted them and gently, but firmly examined their papers before performing a quick search. They wanted to take Art's pistol and, after Alice had intervened, he reluctantly allowed them to keep it in custody. He felt naked without it.

"Odd," he said, as they stepped into the house. He had just felt – and blocked – a very light telepathic peek. Someone in the house was a telepath and had just tried to peek at them. "I didn't know that telepaths were being added to bodyguard teams..."

"The Senator insisted," the butler said. He had an English accent that would fool anyone who hadn't spent time in England. For reasons beyond Art's comprehension, the men and women who were wealthy enough to hire butlers were insistent that they had to be English, or close enough to English to fool a casual observer. "The man has enemies and refuses to take chances with the safety of his family."

"Wise of him," Art observed, neutrally. The butler was leading them up the stairs and Art was glancing around, trying to fix the route in his mind. The interior of the house, at least, was surprisingly tasteful. "Does the Senator get many death threats?"

The butler didn't answer. Instead, he knocked on a wooden door and opened it a moment later. "The Senator will see you now," he said, ushering them through the door and closing it after them. "Please don't hesitate to call if there is anything you need."

Senator Walker proved to be a genial man, with short white hair and a smile that didn't quite touch his eyes. His handshake was strong and firm, without any silly dominance games, although that might have been because he knew that Art was a Marine and probably stronger than him. Art tried to read the Senator's emotional state, but all he picked up was extreme agitation and near-panic. The Senator hadn't called them to discuss the Telepath Corps at all! He was tempted to probe deeper, yet there was no time. The Senator was already waving them to chairs and offering them coffee from a side table, playing the good host.

"Thank you for coming," Senator Walker said, as he sat back in his own chair. "I understand, do I not, that you have both agreed to be guided by the professional ethics of the Telepath Corps?"

Art looked at Alice, and then back at Senator Walker. "I have agreed to abide by the ethical instructions given to us," he said. Registered telepaths operated under similar rules to doctors; they were bound not to discuss what they saw in a person's mind, without a warrant or permission from their target. "I believe that that should suffice for you."

"And I am not a telepath," Alice added. "What can we do for you?"

"You must understand that this is a delicate matter," Senator Walker said. "I must ask you both for your word that you will keep what we discuss to yourself."

Art frowned. He would have been offended, had he not sensed the fear underlying the Senator's words. Something was *terrifying* the Senator, one of the most powerful men in America. Logically, it had something to do with telepaths, perhaps even the mystery telepath who had joined his bodyguards. Somehow, Art doubted that he wanted a quiet, off-the-record briefing.

"I won't talk about it, provided that it does not include criminal activity," Art said, finally. Alice seconded him a moment later. He repeated Alice's question. "What can we do for you?"

The Senator hesitated, reluctant to speak. "When I was a younger man," he said, finally, "I had an affair with one of the young ladies who worked in my office. I was a very junior congressman at the time and I didn't think about the consequences as much as I should have done. I was young, my wife and I were going through a bad patch and I thought that I could get away with it. The girl was younger than I, with long red hair and a smile that could start a party at a hundred yards. Oh, and she had the most remarkable breasts."

Art had to hide his smile at the sudden flash of emotion from Alice. She wasn't at all happy at the comment. Art reminded himself to look away from her and focus on the Senator. Even without doing a surface peek, he should be able to tell if the Senator was lying to them.

"Nature took its course and she got pregnant," the Senator continued. "I was shocked to hear about it and even more shocked when she decided that she was going to keep the baby. I had repaired my relationship with my wife and I was in line for a more prestigious position. Mirabelle refused to listen to my pleas, although she did promise to keep the baby's parentage to herself. I set up a trust fund for her to ensure that she lacked for nothing and I set up another for the child. I watched from a distance as she gave birth and brought my child up as a single mother. And I was proud of him. He grew up into a strong young man."

"This is very interesting," Alice interrupted, "but can we get to the point?"

The Senator nodded. "A few months ago I received a letter addressed to my personal mailbox," he said. "The letter informed me that someone knew about my bastard child and that if I didn't pay up, the entire world would know about him soon afterwards. I swear to you – no one apart from the mother and I know the truth behind his parentage. Only a telepath could have ferreted out the truth, either from me or his mother."

He hesitated. "I paid," he admitted, finally. "I followed the instructions and paid a hundred thousand dollars for their silence. A few weeks later..."

"You got a second note, demanding more money," Alice said. The Senator nodded, once. "Why didn't you call us in at once?"

"The note made it clear that if I went for help, the telepath would know and my secret would be out," the Senator said. "I received no less than five demands for money and I have paid out nearly two million dollars."

Art laughed and fought desperately to turn it into a cough. "Sir, with all due respect, why didn't you confess the truth at once?"

The Senator scowled. "I may be putting my hat in the ring for the next election," he said. "There are already people – political allies – suggesting that I should run for President. I have not yet committed myself, but I am tempted. A scandal like this would blow my campaign out of the water before it has even begun, to say nothing of destroying my relationship with my wife and my son's life. And I love my wife. I would never do anything to hurt her."

But you have, Art thought, coldly. *You cheated on her and had a child with another woman.*

Alice cleared her throat. "So," she said, "what has changed?"

The Senator looked up, surprised.

"You paid out more money than most people will ever see in their lives to keep your unknown blackmailer quiet," Alice said. Art nodded. It had never occurred to him to ask that question. "Why have you suddenly decided to call for help?"

"The latest demand wasn't a demand for money," the Senator said. He picked up a sheet of paper and passed it over to them. "The bastards demanded...well, read it for yourselves."

Art skimmed the handful of typewritten lines quickly. The unknown writer hadn't asked for money, but for a certain political decision. The Senator had been ordered to push through much harsher controls on telepaths – including mandatory use of the telepathy-suppressing drugs – or his secret would be revealed. As one of the senators appointed to the Oversight Board, the chances were good that the Senator could get the stricter controls passed.

"Weird," Art said, puzzled. "Why would a telepath want stronger controls placed on his fellow telepaths?"

The Senator shrugged. "The crucial vote is in two weeks from today," he said. "You have to find the bastard by then, or I will have to give him what he wants. Do whatever it takes to uncover him. Do you understand me?"

"Perfectly, sir," Alice said. Art could sense the distaste hiding behind her smile. "We'll be in touch."

She didn't speak another word until they were back in the car and heading out of the grounds. "That son of a bitch," she said, angrily. "How *dare* he expect us to serve as his personal police force?"

Art frowned. "He is a Senator and he is being threatened by a telepath," he said, mildly. Alice looked lovely when she was angry, at least when the anger wasn't focused on him. "Catching the bastard will look good on our report sheets..."

Alice started to say something angrily and then broke off as her cell phone rang. "Spencer," she said, and listened quickly to the speaker. "You're sure?"

There was another burst of chatter. "All right, I understand," Alice said. "We'll start heading to New York now."

She closed the phone and looked over at Art. "We have to go to New York," she said. "A fast plane is already being prepared for us. There is a...situation there."

Chapter Twenty

Last night's broadcast of the Jenny Dean Show – the successor to Oprah Winfrey and other such programs – featured several couples who had been torn apart by telepathy. Two of them were couples where one partner had developed telepathy and discovered that the other was hiding a guilty secret; the third was a couple where both partners had developed telepathy and found themselves unable to tolerate the other's company. The friends and neighbours of the third couple were surprised and unanimously agreed that they were a good and loving couple.

-AP News Report, 2015

Tiffany Fieldstone was happy and wanted everyone to know it. An hour ago, she'd closed a deal for her bank that would ensure that it made a vast profit at the end of the year, practically guaranteeing herself a bonus when the time came for bankers to be rewarded. If that wasn't enough, her manager had hinted that a slot was opening up on the board and that she – *Tiffany Fieldstone* – might be considered as a possible candidate. At thirty-one years old, still young and attractive, she knew she could climb high. If the board voted against her, she knew that her record was good enough to allow her to walk into a job with any other bank on Wall Street.

She smiled at the reflection of herself in the restaurant window. She knew she looked hot, if only because of the way some of her partners in the latest banking venture had spent most of their time staring at her low-cut dress rather than the figures. Not that there was anything wrong with the figures, of course, at least not as far as Tiffany was concerned. Even if their venture went bust, the bank's ass would be covered – and so would her own. She ran her hand through her blonde hair and winked at her reflection. The young interns in the offices below her might catch the eyes of her male counterparts, but how could they ever match her?

"Ah, welcome," the manager said, as she stepped through the door. Sven claimed to have been descended from Italians who had escaped Mussolini seventy years ago, but Tiffany did not know or care if that was actually true. All that really mattered was that Sven's Diner served up excellent Pizza – it would have gone bankrupt swiftly in New York if it had served substandard Pizza – and that it was well away from her workplace. And it didn't hurt that Sven was a handsome man without any of the pretensions so common in the more upscale eateries. He didn't spend his time staring at her chest. "Your normal table is ready for you, my dear."

"Thank you," Tiffany said, as she took off her fur coat and placed it on the coat hook. The burning fire in the grate seemed to welcome her as she sat down. Briefly, she caught a glimpse of a hooded man sitting at another table, but he wasn't looking at her and so she ignored him. Besides, the menu was right in front of her. Tiffany could be decisive elsewhere, even to the point of being brusque and impolite, yet Sven kept her from making her mind up quickly. So many of his dishes were simply wonderful and she had over two hours to choose and eat. She skimmed down the menu and finally decided on a loaded pizza. It was a special day for her after all.

She placed her order, suddenly realising that the hooded man had turned and was looking at her, before glancing away for a second. Tiffany realised that he had been staring at her and smiled to herself. When he looked back at her, she treated him to a smile that would have melted the heart of the coldest man in the world, wondering if he would have the nerve to ask her out. The man smiled back, rather weakly, and Tiffany met his eyes. A moment later, a wave of dizziness swept through her...

"Hey, are you all right?" Tiffany looked up in surprise. Her food was in front of her and Sven was looking down at her, concerned. "You just...were staring into space for a few minutes."

Tiffany rubbed her forehead, confused. She'd been on top of the world a moment ago and now her head felt as if someone had filled it with cotton wool. The man who had been staring at her was gone and, no matter how hard she concentrated, she couldn't come up with any impression of what he actually looked like. She smelt the pizza and smiled, pushing the question of the man and her dizzy spell out of her head. Somehow, she never thought of him again while she was eating.

Sven had excelled himself, as usual, and Tiffany enjoyed the meal as much as she had her commercial victory a few hours ago. Normally, she would have gone for a walk before returning to Wall Street, but this time she had the impulse to return to her office and congratulate herself in private. Her head kept spinning and it crossed her mind that she should visit the company nurse, before she decided that it was only a small headache. She'd had worse when she'd been cramming for her exams. Besides, the last thing she wanted to do was appear weak, not when there was a chance at joining the board.

Her office – instead of a cubicle – was a sign that she was a senior and respected employee of her company. A junior employee was easy to replace – thousands entered Wall Street every year – but someone like herself, with a record of making profitable deals and transactions, was irreplaceable. She mentally patted herself on the back as she sat down in her comfy chair and stared up at the ceiling, grinning to herself. No matter what she did, or how outrageously she performed, they wouldn't dare fire her. She'd just go into another firm and make them vast amounts of money instead. The thought of money fired her mind and she placed an email to the financial department, ordering them to send her a hundred thousand dollars in used notes. The director argued and she cut him off. She was a senior banking employee – how dare he stand in her way? The money arrived barely twenty minutes afterwards...

It crossed her mind that she really should take the money out of the building. It wasn't easy to pack it all in her briefcase, but somehow she managed it, even though she had to secure the case with an extra strap. Walking to a beat that only she could hear, she walked down the stairs swinging her hips and out towards the great glass doors that invited people into the building. A second later, the alarms went off and a security guard jumped up from behind a desk and ran towards her. The shock snapped Tiffany back to herself and she recoiled in horror, her brain unable to reconcile common sense with what she'd been doing, too late. The security guard knocked her to the floor – the briefcase burst open, showering money everywhere – and cuffed her hands behind her back. Tiffany, still in shock, offered no resistance.

Her last sight, before the darkness descended on her mind and she blacked out, was of a hooded man making his way away from the bank.

***

Art was feeling more than a little jet-lagged and would have done anything for a hotel bed – or even a barracks bunk – and a few hours of uninterrupted sleep. He had tried to sleep on the plane, but that had proven difficult, not least because of the presence of Alice far too close to him. He couldn't help feeling her thoughts and feelings in his mind and some of them, he knew, were too close to his own thoughts. He wanted to ask her out, yet...what kind of relationship could they have? The Telepath Corps had learned about quite a few married couples who had separated after one of the partners had become telepathic. The non-telepath might have trusted the telepath, yet there would always be a quiet nagging doubt.

"All right," he said, once the local NYPD officer had introduced himself. The officer had been relieved to see them, much to Art's surprise. The Telepath Corps had jurisdiction over all crimes involving telepaths, but local cops – or, worse, the FBI – often baulked at allowing any outsiders onto their patch. "What's happened here?"

He peered through the one-way mirror into the interrogation room. A mature blonde woman was sitting on one of the chairs, her hands cuffed to make it impossible for her to leave the chair. Her face was streaked with tears and she looked to be in shock, although that might have been because of her sudden transition from successful businesswoman to common criminal. Art reached out for her mind and touched a rolling mass of fear and confusion.

"Her name is Tiffany Fieldstone," Inspector Jordon said. "She is – was, I suspect – one of the stars at her Wall Street bank. She was attempting to take a hundred thousand dollars out of the bank, apparently unaware that the money was tagged by the accountants and would trigger alarms when she tried to walk out of the building. She was arrested by the local security guard and started ranting and raving about how someone had *made* her do it."

Art frowned. "And do you believe her?"

"I don't know," Jordon admitted. "She's smart; her manager says that he cannot believe that she would be so dumb as to take tagged money through an alarm. With a little care, she could probably have smuggled twice as much money out of the building without setting off any alarms at all, yet she does something stupid. On the other hand...can someone be made to do something like that?"

"It's possible," Art said. He didn't want to talk about it. He'd developed the power after the Harvard Blast, but every time he used it he found himself sickened by the potential. If someone had developed it without Art's sense of morals – he found himself thinking of Leo Davidson and shivered – the results would be unpleasant. "It requires a powerful telepath and a great deal of concentration."

"Right," Jordon said. For the first time, Art picked up the flicker of fear that was becoming depressingly common. Jordon seemed unsure of what to do. "Can you verify that?"

"I'd have to peek inside her head," Art said. "If I confirm her story, we can take her for treatment and make sure that the mystery telepath didn't leave any unpleasant surprises inside her mind. If not...well, you can arrest her for grand theft and throw the book at her."

Jordon frowned. "Will she be held responsible for what she did if someone forced her to do it?"

"No," Alice said, flatly. "Legally speaking, she would be in the clear."

Art nodded. "Yep," he agreed. He winked at Alice as Jordon headed over to the door to arrange for an interview. "We have a blackmailer near Washington and a mind controller here. Do you think that the two are connected?"

"Not unless the second is intended to confuse us," Alice said, practically. "The blackmailer thought through his plan very well. He made sure that even if his target decided to try to catch him, it would be impossible for him to be identified.

The mind controller, on the other hand, didn't realise that no one, not even a senior banker, would be able to take so much money out of the building without being stopped. He's powerful and dangerous, but he's not very smart."

Art would have pressed the issue a little further, but Jordon returned before he could say anything. "Miss Fieldstone has agreed to see you," he said. "Unless you have any special requirements, I suggest that you use the current interview room."

"It will suffice," Art said. He nodded to Alice and allowed Jordon to lead him through a pair of sealed doors. The police station didn't strike him as particularly secure, but then he doubted that New York's gangs were going to lay siege to it, as had happened in Iraq and Afghanistan. There, a well-built police station was the difference between life and death. "Leave us alone, please."

Tiffany lifted her eyes as Art entered the interrogation chamber. Art didn't need to be a telepath to know that she was on the verge of collapse. He scowled as he took in the cuffs that held her to the chair. It was obvious that she posed no physical threat and the cops should have removed the cuffs, or at least loosened them. Her hands had to be going stiff by now. Of course, there were politics involved; he suspected that her former employers had been pressing for the police to come down as hard as possible.

"My name is Art," he said. Tiffany merely nodded slowly, as if it hurt to even move. "I am a telepath with the Telepath Corps, licensed to perform telepathic peeks for legal purposes. I need your permission to probe your mind and find out what happened."

He tried to push as much reassurance into his voice as he could. "We can find the person who did this to you," he added, "but you have to help us. Please let me in."

"My career is ruined," Tiffany said. She had a whispery voice, the result – Art figured – of too much crying while she'd been in the cell. If she had been influenced, if she had been forced to act against her will, it might well have broken her. But then, she hadn't been directly controlled; instructions had been implanted in her mind, leaving her helpless to resist or even to know what was going on. Her mind had been pulled into a pretzel. "I..."

"It's going to be all right," Art said. "Please will you allow me to peek into your head...?"

Tiffany nodded. Art reached forward gently and placed his hands on her forehead. Maybe it wasn't quite the original Vulcan Mind Meld, but physical contact allowed for a deeper peek. Tiffany's mind was a churning vortex of confusion, with thoughts and memories spewed up for brief inspection and then falling away, leaving Art wondering if her experience had driven her insane. He braced himself – contact with a mad mind could drive *him* insane – and pushed forward. A moment later...

He saw it, clearly. Tiffany's mind was no longer natural. Someone had reached into her mind and stamped around inside, wreaking havoc within her thoughts and twisting her mind to the point where she no longer knew right from wrong. Her mental curves had been flattened, as if the unknown telepath had forced them to remain within set limits, and a whole series of mental commands had been inserted into her head. She wouldn't have been able to tell the difference between then and a normal thought and – like a post-hypnotic suggestion – she would have found herself compelled to justify her actions to herself.

I believe you, he sent, hoping that she would hear his mental comment. *Show me what happened...*

Her memories crashed around him. Her unknown tormentor had been careful, careful enough to program her mind to refuse to remember him. Art had peeked into the minds of a handful of people with repressed memories, yet they hadn't been able to hide anything from him so effectively. But then, they'd wanted to help him – and they had known that he might see the memory, but they wouldn't. Tiffany, on the other hand, had been programmed to hide the memories. The only consolation was that the job wasn't done very well.

Art was walking beside Tiffany – no, he was *in* Tiffany – as she crowed over her success. She walked into the eatery and *he* was there. Tiffany's eyes just passed over him, as if she refused to recognise his very existence. Art realised that

Tiffany had to have been targeted some weeks, perhaps even a month or two, ago. It was the only explanation for how her mind had been rewritten. The Tiffany he was following had slipped into a fugue state...and orders slid into her mind. Art watched helplessly as Tiffany's mind was violated – raped – in front of him. He reminded himself that they were memories, that they couldn't harm him, but it didn't help. He felt a cold burning anger deep inside him. He wanted the bastard's head on a platter and his balls in a vice.

He looked back, flicking through the memories until he came up with the best image of the man's face. He wasn't a handsome man, but if he was powerful enough to control people, he probably didn't need to be handsome. He wore a hood at all times, yet Art could see greasy dark hair and an unpleasant, very pale face. Art memorised the face and scowled, promising the unknown telepath a reckoning. He would catch him and throw him in jail...

Tiffany's mind jerked and Art fell out of her. "It's all right," he promised, as her eyes started to fill up with tears. Art raised his voice. "Someone go find the handcuff keys and free her."

Jordon and Alice entered, followed by a pair of female police officers. "Take her for a shower and then prepare her for transport elsewhere," Art ordered, briskly. He turned to look at Jordon. "She was telling the truth."

"Right," Jordon said, slowly. "How do you intend to catch him?"

Art smiled. "First, I'm going to get one of your officers to help me draw up a picture of what he looks like," he said. He held up a hand before Alice, at least, could point out that such a powerful telepath could make sure that no one saw him properly. "And then we're going to load that image into every camera in the city. He's somewhere around and I intend to catch him."

Chapter Twenty-One

A source within the NYPD confirmed that an unnamed woman was telepathically forced into committing criminal offenses. There has been no comment from the Telepath Corps, but Senator Thomas Wallis stated that incidents like this – and the others that will soon take place – make the case for mandatory testing for telepathy and, if telepaths refuse to go to Alaska, mandatory drug administration to suppress telepathy.

-AP News Report, 2015

"You know," Lieutenant Jennet said, "I've heard that they can put images in our minds."

"I think they'd have to work on you," Lieutenant Singh countered, gruffly. "You have no mind to influence."

He smiled at his friend's consternation to cover his own concern. The last thing he'd expected to find himself doing was guarding a building full of telepaths. Professor Zeller had refused, for whatever reason of his own, government protection, even though the telepaths received more death threats daily than all of their previous clients had received in a month. Instead of requesting the Secret Service, or an FBI Close Protection Detail, Zeller had hired Celebrity Protections Inc. and charged them with defending his mansion. It was both an easy task and a very complicated one.

The telepaths didn't seem too willing to actually leave, which meant that the bodyguards didn't have to worry about escorting them to the shops and public appearances, but they seemed to attract protesters like a politician attracted lobbyists. Friends and relatives of the people killed at Harvard, religious freaks and civil liberties nuts – strange bedfellows all – were camped some distance from the mansion, protesting the mere presence of telepaths in their society. Thankfully, they didn't seem inclined to cause a riot – Harvard had probably dissuaded even the most hardcore trouble-maker from picking a fight – but they were a noisy distraction, particularly when they pressed close to the walls and started shouting at the telepaths. Some of the protesters were packing heat and had even unloaded a few rounds towards the building before vanishing back into the crowd, defying the bodyguards to catch them. Singh's superiors had asked the state police to disperse the protesters, or at least to force them to move further away, but the police were dragging their feet. Singh scowled at the memory. Normally, the state police would come down like a ton of bricks on anyone involved in a firearms offence, yet now they were prepared to let it pass by. The telepaths were a political hot potato.

At least they didn't seem inclined to poke into the minds of his subordinates, although there was no way to know for sure. Quite a few operatives had flatly refused to join the protective detail, citing mental privacy as the reason, and Singh's superiors hadn't tried to push the issue. Quite a few people came to the company after rather…questionable military or police service and they had their secrets. They wouldn't want to share them with anyone, particularly a telepath. They'd all seen the latest soap operas where telepaths – accidentally or purposely – revealed secrets and ruined lives. He'd had less cooperative clients in the past.

"They're smart enough to know not to play games," he said, as he turned back to the radio. The visible patrols were only half of the defences. He'd placed a heavily-armed team in one of the outlying buildings, ready and waiting for anyone who wanted to try and take out the telepaths. It seemed that everyone wanted the telepaths dead, from the latest version of Al Qaida to home-grown militia movements. The threats had included everything from sniper fire to an airplane being rammed into the building. "You may be all that stands between them and death at the hands of another outraged mob."

He glanced up as a white van came into view and rolled his eyes. Professor Zeller – to add to his other problems – didn't seem to understand the concept of clearing all deliveries with his security guards first. He had a habit of ordering complex equipment from halfway across the country and having it delivered to the door, where the security guards had to search it – often without understanding it – before it could be cleared for entry. The first time a van had turned up, Singh had reacted swiftly and held the driver at gunpoint, convinced that the vehicle was a bomb. After that, he had grown a little more careful, although he was unwilling to compromise his client's safety any more than strictly necessary. A driver who shit himself when he found himself staring down the barrel of two guns – and others out of sight – wasn't a problem compared to losing the client. His superiors, at least, had backed him up on that one.

"It's another delivery for the madman in the building," he said, with a droll smile. He'd have to inspect it personally, of course, and confirm it with Professor Zeller. Judging from the time, the Professor would be giving one of his lectures at the moment, addressing scientists who had come from all over the world to study telepathy. After so long in the scientific wilderness, the vindication Professor Zeller felt was understandable, even if it did make him seem a pompous ass from time to time. "You'll have to check the manifest and compare it to what the Professor ordered and…"

Time seemed to slow down as the white van pulled into the gatehouse. Combat instincts Singh hadn't used since he had mustered out of the 10th Mountain Division were screaming at him, telling him that something was badly wrong. The van was wrong. He opened his mouth to shout a warning, but it was already far too late. A moment later, the van disintegrated in a tearing ball of light that picked him up and carried him away in a wave of sound and fury.

***

"…So when considering communism," the lecturer said, "we are faced with the problem that, in order for communism to work, people must behave in a certain way. Specifically, they must behave in the interests of the entire community, rather than in their own self-interest. Unluckily for those who regard a communist society as a workable society, people don't act that way. They will generally act in what they see as their own best interests."

Elizabeth scowled to herself. Professor Zeller had hired tutors for the younger telepaths – she had to admit that they could be interesting – and he'd insisted that some of the older telepaths sit in on the lessons. It hadn't taken her long to realise that the Professor had wanted them to listen to the words and know how often the visiting speakers lied to their students. This speaker, at least, believed what he was saying.

"The people who developed the basis for communism considered themselves smarter than the vast crowd of individuals who made up their society. They regarded the common herd as being too stupid to understand where their own best interests actually lay. When communists took power, they found themselves faced with the fact that the human herd refused to naturally follow the elite – as they considered themselves. They were faced with a choice between *forcing* the common herd to follow them – or giving up on their dreams. Very few communists chose to give up. They *knew* they were right.

"Accordingly, they developed the tools for forcing their views on society," the speaker continued. His words were dispassionate, but Elizabeth could sense his underlying disgust. "They created a system intended to enforce their views and remove anyone who dared to object. Again, in theory, the idea should have worked out well. In practice, the system became warped by its own nature. Disaster was just waiting to happen…"

The entire building shook. Elizabeth came to her feet as she sensed the sudden swell of alarm from the other telepaths – and the naked shock from the speaker. She turned to the window and saw a massive fireball rising up from the gates, just before it occurred to her that showing her face at the window might be suicide. She dropped to the ground and shouted at everyone else to get down, just before the first gunshots broke out. It hadn't been that long since Harvard and she knew what it meant. They were coming to kill the telepaths!

I told you so; Leo's voice spoke in her mind. He was broadcasting directly to every telepath in the building, unheeding of who might be listening. *We have to get out of here before they kill us all…*

***

John found himself laughing as the first explosion went up, exactly as planned. The Lord was with them today. The telepaths hadn't bothered to think through their defences very carefully, even though they had to know that they were under threat. They'd only established a single guardhouse and a handful of guards. The bomb would have taken them all out – a regrettable price for exterminating the telepaths. Besides, they'd chosen to take the contract and defend the telepaths, even though the telepaths had been touched by evil. It made them guilty and so they deserved to die.

He pulled his assault rifle out of his bag and shouted for his formation to form up on him. The protesters – useful idiots, the lot of them – were scattering in all directions. Some of them had been injured, perhaps killed, by the bomb, but John didn't care. He hated liberal protesters anyway; boys and girls who had never done a day's work in their lives, yet who felt themselves qualified to pass judgement on men and women who actually worked for a living. They deserved to understand that the universe was not always fair and government bailouts didn't always save the world. He kicked one of the fallen protesters out of his way as the Army of the Lord formed up on him. She reminded him of his wife.

They had been younger when they had married, young enough not to understand that they were making a mistake – young enough not to take anything for granted. Debbie had told him that it was safe for him to sleep with her and yet somehow she'd gotten pregnant. He hadn't realised until much later that she'd wanted to entrap him into marriage. Like all women, she wanted a man to provide for her, but unlike a good woman she wanted to have the man without performing her wifely duties. The marriage had started out badly and then gone downhill. Every day – every fucking day – she'd been there, carping and complaining; the house wasn't right for her, the kids needed new clothes, he wasn't bringing in enough money and he was drinking too much. Of course he was drinking too much! What man wouldn't with a shrew for a wife and two screaming kids, one of whom he was sure wasn't actually his. And then he'd snapped and lifted a hand to her.

She'd fled with the kids to the authorities and the damned liberals in the courtroom had taken her side. John had found himself enslaved by the law, forced to sign over most of his pay without even being allowed to see his kids. Debbie had gotten what she wanted and he was her slave. The one time he'd gone to see his kids – as a father should, on his oldest son's birthday – the police had arrested him and he'd had to spend a week behind bars. How could they do that to him?

But perhaps it had been a sign from the Lord, as he'd been introduced to the Church by a fellow inmate. John had taken to the Church at once and thrown himself into study, rising rapidly within the ranks. The country was the way it was because godless liberals had thrown god-fearing men out of power and replaced them with a witches' brew of homosexuals, communists, feminists and work-shy politicians who kissed up to big business while penalising the little man. And now they had telepaths. Soon enough, they would have a thought police force that would root out all who dared to believe in the American Dream.

Yet there was hope; the Church, a congregation of god-fearing men, would take back their country. All they had to do was kill the telepaths before they could be used against true patriots.

He smiled at the thought as the formation advanced. John had never been in the army – the recruiting station had rejected him, although he liked to claim that he had gone to Boot Camp and had been thrown out after refusing advances from a lesbian in a man's uniform – but the warriors had drilled and drilled until they could move as a unit. They'd broken several federal gun laws in order to arm their force, yet no one in the Church cared. The gun control laws were just another plot to disarm the true patriots.

"Kill them all," he shouted, and his men took up the cry. "Kill them all!"

***

Elizabeth could feel the minds advancing towards the building as she ran down the stairs, trying to keep her balance. The sound of shooting was growing louder, but her telepathy couldn't pick up any sign of what was actually going on. The attacking minds were brimming with hatred and hostility, yet there was a coldly-focused element to their thoughts as well, concentrated on killing the telepaths. She reached the bottom of the stairs as the gunfire finally died away. For a moment, she hoped that the attackers had all been killed, but she could still feel their hating minds.

What did we do to them? she thought, as she reached the panic room. Leo was there, along with Valentine and most of the other younger telepaths. There was no sign of Professor Zeller. *What are they going to do to us?*

Kill us, of course, Leo thought back at her. None of them were speaking aloud, yet as their minds interlinked she could feel their fear calming, to be replaced by rage. She remembered Harvard and shivered. How much power could they tap into if they really tried? *They want to kill us all. Can't you feel it?*

Elizabeth shivered. The hatred was growing, yet there was also a form of anticipation…

A moment later, the entire building shook again.

***

John let out a glad cry as the explosion blew through a section of the mansion. It wasn't *right*, telepathic voyeurs being given such a building when true patriots had to scrabble in the dirt to live, but the joke was on them. Their telepathy had made them a target and flames were already licking at the remainder of their mansion. And most of their guards had either fled or died quickly. Perhaps some of them had been covert patriots, serving the enemy until the time had come to switch sides.

"Come on," he ordered. Entering the burning house was dangerous, but he knew that there wouldn't be long before the federals responded to the attack. The Church had promised to delay the federal response for as long as possible, yet there was no way to know if they would succeed. The federals were good at responding to threats to their power. "We have to kill them all."

***

Within the panic room, the combined mind of the telepaths was settling down into colder – deadlier – patterns. Elizabeth wanted to take the lead position herself, but Leo – who had been building the gestalt – nudged her aside. Their combined powers allowed for far greater abilities than anything they could muster on their own. The attackers all wore tinfoil hats and Mind-Lock Amulets, but they provided no protection at all.

Look, Leo proclaimed to the group. *They have the support of the government! They intend to kill us*!

Elizabeth looked, and shivered. The intruders certainly believed that they had the support of the vast majority of mundane humans. They had help from agents within the government, so much so that the telepaths didn't dare rely on anyone. The government would either draft them or force them to take telepath-suppressing drugs. The growing consensus, led by Leo, was for escape and revenge. If the mundane humans refused to allow them to live free, they would fight...

Now, Leo said. They reached out as one, reaching into the minds of the attackers. Twisted and perverted by hate as they were, it was easy to influence them, even without telepathy.

***

"John?"

John turned. Debbie was standing there, completely helpless and alone. Somehow, it didn't occur to him to wonder what she was doing there. He knew it was her, right to the core of his being. Hatred surged up within him and he turned, lifting his gun and firing right into her heart. He laughed as she died and kept firing, as if he was wiping away every last part of her. Her face refused to fade, no matter how much he fired, yet he didn't care. He was still laughing when four hammer blows stuck his body and he fell away into the darkness.

***

One by one, the intruders died. It wasn't pretty. The telepaths reached into their minds and turned them on each other. Elizabeth shivered in disgust at some of their memories, even as she played with their minds, manipulating them. It was easy and some of the telepaths, she realised, revelled in their power. The consensus they shared meant that hardening attitudes spread from mind to mind like a virus. Only Valentine, whose mind remained a locked box, seemed reluctant to share in their consensus.

"Time to leave," Leo said, verbally. The shock of actually hearing his words brought them out of their shared mentality. Elizabeth wanted to be sick at what they had done, even if it had been in self-defence. Harvard had been one thing, but this was worse. They'd mentally raped their attackers and torn their minds apart. "There will be others coming soon."

Pulling telepathic invisibility around them like a shroud, the telepaths ran up the stairs and disappeared out into the countryside.

Chapter Twenty-Two

This just in – a group of unknown terrorists have attacked the Zeller Institute and killed at least forty people. First responders who reached the building reported that most of the security guards and building staff had been killed, but there is – as yet – no word on Professor Zeller or his telepaths...

-AP News Report, 2015

Roger had visited the Zeller Institute twice before, once as part of a group of reporters who had been chosen to witness the opening ceremony and once for a private interview with Professor Zeller. For a man whose primary talent seemed to be annoying people – at least until his theories had actually been proven to have some basis in reality – Professor Zeller was quite a remarkable self-publicist. Back then, Roger had been impressed with the building. It had really been quite remarkable.

It wasn't so remarkable now. Where the gatehouse had been, there was nothing more than a crater and a great deal of debris. The white-clad FBI officers poring through the wreckage would have their work cut out for them. The bodies outside the grounds – the intact ones had been covered with shrouds – weren't a pleasant sight. Some of the protesters had been in their teens, too young to die in an act of violence. He turned and looked up towards the building itself. Part of it was a burnt-out wreck; the fire department had responded quickly, but the flames hadn't been quelled easily. The remainder was badly damaged and, apparently, deserted.

"At least fifty dead," the FBI officer said when Roger approached her. Agent Evens looked shaken by what she had seen, although it didn't seem to affect her ability to issue orders to her subordinates and keep on top of the crisis. It might not matter. The terrorists were long gone and the telepaths might well be dead. "Some of the remains may never be identified."

"And they were just protesting," Roger said, in dismay. There were countries where anyone brave or stupid enough to protest would be gunned down by their government or arrested and sent to prison for the rest of their lives. In America…there was a right to protest peacefully, although the key word was *peacefully*. The protest at Harvard had been bad enough, but in its way this was worse. "What did they do to deserve this?"

Agent Evens shrugged. "I think they were just collateral damage," she said, flatly. "We've picked up several protesters who had the sense to run when the shooting started. They're saying that some of their fellow protesters drew arms and opened fire on the remainder of the guards. The bastards snuck up to the building under cover and then launched their attack without caring about the people caught in the middle."

Roger looked up as a deafening crash echoed out from the building. Part of the roof had just collapsed inward, smashing through weakened floors and ceilings. He hoped that everyone had been evacuated before it had been too late. People didn't always react rationally during a crisis, when they had to think quickly and clearly. It was far more common for people to gibber with shock and be unable to think logically. He wondered, suddenly, how the telepaths had reacted. Had they known that they were under attack?

"I think so," Evens said, when Roger voiced the question. She led him up the road towards nineteen covered bodies, lying on the grass. "Take a look at this…"

She pulled one of the sheets away and Roger recoiled. The dead man clearly hadn't looked very pleasant in life, but in death he was appalling. His eyeballs had been pulled out and, from the blood on his hands, it was apparent that he'd done it to himself. Roger stared for a moment and then had to turn away, swallowing hard. The expression on what remained of the man's face would haunt him until his dying day.

He moved from body to body, shaking his head in disbelief. Many of the terrorists had clearly turned on their fellows. Others had killed themselves, apart from one unmarked body with an uncertain cause of death. It looked almost as if the fellow had died peacefully. Roger found that the most alarming of all.

"It may have been the result of a telepathic blast," Evens said. "There have only been a handful of people killed by telepaths, at least killed by mental powers, so we won't know for sure until we do the autopsy. And then the results might not be certain anyway. It could just be a coincidence."

Roger snorted. "Not here," he said. "Not after what happened to the others."

"It's the first thing a defence attorney will raise," Evens predicted. "Do you know that we have a handful of unexplained deaths that might – I say might – have been caused by a telepath? The problem is that we have no way to be certain. There are a handful of cases of cerebral haemorrhage that have never been satisfactorily explained. Most of them appeared prior to telepaths entering the public mindset, but we don't know for sure when the first telepath actually appeared. There could have been a telepathic killer wandering around for years without us even being able to deduce his presence."

"An untraceable killer," Roger said, with a shiver. "How do we deal with someone like that?"

"We're working on it," Evens said. She looked down at her hands. "I think..."

"Agent Evens," a man called. "You have to come see this!"

Evens ran and Roger followed her. After all, she hadn't told him not to follow her. The man was waving to a stretcher that had been pulled out of the building, a stretcher that was holding one very familiar person. Professor Zeller had been found, his pale face sending chills down Roger's spine.

"He seems to be in a coma," the man said. Roger looked for a nametag and saw nothing. He clearly wasn't FBI, as he didn't seem inclined to object to Roger's presence. Or maybe he did and he had clearly decided not to make a fuss. "We need to transport him to the nearest facility ASAP."

Evens nodded. Roger wondered if she appreciated the irony. Professor Zeller's mansion had the finest collection of equipment in the state for monitoring a person who needed mental care, yet it had all been destroyed by the terrorists. He looked down at the staring eyes and shivered. Professor

Zeller's body might be there, but his mind had long since departed. It was not a pretty sight.

"We've searched the entire building," the man continued. "We found a number of other bodies, including three of the telepaths, but the remainder appear to be missing."

"If that's the case," Evens said slowly, "where the hell have they gone?"

***

"What the hell is this place?"

Elizabeth wanted to scream, but she didn't dare shout, or even broadcast mentally. Leo had warned them that the government was probably already looking for them and even telepathy had its limits when it came to hiding them from remote sensors. They could fool the minds of anyone who happened to be in range, but that wouldn't last. A single automated system connected to an operator out of range would pick them up easily, if they gave it the chance.

"It's a hiding place," Valentine said, easily. Unlike the other twelve telepaths, even Leo, he seemed unmoved by the danger. Elizabeth privately suspected that he was enjoying himself. "We can rest here and recuperate before we move onwards. The people who own this building don't have the slightest idea that we're here."

Elizabeth scowled. Valentine had led them to the large house – it didn't quite earn the title of mansion – and used his telepathy to convince the small staff that the telepaths weren't actually there. Elizabeth had been impressed – and horrified – by the skill both Leo and he had displayed. They had forced the staff to accept a contradiction; the telepaths were not there, yet they had to provide food and drink for them. By the time their minds reasserted themselves, Leo had assured them, the telepaths would be long gone.

"Right," Elizabeth said. "And you don't think that we might attract attention?"

"Not as long as we avoid doing anything stupid," Valentine said. He'd insisted, as soon as they left the mansion, that they dump their cell phones and anything else that might carry a microchip. It would have been embarrassing to make a phone call and discover that it brought the government swooping down on their heads. Two of the telepaths had protested until Leo had reminded them of the danger. "We're not going to be here for long."

Leo nodded. "We have to get down to the city," he added. "The government is probably already setting up road blocks and other traps…not that we have to worry about them, of course."

"Once we're in the city, we can hide for years if necessary," Valentine said. "I didn't pick this place entirely at random. The servants have access to a van that can carry us all down to the city, while our powers will ensure that any cops who try to stop us walk away with the correct impression. We can even get one of them to drive it and make sure that there isn't even the slightest thing that will make them suspicious."

"We have to move quickly though," Leo added. "They might have called in their tame telepaths by now and we won't be able to fool them so easily."

That thought brought conversation to a halt. The telepaths showered and changed rapidly into different clothes – stolen from the staff – before watching the news. Both CNN and Fox carried stories about the terrorist attack on the Zeller Institute and for once they had the same slant. Acts of terrorism on American soil were unacceptable. There was no warning about the missing telepaths, which struck Elizabeth as odd. Either the government thought that they were still buried somewhere in the wreckage, or they were keeping it to themselves to avoid panic. She hoped it was the former. She didn't want her parents to see their daughter hunted by the government across America.

She was feeling a little better when they boarded the van and discovered that it had a small bar that was well supplied with alcohol. Valentine warned them not to drink any, reminding them that a drunken telepath could lose his mental blocks and wind up attracting attention. Leo didn't argue with him, although three of the other telepaths did, wanting something to take their minds off what they were going through. Valentine won the argument and went forward to program the driver. Without his beard – he had shaved while at the house – he looked different enough to be unrecognisable. As the van lurched into life, Elizabeth allowed herself to relax. Whatever else happened, the die was cast.

"Trouble," Valentine announced, thirty minutes later. The spark of alarm that flared through Elizabeth's mind was shared by the others. "This is a small roadblock ahead of us and cops are waving people down. I suggest that we get ready to focus our minds."

Elizabeth nodded, feeling the consensus building around her. Their minds reached out and sensed the presence of seven policemen, as well as four men they'd arrested, their thoughts slurred by the presence of too much alcohol. Elizabeth felt a flicker of concern without recognising its source; the drunken drivers might be too drunk to be easily influenced by telepathy. They might end up warning the police that something was wrong.

We should kill them, Leo thought. Elizabeth sensed his injured pride and fury. *They send their minions to kill us.*

No, Elizabeth sent back, before she could hesitate. An emotional argument wouldn't work, not against Leo and Valentine. They needed cold logic. *Dead policemen will attract attention and point them towards us.*

There was another concern. Mental control tended to have unfortunate effects on the victim. They didn't handle a new situation very well or a situation where they might have to make decisions in a hurry. An outside observer might realise that there was something badly wrong with them, even if he didn't know exactly what had happened, or why. A policeman, trained to watch for signs that a suspect was on the verge of doing something stupid, might just realise the truth. And then they would have to do more than just wipe his mind. If they handled him too roughly, the Telepath Corps would know what had happened and why.

Brace yourself, Valentine sent. His mind focused on the policeman as he walked up to the driver's window, peeking into the policeman's mind. He'd been ordered to set up a roadblock and search for people who matched a certain description – their description. Elizabeth shivered again as the implications flickered through her mind. The cop had been told to take them alive, but he was nervous and had already come close to drawing his gun in anger once today. *Here we go…*

The cop entered the mental field and the combined mind went to work. He didn't see the people in the rear of the van – thankfully, the tinted windows made it impossible for anyone else to see in – nor did he realise that anything was wrong with the driver. Instead, he made a show of checking the driver's licence and then waddled off back to his car, relieved that he hadn't found the telepaths. Elizabeth watched his thoughts for a moment longer, as the driver pulled away from the checkpoint, and shivered. Leo had told them, time and time again, that they were the superior race. With power like that, what could they not do?

And what would the government do to stop them?

***

The President had known that it was going to be bad the moment the Telepath Corps Oversight Commission called for a meeting. He'd been involved in delicate negotiations with the Prime Minister of India – the world went on, even if telepaths had appeared and started to upset the balance – and his staff knew not to pull him out for anything less than an absolute emergency. Besides, sharing notes with another world leader was always interesting. Very few Americans who had never been President could understand the stresses and strains of leadership.

"They're all gone?" He said, once the FBI Director had finished outlining what had happened at the Zeller Institute. "All of them?"

"Yes, Mr President," the FBI Director said. He was the President's personal choice for the position and was clearly aware that he could be dismissed for this failure. It was hardly his fault, the President knew, but public opinion had a nasty habit of demanding scapegoats. "We have thirteen powerful telepaths completely unaccounted for – no bodies, no nothing. They've gone rogue."

The President stared down at his hands. "What the hell happened?"

"The preliminary reports on the bodies – the terrorist bodies – were able to identify a handful of them," the FBI Director said. "They had criminal records, although nothing too serious; most of them served a few years in jail for possessing an illegal weapon. The bad news is that they were all members of the Church of the Rapturous Awakening. We have quite a file on them, Mr President; they believe that there will be a disaster soon, after which New World Order will fade away and the true Americans – by which they mean people who share their beliefs – will come to power. Quite a few of their members have been involved in criminal acts of one kind or another, but we have never been able to pin anything on the Church itself."

"And they attacked the Zeller Institute," the President said. "Why?"

"The Church's official position on telepaths is that they're drawing on satanic power and are therefore devils and demons," the FBI Director said. "It is possible that one or more of the terrorists was urged to attack the institute by the Church's senior leadership, but as they all died we're unlikely to be able to prove it. That isn't the worst piece of news, however; the telepaths may pose a more dangerous threat."

He passed the President a slim file. "The Zeller Institute didn't vet its telepaths with the Telepath Corps or even us," he added. "We only obtained their records in the aftermath and…well, this guy surprised and alarmed us. He called himself Cyrus Valentine – and had the papers to prove it – but we know him as Alvin Greenwood. He's, Mr President, one of the people we'd very much like to have a few words with one day."

The President frowned. "He's an anarchist *and* a mercenary?"

"They don't seem to go together very well," the FBI Director agreed. "The short version of his story is that he was recruited by the CIA" – he paused to look at the CIA Director as he spoke – "and trained as an agent of influence – ah, he would be inserted into a foreign country and work to destabilise their government. It was all very secret and…"

He broke off. "Greenwood was involved in the attempt to support a Kurdish-led uprising in North Iraq during Clinton's time in power," he added. "The attempt was cancelled at the last moment, the promised support didn't materialise and the Kurds were brutally slaughtered. Greenwood went rogue, Mr President; he vanished somewhere into the underground and only rarely surfaced, often in some of the worst parts of the world. He takes whatever money he can get, but he isn't loyal – not really. He's too dangerous to be trusted by his employers."

"And now he's a telepath," the President said, grimly.

"Yes, Mr President," the FBI Director said. "In hindsight, he has been working away at young Davidson for months. And now he has thirteen telepaths under his control. We have to find him before it's too late. He has a grudge against this country and a complete lack of scruples. He could do more damage in a month than Al Qaeda could do in fifteen years of war."

Chapter Twenty-Three

In an update to the terrorist attack on the Zeller Institute, thirteen young telepaths have been found to be missing, perhaps on the run. The government has issued an appeal for them to come forward to safety. Sources within the government have hinted, however, that the telepaths are wanted on charges of terrorism and may be arrested as soon as they show their faces...

In other news, Wall Street is on alert after the Telepath Corps confirmed that Tiffany Fieldstone, who was arrested on suspicion of theft, was mind-controlled into committing the crime. Her employers refused to comment.

-AP News Report, 2015

"FBI! Don't move!"

Art watched as the SWAT team stormed the apartment, wishing he could be up front with good men behind him. Or perhaps not; in Afghanistan, when going into hostile territory, they'd started by throwing in grenades and then firing rounds at anything that looked suspicious. He doubted that the NYPD would look kindly on using such methods within the confines of New York City, while the public would be horrified by the mere thought.

"Clear, sir," the SWAT team leader said. In the haste to get the operation mounted, Art hadn't even caught his name. "The bird has flown."

Or was never here at all, Art thought sourly. Two days of crunching through every piece of CCTV footage in New York and trying to match it with the memories he'd pulled from a handful of minds had left him dubious about their prospects for success. The mind controller they were searching for might well have left the city by now, relying on his talents to shield him from detection, or he might have burrowed underground and pulled in the hole behind him. Art could imagine a dozen ways a telepath could hide, even from a determined search, and few of them would give the searchers any clues.

He nodded to Alice and they headed forward, walking up the stairs towards the isolated apartment. The building's landlady was in breach of a number of health and safety laws, but her tenants had never complained; for most of them, it was the best accommodation they could ever hope to have. They paid in cash and were rewarded with a blind eye to any of their misdeeds. The chances were good, Art decided, that the building's other tenants – who would be being rousted out of their apartments right now – were probably involved with drug dealing or even smuggling. The NYPD had a warrant to search the entire building and he suspected that they – and the local courtrooms – were going to be busy for the next few days.

"It's completely clear," the SWAT Leader assured Art, as they entered. "There's no sign of him at all."

Art nodded and, slowly, opened up his mind. The SWAT team didn't include a telepath, an oversight he had had no time to rectify. Besides, a telepath who wanted to use his talent would be blinded by the surge of emotions from the unlucky souls who got in the SWAT team's path. He doubted that drug dealers would be brave and respond to the intruders calmly, but a telepathic mind controller might be a different story. His mind expanded, searching for the mental *stillness* that might conceal another telepath, and he relaxed slightly when he found nothing. The mind controller could have been hiding under their very noses, broadcasting *I'm not here* signals to anyone in the area.

"Check with the monitoring team," he ordered. He keyed his radio. "Agent Graves...is there anything from the probes?"

The probes – microscopic surveillance devices – had floated into the apartment along with the SWAT team. Art had argued for their inclusion because they could not be fooled by a telepath, no matter how hard the telepath tried to control them. The minds back at the NYPD station couldn't be tricked into believing that the apartment was empty, or so Art hoped. If the mind controller was powerful enough to influence people at such a distance, resistance would be completely futile.

"Negative," Graves said. He was a cranky old man, well past his prime, but he had stayed current and he did know his stuff. "There's no sign that he is here."

"Good," Art said, and then changed his mind. "Bad. Get the forensic team up here and have them take the place apart room by room."

He closed his mental shields and started to look around the room, searching for something out of place, something that would provide a clue as to where the mind controller had gone. He'd been skilled at that in Afghanistan – he'd actually wondered if it had been an early form of telepathy peeking out of his mind – but that was in the middle of a war zone. Now, there was nothing that seemed to be obviously out of place. The room was a mess, yet Art couldn't blame the mind controller for that – his own room was a dump. He'd never dared take Alice or anyone else to his new apartment.

The apartment smelt funny, he realised, after a moment of consideration. It was easy to see why. Massive piles of unwashed clothes lay everywhere, some of them clearly more expensive than Art would have expected anyone who lived in the apartment to be able to buy. He leaned down, without touching anything, and frowned. Most of the clothing was clearly designed for a woman – in fact, if he was any judge, several women. There were used panties and bras within the pile, simply abandoned. He guessed that the mind controller had been bringing women home, having his way with them, and then claiming their underwear as a trophy of each conquest. He'd known a Marine who behaved in much the same way, although *he*, at least, had seduced the women fairly.

He stepped into the kitchen and recoiled from the smell. There was an overflowing bin, filled with used takeaway containers and bottles of soda pop – no alcohol, he noted. That made sense; very few telepaths continued to drink after discovering that it weakened their mental shields and left them vulnerable to every stray thought in the area. The kitchen sink was blocked – Art didn't want to *think* about what might be blocking it – and half-filled with washing water. It looked as if the suspect had fled the building before the SWAT team arrived, which was interesting. Had someone at the NYPD warned him and, if so, had that person been mentally programmed to pass on a warning?

Art shook his head as he stepped back into the hallway to allow the forensic team to get to work. The mind controller was dangerous – no doubt about it – but he didn't seem to be particularly clever. It would have been easy for him to program some of the people in the building – perhaps even the landlady herself – to clean his apartment for him; come to think of it, he could have probably moved into a finer apartment without tipping off the NYPD. All he seemed to want was money and sex. If Art hadn't known already, he would have been sure that their target was a man – a young man.

"I'm going to talk to the landlady," Alice said. "I'm afraid the vultures have already started to gather."

Art scowled. The NYPD had thrown up a cordon around the apartment block as soon as the SWAT team moved in, but someone had clearly had the presence of mind to call the media and sell the story for a few bucks. A person with a cell phone or a video camera might well have been able to take some footage to attract their attention and, after the dramatic disappearance of some of Zeller's telepaths, the press would draw a link between the two events. The thought had crossed Art's mind too, although he had reassured himself that the mind controller had clearly been active a long time before some of Zeller's pupils had vanished into the underground. That meant, at least, that it was a telepath no one else had ever met.

The thought of Zeller's pupils was a worrying one. Art had access to the classified alert that had been passed to the Telepath Corps, a warning that the rogue telepaths might have linked up with anti-government activists. That wasn't good news. Art had rather liked what he'd seen of Elizabeth, but Leo certainly had the personality to be a major pain in the ass. And if he wanted to cause trouble, he certainly had the power to do it.

"Captain," a woman's voice called. Art looked up to see Doctor Waianae shouting at him. "Can you come and look at this please?"

Art nodded and stepped back into the apartment. Doctor Waianae was Japanese-American, a short elfin woman with a slim, almost boyish figure. Her porcelain face concealed a surprising amount of insecurity, although she never lacked for male companionship. Art had sensed Alice's reaction to her and had been forced to conceal a smile. The Doctor might feel that her small breasts and tiny figure were unattractive – a result of growing up in a world where large breasts and curvy figures were taken for granted – but he knew that men found her desirable. He didn't know why she worried so much about her life.

"This is one of his shirts," the Doctor said, briskly. "Can you pick anything off it?"

Art shook his head. He blamed the media personally. A fake telepath had claimed to be able to feel psychic impressions off an item that had belonged to someone else, but the claim had never been verified and the faker had refused to be tested under controlled conditions. Perhaps it was possible – after all, you could tell a great deal about someone by what they bought and used regularly – but no one in the Telepath Corps had developed any such ability.

"No," he said, flatly. The Doctor's cool professionalism hid a multitude of other feelings, including an unwilling attraction to Art personally. He tried to push that thought aside. "What can you tell me about him?"

"Young, probably no older than twenty-five," the Doctor said, briskly. "He took no precautions at all; we took prints and DNA samples and we're running them through the databases now. If he's ever been arrested and fingerprinted, we will have him and the people he brought back here. And he had a drugs habit."

She nodded towards one of the opened cupboards. Art could see a small bag of white powder inside, as if someone had just tossed it carelessly into the compartment. That was odd for a telepath, not least because drugs – like alcohol – weakened the mental shields. On the other hand, if one spent most of one's life smashed out on drug trips, the chances were good that one might not notice – at first – when telepathy started to appear. Why not? It could easily be dismissed as yet another drug induced hallucination.

"It might not be his, of course," the Doctor added. "He might well have used his powers to assert control over the drug gangs in the area and made them his slaves. Or he could have pushed them into providing him with drugs for his victims. A drugged mind would be even less able to fight back."

Art nodded, sickened. "How many women did he bring back here?"

"We're uncertain as yet," the Doctor admitted. "We're picking up dozens of separate DNA signatures in the room. The chances are good that most of them are his victims, women compelled to come with him, sleep with him and then forget the experience. The bastard must have been living a dream."

Art sensed her disgust and understood. A normal rapist could be caught and convicted on the strength of his victim's testimony. A mind controller, on the other hand, could leave the women convinced that they wanted him, or make them forget the whole experience afterwards. Indeed, the more Art through about it, the more he was convinced that that was what the mind controller would do. Why take the risk of being identified when he could wipe their minds and send them home happy and ignorant?

"We may manage to identify some of his victims," Art agreed. As he spoke, it occurred to him to wonder if that might be the best thing to do. Surely it would be better to leave matters undisturbed. How could he explain to someone that they'd been raped and then made to forget the experience? On the other hand, their memories might one day surface, leaving them confused and terrified. "They might give us a clue where to look for him now."

He shook his head. "Send me a complete copy of your report," he ordered, finally. "I'll be downstairs with the others."

Outside, half of the building's population were in handcuffs, sitting on the ground and waiting for a police van to come to take them away. The NYPD had been through most of the building and found more than enough evidence to convict various occupants – including the landlady – of all kinds of charges, mainly drug possession and distribution. Art knew nothing about the economics of the drugs trade – at least outside Afghanistan, where the Marines had been involved in capturing or killing drug barons and the terrorists their money supported – but it struck him as stupid to keep all of one's drugs in one's own apartment. The gang members clearly hadn't been expecting the police raid.

He looked over at the landlady, who was cursing at Alice. She was a fat ugly woman, wearing a dress that should have left rather more of her body to the imagination. Art had disliked her on sight and the brief contact with her mind had left him feeling sick. Maria was the runt of the litter, the fat sister who had always been overshadowed by her three thin and pretty sisters, all of whom had made good matches and escaped the streets. She had moved from man to man, the last of whom – her least worthless husband – had left her the apartment building. And now even that was taken from her...

Art staggered as her thoughts and feelings crashed through his mind, then stabilised himself, rebuilding his mental blocks piece by piece. Maria – the landlady – clearly had a very minor telepathic power herself, or perhaps the force of her resentment was so strong that she was somehow able to slip into Art's telepathy and bombard him with waves of emotions. As soon as he could trust himself to move, he walked over to her and placed a gloved hand on her shoulder. She looked up at him resentfully.

"You're going to lose your building," Art said, flatly. There was no way around that, unless someone went to bat for her and somehow he doubted that anyone would be willing to do that. The chances were good that she was looking at some serious jail time. "I need your help. If you help me, I will help you."

Maria swore at him in a language Art suspected was Italian. He didn't know enough to be sure, although several of the words were familiar. "Get fucked," she said, finally. The concentrated venom in her voice made his head spin. Behind it, hope and fear warred in her breast. "Why should I do anything to help you?"

"Because I'm the senior officer here," Art said. It was stretching a point, but the Telepath Corps did have jurisdiction and Alice would back him up, if necessary. "I can make the difference between you going to jail and being released as a victim of a mind controlling telepath."

He smiled at the churn of emotions playing out across her mind. "Right," she said, finally. "I have had enough of promises from pigs. What guarantee do I have that you will keep your word?"

"None," Art said, honestly. "You don't have much of a choice, though. Do you?"

Maria glared at him, and then nodded. "All right," she said. "What must I do?"

Art pulled off his glove and touched her forehead. The physical contact made the link stronger and the intensity of her hatred and fear crashed against him, almost throwing him back out of her mind. Slowly, he concentrated on her mysterious lodger and skimmed through her memories. There wasn't much – like he'd done to his other victims, the mind controller had fiddled with her mind, making it impossible for her to recall much about him – but there was a clue. The mind controller had been addicted to women. He'd brought women off the streets – some clearly whores, some clearly wealthy women – and fucked them, before releasing them back out into the wild. Art was almost relieved. At least they weren't dealing with a killer.

He broke the contact and nodded at Alice. "I think we know where we have to go next," he said, finally. A few hours of research with the NYPD would confirm it for him and then they could act. The mind controller, it seemed, had been fond of a particular speakeasy. Art snorted at Maria's mental tone. Speakeasy indeed – the last time he'd heard anyone use that word had been during a documentary about Prohibition. "And then we can set a trap."

Alice nodded. "All right," she said. He caught a whiff of her mental state and smiled. She didn't like Maria any more than Maria liked her. "Let's go."

"One moment," Art said. He looked down at Maria and resolve crystallised in his mind. "A few debts have to be paid."

He called over one of the senior NYPD officers and issued orders. Maria would not be arrested, at least not formally. She would be taken to a place where she could find a second chance, if she chose to take it. If not...he suspected that she would soon find herself in trouble again. The Telepath Corps might not approve of his choice, but then...the telepaths had to pay their debts.

How else could they become good members of society?

Chapter Twenty-Four

Rumours have reached us that a large number of Indian telepaths have attempted to defect to the US and Britain following an official decision of the Indian Government that all telepaths are to be drafted into an Indian version of the Telepath Corps. The news follows rioting in several Indian cities against lower-caste telepaths, including a handful of untouchables who have revolted against the superior castes. There has been no official statement from the White House or Downing Street...

-AP News Report, 2015

"I feel," Alice subvocalised, "like a bloody whore!"

It was the fourth day she'd worked at Paddy's Pub – a warehouse that had been purchased by an immigrant and turned into a drinking den. Paddy, a man who was clearly proud of his roots, had filled the entire room with Irish pictures and decorations, while insisting that his bar maids wore green uniforms that showed off most of their bodies. It was about as authentic as some of the 'genuine' Native American artefacts she'd seen sold to gullible tourists, but few of the clientele seemed to care. Paddy, by accident or design, had started his business on a borderline between two of New York's gangs and the pub served as neutral ground.

She'd expected that Paddy would demand references and proof that she had a right to work in America, but instead she'd just been handed a uniform and told to put it on, before reporting for her first shift. Paddy, it seemed, had no intention of either reporting his takings to the IRS or paying his bar maids anything like a living wage. The other girls, who ranged from sixteen to twenty-seven, were all hopeless, their lives destroyed by drink, drugs and the sheer drudgery of their day to day existence. It was a side of America that Alice had never really believed existed until she'd seen it, the perfect place for a rogue telepath to hide.

"And you look like one too," Art sent back. He was waiting in an unmarked van, two blocks away from Paddy's Pub. They'd chosen not to involve the NYPD any more than strictly necessary, if only because the various gang leaders and criminal masterminds in the area would probably have their own hooks into the department. "I thought that that was the point."

Alice wanted to scowl, but she kept smiling at a sailor who was beckoning her over to sit on his lap. The CIA wasn't the most woman-friendly organisation in the United States, yet nothing she'd endured at Langley – including the suggestion that she was too young and inexperienced to be trusted with a proper position – was anything like what she'd gone through in a few hours at Paddy's Pub. Her bottom had been fondled or pinched more times than she could count, her breasts had been groped several times – at least she'd been able to slap the gropers, to general hilarity – and she'd been propositioned at least five times an hour. It was easy to see why. The other girls, all of whom needed the money desperately, would be happy to do anything for cash. She'd heard a sixteen-year-old talking quite openly about giving up her ass for money, telling her co-workers about a man who was prepared to pay her a hundred dollars for anal sex. Alice knew that the girl wouldn't last long. By twenty, she'd be worn out and heading for the gutter.

Art's idea had been simple enough. The FBI had managed to identify several of the mind controller's victims and most of them had one thing in common. They were young and they were blonde, just like Alice. If the mind controller liked coming into Paddy's Pub and trawling for girls, he would see Alice and be tempted to use his powers on her. Alice had reluctantly allowed Art to place a handful of mental blocks in her mind – hopefully preventing the mind controller from peeking and realising that it was a trap – but she knew that the whole plan hinged on a long shot. The mind controller could be halfway to Australia by now.

She pushed her doubts aside as she felt a hand start crawling up between her legs. Quite calmly, she stepped forward and left the groper behind. She wanted to draw her hidden weapon and put a bullet through his head, but that would have solved nothing. If the man had decided to make a fuss, the bouncers would have tossed him out on his ass. They were the only thing between Paddy's Pub and complete anarchy. Picking up a handful of empty glasses, she carried them towards the rear of the pub and into the kitchens. It, like the flat that had housed the mind controller, would never pass a health inspection. She had already resolved not to eat anything produced in the kitchens. The staff, underpaid illegal immigrants from China or Mexico, took the glasses from her and waved her towards the restroom. Alice was tempted, but she didn't like the restroom, not when half the staff were shooting up and the other half were smoking themselves to death. Besides, it was all part of the Blonde Princess act. The mind controller would get off on the thought that he might be the first to score with her.

The thought was unpleasant, but it had to be faced. The FBI had attempted to profile the mind controller from his apartment and while most of their conclusions had been obvious – they'd stated that he liked women, which was clear from the clothes in his apartment – they had made a number of good insights. Or so Alice hoped. She had very little faith in professional profilers. They sometimes made bad mistakes and, because they were taken seriously, others got hurt in the crossfire. They'd claimed that he liked to take women who would normally have been completely out of his league, ones that others in his circle would never be able to touch. By acting as if she would never give herself to anyone, Alice should have made herself a target – or so the theory ran. If they were wrong...she didn't intend to stay here forever. One more week and then she would leave, blowing the whistle on Paddy and his Pub afterwards. The NYPD could raid it and perhaps give the girls a chance of a better future.

She stepped back into the main bar and was instantly assailed by deafening heavy metal music as some of the girls got up on stage. Alice had flatly refused to dance on stage when Paddy had asked and he hadn't pressed the issue, much to her surprise. Or maybe it wasn't such a surprise after all. Paddy had more girls willing to strip naked on stage than he had places, so he might be happy to leave her as a barmaid. Besides, if she ever did weaken, he'd be able to charge extra for her first show. She took one look at the girls, shivering at the thought of ending up like them, and then turned back to her job. There was a tray of beers that had to be taken to a table...

Alice froze. Just for a second, she had felt someone touch her mind. She looked up and saw a hooded man standing in the shadows at the edge of the room. It took everything she had to pick up the tray and walk towards the table, already aware that the mind controller was starting to slip into her mind. She prayed silently that the mental blocks would hold. If they didn't hold, she would be exposed. The mind controller might tip Paddy off before Alice could escape or call for backup. She keyed the hidden signal in her dress – sending an alert to Art – and then started to unload her tray. Strangely, none of the men at the table – all gang members spoiling for trouble – attempted to grope her. Once she had finished unloading her tray, her body moved of its own accord, heading for the person in the shadows. If it hadn't been for the mental blocks, she realised, she would never have known that something was wrong.

Up close, there was nothing strange about the mind controller, apart from a gaunt face and piercing eyes. Alice felt her body shiver under his gaze, turning and walking out of the door and into the cold night air. She was aware that he was following her, yet she couldn't turn her head or break out of his control. Her body was moving against her will, swinging her hips in a saucy manner she had never used before, even with her first boyfriend. She hoped that Art was following them and would be in position to intervene soon.

Her treacherous body stepped into a building and up a flight of stairs she'd never seen before. She guessed, as the mind controller moved ahead of her, that he'd already secured a new apartment, either by paying cash or simply using his powers on the owner. It was definitely a nicer apartment than the previous one, but somehow she doubted that she would have time to admire it. He walked past her, threw himself onto a chair and turned his gaze on her body. Slowly, her hands moving against her will, she started to play with herself. One hand started to stroke her breasts; the other reached down into her panties, provoking a strange response from her body. She was surprised that she wasn't panicking, although she guessed that he was using his powers to keep her calm. At least he didn't seem to get off on terror and fear.

The thought was no consolation. Her hands were already removing her top and revealing her breasts to his hungry eyes. A moment later, she started to inch her pants down. She saw the bulge in his pants and shivered. If Art didn't come quickly, she was going to be forced to go all the way with him. And yet she still could not panic.

***

Art had watched in astonishment and dismay as Alice walked out of the club, followed by a man wearing a hood. The mental feel of the mind controller had been shocking. It was clear that most of his development had followed a very different course to any other known telepath, as his mind seemed completely chaotic. He was also very dangerous, not least because he wasn't entirely sane. Art followed him at a distance, relying on his own powers to keep him hidden from view. He didn't even dare draw his pistol and shoot the mind controller in the head. The spark of emotion might have tipped the bastard off.

He took a moment to fall back as Alice was forced to enter another apartment block, almost indistinguishable from his previous house. He guessed that everyone within the building had been programmed to serve as the mind controller's guards – if not his servants – after he'd lost the previous apartment, which meant that they might alert his target. The door slammed closed and Art held himself back for a few moments, just to allow the mind controller to reach his apartment, before pulling out a lockpick he'd used in Afghanistan. The apartment locks yielded easily to his pressure and the door opened, allowing him entry. He pulled a small terminal out of his pocket and checked on Alice's signal. Art had been careful not to tell her that she had been carrying a transponder as well as a radio. What she didn't know couldn't be read from her mind.

The terminal said that she was upstairs, so he followed her, opening his mind as far as he dared. There were faint traces that suggested that there were others in the building, but no one waiting in ambush. He reached for his pistol and checked it quickly, before pausing in front of the mind controller's door. The sign on the front read ZELLER, which made him jump. Was it a coincidence, a joke or a sign of a genuine connection? Professor Zeller was still in a coma, according to the latest report from the Telepath Corps. All attempts to probe his mind had been useless, of course. Whatever perversion of telepathic talent he had that made peeking into his head impossible had doomed him to remain in a coma. No telepathic mind healer could help him return to himself.

Art listened carefully, wondering just what was going on. He could hear the sound of someone breathing deeply, a harsh masculine sound. It dawned on him that his caution might have led to Alice being forced into sex, just as so many other victims had suffered. Angrily, throwing caution to the winds, he kicked the flimsy door and it shattered. Inside, a naked Alice was performing a seductive dance, while the mind controller was sitting on a chair, playing with himself. Art hesitated, just for a second. It was almost too late.

FREEZE! The mental command blasted into his skull. It hurt, sending unpleasant tendrils of pain running through his mind. A non-telepath would have frozen, unable to move, perhaps even unable to think. Even a telepath who had skirmished with other telepaths found it hard to move, but then none of the drills the Telepath Corps had carried out had risked serious damage. Art realised, as the pressure on his head swelled into a hellish nightmare, that even a victorious skirmish might leave him with serious mental damage. The thought was paralysing, far worse than wounds he might have suffered on Afghanistan's plains. He could have taken the thought of losing a leg, or an arm, but not his mind.

He's pushing at you, idiot, Art thought to himself. The mental battle was taking place within his skull. He pushed back hard, reaching out with his own talent to slash into the mind controller's mind. A name – an insistence of identity – flickered through his skull. The mind controller was called Henry. There was no hint of a surname. Henry's thoughts and feelings – his surprise and rage at being violated – raged back at him, daring him to keep pushing into his mind. Memories flared open...

...He was lying on the ground, his chest hurting from the beating. An overweight man was staring down at him, slowly returning his belt to his waist. The young man was in so much pain, yet he didn't dare cry out, knowing that it would merely mean another beating...

Art winced. Henry was fighting back, hacking away at Art's own memories. For someone who had never encountered another telepath, he seemed to understand mental combat far better than Art. But then, Art had never fought another telepath to the death...

...The Drill Sergeant is laughing at the clumsy recruit; the other recruits are laughing. The entire Marine Corps is laughing at Little Art, who cannot fight, or fuck, or shoot straight. The merest exercise is impossible for him; guns shatter in his hands, he cannot bring himself to fight the foe, even on training grounds. When he is dismissed, it is almost with relief. He was never cut out to be a Marine.

Art felt cold anger flaring through him. It hadn't been that way at all. His anger gave him new strength and he pushed back, allowing his anger to slash deep into his foe's mind...

...The woman is laughing at the skinny young boy. Why would she want to go out with him, let alone allow him to share the pleasures of her body? Her boyfriend comes over and beats the skinny boy up, laughing at him for daring to even think of touching his girl. The pain and rage flare up within him and lash out, ripping the jock's mind apart. For the first time, the boy has touched the power he possesses and loves it...

...One girl, a dozen girls, a hundred girls, so many that even he loses count. The girls who rejected him when he was a powerless youth go first, compelled into his bed and made to perform shameful acts. Later, when he leaves school and flees into the underground, there are others, girls who can give him money as well as sex. He's a simple man. All he wants is money and sex. Even when he first hears of telepaths, other telepaths, it never occurs to him to draw a link between his gift and theirs. He is special...

Art felt a vein pounding away in his forehead. It was stalemate. He couldn't dislodge his opponent and his opponent couldn't dislodge him. He'd fucked up, part of his mind reminded him; the battle would be decided by endurance and the winner would be the one who collapsed last. Except that even the deadly embrace would leave him with mental damage...he couldn't retreat and he couldn't advance. A moment later, the fight ended suddenly.

He opened his eyes in disbelief. Alice had knocked the mind controller – Henry, he reminded himself – out with a bottle she'd found on the side table. The grip that had threatened to overwhelm and destroy his mind vanished, leaving him spinning dizzily. He finally collapsed to the floor, stunned. The pain, perversely, helped him to focus. A moment later, he was aware of strong arms rolling him over and warm lips pressed against his. With their touch, there came an awareness of identity. Alice was kissing him.

"You're an angel," he said. She was still naked, save for her socks. He knew that there was a problem, but he couldn't comprehend it, not with his head still spinning. "You saved my life."

"You cut it very fine," Alice countered, grimly. She sounded shaken. Art tried to reach for her mind, but all he felt was a roaring pain at the back of his head. "A few moments later and..."

She shuddered. "But he's out of it now," she said. "That mad plan of yours worked."

"Good," Art said. Every word was an effort, but at least he could *think*. Maybe there was no permanent damage after all. "Call it in; get someone to come take him off our hands and shoot him with sleepers. We need him secure before..."

The darkness rushed up suddenly and bore him away into nightmares.

Chapter Twenty-Five

Saudi Arabia reported the world's first major case of telepathic terrorism when an unknown telepath broadcast feelings of hatred and fear into one of the country's major cities. The resulting chaos, perhaps inspired by the Harvard Blast in America, took the lives of over seven hundred men and women. Particularly targeted were the religious police, who were torn apart by howling mobs in the streets. Saudi Arabia, which has refused to consider rescinding the fatwa against telepaths, is bracing itself for further attacks.

-AP News Report, 2015

"You have to admit that the view here is great," Leo said. He grinned as he lay back on the bed. "We have to rebel against the system more often."

Elizabeth rolled her eyes. The penthouse suite on top of the skyscraper belonged to an oil millionaire who was currently in Texas, attending to business. The five telepaths – the remainder had headed to New York, instead of Washington – had walked through the building, convinced the servants that they were guests of the owner and had received the run of the place. None of the servants would remember them when they left.

"And the lifestyle of the rich and powerful," Leo added. "We could have this for ourselves once we win the war."

Valentine shrugged from where he was sitting, gazing out into space. "I was in touch with a few of my contacts," he said, slowly. While four of the telepaths had remained in the penthouse, waiting for the word, Valentine had been out on the streets looking for allies. Leo had expressed a hope that Valentine would find other rebellious telepaths, but Valentine had referred to contacts in the underworld, people who lived their lives in hopes of frustrating The Man. "They're impressed with what we've done so far, but they want more."

Elizabeth frowned. "And what have we done so far?"

"My point exactly," Valentine said. He smiled, without humour. Unlike the other three, he refused to show them what he was feeling, let alone thinking. He was older than them and perhaps mental privacy was more important to him, but it made it harder for Elizabeth to trust him. "Some of them feel that we're just another band of runaways, while others fear that we're working for the federal government and intend to arrest them when we meet them."

"We're on the run from the federal government," Leo protested, pulling himself to his feet. "Don't they know that?"

Valentine shrugged expressively. "It wouldn't be the first time that someone in authority managed to slip an agent into the underworld and maintain him there for long periods of time," he said. "The FBI has undercover agents in most anti-government militia movements and criminal rings in America. The only ones that are fairly safe from penetration are the ones that demand a high entry price and even they are not immune to having their members turned, either because they want out or because they have been threatened by the law. I don't blame them for feeling a little paranoid."

"The FBI has agents everywhere?" Leo said. He sounded dazed. "How the hell do they manage that?"

"They wipe a person's record and create a new one," Valentine said. "There's no shortage of ways to do it. Many of the gangs are always looking for new members and muscle. The infiltrators get plenty of training and support, everything they might need to slip into a gang. The FBI cannot condone infiltrating the gangs that demand that a person kills someone in exchange for a position, but the others...if the government believes that they could be dangerous, they get infiltrated."

He grinned. "They have agents in right-wing militia groups and left-wing protest groups," he added. "If there's a protest march planned that might be inconvenient, it gets diverted or pushed into senseless violence. The riot at Harvard only went so badly wrong because there were people in the crowd who wanted to produce an excuse for cracking down on telepaths."

Elizabeth remembered the riot and shivered. There might have been government agents in the crowd, but the feelings they had produced had been all too real. She'd killed then, she knew; hundreds of people were dead because of her, including many who hadn't been trying to kill her. She wondered if she would ever wipe the blood off her hands. There were times when she envied Leo. His belief that telepaths were the superior race gave him a mental framework for dismissing the lives of ordinary humans. Elizabeth didn't have that luxury.

"Why?" she asked, hoping to divert attention. "Why would the government bother to infiltrate a few harmless organisations?"

Valentine grinned. "The political organisations, left and right, exist to challenge the government," he said. "It doesn't matter if they're right-wing nuts who believe in returning the Ten Commandments to the courtroom and prayer to public schools, or left-wing nuts who want to ban nuclear energy and disband the military; they both challenge the government and the men who run it. Their mere presence is a threat to the government and governments always concentrate on securing their power first. They waste no opportunity to embarrass, discredit and eventually disband any such organisation."

He winked at her. "Which is lucky for us. It gives us thousands of potential allies, if we can convince them that we are worth supporting," he added. "They've been stung before, so they will be careful at first. We have to prove ourselves to them."

"We don't have to prove ourselves to anyone," Leo snapped. He stroked his chin, where he was trying to grow a beard to fool the CCTV cameras that were already doubtless looking for them. It wasn't working very well and Valentine had already been talking about obtaining a fake beard for him. "We're telepaths! They should be coming to us and begging for support."

"I'm afraid they don't actually see it that way," Valentine said. "They need proof before they risk exposing themselves and it has to be dramatic proof, the kind of proof the FBI would never sanction. We have to make our position clear in no uncertain terms."

"You're talking about carrying out a terrorist act," Elizabeth said slowly. She still had nightmares about the minds she'd sensed snapping out of existence at the riot, killed by her – even if she hadn't meant to do it. "How many people do you want us to kill to make the point clear?"

"Well, that's rather up to you," Valentine said. He grinned at her unpleasantly. "How much of a show of power do you want to make?"

"One that will make them back off and leave us alone," Leo said. The icy determination – and hatred – in his mind shocked her. Elizabeth had known about his beliefs, but the new feelings washing through his mind were worse. "We could start by crashing a few aircraft and then perhaps picking off a political leader or two from a distance..."

"And that wouldn't win us any friends," Elizabeth snarled. She didn't want to kill anyone again. "The mundane humans would be screaming for the government – and the Telepath Corps – to hunt us down as dangerously insane terrorists and they'd be right! We'll just make them more scared of us, more determined to wipe telepathy out whatever the costs...if we are a separate race, we could be looking at extinction. They won't let us set up home in Alaska after we have killed a few thousand people, will they? They'll put us on Death Row and execute us."

"We are the superior race," Leo said, firmly. "We can win..."

"Oh, give it a break," Elizabeth snapped. "You're a telepath, not Superman. The last time I checked, a speeding bullet could catch us before we even turned to run and our skin isn't exactly made of armour. Reading minds isn't that great an advantage in a tactical situation – is it? Maybe we can send soldiers running away from us, or get them fighting each other, but we can't influence robots or drones. They'll send an unmanned aircraft overhead and drop a missile on our heads and that will be the end of us!"

She realised that she was shouting and lowered her voice. "We are not gods," she said. "We cannot afford to provoke a war of extermination."

Years ago, while she'd been in college – it felt like a lifetime ago – she'd studied the Perfect Heresy, the rise and destruction of the Cathar Religion in France. They'd struck her as wonderful people, far superior to the Catholic Church

– particularly after all the priestly abuse scandals – and yet they'd been destroyed by the Christians. Having right on one's side was no guarantee of victory. And there were plenty of other examples of a race being threatened with extermination by an outside force. Hitler and the Jews were merely the most prominent.

"We need to make it clear that we can live in peace with them," she said, finally. "If we start by committing mass slaughter" – *again*, her mind whispered – "they will have no way out of the crisis, save by slaughtering each and every telepath down to the very last man, woman and child. You said it yourself" – nodding to Valentine – "that government show a much smarter and deadlier side of themselves when their power is seriously threatened. We are going to threaten both that power and their reason for existence, protecting the American population."

Leo stared at her as if he had never seen her before. "And you suggest...what? We cannot stay here forever. Even if the rich bastard who owns the place stays away for a few more months, we are consuming more food than they would over the same period of time. Someone might notice and then realise where we are. What do you suggest we do?"

"We cannot stay hidden forever anyway," Valentine added. "That redneck fool senator is already talking about mandatory telepathic testing and drugging for telepaths who refuse to join the Telepath Corps and be indoctrinated into service to the government. It won't be long before they bring in ID cards and random sweeps for subversives and unregistered telepaths, including us. And then where will we be?"

He leaned forward. "There is an election coming up in a few months," he reminded them. "The person who wins that election will be the person who shapes the government's response to telepathy. Do we want to risk hiding until we discover that the next President is someone who intends to make such mandatory precautions real?"

Elizabeth stared down at her hands. She hadn't realised, because they had all been so close back at the mansion, that Leo had brought his strongest supporters to Washington. She had wanted to go with him to keep an eye on him, but it suddenly crossed her mind that four telepaths on one would be quick and decisive. If Leo started to wonder about her loyalty, he might well kill her or try to rewrite her mind...

"We cannot start by killing people," she said, trying to conceal her inner thoughts. Luckily, she would have known if anyone had actually been reading her mind. Being so exposed to one another had made them all more sensitive and more tolerant. "If we kill political leaders, it will turn them into martyrs rather than the criminal traitors they are. We need to embarrass them instead. That shouldn't be too difficult. The way they have been pushing for controls on telepaths suggests that they all have their guilty secrets. We peek into their minds, discover their secrets and then expose them to the world."

"We can hardly step forward and tell everyone without getting arrested," Leo sneered. "That is an absurd idea and..."

"No, we can't," Valentine agreed. "On the other hand, we can definitely use one of the underground internet newspapers to spread the word. Quite a few of them have links to the more respected newspapers and television programs, so the word would spread quickly. If the political leader tried to sue, he'd discover that it would be impossible to save what remained of his reputation..."

He grinned. "Best of all, we wouldn't have to show ourselves so openly," he added. "They'd know what had happened, but the world wouldn't know – which would make them wonder what else we might know that we have decided to keep to ourselves, so far. They'd be hit by their own inner demons..."

Leo laughed. "Anyone would think that they had something to hide," he said. He grinned. Elizabeth blinked in alarm at the sudden burst of dark amusement that flickered through his mind. "I have a better idea. There are always political press conferences going on around Washington. Let's crash one of them and make the bastard confess to his sins in public."

He looked up at Valentine. "Wouldn't that convince your contacts that we are to be trusted?"

"Probably," Valentine said, slowly. "They'd certainly be delighted at embarrassing a politician. We'd have to check with them first, though; they might have particular targets in mind. I'll see to that now. Everyone else can get a rest and we will move out tomorrow."

Elizabeth frowned inwardly, pulling her own mental shields around her. She still didn't trust Valentine, even though Leo seemed to trust him completely. It would have been easier if Valentine showed his emotions to the other telepaths, but his mental shields had strengthened in the last few minutes. She had the distant feeling that she understood – too late – how he was manipulating Leo. He showered Leo in tales of government misconduct and offered to help make his dreams real. Leo probably hadn't needed much persuasion. He'd been convinced he was a superior form of life before the first telepaths had sprung into existence.

She shook her head at Eugene, who had sent her an unspoken invitation to share his bed, and walked into the room she'd claimed for herself. She hadn't risked having sex as a telepath – indeed, she'd curtailed physical contact as much as possible, like almost every other telepath – after hearing about some telepaths who became so closely entwined in one another that it had proven impossible to separate them into two separate minds. They might have been the lucky ones. Other telepaths – or telepath-mundane pairings – had failed because they'd suddenly learned all of their partner's innermost secrets. Eugene was a nice boy, in his way, but he was very definitely a loyalist. He would have told Leo if he knew about Elizabeth's doubts.

The room she'd claimed for herself had clearly been designed for a pre-teen girl, or perhaps a very soppy teenage girl. It was covered in pink; pink wallpaper, pink furniture and a pink bed. Elizabeth had laughed when she'd seen it, but after two days of sleeping in it she'd decided that she positively hated the colour pink. The laptop on the desktop was useless. The room's owner had put a password on and Elizabeth's poor computer skills couldn't unlock it. She shook her head, pulled back the sheets and settled down into bed. At least the pink mattress was comfortable. The maids had changed the linings for her on Elizabeth's command, although they hadn't been able to change the colour. Or perhaps there were simply no other colours.

She started to breathe deeply, focusing her mind. Professor Zeller's old exercises – she wondered, briefly, what had happened to the Professor – still worked, allowing her to sleep in reasonable comfort. She hoped that her nightmares weren't being broadcast to the others. There was no such thing as privacy at night any longer, not in a world that included telepaths. She closed her eyes and started to think...

Leo had gone off the deep end, aided and abetted by Valentine. It was clear, just from his mental tone, that he actually believed most of what he was saying. Elizabeth had hoped that she could talk him into settling for less than total victory or defeat, but that was looking increasingly unlikely. Quite apart from Valentine whispering poison into his ear, the government *was* looking for them and wouldn't be too happy when they found them. It occurred to her that she could simply walk away and vanish into the shadows, relying on her own telepathy to keep her hidden, but Valentine was right. The government would be searching for them and, eventually, it would start mandatory testing for telepathy.

And Leo's actions would probably make that inevitable.

Elizabeth's thoughts chased themselves uselessly, around and around. If the telepaths frightened the normal humans enough, perhaps they would be left in peace – or perhaps it would be war to the knife. If two telepaths, linked together and panicking, had been able to wreak havoc in Harvard, she knew that thirteen would be able to cause vast damage, perhaps even break the telekinetic barrier. They could lay waste to an entire city...

No, she thought. That couldn't be allowed. If the embarrassment campaign worked, there would be no need for mass slaughter, no need for a war that could only end in genocide. She had to believe that it was possible, because otherwise there would be no home for her. She wished Professor Zeller was with them. His wisdom might have helped them find a way out of their predicament. Slowly, unwillingly, she fell into a fitful sleep.

***

"There's still no trace of them?"

"No, Mr President," the FBI Director said. "They haven't shown themselves at all. We have had no luck in tracing them to their final destination."

The President scowled. There were thirteen rogue telepaths, among the most powerful in the world, loose in America. God alone knew what they were planning. The entire country had been placed on alert, watching for them. Once they were found, perhaps they could relax a little.

"And Professor Zeller?"

"Still no change," the Director said. "His coma remains unbroken."

The President nodded, reluctantly. He had hundreds of questions for Zeller.

And it looked as if they would never be answered.

Chapter Twenty-Six

The European Union today announced the development of a Euro Corps of Telepaths, who would be charged with supporting counter-terrorism activities and border security. Rumours have emerged from Brussels that the Euro Corps was brought into existence through the combined efforts of France, Germany and Britain – and over the objections of most of the European Parliament. Telepaths in France and Britain have helped expose and capture many terrorist cells in both countries...

...Russia accused the Chinese Government of allowing a telepath to peek into the mind of the Russian Ambassador to China, following a small border dispute two weeks ago. The Chinese denied the claim and accused Russia of attempting to undermine the Chinese Government...

-AP News Report, 2015

Senator Curtis Hughes was a beefy black man, elected twenty years ago to the Senate and, so far, hadn't even been worried by the Tea Party Movement. Roger disliked him on sight, as did many others in the media, even though they knew that Hughes had been quite successful at pleasing his constituents. Rumours of scandals plagued his career, as they did to all political figures in the world, but somehow nothing had ever stuck to the man. He'd been quite willing to unleash an army of lawyers on anyone who dared to repeat some of the more outrageous rumours, including the one that linked him to organised crime and voting fraud.

He scowled as he stood in the press pit and watched as the Senator outlined his plans for the future, including a possible bid to become the Democratic Candidate for President. There were several other major figures in the party considering a run for President themselves, so it was clear that Hughes didn't want to show his hand too soon. Roger had never quite understood the process, but he did understand that the prospective candidate had to bring in enough funds, without exposing himself to the media for too long. The longer his name was in the public eye, the greater the chance of some of the mud that would be thrown at him sticking It wouldn't be the first time a seemingly inevitable victor had been derailed by the sudden discovery of an embarrassing fact.

The Senator was, of course, talking about telepaths. "I say to you all," Hughes thundered, "that the use of telepaths in law enforcement is quite unacceptable! Can a telepath tell the difference between a fantasy and reality? How long will it be before the Telepath Corps becomes the Thought Police, poking into our minds and using whatever it finds as evidence against us?"

Roger shrugged, jotting down the high points in his little notepad. As he understood it, from his interviews with Professor Zeller's pupils, a telepath could easily tell the difference between a false memory, one born from a fantasy, and a true memory. The false memory would lack the hundreds of tiny impressions that the true memory would have – everything from temperature to ambient feelings. But the Senator was speaking to men and women who were scared of telepaths, worried that their innermost thoughts and feelings would be brought out on display. They might have good reason to worry. Only five days ago, a telepath – a thirteen-year-old girl in school – had been exposed, using her powers to read minds for her own amusement. The courts were still arguing over what, if anything, she could actually be charged with. Could she be charged with invasion of privacy or worse?

"And I pledge that should I be elected, I will ensure that every known telepath is told to go to Alaska and live there, or take sleeper drugs to dampen their telepathic powers," Hughes continued. Roger lifted an eyebrow, wondering if he'd misheard. No, the other reporters were reacting as well. It was rare for political candidates to make such blunt statements, if only because their rivals would have a field day making fun of it. A statement in favour of one issue would ensure that everyone who was *not* in favour of that issue would line up on the other side. But then, telepaths were only a tiny percentage of the population. Losing their votes wouldn't matter a damn if the remainder of the population voted for him. "They will be taught to control themselves or be separated from normal people."

Roger listened to the remainder of the speech, but there was little else of interest in it. As always, the Senator took questions from the media, carefully picking out the reporters who were sure to ask favourable questions. Roger rolled his eyes cynically; reporters always had their political favourites, the candidates they would root for, ignoring all traditions of journalistic neutrality. The first question was harmless, one about how the Senator treated his constituents; good for nothing more than a sound bite. The second was political dynamite.

"Senator," a voice said, "is it true that you're having a relationship with a woman called Yolanda who is not your wife."

There was a stunned pause. A moment later, the Senator started to speak. "Yes," he said. Roger stared in disbelief. By the look of him, the Senator couldn't believe the words coming out of his mouth either. "I fell in love with Yolanda after my wife rejected my advances. I had tried to introduce her to some of my favourite sexual games, but she refused to play. Yolanda loved experimenting with me, although we sometimes went too far and I had to pay for her to get an abortion because an illegitimate child would have ruined my prospects of becoming President ..."

Roger – the entire press pool – just stared as Hughes destroyed his political career. The words just kept rolling out; he'd committed adultery on many occasions, he'd accepted bribes, he'd spread lies and nonsense about his rivals, he'd used blackmail and threats to ensure that his state got a large slice of the federal pie...there seemed to be no end to the confession. He was even talking about taking drugs as a young man and using prostitutes before he married his wife. The live feed from the event would be on CNN and Fox by now, he knew; none of the Senator's army of lawyers or PR men would be able to stop it from going viral. The entire country would see it by afternoon.

"Fuck me," he said, as the confession finally came to an end. He couldn't help but notice that the army of supporters and assistants behind the Senator was a great deal smaller. Men and women who had believed in him had been disillusioned forever. Whoever ran against Hughes in the next election would not lose, even if he had his own scandals to overcome. "What the hell just happened?"

***

Elizabeth watched from the sidelines as Senator Hughes collapsed on the stage. She hadn't meant to make him collapse, but there had been a sudden unexpected pressure in his mind, throwing her back into hers. A moment later, he'd just crashed down into darkness. She hoped that she hadn't killed him by accident, although after what she'd seen in his mind she found it hard to care. A world that had nothing but telepaths wouldn't have such dishonesty in high places. It would be impossible to hide such a mind for long.

Come on, Leo sent. She'd insisted on doing the probe herself, knowing that Leo might well lose control and seriously hurt their target, instead of just humiliating him. It helped that the Senator had been terrified of telepaths, not without reason. His list of crimes seemed never-ending. *We have to get out of here.*

Elizabeth nodded and led the way out of the crowd. Hundreds of others were leaving, some already using their cell phones to call their resignations into the office. Others – citizens who would have voted for Hughes in the election – looked angry. How could they vote for him now? She wondered if they'd just switch *en masse* to the other party, or if they'd just stay home in disgust. The general mind tone was full of sudden anger. Hughes would be lucky to be elected to Assistant Garbage Disposal Officer if there was an election tomorrow.

"I expected him to have support from the Telepath Corps," Leo muttered, as they kept walking. They could already hear the sounds of sirens heading towards the stadium. Someone had probably called the police and suggested that Hughes be taken into custody before his former allies in the criminal syndicates realised what had happened and sent assassins after him. Or maybe someone had realised what had happened and sent the police after the rogue telepaths. "They should have guarded him."

Elizabeth shrugged, remembering the only Telepath Corps member she had ever met. "They might have had a peek themselves and discovered the truth about him," she said, thoughtfully. "Hughes clearly decided that telepaths, even telepaths who were supposed to be on his side, were a liability. I think he's just learned the error of his ways."

Leo chuckled as two police cars drove past them. Elizabeth sensed the presence of a telepath in one of the vehicles and pulled her own mind inward, concentrating on hiding. The other telepath didn't notice them, his thoughts intent on something else. There was no way to know what without risking a probe and that would have certainly alerted him to their presence.

"And what will happen," he asked, "when the Telepath Corps starts peeking into the heads of the people they are supposed to guard?"

Elizabeth smiled. Walking like this, almost as if they were two young lovers, made the world seem almost normal, just as it had been before her powers exploded into life. The illusion was shattered as they walked into a small café and met up with the other three telepaths, led by Valentine. Their thoughts were calmly focused, but glittering with victory. They had succeeded. Their task hadn't been as dangerous as peeking into the Senator's mind and forcing him to spill his secrets in front of a captive audience, but it had been richly rewarded.

"Success," Valentine assured them. "We got everything we wanted from the targets."

Leo nodded. "And then I am afraid the next step in the plan is for you, Liz," he said. Elizabeth nodded. She disliked that part of the plan, but it was necessary. Besides, it would keep her away from Valentine for a few hours. "Good luck."

***

Gary lived for computers. As a youth, his parents had bought him an old Windows machine that had been destined for the scrap heap. Gary had, instead, bought a handful of books on computers and somehow managed to repair and vastly improve the old machine. Other computers followed after his parents realised that he had a talent, each one expanding his knowledge of both computer hardware and software. Gary became a master programmer, cutting his teeth on Linux and other free programs, before expanding outwards into computer hacking and even mischief. He wasn't political, although he had once helped hack into a congressman's computer after the man had demanded greater controls over the internet; his only concern was keeping access to his beloved computers. His apartment was crammed with the machines. When he ran them all simultaneously, as he did most of the time, he had to use air conditioning to keep the room cool.

The knock on the door reminded him that the real world sometimes intruded on his existence, an existence that was more in cyberspace than in reality. Given a choice between the cold greyness of reality – where a fat nerd like him would be mocked relentlessly – and the warmth of cyberspace, he knew where he wanted to live. Girls didn't mock him in cyberspace – one of his proudest achievements was discovering how to unlock the passwords of a hundred different porn sites and spreading them over the internet – and he could have them whenever he wanted. It was so much cleaner than living with an actual girl, or so he told himself. The girl at the door took his breath away.

She was young, shapely and adorable, just like his favourite porno star. When she passed him the small hard drive containing a list of computer servers and passwords, he knew that he was in love. He'd been told, by one of his contacts, that there might be a chance to hack into servers that – so far – no one had been able to access, but they hadn't mentioned the girl. He would do anything for her. He took the hard drive back to his lair and – feeling nervous at even making a tiny pass at her – beckoned for her to follow him. He expected her to leave, but instead she followed him into the room.

He knew she was impressed because her mouth fell open. Grinning, he sat back down in his chair and picked up the cyber-glove that allowed him to manipulate objects within cyberspace. Very few people could use a glove naturally, but Gary – whose early experience had given him a freakish insight into how computers thought and reacted – had no problems using one. The girl looked suitably impressed as he linked up the hard drive to the computer network and started to examine it. It wouldn't be the first time someone had given him a virus, but most computer viruses couldn't thrive on his machine. It would need to be a virus designed specifically for his computer and he had been careful to make sure that no one had the information that would allow them to create one.

The data fell open in front of him and he smiled. He didn't know how she'd done it – he was sure that it was all her work – but the passwords of some of the most secure databases in the world lay in front of him. The secret databases of the banking sector, the insurance companies, the military-industrial complex, the state department...they were all open to him. He was barely aware of time passing as he started to poke through the internet, slipping through links that led to proxy servers and then into his destination. Secure firewalls that had daunted the most determined hackers fell open at his touch. They could hide nothing from him.

"All you have to do is spread this far and wide," the girl said. Her voice sounded unbearably sweet in his ear, like the voice he'd ripped from a porn star and used for his alarm clock. "I want the entire world to know about it."

Gary, who would cheerfully have killed for her, nodded. "Yes," he promised. He knew that there was no way that a major babe like her would deign to kiss him, but at least he could dream. "I will make sure that everyone knows."

***

Elizabeth looked up at the wall of computers and fought hard to keep herself from bursting into laughter. It looked like a computer geek's paradise, which she supposed it was, in a way. Gary seemed to live a twilight existence, having long since hacked into the power companies to make sure that they kept feeding his computers electric power without noticing that they were doing anything of the sort. Valentine had told her that Gary was unlikely to give a damn about politics, but like all such outcasts, a pretty girl could get through his defences with ease.

She looked down at his mind and realised that Valentine had been right. Gary was easy to manipulate, even without telepathy, especially when she looked so much like his dream girl. She'd caught a glimpse of the image surrounding her in his mind and found herself smiling at how pretty she looked. She'd pushed a handful of other commands into his mind while he was distracted, covering her tracks. Even if the Telepath Corps peeked into Gary's brain, they'd only see the porn star he admired. She wondered if they'd waste time trying to track her down.

The plan was simple enough. The most powerful firewalls in the world couldn't stop someone who had the right password, the passwords that Valentine and the rest of his team had been systematically pulling out of the right minds. The data that Gary found would be dumped out onto the web, creating a security nightmare for their targets. Even if they managed to wipe it out of the web, no one would ever trust their security again. The damage would be considerable, or so she hoped.

Gently, she touched Gary's mind and implanted a fantasy, and then left the apartment. She hadn't realised how warm it had been in there until she walked out, back into the outside world. Gary seemed to live in a hothouse. She would have been surprised if Texas was any hotter. Shaking her head, she went outside and headed back to the meeting point, where the others were waiting. If anyone managed to trace the hacker back home, all they would find would be Gary. Oddly, exposing him like that caused her a pang of guilt. Gary had been a genuine innocent, without any fear of telepaths, or even hatred. All of his emotion was reserved for his beloved computers.

"Hey," Leo said, as she walked in. He was grinning unpleasantly, his mind flaring with malice. "Take a look at that."

Elizabeth glanced up. The television had been set to Fox News and the presenter was talking about Curtis Hughes.

Leo clicked a switch and the volume came up, allowing them to hear what he was saying. The Senator's career had come to an end. It seemed likely that he would never be free again; at least once all of the criminal acts he had admitted to committing were proven. She hoped that other political leaders took note. They could all be targeted by rogue telepaths. Maybe they'd see sense...

Or maybe they'd just become more determined to hunt them all down.

Chapter Twenty-Seven

Official Washington is reeling today after the shock confession of Curtis Hughes, formerly one of the prime Democratic candidates for the Presidency. Hughes, whose confession was broadcast live to the entire country, claimed responsibility for a multitude of criminal acts and has been taken into custody by the FBI. His angry political workers have deserted him in droves, two of them even going so far as to start a recall election. A spokesman for the Democratic Party pledged a full investigation prior to the DNC.

-AP News Report, 2015

"So," a voice said. "How are you feeling today?"

Art's eyes opened and he found himself staring up at a pair of naked breasts. For a moment, he was completely stunned and then he remembered. After handing the mind controller – *Henry the Mind Controller*, part of his mind whispered mockingly – over to the FBI, they'd gone back to their hotel and fallen into bed together. It had been a long time for both of them and they'd spent half of the night making love.

"Very good," Art said, reaching for her. Alice came willingly and he felt her breasts pushing against his chest. He sensed her desire as she touched him, feeling the emotions running through her body and mind. "And how are you today?"

She kissed him and, for a long moment, all thought was forgotten. Art could feel her pleasure as he touched her, caressed her and finally slipped inside her, allowing him to ride her orgasms until he reached his own climax. Oddly, he was sure that she could feel him as well, even though it should have been impossible. Perhaps his telepathy had opened up a two-way link between their minds. For a second, he remembered the two telepaths who had merged into one being and almost drew away, before deciding that there was no better way to go. It didn't happen; when they separated, they separated permanently.

"I think we'd better get a shower," Alice said, afterwards. She pulled herself off the bed and staggered towards the bathroom. "They want us back in Washington ASAP."

Art blinked at her, and then reached for his cell phone. It was blinking away with an urgent message, ordering him to report back to Washington and the Telepath Corps as soon as possible. He opened his mouth to complain about her leaving him to sleep, before realising that it would be churlish. Besides, he wasn't too unhappy about the delay. He was still smiling when Alice left the shower – wearing a dressing gown and her hair down – and ordered him into the shower. He winked at her and held up the cell phone.

"I wanted to make sure that you were all right," Alice said, by way of explanation. Art remembered the mental conflict with the mind controller and shivered. There didn't seem to be any permanent damage, but there were gaps and flickers of pain running through his memory. He recalled how the Telepath Corps had used stress-inducing techniques to help awaken new telepaths and shivered. He knew how they felt. "And besides, I wanted to take you to bed."

Art caught the towel she threw at him and stepped into the shower, troubled. He hadn't used his telepathy to force Alice into bed, yet there was a quiet nagging doubt. Had he done it unintentionally? The mind controller would have forced her into bed without a second thought, but Art...how could he know if the feelings she had for him were real, or something he had created in her mind? He turned on the shower and felt warm water sluicing him down, washing away the sweat and stains of sex. There truly was no way to know, apart from asking another telepath to probe her mind, and even that might not be conclusive.

You'll find out when you die, a voice whispered in his mind. *You'll know if you had a lover or if you're nothing better than a filthy rapist...*

Art shook his head angrily and turned off the shower, towelling himself down as he stepped out and studied himself in the mirror. There were no obvious signs of injury caused by the mind controller, although the scars he'd picked up while on active duty still showed clearly. Alice had kissed them all, one by one, and he'd loved her for it. A soldier's wife had a hard life and far too many marriages and relationships were broken up by the stresses and strains of combat.

"...The New York Stock Exchange is shivering after multiple hacking attacks on various banks and other companies left their secrets open for all to see," the television said. Art frowned – he hated television in the morning, although it was closer to noon – and stepped back into the bedroom. Alice was sitting on the bed, watching CNN. "It has been discovered that several banks do not have the financial reserves to cope with a sudden run on their money. Furthermore, they have continued to invest in toxic stocks, despite the lessons of 2008. As the word spread, thousands of investors and private citizens have started a run on the banks, demanding their money before the banks run out of reserve cash."

Art blinked. "What the hell?"

Alice tapped her lips and switched to Fox. "...Been confirmed that a group of rogue telepaths obtained the passwords for the State Department and the Pentagon's innermost computer databanks and spread the word to the hacker community. In a deliberate repeat of prior politically-motivated hacking, the telepaths have been broadcasting the secrets to the entire world. It may be days before we obtain a complete list of secrets, but highlights known to be on the web include a secret plan to offer sanctuary to Saudi and Iranian telepaths and a military operations plan for withdrawal from Afghanistan..."

"My God," Art said, in astonishment. "Who did this and why?"

"The Pentagon spokesman, General Harrison, stated that the combined telepathic and hacking attack was an act of terrorism," the speaker continued. "Whatever the motivations of the key players, they have successfully weakened the United States and embarrassed the country in front of the world. The White House has not yet commented, but sources within the FBI have stated that hunting down and capturing the telepathic terrorist – or terrorists – has become the first priority for the FBI..."

Alice clicked off the television. "I spoke to Washington," she said, wryly. "They want us back there for a meeting. It seems that the faecal matter has definitely hit the fan."

Art nodded. He'd been a young Marine during the last financial crisis and could still remember how his parents had come alarmingly close to losing everything. The Marine recruits had wondered if they'd be called out onto the streets to keep the peace, although in the end that hadn't been necessary and they'd gone to Iraq instead. If it had happened again, with government budgets so tight, he doubted that there could be another bailout. Besides, if the bankers had been taken insane risks again, the country would not be inclined to let them get away with it.

"No arguments," he agreed. "I take it that they have already arranged for an aircraft?"

Alice winked at him. "How did you guess?"

***

The Telepath Corps had decided not to build a prominent headquarters in Washington, even though all of the other intelligence agencies had their own headquarters near the centre of power. It had been pointed out by various PR experts that most people preferred telepaths out of sight and out of mind – particularly the latter – and having a large and expensive government building would only provide a focus for tension and riots. For the moment, the Telepath Corps was operating out of a CIA installation near Washington, although as the separation between the two organisations got wider, they would probably have to move.

Art allowed Alice to precede him into the briefing room, giving him a chance to catch his breath and focus his mind. Inside, the room had been equipped for video conferencing, with the three Senators who served as the Oversight Committee and the President himself displayed on the screens. Doctor Sampson, Agent Evens and a handful of people Art didn't know made up the remainder of the conference. Agent Evens nodded to him, her thoughts agitated; her transfer to the Telepath Corps hadn't been entirely willing. And she wasn't a telepath herself.

"All links secure," the technician stated. "You may speak freely."

Art concealed a smile. The United States was good at creating secure communications networks, at least under normal circumstances. The NSA had designed powerful encryption programs that should have made it impossible for anyone to listen in to their conversation, at least under normal circumstances. What would happen if a telepath obtained the encryption algorithm or even managed to listen in telepathically? Professor Zeller had started out working with remote viewers after all and that part of the program had remained firmly with the CIA.

He looked up at the President, who looked pale and tired, and at the three Senators. Senator Walker – the blackmail victim – seemed deeply worried, leaving Art wondering if there was a connection between the blackmail attempt and the current crisis. Senator Wallis looked calm and composed, yet there was something in his face that Art didn't like. He could tell, even without telepathy, that the Senator was trying to find a way to game the current crisis to his advantage. Senator Gillian Forrester, a woman Art had never met in person, just looked harassed. Her constituents would be demanding action.

The President opened the discussion. "Yesterday saw the first outbreak of what we have come to call telepathic terrorism," he said. "I don't think I need to remind anyone that this situation is already highly volatile and could become much worse. Agent Evens – the floor is yours."

Agent Evens nodded. "Thank you, Mr President," she said. If she was intimidated by suddenly finding herself speaking to people who were normally well above her pay grade, she didn't show it. "The most notable event was the shock confession of Curtis Hughes. After he recovered from the shock, Hughes claimed that a telepath made him confess to his crimes and other...misdeeds. A telepath from the Telepath Corps was invited to peek into his mind and confirmed that he was pushed into admitting the truth. The telepath also discovered that what he admitted *was* the truth. He wasn't forced into lying about imaginary misdeeds."

Art frowned at the thought. Could Hughes claim to have been forced to lie? Perhaps not – even if a telepath's report wasn't considered legally admissible in court, the reporters were probably already trying to verify the story. His mistress would sell her story to the highest bidder and retire, once the quickie book and movie deals came through. She'd have to move fast, though; scandals didn't have a long shelf life before they were replaced by the next set of scandals.

"The second attack, however, was considerably worse," Agent Evens continued. "The telepaths obtained passwords and access codes for hundreds of secure databases and passed them over to a hacker from the online community, a young man the FBI's Computer Crime Division has been struggling to build a case against. We have that case now, but too late; the information he retrieved has already been distributed onto the net and has spread abroad. The results have been...worrying."

She nodded to one of the men Art didn't know, who scowled. "The key to keeping our financial system working is public confidence," he said, gruffly. "The public faith in banking has been low for the last few years, ever since the financial crisis in 2008. That has, in turn, hampered development, investment and future profit. Bankers are regarded as the lowest level of life form imaginable. We were working to attempt to rebuild trust, but the release of secure databases has shattered all of our work. The world now knows that parts of the banking system are still hollow."

The President frowned. "Can't we hold it together?"

"Not easily, Mr President," the speaker said. Art winced at his mental tone. Deep inside, the man had already given up. "The problem lies in the public's perception of the banks and their stability. If the public remains calm and refuses to panic, we can patch up the holes and keep the overall system going. The public, however, is not calm. The word is spreading that the banks are failing – each rumour only adds to the panic – and the public is trying to withdraw their money, which leads to others trying to withdraw their money as well..."

He shrugged. "The bottom line is that we may be looking at another financial slump, perhaps worse," he concluded.

"We do have emergency powers to try to slow the crisis, perhaps hold it back long enough to keep the system together, but they are unreliable. And then there is the effect of the attack in the first place. It made us look like fools."

"True," one of the other unnamed men said. Art realised that he was from the State Department. "The release of various secret documents from secure databases will have long-term implications for our security, as well as our relationships with other countries. Like Snowden, only worse."

"That's a long-term concern," the President said. "Who is responsible for this?"

Agent Evens bowed her head. "It would seem that the attack was carried out by the telepaths who escaped from the Zeller Institute," she said. "We captured the hacker and peeked into his mind, finding only vague and unhelpful memories caused by another telepath. However, we checked the entire apartment and found DNA evidence – the person who visited the hacker and convinced him to help was Elizabeth Tyler."

Art winced. He'd known that Leo was capable of doing something stupid, just to prove his own belief that telepaths were superior to normal humans, but he'd thought better of Elizabeth. She had been reluctant to assert any superiority and had been traumatised by what had happened at Harvard. Indeed, the more he thought about it, the more he wondered if the whole idea had not been hers. She wouldn't have wanted to kill anyone else. Leo, on the other hand, could blithely have killed thousands of people if it suited his aims...and he was allied with one of the most dangerous free agents in America.

"Which means that all thirteen of them have become terrorists," Senator Wallis said. "Mr President, I don't believe that we can delay any longer. We need to catch those...people before they get out of Washington, or before they cause even more havoc."

"Yes," the President said, dryly. "Now, where do you suggest we start looking for them?"

"We have a plan, of sorts," Agent Evens said. "The problem, however, is that they may have left Washington. If so, the task of hunting them down becomes a great deal harder. They can interfere with the minds of non-telepaths and we don't have that many telepaths in the Telepath Corps..."

"So we draft them," Senator Wallis said, sharply. "We order all of the registered telepaths to join the Telepath Corps for the duration of the emergency. We give them some training and add them to hunter teams. They can tell if someone is attempting to manipulate their minds and call in back-up from the Telepath Corps."

Art exchanged a glance with Alice. He had to admit that the plan was sound, at least in theory, although it might take weeks before the terrorists were hunted down. The anarchist they had with them would know all the tricks and where to hide, places that would be overlooked or ignored by the searchers. And telepathy gave them a major advantage, perhaps two; they would know where the searchers had been and slip into the cleared areas. Washington couldn't be sealed off like a city in Iraq, not if the President wanted to remain in power. He had to admire whoever had come up with the plan. The chances were good that half of the American population would hail them as heroes.

The President looked over at Art. "Captain Russell," he said, "is that plan workable?"

Art flushed. He had never imagined that he'd be in a position to advise the President, not after he'd developed telepathy and had been recalled to the United States. The vague dream of rising to the top of the Marine Corps had always been nothing more than a dream, but now...all of a sudden, he realised what that meant. The wrong advice could do more than merely end his career. It could get people killed.

"The plan is sound," he said, reluctantly. "I think, however, that it will require considerable training before a civilian telepath is ready to join the hunt. We need to get started sooner rather than later."

"See to it," the President ordered. He stared down at his hands. "I will have to address the nation in an hour. It would be nice to give them some hope."

***

"My fellow Americans," the President said, an hour later. The cameras followed his every word. "We know now that the current economic crisis facing the country was caused by a group of rogue telepaths, who invaded minds and caused them to act in ways not suited to the country's advantage. They have attacked our country and weakened the government."

He paused. "After consultation with Congress and the Senate, in order to deal with this nightmare, I have ordered the drafting of every registered telepath into the Telepath Corps," he continued. "All telepaths will be given training and then put to work to counter the terrorists and make our country safe again. I ask for all telepaths to respond to the call. Your country needs you. Your friends and families need you.

"This country has endured many a crisis," he concluded. "We have survived them all and we will survive this one too. Goodnight – and God bless America."

Chapter Twenty-Eight

The President's decision to draft telepaths has been met by mixed responses from the public. Many have applauded the President's decision, but both civil liberties and privacy advocates have questioned the use of the draft – the first since Vietnam – for recruiting telepaths to the government's side. Public opinion is, in fact, divided on the so-called telepathic terrorists – they have a surprising level of support from many on the internet, including those who used to work for Curtis Hughes. Others say that forcing him to confess in public was cruel and a foretaste of what humanity might expect in a world dominated by terrorists...

-AP News Report, 2015

"Welcome to the lair of the revolution," Valentine said, as he waved Leo and Elizabeth into the warehouse. "A third of the anti-government activity in Washington passes through this warehouse, from smuggled guns to propaganda leaflets that the feds would snatch and destroy if they got their hands on them. Your presence here is a sign of trust from the leadership."

Elizabeth frowned. Valentine talked a good game, but the warehouse just wasn't that impressive. On the outside, it looked as if it was permanently on the verge of falling down, with a handful of homeless people gathered around it. On the inside, it was dark and grimy, with hardly any lighting worth the name. It struck her as more of a hideout for junior criminals than the heart of the resistance that Valentine kept talking about.

"Of course it's not that impressive," Valentine said when her doubts began leaking out of her mind. "What were you expecting? Perhaps you wanted bright lights and a sign reading SECRET MEETING HERE?"

Elizabeth realised with a start that Valentine's telepathy was growing stronger, but then they were all growing stronger. Being on the run forced them to develop stronger telepathy; God knew it was their only advantage. In the two days since they had launched their first offensive – as Leo had, rather grandly, called it – they had come alarmingly close to being captured twice. If the policemen had had a telepath with them, the game would have been up.

Elizabeth flushed at his tone. "The underground knows that the only way to remain alive and free is to keep operating on the down low," Valentine added, dryly. "They cannot risk being detected by the feds, or they'd come down on their heads like a ton of bricks. They know what they're doing."

"Fine, good, glad to hear it," Leo said, tartly. They stepped into the main warehouse and stopped. There was no one there. Elizabeth reached out with her mind and sensed nothing. "Why did we come here?"

"The feds have been desperate to locate us ever since we embarrassed them," Valentine explained. "We're here because they need us to check out the loyalty of some of their people. The government is offering ten million dollars for our heads – preferably without the bodies attached – and they are worried that some of their people will take the shot at instant wealth."

"Oh," Elizabeth said. "I thought you trusted these people?"

"I trust the leadership, even if we don't always agree," Valentine admitted, "but what about the others? The junior members, the ones who might only be playing at being rebels who want to smash the system; the ones who have questionable periods in their past; the ones who may have ulterior motives of their own...we cannot trust them all."

He grinned. "There's an old military saying that says the largest trustworthy group is around fifty men," he added. "After that...there are going to be divided loyalties, whatever else happens. You don't get old in this business by taking chances."

Elizabeth frowned. "But how can they trust us?"

"The government has put a massive price on our heads," Leo pointed out, sharply. He sounded tense and Elizabeth wondered if Valentine had told him something more about the meeting than he'd told her. "They can trust us not to want to betray ourselves to the government, not after they started drafting telepaths into their army..."

Valentine looked up as a noise echoed through the warehouse. "You two go into that room and get ready," he said, pointing to a dusty door. Elizabeth stepped over to it and discovered that the room inside was surprisingly clean and untouched. It had no windows and so they could turn on the lights. The person who had originally owned the room had a fondness for an Indian model, one with long brown legs and dark eyes to die for. Elizabeth ripped the calendar down and dumped it in the waste bin.

Twenty minutes passed slowly. Elizabeth could hear chatter outside, but it was impossible to read thoughts at that distance, at least without being able to see the person. She strained her mind and caught flickers of emotion – nervous eagerness mixed with trepidation – but sensed nothing else. Leo took a chair and sat down on it, his mental shields drawn tightly around him. She couldn't read anything from his mind at all.

The door finally opened and Valentine came in. "They have agreed to come in one at a time and be interviewed," he said. "We didn't tell them that they were having their minds read – it would only have upset them. If one of them is a bad apple, someone working for the feds, freeze them and hold them. We can deal with them in a manner that will terrify anyone else who is even thinking about infiltrating our organisation."

"Of course," Leo said, too loudly. "When do you want to start?"

Elizabeth took one of the other chairs as Valentine went back outside. A moment later, he came in with a young man who was clearly determined to shock. He had shaved all of his head, apart from a single shock of hair in the exact centre of his skull, which he had dyed bright green. He had so many rings on his fingers that Elizabeth shivered, knowing that she would have been nervous around him if she'd seen him before she became a telepath. The sudden flush of lust through his mind as he saw her shocked and repelled her, even though she had thought she was used to such involuntary male thoughts. Men, particularly young men, couldn't help themselves when they saw a pretty girl.

Leo winked at her and reached out with his mind. Elizabeth followed him a second later, suddenly becoming aware of the young man's puzzlement. He didn't understand what was going on, or why he was there and part of him was worried about it. His memories rose up in front of them and they swam through them, realising how the boy had grown up with an abusive mother and no father. He had no idea who his father had actually been, something that had nagged at him as he grew older. He'd drifted into the movement by accident, but had been an enthusiastic participant, once he realised that he was allowed to cause as much trouble as possible. He'd thrown stones at policemen, turned protests into riots and much more. Darker memories flared around them and Elizabeth looked away. She didn't want to probe too closely.

"Loyal," Leo said, finally. He touched the young man's mind, blurring it so that he wouldn't recall what had happened. "Send in the next one."

The second person was a girl who didn't seem to have a single cell in her brain. Elizabeth had cracked jokes about dumb blondes before, but this one really was dumb – and, for some reason, she had dyed her hair blonde. She was possibly the stupidest person that Elizabeth had encountered, someone so caught up in the romance of being part of an underground movement that it honestly hadn't occurred to her to question it – or, for that matter, to develop any politics of her own. She could have been a fascist or a communist, a socialist or a libertarian – she just didn't have any convictions at all. Elizabeth rolled her eyes as other memories rose up and knew, somehow, that Cholula would burn herself out before too long.

But she was loyal, if only because she didn't have the imagination to be anything else.

The night wore on as seven more people were paraded before the telepaths. Elizabeth had sometimes wondered what pushed a person into the underground; now she knew, in so many ways. Some had the conviction that they were doing the right thing and that they had to fight against the system; some believed that it was the gateway to future power and position for themselves. A handful just liked the free drugs and even freer love. The parts of the movement that connected to the colleges and college students encouraged throwing away old taboos, helping the ones who would become true anarchists to lose their inhibitions, just so they could rebel against society and strive to bring it down.

The eighth person was different. She looked like a teenager, complete with tight jeans, short top without a bra and a weird hairstyle, but her thoughts were too ordered to be real. Elizabeth and Leo shared a glance and then reached out, realising in a moment of shared horror that they were looking at an undercover police officer. The policewoman wasn't a telepath – or else the game would have been over at once when she sent for help – but she recognised them. Elizabeth tore through her memories in a panic, feeling the cool contempt the policewoman felt for the people in the movement and her certainty that the movement was being exploited by enemies of America. Elizabeth saw the movement as the policewoman saw it and recoiled. It was nothing more than a group of silly children playing games.

FREEZE, Leo sent. The policewoman shivered and froze, unable to resist the telepathic command pouring into her mind. Valentine leapt up at once, heading out to warn the others that they had caught a spy and that their bases would be compromised. *YOUR MIND IS OURS.*

Elizabeth watched as he dug into the policewoman's mind, pulling out everything she knew about them. The policewoman – her name was Cheryl, it seemed – had been placed within the movement a year ago and she was looking forward to leaving when her time was up, as she hated the movement. Elizabeth ignored that and pressed onwards; she'd been warned to watch for the telepaths, Valentine in particular. She hadn't been told why, much to Elizabeth's frustration, which suggested that someone knew that she might encounter the telepaths in the future.

Leo had been more practical. He checked through her mind for any radios or other emergency supplies, and then carefully removed them from her clothes. A tiny button, it seemed, was a distress bleeper, something that would have had the Washington PD crashing in on the meeting within minutes. Another device was a tiny recorder that wouldn't have been fooled by any telepathic illusions. A third was a device that, after some prodding, her mind finally admitted was a portable DNA sampler kit. Elizabeth was horrified and yet relieved. At least they'd caught the spy before she could get a word out to her superiors.

True, Leo sent. Elizabeth didn't like the sense of grim resolve echoing through his mind, followed rapidly by a darker feeling she *really* didn't like. Leo seemed to be considering extreme options for dealing with the spy. *On the other hand, they will suspect something when she fails to report back after the meeting...*

Valentine returned to the room. "We have gotten the others out of here," he said, grimly. "They know about the danger now, but we'll have to act quickly. This bitch may not be the only one inside the movement."

"She's the only one she knows about," Leo said, calmly. His mind started to slip into the policewoman's mind, issuing new commands. Elizabeth felt the policewoman's horror as her body went limp, no longer responsive to her commands. "I think that we can have some fun with her before we wipe her mind and dump her."

Elizabeth stared at him in horror. "What are you...?"

Leo ignored her, concentrating on the policewoman, who stood up at his mental command. A moment later, her body started swaying in time to an imaginary beat, while her hands reached under her shirt and clasped her breasts. Elizabeth recoiled as the policewoman's hands started to remove her shirt, leaving her breasts bobbing in the open air. Leo's mind was pushing against hers now, causing all kinds of reactions; the woman's mind was suddenly torn between a sickening arousal and outright terror. She started to cry silently as her hands reached down to her jeans and pushed them down, stepping out of them and then reaching for her panties. The thin silk was already stained with her unwilling arousal.

"No," Elizabeth said, flatly. She reached out with her own mind, only to discover that both Leo and Valentine were controlling the girl. She couldn't free her from her sudden enslavement. "I won't let you do this, not to anyone."

She touched Leo's mind for a second and was nearly sick. She had never realised just how deep his contempt for mere mundane humans truly ran, even though he'd been prepared to kill to achieve his goals. He thought he had the right to take the policewoman – to rape her – because he was superior – and because he'd been denied it when he'd been a mundane human himself. If he cared about the policewoman's horror and terror, her own thoughts and feelings, it was only to enjoy her forced submission to his will. Elizabeth saw – and cursed herself for not seeing it earlier – just how far gone he truly was. A world dominated by Leo, or people who thought as he did, would be a nightmare.

"She would have betrayed us," Leo said. The policewoman was still moving at his command, removing her panties and then bending over the chair, ready to be raped. Tears were still dripping from her eyes, but she was allowed no other movement. "You know that – she would have sentenced us all to death without a second thought. It is right that we punish her before..."

"And we are the superior beings," Valentine added. His mocking voice echoed in the still air. "Why should the inferior not submit to us?"

Elizabeth stared at him, finally understanding why the policewoman had been warned to watch for Valentine in particular. He'd been carefully manipulating Leo ever since they had first met at the Zeller Institute, wearing away at what remained of his humanity until nothing was left, but the broken man convinced of his own superiority. And Elizabeth had helped; she'd helped them flee the Institute and helped them to carry out acts of terrorism against the country. And all of it had been meant to do nothing more than spread chaos. The fact that it made it impossible for Leo and his allies to expect mercy was only icing on the cake.

"I thought we were supposed to be better than them," Elizabeth said. She gathered herself, knowing that if they both decided to attack her, she'd lose quickly. At least Leo had stopped fumbling with his pants. The frustrated rage was bubbling up within him, threatening to overwhelm his mind and what remained of his rationality. "How are we superior if we force them to have sex with us?"

Leo looked up at her and she recoiled, transfixed by the wave of emotion pouring out of his mind. A mixture of lust, anger and even misogyny, memories of a life spent knowing that he was smarter than most of his contemporaries, yet also knowing that his contemporaries rejected him and the girls he lusted for chose to go with the dumbass jocks rather than smart boys who wouldn't harm them. Elizabeth had never known just how deep his feelings ran, or how well Valentine had played on them. There was no hope of appealing to reason now. He wouldn't listen to her...

She lashed out with her mind, aiming at the policewoman and hoping to shatter the bonds Leo had placed on her mind. A second later, a wave of mental force from Leo sent her stumbling backwards to the floor, while Valentine leapt at the naked policewoman and knocked her down himself. Leo was on top of Elizabeth a second later, his mind boring down into hers and trying to knock her out; Elizabeth, suddenly thinking that he might want to rape her, found new strength and lashed back. Leo seemed to recoil from her mental blast, but before Elizabeth could capitalise on her success she felt Valentine behind her. A moment later, a blow landed on her head and she fell back to the ground. Strong arms gripped her, rolled her over and started to tie her hands behind her back.

"I told you," a voice said, as if it was echoing from a far distance. She heard an ominous click, but she couldn't identify it through the pain in her mind. It seemed impossible to focus her mind on anything. She wasn't even sure what had happened. No, she knew that; someone had hit her from behind. She was trapped and helpless. "I told you that she didn't have what it took."

"I thought she would come around," a second voice said. The hands were working on her legs now, tying them together. She could barely feel anything through the roaring in her mind. It dawned on her, suddenly, that her telepathy had gone wonky. She was reading far too many minds at extreme range. "I liked her."

"There's no time for that in a revolution," the first voice said. It sounded ruthlessly practical. "You're going to have to be much more ruthless than that if you want to win."

A moment later, Elizabeth felt another searing pain on her forehead...and then there was nothing but darkness.

Chapter Twenty-Nine

The financial panic continues to spread with reports of additional banks going under or calling in their markers. A number of banks have foreclosed their loans to foreign countries, resulting in a tidal wave of default racing through South America and Africa. The Fed ordered many banks to slow their trading and appealed for calm on Wall Street, promising that everything could be sorted out in time. Their words do not impress, however, and massive protest marches are expected in many American cities...

...In the meantime, a viral broadcast from the telepathic terrorists has hit YouTube and spread across the internet...

-AP News Report, 2015

"This isn't working out too well."

Art couldn't disagree. The United States possessed around four thousand registered telepaths. Of those, roughly two-thirds were powerful enough to be useful and, at the same time, capable of controlling their powers and surviving for extended periods in normal society. Those telepaths had been drafted and ordered to report to the nearest draft office for processing, but many had simply refused the call. Others, who had wanted to keep their newfound power a secret from their family and friends, had been exposed and were furious at the government. Their lives had been ruined by the call from the draft board. A handful of civilian telepaths were even planning to sue the government.

He looked up at the map of Washington pinned out on the wall. The government had had to go back to pen and ink in a hurry and not everyone was adapting well, but until their computers and databases could be secured there was little other choice. The government had been crippled in many ways – the central IRS database had been wiped, leaving no solid record of taxpayers – and the repercussions of the damage were still being felt. Even if most of the lost data could be restored from back-ups, it would still be incomplete.

The Telepath Corps had deployed its active strength to support the more mundane law enforcement teams, but Art had no illusions as to the difficulty of their task. Washington was a massive city and the telepaths couldn't be everywhere at once – besides, Leo and his band of merry men might well have abandoned the city by now. Worse, the residents of Washington didn't like the idea of mandatory telepathic probes – even gentle peeks to prove that they weren't telepaths themselves – and outright chaos seemed permanently on the verge of breaking out. It could have been worse. Across the world, governments had dissolved into chaos or had been overthrown as the economic shockwaves smashed bastions that had seemed unbreakable. Even the more stable countries were having problems.

And the public paranoia against telepaths was growing stronger. In the two days since the economic attacks, several telepaths had been shot, including a pair from the Telepath Corps. One of the assassins had been caught and had been revealed, when another telepath had peeked into his mind, to have been a man who had cheated on his taxes and had been convinced that the telepaths would find him out. Art hadn't been able to understand it when he'd found out. Cheating on one's taxes was bad – or so he tried to convince himself – but it wasn't exactly the crime of the century. How guilty had the man felt that he'd been prepared to commit murder in hopes of covering it up?

"No," he agreed, slowly. The problem was that most of the telepaths who wanted to be involved in law enforcement or intelligence-gathering had already signed up with the Telepath Corps. The remainder were either sullenly agreeing to work or simply working under duress, their irritation and frustration shimmering out into the mental field. Art knew that they didn't dare put an unwilling telepath out in a position where they could do considerable harm, yet how much choice did they have? "This isn't going well at all."

"And then there's this march," Alice added, flatly. "The government refused to try to block it."

Art scowled. A day after the President's broadcast, rumours had begun circulating in Washington of a massive public protest against telepaths and telepathic intrusion in law enforcement. It was billed as a March for Mental Privacy and was likely to attract most of the population of the city, instead of just the usual ragtag gangs of students and others with limited knowledge of the real world. The public anger was palpable in the wake of the economic shock and conspiracy theories were running wild. The latest was that the telepathic terrorists were actually working for the Telepath Corps, causing havoc so the Telepath Corps could take over the government. It was nonsense, of course, but people were starting to believe it.

"Yeah," Art agreed. He shook his head in disbelief. This was America, not some godforsaken country in the Third World. What were they thinking?"

He looked up at the CNN broadcast from Washington and shuddered. Leo had released a video onto YouTube and it had spread wildly, moving from site to site ahead of any attempt to shut it down and wipe it from the internet. It was a mixture of threats and raving paranoia, claiming that telepaths were the superior race and, at the same time, the government had attempted to wipe them out. It had been picked up by the major news networks and had helped spread panic around the world. There were other statements that purported to come from the terrorists, but the video was the only one Art believed. It had the right mixture of arrogance and pompous self-justification that he had come to expect of Leo.

Alice stepped up to him and took his arm, giving him a kiss. "I think that they were worried about their freedoms," she said, tiredly. He could sense her frustration every time their bare skin touched. "And if Leo wins, will they have any freedom at all?"

Art scowled. Once the first telepaths had entered the public eye, it hadn't been long before people had started writing novels and producing television programs about what living in a world dominated by telepaths might be like. Art had read a couple of them and declared them nothing more than airport reading, but some of the books had dripped paranoia, claiming that telepaths would want to be worshipped and would know – instantly – if their servants were harbouring any rebellious thoughts. The optimistic ones – if such a word could be used – had ended with telepaths being killed or neutralised by tailored viruses, while the pessimistic ones could have given the Draka books a run for their money.

"I don't know," he admitted. Detective work came hard to him. He would have preferred a visible enemy he could shoot. Even running counter-insurgency in Afghanistan was preferable to this. "I just don't know."

***

Crowds had been gathering outside the White House all morning, even though the protest wasn't officially scheduled for several hours. Roger watched from the safety of the press pool as the protest organisers started handing out placards and signs for the protesters to carry, a strange mixture of anti-telepath statements and demands for mental privacy. The crowd was the largest one he had seen in his entire life, far larger than the protest march at Harvard or even back before the Iraq War. Telepaths touched everyone in the United States; no one, whatever their feelings, could remain immune.

He glanced up as a police helicopter clattered overhead, watching the protesters from high above. The policemen gathered at one end of the protest looked concerned; those who weren't wearing masks and body armour to protect their bodies. Roger had heard through the grapevine that the march had been banned and the protesters had gathered anyway, daring the police to do anything about it. Nothing had been confirmed, which suggested that it was just a rumour, but still…the air smelt of trouble. He remembered Harvard and shivered. The crowd didn't seem to care about the danger.

From high above, he knew, the crowd would look like a single living creature. Roger had protested himself while he'd been in college and knew how it felt to be part of a greater entity. A crowd knew nothing of common sense, or even of self-preservation, not once the mob mentality had taken over. People who would otherwise be smart enough to stay out of trouble would be lobbing rocks at the police and breaking windows, as if wanton violence and destruction would help them achieve their aims. A telepath wouldn't have been able to operate near the crowd, he hoped; even for a non-telepath, the waves of concentrated feelings were almost overpowering.

He made his way through the fringes of the crowd, trying to ignore the blaring music someone had set up from a vehicle they'd brought into the street, towards the protest leaders. They were unfamiliar, thankfully, but when he asked they refused to be interviewed, citing privacy concerns. They assured him that the protest wasn't about a minor issue and the people who had come to the protest were more important than the leaders. That was odd – normally, protest leaders loved the spotlight and had to be pushed out of it – but Roger was forced to accept it. They seemed unwilling to comment further, on or off the record, and they refused to be filmed. He decided not to point out that the entire march would be under police surveillance from high above.

The stewards were working on the crowd as he slipped back to the press pool. The crowd started to chant loudly, ringers among them shouting out the words, knowing that others would be swept up in the wave. "WHAT DO WE WANT? MENTAL FREEDOM! WHAT DO WE WANT? NO MORE TELEPATHS!" Roger shivered again as the noise echoed out over Washington. It looked as if the entire city had come out to join the protest march. The crowd started to move, heading past the White House and up through the inner core of Washington. The noise was shaking the entire area. Roger hoped that the congressmen and senators were taking note. The crowd was in an angry mood and wasn't likely to vote for them in the future.

And then it all went to hell.

***

Art had been – mentally, at least – cowering away from the noise in his mind. The crowd seemed to have turned into a single massive psychic broadcaster, blasting their unholy din into his mind and into that of every other telepath in Washington. Art could sense flickering headaches all over the city through the mental waveband, telepaths feeling the noise and suffering because of it. He pulled his shields as tightly around his mind as he could and tried to hold out. Alice and the other non-telepaths were lucky. They might be deafened if the noise grew much louder, but at least they wouldn't be risking mental damage.

And then he sensed it. There were sly intrusive thoughts, beaming out into the crowd. He glanced up, sharply, realising that an unknown telepath – several unknown telepaths – were beaming violent thoughts into the crowd. The emotions were bitter and twisted, yet they would somehow be amplified by the crowd, spread from person to person like a virus. The crowd's mass mental tone was shifting, growing uglier and more violent by the second. Art reached for his radio, desperately trying to sound the alert, but it was already too late. No one saw who threw the first punch, yet within seconds the crowd was turning on itself and everyone else. The crowd-monster was convulsing in pain as alien thoughts lashed into its combined mind...

A fist slapped Art's face and he fell back. The crowd wasn't the only group affected, he realised in horror; the telepathic memes were being broadcast into the police and watching civilians as well. Alice was staring in disbelief as her hand moved, seemingly of its own accord, to slap Art again. Art caught the hand and, using the sudden mental contact, pushed the maddening thoughts out of her head. She stared at him and then jumped back as one of the police liaison officers tried to take her head off with his truncheon. Art flattened him with a punch and then looked around, down into hell. The police lines had collapsed into an orgy of violence and rape. Several policemen were firing randomly into the crowd, some lost in the madness, others aware of what was happening, yet unable to stop it.

Art took Alice's hand for comfort and opened his mind just a tiny fraction, hoping that he could survive the mental maelstrom long enough to locate the telepaths responsible for the growing disaster. The impact of so many minds thudded into his soul, but somehow he held himself together long enough to sense the enemy minds. He didn't recognise their mental touch, which suggested that they were either some of

Zeller's former pupils or completely new terrorists. Locating them was difficult, but somehow he managed it.

"Come on," he snapped, and pulled Alice with him. He pulled his mask on as tear gas canisters started to explode, although there was no way to tell if some of the police had regained awareness or if they had just started firing them off at random, still caught up in the nightmare. Art skirted the edge of the crowd, knowing that to try to wade through it would be suicide, and cursed under his breath as a body fell in front of him. A man large enough to be a sumo wrestler had blocked his path, maddened eyes overflowing with hatred and rage. Art didn't hesitate. He drew his pistol and shot the man in the leg.

Alice followed him as he came up to the press pool – the reporters were fighting each other, smashing their equipment in the process – but it wasn't them who caught his attention. The enemy telepaths were broadcasting their thoughts out to the crowd, which meant that they were detectable – no amount of telepathic shielding could hide them. They had to have slipped in while hiding in one of the media vehicles, Art realised, or else they might have been caught ahead of time. He lifted his gun and pointed it towards the three telepaths. Leo himself, sadly, wasn't there.

"Stop it," he barked. Even in his best parade-ground manner, it wasn't loud enough to be heard over the riot. The backwash of emotions was chilling – he was sure he could sense minds just snapping out of existence, either dead or losing themselves completely. They might never recover from what had been done to them. "Stop it now!"

The three telepaths looked up at him in shock – they hadn't expected to be caught – and reached out for him with their minds. Art had expected that and pulled the trigger at once, blowing a hole through the first telepath's head. The other two fell backwards in shock – their minds had to have been linked to allow them to survive the crowd and broadcast poisonous thoughts into the ether – and collapsed, blood leaking from their ears. Art hoped – even though he knew they needed information – that the shock had been enough to kill the bastards. He had no idea how many people had died in the riot, but it had to number in the hundreds, at least.

He checked both telepaths, reassured himself that they were out of commission for the moment, and then keyed his radio. "You need to send in reinforcements," he ordered, hoping that the reserve forces hadn't been contaminated by the mental broadcast too. His mind felt musty as he rebuilt his shields. "I've stopped the broadcast, but we need help."

The crowd was slowly coming back to its senses. Very few of them had come for violence and, as the alien thoughts faded out of their minds, they stared down in horror at what they had done. The police were no better. They'd turned on themselves in an orgy of violence, or worse. Art looked away from one of the police officers. He was hopelessly confused, yet unable to deny the evidence of his eyes. The poor bastard had murdered his partner.

Slowly, order was restored with the help of Marines from the nearby barracks. Art found himself in the odd position of issuing orders to officers he would have saluted months ago, but there was no time to worry. There were thousands of injured people and hundreds – perhaps thousands – of dead bodies. The streets of Washington had run red with blood. Sickened, Art saw to the transfer of the two captured telepaths to the Telepath Corps and then joined the rescue teams. He owed it to the people he had failed to save.

***

Roger came back to himself slowly, feeling the strange unwanted thoughts fading out of his mind. He found himself looking down on a scene from hell. Kristy McHale, a bitch of an anchorwoman, lay in front of him, her skull smashed in by a rock. No, by a camera, the same camera he held in his hand. Sickened, unable to believe his eyes, Roger slowly collapsed to his knees. What had he done?

He'd killed her. There was no way around it. He'd murdered a woman he didn't like – hated, in fact – and part of him had enjoyed it. The nightmarish thoughts at the back of his mind mocked him. He'd killed her and he'd loved every last moment of it. He told himself that even the Wicked Bitch of the West – as she had been called by her enemies – didn't deserve such a fate, yet it was hard to convince himself of that. It was so hard to even think clearly.

"Dear God in Heaven," he said, finally. For the first time, he realised just how far the madness had reached. He had been far from the only victim. "What happened?"

He had a feeling, somehow, that he already knew the answer.

Chapter Thirty

At latest report, over two thousand people died in Washington, with far more than that either injured or maddened beyond immediate recovery. The city is under martial law; Marines from Quantico have joined the Washington PD and National Guard in maintaining order in the wake of the chaos. The President has appealed for calm and is, according to official statements, in a secure and undisclosed location.

-AP News Report, 2015

There was a dull roaring in her head, a sense that she was on the verge of fading back into madness and pain. The headache was lurking at the edge of her perception, yet every time she thought about it, she felt new twinges of pain tearing her mind apart. She wasn't sure if she was alive or dead, or trapped endlessly in a hell within her own mind. The darkness seemed to be alive in its own way, pulling her towards oblivion. She wasn't even sure who she was, or what she was doing…or what had happened to her.

Elizabeth, a voice said, in her mind. *Your name is Elizabeth.*

The thought was like an anchor for her. She clung to it gratefully, even as the pain seemed to grow stronger, a permanent ache in her head. The thought somehow made her stronger; if she had an ache in her head, she definitely wasn't dead, nor was she in Hell. Elizabeth focused, trying to concentrate on her own memories. Thoughts and feelings roared around her, yet it was hard to recall what had happened before she had collapsed. Her mind had been traumatised, she realised, and she was unable to remember because her mind was trying to protect her. The thought was galling, yet…where was she?

As if the thought was a key, her eyes sprang open. She hadn't even been aware that they were closed until daylight flared into her mind, sending a wave of pain screaming through her body. Elizabeth wanted to scream and discovered to her horror that no sound came out of her mouth. Her mind raced, unable to decide if she was deaf or mute or…she realised, a second later, that someone had gagged her. The thought was such a relief that she almost fainted back into the darkness. She wasn't deaf.

All right, she thought, focusing on her own mind. *What happened?*

Her mind stubbornly refused to unlock and reveal its secrets. Instead, she heard a moan and turned around. For the first time, she realised that her hands and feet were bound, bound so thoroughly that she could barely move. She managed, finally, to twist her head and look towards the source of the moan, a naked girl lying on the floor. She, too, was bound and gagged; her eyes were wide with panic. The sight finally unlocked her memories and Elizabeth nearly fainted again. Leo – the man-boy she had liked enough to trust, at least to some extent – had tried to rape the other girl.

The memories were vague on precisely what had happened. Someone had hit her, she suspected; she certainly felt concussed. Who had it been? Leo had been in front of her and besides, he'd resort to telepathic power rather than a physical struggle. Had it been Valentine or someone else? If so, who could it have been? And where were they now?

A nasty thought ran through her head and she checked herself as best as she could. No, she was still fully clothed, which was a relief. And she was stuck. If Leo and the others had abandoned her, they had left her alive only to starve to death. She doubted that they would come back for her, not if Valentine was calling the shots. Leo might be sentimental towards a fellow telepath – it explained why she'd been left alive, at least – but Valentine had no conscience. The real surprise was why he'd left her alive in the first place. Had it been just to please Leo?

She scowled to herself, feeling the gag pushing uncomfortably against her lips. In the movies, the damsel in distress could always free herself – if she wasn't waiting for the prince to come and free her – but real life worked differently. A few moments of struggling convinced her that whoever had tied her hands knew exactly what he was doing. She could barely move, let alone break the ties or unpick the knots. The movies had made it look easy…

A thought crossed her mind and she reached out with her telepathy, only to recoil as a sudden headache blasted back into her mind. She hadn't even noticed the absence of pain until it returned. Her telepathy was useless, perhaps permanently. The thought didn't distress her as much as she would have thought. It wasn't as if the telepathy had been useful for her. She'd been used, by Leo and the others, to help spread terror across the country. What did it say about her, she wondered, if the only reason she'd turned against them had been having her nose rubbed in just how evil they were?

There was another moan from the other girl. When Elizabeth looked over at the undercover policewoman, she found that she was giving her a reassuring look. Elizabeth would have laughed, if she could; she'd helped get the policewoman into the mess and the policewoman was trying to comfort *her*? The thought only made her more determined to escape, but how...?

Slowly, she pushed her tongue against the tape Leo had placed on her mouth. It was hard – the taste was horrible and she wondered if the glue was poisonous – but somehow she managed to keep it up. It was painstakingly slow, but eventually she was able to work off the gag and spit out the rest of the glue. At least she could breathe normally...the policewoman made another sound and Elizabeth realised in a flash of understanding that they *could* get out. It was hard to crawl towards the policewoman, but eventually she found herself in a position to start working on the ropes binding the policewoman's hands behind her back. She bit the poor girl several times before finally biting through the ropes. A moment later, the policewoman was able to stand up, free her legs and then remove the gag.

"Thank you for saving me," she said, as she started to unbind Elizabeth. "They didn't touch me after knocking you out."

"Good," Elizabeth said. How had the policewoman known that she had needed the reassurance? Had she developed telepathy after her capture? "What do we do now?"

The question brought a wave of despair running through her mind. Where could she go now? She couldn't go back to

Leo, Professor Zeller was in a coma…and besides, she was still a wanted criminal. Perhaps it would be best to surrender to the authorities and let them decide her fate. Even Death Row would be preferable to a life on the run, with everyone trying to hunt her down.

"You'll be fine," the policewoman assured her. "I'll speak for you. You risked your life to save mine."

Elizabeth was still puzzling over that when the policewoman, having recovered her clothes from where she'd been forced to dump them, picked up her radio and called in to her office. Ten minutes later, a single police van arrived, with two police officers and a single telepath. Her own telepathy wasn't working properly, but she didn't need it to sense the policewoman's consternation. Her call should have brought a small army of policemen to her aid.

"All hell has broken loose up near the White House," one of them explained. "The entire department has been sent there. We were only cut loose because you mentioned a prisoner from the enemy side."

"Yeah," the policewoman said. She looked over at Elizabeth, sympathetically. "I'm afraid we're going to have to arrest you for the moment, but everything will be all right."

"No, it won't," the telepath said, as the policeman slipped cuffs onto Elizabeth's wrists, locking her hands behind her back – again. "I'm afraid that nothing will ever be the same again."

***

Alice frowned as she studied Elizabeth Tyler through the one-way glass. The girl had been attractive when they'd first met, back when Professor Zeller had announced the birth of a whole new set of telepaths, but now she looked beaten down by events. The Telepath Corps doctors, the most experienced in dealing with telepathic patients, had inspected her and reported that she was basically fine, apart from some malnutrition and minor injuries. They hadn't been able to explain the odd mental effect surrounding her.

It was weird, but the more Alice looked at her, the more she was sure that she knew what Elizabeth was feeling, perhaps even thinking. The report from the captured policewoman tended to confirm it, and she – like Alice – was no telepath. Somehow, Elizabeth was broadcasting her thoughts and feelings to anyone within range, even if they weren't telepathic. It wasn't a pleasant feeling, even though it was clear that the girl had no idea what she was doing. Had a single bump on the head inverted her telepathy?

"It would appear so," Doctor Sampson said, when she asked him. They stood together, watching the girl. Elizabeth had been left in the interrogation room alone, her hands cuffed to the chair, while the Telepath Corps argued about what to do with her. Technically speaking, she was a terrorist, yet she'd risked her life to save the undercover officer. The courts were going to have fun deciding what to do with her. "Everyone seems to know what she's feeling, if not thinking. I think the rest of her life is not going to be fun."

Alice frowned and quirked an eyebrow at him, puzzled. "Most telepaths are capable of putting up mental shields to prevent themselves from being bombarded by outside thoughts," Sampson explained, dryly. "Miss Tyler, on the other hand, may not be able to prevent herself from broadcasting her thoughts. She will have no privacy for the rest of her life, even if she lives away from other telepaths. Even a non-telepath will be able to pick up on her thoughts."

"I see," Alice said. The thought was sickening, in a way. She knew that Art – she had stopped thinking of him as Captain Russell at about the same time they'd started sleeping together – could read her mind, but she trusted him not to peek more than strictly necessary. Besides, having a lover who could tell when she was happy – and what gave her pleasure in bed – was wonderful. But being unable to prevent it from happening? Who could endure such a life? "Is there nothing we can do for her?"

"We could try injecting her with sleeper drugs," Sampson said. "The problem is that we don't fully understand what's happening. Professor Zeller used to claim that all humans were broadcast telepaths, yet no one had the ability to pick up on thoughts – at least not until the first telepaths came into existence. Yet what she's doing tends to run counter to that, at least to some degree. She's broadcasting her thoughts to anyone within range."

Alice considered it. "Telepaths are capable of mentally altering a person's mind," she pointed out. "Perhaps the ability is a warped version of that – she can't stop herself from broadcasting her thoughts, rather than mental commands."

"Could be," Sampson agreed. "Which does rather lead to the next question – what are we going to do with her?"

"The only thing we can do," Alice said. "We get her to work with us."

She grinned, nastily. "At least she won't be able to hide anything from us."

***

Elizabeth sat on the hard chair, feeling the throbbing in her head slowly recede. After two tries, she had given up on using her telepathy, not after developing a massive headache that had come close to killing her. Or so she had felt. She wasn't able to read any minds, even that of the doctor who had examined her or the female officer who had escorted her to the shower and toilet. Her head just felt delicate, as if she'd been drinking too much the night before. The bumps and bruises on her body didn't help.

She looked up as the door opened, revealing a blonde woman who was oddly familiar, although it took her a few moments to place the face. The woman had visited Harvard when Professor Zeller had made his announcement to the world and again after the Harvard Blast. She didn't seem much older than Elizabeth herself, but her face was tired and worn. There was a nasty glint in her eye that Elizabeth didn't like at all.

"Good afternoon," the woman said. "My name is Alice Spencer and, for the moment at least, I am...charged with dealing with your case. Do you know what happened this morning?"

Elizabeth shook her head. "I was a little tied up at the time," she said, sardonically. She hadn't even realised how much time had passed until they'd escaped the warehouse. "What happened this morning?"

"Your friend Leo and his gang attacked a protest march," Alice said, flatly. Elizabeth realised, in a flicker of horror, what had happened. "They broadcast memes — I don't pretend to understand how — into the crowd. The result was a bloody riot and mass slaughter. The death toll, so far, is upwards of two thousand people."

Elizabeth felt sick. They'd discussed the possibility when they'd been on the run, but she had thought that she'd talked Leo out of using it. Valentine, on the other hand, must have encouraged him to try it…and, without anyone to hold him back, Leo would have taken the idea and run with it. Every mind that accepted the memes would start broadcasting them onwards, as well as physically attacking everyone within reach. Unlike most forms of telepathic control, pain and shock wouldn't break the victim free. It might even linger if the telepath was killed.

"Whatever Leo is up to, it has to be stopped," Alice snapped. Elizabeth couldn't disagree. "We need you to help us catch him. Where is he now?"

"I don't know," Elizabeth said. Briefly, she outlined their hiding places, but she knew that Leo and Valentine would have the sense to move, once she deserted them. She might have managed to get a telepathic message off before they knocked her out, although she didn't know who she would have tried to call. Telepathic communication only worked when done between two telepaths who actually knew each other. And besides, whatever they'd done to her head, it had killed her ability to send messages. "I really don't know."

Alice nodded. "I believe you," she said. She smiled, a smile that left Elizabeth wondering what she'd missed. Alice wasn't a telepath, unless she'd developed telepathy since last they'd met. Perhaps the chair was a lie detector in disguise. "Which leads to the next question, doesn't it? What does Leo want?"

"I don't know if it is Leo any longer," Elizabeth admitted. She started to tell them about Valentine. As she spoke, she had the odd impression that Alice already knew most of what she was telling her. "Leo thinks that telepaths are superior and wants us to rule the world; Valentine...I don't know what Valentine wants, except that he has been manipulating Leo ever since they first met."

"Yeah," Alice said. "He's the one with the knowledge that makes him dangerous."

Elizabeth frowned. "What do you mean?"

"Later," Alice said. She looked down at Elizabeth for a long moment. "You know that you're in deep shit, right?" Elizabeth nodded, reluctantly. "You could be charged – hell, you *have* been charged – with terrorism and economic warfare. The chances are good that they will end up filing charges of treason as well – the information you leaked from the Pentagon cost lives and money. You need to work to earn a pardon, if that is even possible."

"I know," Elizabeth said. She felt the bitterness welling up within her and tears starting to form in her eyes. "I was wrong. I...I was wrong."

Alice, oddly, reached out and placed a hand on her shoulder. "Yes," she said. "Everyone makes mistakes when they're young and so sure that they understand the world. Your mistakes were just...larger and more damaging to others than most mistakes. You aren't innocent, but you're not completely guilty either."

Elizabeth snorted, bitterly. "Not completely guilty," she echoed. "Thanks."

"Don't thank me," Alice said. She stepped back and smiled. "The choice is yours. You can help us track down your former friends and allies, or you will be transported to a holding pen prior to a short trial. The population wants blood, Miss Tyler; they will be happy with your blood, if it is offered to them."

"I know," Elizabeth said, again. "How long will it be before they come for your blood too?"

Alice shrugged. "It's already started," she said. "Protests outside Telepath Corps facilities have turned into riots; gunfire has claimed the lives of several telepaths...we even intercepted a stream of mail bombs sent to Alaska and the telepath towns there. If you have any loyalty to your country, or your people, or even your type, help us now before this gets out of hand."

Elizabeth didn't really need to think about it. After what Leo had tried to do – and what he'd done in Washington – she no longer believed in his cause. Telepaths weren't superior to anyone else, any more than a woman was superior to a man because she could bear children. Telepaths just had an extra ability. Maybe one day the entire human race would be telepathic, but until then…they would have to live together. And Leo would make that impossible. He would provoke a war that would only end with one side exterminated or enslaved. He had to be stopped.

"I understand," she said. "Whatever it takes, I will do it."

Chapter Thirty-One

In the wake of the disaster at Washington, seven states have introduced emergency legislation banning telepaths – registered or unregistered – from residing within their borders. These unconstitutional measures are expected to pass through state legislatures within the week. They may not be in time to save hundreds of lives as a number of real or suspected telepaths have been shot dead over the last two days, while others have gone into protective custody. The ACLU has fractured over the last two days, with no coherent response to emergency pleas from civil liberties campaigners...

-AP News Report, 2015

"So," the President said. "What do we do now?"

He had always disliked the emergency bunker. Located twenty miles east of Washington, hidden under a farm that had been – covertly – federal property since the 1970s, it seemed cold and sterile to his gaze. It was a chilling reminder that he'd been forced to flee Washington and even though he knew that the President had a duty to remain alive and free, it was galling. At least he wouldn't be running for re-election. His opponents would have made much of any flight from Washington, no matter how necessary. They'd have said that the President had abandoned the citizens of Washington to their fate and they would have been right.

There was a long pause. Nine men and women had joined the President's videoconference call, yet no one seemed willing to commit themselves to anything. The Vice President seemed to be the most unwilling of all, not least because he was hoping to make a run at the Presidency himself – if there was a next election. The President had never seriously considered that there might not be another election, or another President, but now he wondered. After what had happened in Washington, after Harvard, how long would it be before the fundamental glue holding America together melted?

"Perhaps we should look at the results of the disaster," the President snarled. "There are only thirteen rogue telepaths, just *thirteen*, and look how much damage they have done to us! Just thirteen men and women have brought us to our knees. What happens when they decide to do something even worse?"

The FBI Director coughed. "There are only nine left now," he said. The President looked up, hopefully. There had been so much to do that he hadn't been able to follow the progress of the investigation. "One is dead, shot through the head by Captain Russell; two were captured and transported to the Telepath Corps holding centre...and one was apparently abandoned by her fellows after she turned on them."

"I see," the President said. He scowled down at the table. "And what have you learned from the two captive telepaths?"

"Very little of use," the FBI Director admitted. "They were kind enough to give us the location that they'd been using for a base, but when we reached it they'd already abandoned it..."

He paused. "I should show you the video instead," he said, grimly. "Mere words cannot describe it."

The President watched grimly as the video sequence began to run. All SWAT and SF force carried tiny video cameras these days, used mainly to allow them to study and learn from their mistakes. A handful had been used in courtrooms as evidence that someone had genuinely been captured while engaged in terrorist operations, or that a person hadn't been the victim of mistaken identity, shot down by his own rescuers. He'd authorised the deployment of the technology personally, believing that it could be used to counter black propaganda run by the enemies of the United States.

The SWAT team had gone in first, followed by five telepaths from the Telepath Corps; their progress monitored by a UAV hanging high overhead. They had met no resistance; the staff in the building had just been sitting on the sofa, waiting for them. The moment the team burst in, the staff members had started to chant and nothing, not threats or pleas, had managed to quieten them.

"WE ARE SUPERIOR," they chanted in brainwashed unison. "WE ARE UNSTOPPABLE."

The President shivered. The Telepath Corps had authorised an emergency peek into their minds and had discovered, to their horror, that the staff members had been brainwashed. No, in many ways it was worse; their minds had been ruthlessly rewritten and then locked in place, beyond any help from mere humans. Even telepathic mental care, practiced by a handful of telepaths who had gone into the medical field, had been unable to help them. They might never recover.

"Miss Tyler has been much more forthcoming," the FBI Director confirmed, changing the subject. The President felt only relief. "However, she was actually knocked out and abandoned by them a few hours before they started their operation in Washington, so while we are convinced that she is telling the truth, there are certain limits to what she can tell us about them. Her telepathy – which appears to have reversed, broadcasting her thoughts and feelings to anyone within range – makes it impossible for her to lie to us."

"But they have moved their bases," the President said, sourly. "Can she tell us anything useful?"

"We're still asking her questions," the FBI Director admitted. "We know, now, that Leo – their leader – is definitely under the influence of the renegade anarchist. We did wonder if the bastard was really a telepath at all, but sadly Elizabeth Tyler was able to confirm that he was definitely telepathic. As to what they want...their goal, as far as we can tell, is to cause as much havoc as possible. There is no real political goal."

The President scowled angrily. "So all they're really doing is lashing out," he said. "What the hell does that gain them?"

"Very little, apart from anarchy," the FBI Director explained. "But then, that's what the anarchists want. We know that the rogue telepaths were involved with checking for FBI operatives within the underground movements and located quite a few, leaving us blind when we need their services desperately. The anarchists want anarchy, Mr President, and they will do whatever it takes to create it."

The President nodded. On his desk was a draft law proposed by the Senate, one that would see the entire country brought under martial law. Everyone living in the United

States would be forced to undergo telepathic screening...and, if they were found to be telepathic – or have telepathic potential – they would be forced to move up north to Alaska. The ones who refused would be transported to internment camps and kept permanently drugged, at least until they changed their minds. It was a violation of everything the United States stood for, yet somehow he knew that it would be passed without opposition through the Senate and Congress. He would have the choice between vetoing it – and perhaps being impeached by an angry Congress – or signing his name to the most inhuman act committed in America since the internment of the Japanese-Americans in 1942. The polling firm had told him that public feeling would be soundly behind the act, once they heard of it, but that was no surprise. He had only to turn on the television and watch the news to know that. There were anti-telepath marches and riots in a dozen cities and plenty more were simmering with anger.

"I understand," he said. He pressed his hand to his forehead. "Is there nothing we can do to catch them before they do something worse?"

The Chairman of the Joint Chiefs of Staff answered the question. "We can be fairly sure that they're still in Washington," he said. "The NSA traced back their second message to a cyber-café in the city, a message sent after martial law was declared and a ring of steel erected around the city. We can search the city thoroughly for them, knowing that they cannot get out without breaking our line. We have considerable experience in searching cities..."

"They'd just have to keep their heads down and the lines would pass over them," the FBI Director disagreed. "Do you have any idea how hard it would be to search a city the size of Washington? It isn't as if you can destroy it as you move through the buildings ..."

"We know what we are doing," the Chairman snapped back. They were all tired and impatient, and guilty. They were watching their beloved country falling apart. "We can do it."

"If there is no other choice," the President said, "then we will have to search the city. If we can't come up with any other options by nightfall, we will start searching tomorrow morning."

He forced his face not to reveal his anguish. The logistics of searching an entire city were going to be herculean, to say nothing of the damage the soldiers would wreak as they moved through the city, even without terrorists and insurgents sniping at them. Or maybe they would have terrorists and insurgents sniping at them; somehow, he doubted that the criminal gangs would allow the soldiers to search their drug dens without a fight. And then there was a prospect of citizens being pushed into resisting the soldiers by the rogue telepaths...

"We'll speak again at nightfall," he concluded. "Until then...well, good luck to us all."

No words had ever tasted so bitter in his mouth.

****

"Do you think they did this to you on purpose?"

"I don't know," Elizabeth said when Art posed the question to her. Simply being close to her was an ordeal, because he could sense her thoughts even through his mental shields. His mind kept reacting as if he were under attack. "I can't see Leo trying to develop the techniques to do this, but..."

Art nodded. As a punishment for a rogue telepath, a defector, he couldn't think of anything better. Elizabeth would have no privacy for the rest of her life, wherever she lived. Depending on what kind of deal was made in the end, he suspected that she would end up living alone, perhaps up in a log cabin somewhere in the woods. He remembered an old friend who had become a survivalist and made a mental note to look him up. Perhaps he would know a suitable property for her.

"On the other hand, he does love the grand gesture," Elizabeth added. "Maybe it's his idea of a joke...and a warning to anyone else who might be thinking of changing sides."

Art tasted her bitterness and nodded. Elizabeth hadn't known what she was getting into and, unlike many others who had been sucked into the terrorist networks, she had at least tried to break free and save a life. An undercover policewoman owed Elizabeth her life, if not more, even though she hadn't been able to discover much before she was caught. The anarchist networks were drawing together; once the police spies and suchlike were eliminated, Art had no doubt that they would be used to cause havoc. Leo would have the grand gesture of his dreams.

He stopped, dead. A thought had just crossed his mind. He should have dismissed it at once, he knew, and yet it was impossible to push the thought back out of his mind. If Leo liked the grand gesture, then...there was one grand gesture that would appeal to both Leo and his secret backer, the number one terrorist target in the entire world. It was insane, it was unthinkable, and yet it was impossible to dismiss. It might just work.

Art keyed his cell phone and called a very special number. "Alice, it's Art," he said. The problem with his idea was that the moment anyone higher up than himself got wind of it, it was going to be squashed without the President ever hearing about it. Art knew what he would do to a junior officer who brought him such a plan and somehow he doubted that anyone higher up the food chain would be enthusiastic about it. "I need to speak to the President, personally."

Alice sounded shocked. "Art...why?" she asked. He couldn't blame her for worrying about him. Unlike some CIA officers he'd met, she was genuinely worried about the men and women under her command. "I can get you a chance to talk to him, but he might not be willing to listen."

"Just let me speak to him for ten minutes," Art said. He winked at Elizabeth, who was staring at him in surprise. She wouldn't like the idea either and he had already resolved not to mention to anyone that she'd been there when he'd thought of it. It would only upset them. "I think I can convince him to listen to me for longer."

In the movies, he would have an instant line to the President and as much time as he needed. In the real world, the President had very little time to deal with anyone, even beings so exalted as foreign leaders and even Senators and Congressmen. The concept of him having more than a few seconds for a mere Captain was absurd, but then he was a

Captain in the Telepath Corps and, to all intents and purposes, the field team leader. Alice might end up as the permanent Operations Director, yet without telepathy she couldn't command telepaths on active service. Art could and did.

He ignored requests – and then outright orders – from various people to tell them what he wanted to tell the President. Alice took some of the flak for it as she cleared the way through a small army of secretaries and assistants, before the President was finally notified that Art wanted to speak with him. The delay didn't amuse Art, who found himself wondering what would happen if – when – terrorists unleashed a major disease in an American city. The entire country could be infected in the time it took to alert the President. Finally, in a secure video room, he had his conference.

"Mr President," Art said. He'd been told that normally any junior officer would be briefed on White House Protocol, but it hardly mattered during a state of emergency. "We need to catch those bastards before they do anything worse and we need to do it without tearing the city apart."

"Of course," the President agreed, dryly. Art *had* done nothing more than state the obvious, after all. The President would hardly disagree that the terrorists needed to be hunted down and killed before they did something worse. "I understand that you have a way to capture them. Do you have a way of peeking across the entire city, perhaps?"

"I'm afraid not, Mr President," Art said. The Telepath Corps had tried linking their minds together and searching for Leo and the remaining rogues, but there had been no sign of them. The telepathic field they'd generated didn't have anything like enough range to scan the city. "We do, however, have another idea.

"We've been proceeding on the assumption that Leo is actually the one in charge," he continued. "We now know that that isn't entirely true. Leo is being manipulated by the older and wiser Alvin Greenwood, whom he knows as Cyrus Valentine. Greenwood – or Valentine – is an anarchist. He delights in causing chaos, both to show the weakness of society and to force the forces of reaction – that's us – into a massive crackdown that he feels will win them more recruits. I think it was him, not Leo, who picked Washington as the target for their madness memes."

"I follow your reasoning," the President said, calmly. There was no trace of agreement or disagreement, but Art had expected neither. "What does that allow us to do?"

Art took a breath. "There is one target in Washington that he would want to target, above all others," he said. "Leo would want to target that target as well, for different reasons. It strikes me that if we played our cards carefully, we could lure the bastards into a trap and destroy them once and for all."

"Right," the President said, calmly. "And what is this target?"

There was a long pause. Art braced himself. "You, Mr President," he said. In a moment, he'd know if he had saved his career, or shattered it beyond repair. "Leo hates you because you brought in all the legislation for controlling telepaths, legislation he sees as an attack on his entire race. Greenwood hates you because you are the personification of authority..."

"Not for half the country, I'm not," the President said, wryly. "Half of the country is composed of sore losers after each election."

"Yes, Mr President," Art agreed. He thought about adding the other reason Greenwood/Valentine would have to target the current President in particular and decided that it would be pointless. "If you were to be exposed, they would use you as their next target, rather than someone rather more vulnerable."

The President stared down at his hands. "The Secret Service is going to hate you," he said, flatly. "I'm not sure if I shouldn't refuse outright."

He shook his head. "I'd have to hold a press conference," he said. "And it would have to be in an insecure area. There would be other dangers, apart from telepathy."

"Yes, Mr President," Art agreed. He hesitated. "I don't think that anyone would hold it against you if you refused..."

"When you're President, you'll understand that sometimes the only purpose of this job is to serve as a punching bag for everyone who has had their feelings hurt," the President said. "It would be nice to be more proactive, just once."

He looked up at Art. "I'll make the arrangements," he said. "And Captain...you must catch these bastards before anyone else gets hurt."

His image vanished from the display. Art sat there, slowly shaking his head. One way or another, he was committed now. No matter how anyone looked at it, protecting a person who had to be exposed to the general public was difficult, even for the United States Secret Service. The President was the greatest target in the world, as far as terrorists were concerned.

One way or another, he knew, the die was most definitely cast.

Chapter Thirty-Two

We have just received word that the President is going to speak from the White House Lawn to the nation. It is expected that the President will address the recent catastrophe in Washington and announce new anti-telepath legislation...

...In other news, Israel has been condemned for deploying telepaths to checkpoints in the West Bank and Gaza Strip. The UN High Commission on Palestine has already condemned Israel for insisting that all aid workers in Gaza undergo a telepathic scan before being allowed to work within the area. Israel, however, has stated that bomb attacks have fallen off since the telepaths were brought in and is determined to maintain the telepaths in position. Islamic Jihad, a spin-off of Hamas, has warned that it possesses telepaths of its own and intends to deploy them against Israel...

-AP News Report, 2015

The President paced the room, staring up at the clock. He'd banished his family to a secure facility on the other side of the country and, after the make-up artist had finished, he'd asked her to leave him alone. He always felt slightly unwell after she worked her magic on his face, even though he knew that it was necessary. Modern-day politics wanted – demanded – that the President be a handsome man, even though the President was wise enough to know that looks weren't everything. The American public had never known, until his death, that President Roosevelt had been in a wheelchair while in office. Perhaps it was for the best. The greatest Presidents in American history could not have been elected in the modern age.

He scowled, wondering how the soldiers he commanded, as Commander-in-Chief of the American Armed Forces, tolerated the countdown to action. The Secret Service had objected, strongly, to the plan, going so far as to enlist the support of most of the Cabinet in their objections. Only the

Chairman of the Joint Chief of Staff had dissented, pointing out that the logic was sound – and besides, the Vice President was waiting in the wings, ready to take over if the worst came to the worst. The Secret Service *still* weren't happy about it, or about the fact that they'd been forced to accept a joint command in Washington. The President told himself not to think about it. Outside of the Telepath Corps, the only people who knew the full details of the plan were far from Washington.

His predecessor, in their private talk before he handed over the Oval Office and wished him luck, had told him that the President was sometimes the sacrificial goat. When things went wrong, the President was blamed, even though most Presidents ended up dealing with problems caused by their predecessors. When things went right, on the other hand, the President would suddenly find thousands of people lining up to claim a share in the credit. The President had laughed at the comment, but somehow – knowing that he was about to step into a pair of crosshairs – it no longer seemed funny. If the plan failed, or if the rogue telepaths struck faster than anyone believed possible, he would be the first President in the new century to be assassinated. He would be the first President ever to die for his country. Even George Washington, the father of the nation, hadn't led troops in battle while he was President.

The Secret Service had told him, in what the President felt was unnecessary detail, just how much could go wrong. He could be attacked mentally, like Curtis Hughes, or he could be attacked physically by a telepathically-controlled thrall. Too many things could go wrong, risking his life and sanity on a desperate gamble; they'd told him that, if he wanted, the whole press conference could be cancelled at the last minute. The President could still back out.

He shook his head at the thought. The unsigned paper still lay on his desk, legislation that harked back to a far less civilised time. Most telepaths were loyal, or chose to remain out of public life; the actions of a mere handful could not be allowed to condemn the remaining telepaths, or the nature of American society would be undermined completely. The President had promised himself that he would sooner die than sign that bill into law and if it took his death to make it unnecessary, he could cheerfully accept it. His lips quirked in sardonic amusement; maybe *cheerfully* was the wrong word. The President had, as a child, wrestled with the issue of God – as most humans did as they grew up – but he had come to no good answers. If he died today, he would discover the truth.

The intercom pinged. "Mr President," a voice said, "it's time to prepare for the speech."

"Thank you," the President said. Everything he did these days was choreographed, unless there was an emergency to deal with, and his schedule was plotted out weeks in advance. There was an entire team of secretaries charged with keeping the President's appointments calendar. "I'm on my way."

When he stepped out of his office, he was met by four armed soldiers, two of whom were telepaths who had donned their old uniform for the duration of the emergency. The President hadn't liked the thought of being escorted by soldiers – it sent entirely the wrong message to the world – but the Secret Service had insisted. Besides, as they'd pointed out, with Washington under martial law, the world would *expect* the President to be escorted by soldiers. He nodded to the leader and allowed them to escort him down the corridor, ignoring the shocked looks from some of the White House staff. They had been in the building since before his predecessor had taken office and would be there long after he had departed. They, too, would not have expected to see the President escorted by soldiers.

The President fought hard to keep his face impassive, even though he knew that his inner turmoil had to be obvious to the telepaths. Was this how soldiers felt before they went off to battle, or sat in place waiting for the enemy to attack? How did they stand it?

***

I should never have agreed to this, Alice thought, as she stared at the bank of monitors that had been arranged in front of her. The Situation Team, a fancy term for the team of operators who would run the entire operation, had been united in their horror at the whole proposal. Even the ones who admired the President for even considering it had been horrified, knowing that far too much could go wrong. Alice had ruthlessly weeded out the timid and the incompetent and those that remained were not shy about sharing their opinions.

Alice watched the screens and shivered. No one knew it – they hoped – but the White House was surrounded by remotely-controlled sensors and security measures. High overhead, four UAVs, so high that they couldn't be seen with the naked eye, were tracking everyone who moved in the open, while tiny robots designed to look like birds or insects provided ground-level coverage. The designers had boasted that nothing, not even an insect, could move without being noted and logged by the system; indeed, they'd had to dial the sensitivity back a little after discovering that it also tracked birds and insects. The testers had had the fright of their lives when, during the early testing period, they had turned the machine on, only to have it scream a warning about incoming missiles and enemy ground forces. It had taken several days of careful experimentation before they discovered the truth.

"You're a madman," she'd said, when Art had finally told her what he had in mind. The argument hadn't destroyed their relationship – at least, she *hoped* it hadn't destroyed their relationship – but it had certainly damaged it. It wasn't just Art's career and the President's life that was at stake, not here; it was the future of the Telepath Corps itself. She knew that the new kid on the intelligence block had enemies, from the older more established institutions to the politicians who feared and distrusted all telepaths. A failure might lead to the Telepath Corps being dissolved before it had even a chance to become established.

"There isn't a choice," Art had countered. "We have to take them all out now, before they have a chance to regroup."

Alice had been forced to concede, reluctantly. The police spies and informers within the underground had been rooted out and killed – apparently, the only one spared had been the one Elizabeth Tyler had moved to save – but the FBI was still picking up rumours of weapons being shipped into

Washington and whispers of grand plans against the military forces in the city. They would have to be insane to try anything, yet she knew, better than anyone else, that a telepath could manipulate someone until they no longer knew the difference between black and white, or right and wrong. And, even after the riot, the military presence on the streets was unpopular. If it hadn't been for the last disaster, half of Washington would be on the streets, demanding an end to military occupation.

She looked up at one particular screen. The tiny robot was watching the recovery effort outside the White House, where the riot had taken place. She knew that the bodies had been recovered, some mutilated in ways that had made hardened police and emergency service workers sick, and taken away, but the remainder of the scene was still horrifying. She'd seen nightmarish sights when despotic rulers had turned on their people, when they had stood up to demand a better way of life, yet this was far worse, as it had taken place in America. How could it have come to this?

***

Check in, Art ordered, silently. There were twenty-seven telepaths, wearing civilian clothes, within the approaches to the White House. No one knew it, outside the security services, but everyone who should have been in the area had been tagged and was being monitored by the security network. The whole system had some pretty dire civil liberties implications, yet Art found it hard to care. They would have to deal with it later, once Leo and his band of rogue telepaths were captured or exterminated.

The mental link between the Telepath Corps members had grown stronger after the riot in Washington, as if they were taking refuge in one another. That had implications of its own, but there was no time to investigate, at least not until the plan had succeeded – or failed. Art knew that few junior officers would have called their superiors idiots to their faces – at least not if they wanted to keep their careers – yet telepathic rapport made it impossible to hide what one person thought of another. They had been united in their horror at the whole plan, just like everyone else, and Art had been their target. He'd been called everything under the sun.

He listened as – one by one – the telepaths acknowledged that they were in position and ready to act. With no way to know how Leo would choose to attack, or what weapon he would use, Art had spread his men out to cover all of the approaches. They were backed up by an astonishing array of firepower and surveillance devices, including some that Art wished he'd had in Iraq or Afghanistan. They would have made fighting the insurgency much easier. Now, of course, there was nothing Leo could do to affect them, or the minds of the men behind them. Most of them were actually hundreds of miles away, safe in military bases and guarded by other telepaths.

The reporter bastards are coming, one of the other telepaths sent. Art couldn't blame him for the disdain – reporters were rarely friends to the military, greeting their statements with artful disbelief while accepting enemy propaganda without question – but it wasn't helpful, at least not at the moment. The media was still reeling from a scandal caused by a reporter who had developed telepathic abilities and used them to reveal secrets many celebrities would have preferred to remain buried. It reminded Art of Senator Walker and his blackmailer, a matter Art had had to put aside until after Leo was captured. At least they could be fairly certain that Leo had nothing to do with that. He hadn't escaped the Zeller Institute until after the blackmailer had already got his hooks into the victim.

Keep an eye on them, Art sent back. Telepathic communication, even between trained telepaths, always carried an undertone of underlying thoughts and feelings. The Telepath Corps would probably end up as an association of equals, something that could never be tolerated in the regular armed forces or even in the intelligence services. *There are few places for Leo and his band of scumbags to operate here.*

He smiled. The government, in the name of public safety, had evacuated most of the area after the riot, although a handful of citizens had insisted on remaining in their homes and defying the terrorists. The entire area was seeded with remote drones and sensor platforms. He doubted that Leo could get close without being detected, no matter how good he was at being invisible. There was no way to fool a mechanical device.

***

Roger shivered as he walked towards the White House with a handful of other reporters, those brave – or foolish – enough to return to the scene of the crime. He'd spent several hours lying on a friend's sofa, feeling as if his body was going to shake itself to death as it slowly burnt out all the fear and panic he'd felt. The memories of what had happened during the riot had faded slightly, much to his relief. He didn't want to confront it, even though the company psychologist had offered to schedule free sessions. Besides, the company's psychologist kept talking about man's inner child and how to release it. For Roger, whose childhood held nothing he wanted to remember, that was enough to put him off psychologists for life.

"I heard that the President is going to order all telepaths executed," another reporter whispered, as if he was sharing a dark secret. Roger shrugged. That 'secret' had been out in the open for days, just another rumour slipping out of emergency sessions in both Congress and the Senate. Roger wasn't impressed. It seemed to him that even if every telepath in the world was to be killed, there would just be a second crop of telepaths soon afterwards – and they would know what had happened to their predecessors. There would be a second, far less merciful, war. "No one likes it, but they see no other choice."

"I doubt it," another reporter added. "They couldn't do that, not with the logjam in the House. I heard that the GOP is planning to introduce a bill banning all telepaths from every state but Alaska. They're all going to be going north."

"I heard that the representatives from Alaska are fighting against it," a third reporter said. Roger wasn't amused. Like the rest of the world, the reporters knew nothing, but rumours and innuendo. "They don't want to be known as the telepath state. Come to Alaska, the PR dudes will say, and have your mind read. The tourist trade will be fucked up six ways from Sunday."

"That might not happen," the first reporter pointed out. "There's that weird little trend from the S&M scene for having a telepath take control of some idiot submissive. Perhaps they'll end up turning Alaska into a paradise for weird mental games and activities."

Roger snorted. "I wouldn't say that near anyone from Alaska," he warned. "They won't see the funny side."

***

The President felt cold as he stepped out into the open air. After being elected President, he had received more than a million death threats in the period between his election and his inauguration alone. He had known that he had made himself a target for every weirdo with a grudge, from the used car salesmen who couldn't make a profit to the fringe groups that believed that all a man needed to live was religion and a gun. And every terrorist in the world would be gunning for him. His mind felt empty, as if he were watching himself from a far distance, the words of his speech long forgotten.

He was barely aware of the reporters in front of him, just behind the line of Marines. They weren't Marines, even though a carefully-worded news report claimed that they were Marine reservists, who had been called up after the disaster in Washington. They were telepaths, wearing ill-fitting Marine uniforms, ready to act to protect the President if necessary. He'd wanted real Marines, but it had been pointed out that having armed men with no mental defences around him was asking for disaster. The President stepped up onto the stage, knowing that the entire world could see him now. How many of them, he wondered, were about to watch a President die?

"My fellow Americans," he began...

***

Art wasn't listening to the speech. His combat instincts, instincts he'd honed in Afghanistan, were sounding the alert, warning him that something was badly wrong. He could see nothing wrong and there was no sign of trouble, yet something was definitely out of kilter. Frowning, he keyed his radio and sent an alert through the network to Alice, even as he started to look for trouble. Something was definitely wrong...

A moment later, he felt it, a mental field that was trying to interfere with his own. It was powerful, yet strangely sloppy, as if the designer was so confident in his own abilities that he had missed a few vital components. Art knew, instantly, who had designed the field and united the minds of his fellow telepaths to produce it. He knew who it had to be.

General alert, he broadcast. Every friendly telepath in the area would hear it. *They're here*!

Chapter Thirty-Three

Iranian telepaths were the spearhead of a successful coup against the Mullahs, who had declared telepathy immoral and ordered that all telepaths be put to death by the religious police. The new regime promised to open its borders, develop democratic institutes and eventually a rule of law. Unconfirmed reports from Tehran claim that former regime loyalists, radical mullahs and corrupt government officials are being ruthlessly purged by the new regime. Thousands are attempting to flee to Iraq or Pakistan, fearing for their lives and – in some cases – their foreign bank accounts.

-AP News Report, 2015

"Mr. President, get down!"

The President had no time to react before he was tackled by one of the telepaths, who knocked him to the ground and lay on top of him. He'd gone through emergency drills before, where the Secret Service had tried to prepare him for the day an assassin got through the perimeter and tried to kill him, but it was still a terrible shock. He hit the ground hard enough to stun, yet part of his mind kept calm and active. It was pure self-preservation. Losing his grasp on what was going on might get him killed. It might even end his political career.

"Stay down," his bodyguard whispered. "They're closing in on us."

***

"I can't find them," one of the operators said. Alice sensed the desperation in his voice and shared it. The President's life and the future of the Telepath Corps – the future of America itself – was at stake, yet they couldn't locate the threat. "They're hiding themselves somehow..."

"Got them," another operator said. "Three of the reporters are not the people they were claiming to be."

Alice cursed. They'd taken every precaution, or so she'd thought, and the enemy had still managed to get into the perimeter. How the hell had they done it? She shook her head, putting the thought aside for the moment. They would solve that mystery once Leo and his gang were safely in custody, or dead.

"Art, it's Alice," she said. "I'm uploading the details to your terminal now. Go get them, tiger."

"Understood," the reply came. "We're moving in now."

***

Roger blinked in surprise as the President was knocked to the ground by a hulking bodyguard in an ill-fitting uniform. A moment later, the fake Marines – if they were real Marines he would have been astonished, as he was sure that no one who had ever been through Marine training would ever slouch while on duty – turned and lifted their weapons, pointing towards the reporters. Others came running from all over the place, carrying their own weapons, even though there was no apparent threat. Roger stared, unsure what was going on, or of what he should do. It almost seemed as though the journalists were about to be shot down on the spot.

"Hands in the air," the leader bellowed. Roger, shocked beyond words, complied with the shouted command. The Marines looked nervous, with itchy trigger fingers. It dawned on him that he could get shot and he concentrated on looking as harmless as possible, even though he was terrified. He'd been at Harvard and the Washington riot, but this looked even more threatening. "Spread out and – no, don't move!"

Three of the reporters were moving suddenly. Roger saw one of them and froze as a chill ran down his spine. He had thought that he had known the reporters, but he saw now that they hadn't been who they claimed to be. They'd been telepaths posing as reporters, using a low-level mental field to convince the reporters to accept them naturally, without panicking or trying to sound the alarm. He sensed, somehow, a sudden wave of mental force directed at the Marines, which was effortlessly dispelled by a second wave of mental force. The Marines, he saw now, were telepaths themselves. The Telepath Corps had used Roger and his fellow reporters – and the President himself – as bait in a trap.

He tried to move, to lash out at the rogue telepaths, but he was unable to even twitch. The mental battle held him and the other reporters frozen; the rogue telepaths, he realised with an involuntary shudder, were using him as a human shield. They had to know that they couldn't escape, but somehow they seemed unwilling to give up and just surrender. The mental pressure in Roger's head grew stronger. How long would it be before he felt mental whispers reaching into his mind, turning him against the Telepath Corps and turning him into yet another mental slave?

"Give up," one of the telepaths said. "You can't escape."

"You should be with us," one of the rogues countered. He sounded as if it was a struggle to breathe, let alone to speak, but then there were only three rogues against nearly thirty telepaths from the Telepath Corps. "You could join us and..."

"No," the telepath said. "You need to give up, now."

****

Art held back from the mental gestalt, watching as the rogue telepaths were trapped in a web of mental force. He wondered if Leo – if it was Leo there – appreciated the irony. He and his fellow terrorists had pioneered the technique, which allowed a number of weaker telepaths to ally their mental powers and crush the opposition. Now, the Telepath Corps used it to hold the rogues in place. The rogues were tough – and confident in their own superiority, which made them tougher – but they couldn't stand up forever.

He scowled. Intentionally or otherwise, the rogues had taken the reporters hostage. Art wasn't immune to the common military belief that the only good reporter was a dead one, but dead reporters would make for bad press. The reporters had almost no mental defences at all, leaving them caught in the mental crossfire, which might lead to mental damage. The whole battle had to be ended soon.

"Snipers; take aim," he ordered. It was an unnecessary order, yet it had to be spoken aloud, just to confirm that the snipers were in place. The USMC had placed forty snipers in Washington, waiting patiently for their chance to shoot a few terrorists. Art hadn't been blind to the dangers of including snipers in the defence plans, but there had been no other choice. "Prepare to open fire."

The rogues sensed the snipers taking aim and reacted, precisely as he had hoped. They pushed out a wave of mental force, hoping to overwhelm the gestalt by sheer power. It wasn't enough; the gestalt pushed back with all the force of thirty telepaths working in concert. The rogues couldn't pull their own gestalt back into place before it was too late and powerful mental commands froze them solid. The reporters collapsed as the mental crossfire came to an end, several leaking blood from their noses and ears. Art keyed his radio and issued a quick order. The reporters would need medical attention as soon as possible.

He ran over to the three telepaths, who had been quickly bound and secured by their captors, and pulled away the hats they'd worn to add to their disguise. They'd been lucky, he realised sourly, using their clothing to help make their disguise believable. The Secret Service would go ballistic when they realised what had happened. Everyone who came near the President was going to require a deep telepathic peek just to make sure that he wasn't an assassin concealed under a mental shield.

"Leo isn't among them, sir," one of the other telepaths reported. Art scowled. A brief glance revealed no sign of Alvin Greenwood either. "The bastard is probably watching events from a distance."

Art keyed his radio, nodding thoughtfully. The entire area was blanketed in sensors. It would be interesting to see who bolted, or if someone was somewhere they shouldn't be. The telepaths shouldn't be able to fool the machines, even if they could fog the minds behind the machines. The operators should be safe from mental interference, although Art warned himself to be careful. Leo had shown a remarkable talent for pushing his telepathy into the fields of the 'impossible.'

He reached down for one of the captives and pulled him into a sitting position. "I don't have time to bandy words with you," he said, sharply. The rogue telepath looked stunned. Art suspected that he, like Elizabeth, might have been having doubts about the terrorist vocation, although it was clear that he had been a willing participant in an assassination plot. "You either tell us what we need to know, or we form a new gestalt and rip it out of your mind. If that happens, your mind will be destroyed and you'll spend the rest of your life with the mental ability of a baby. It's your choice."

Art leaned closer. "You just tried to kill the President," he said, seeing objections and protests forming on the rogue's face. "No one is going to complain if we rough you up a little before sucking everything worthwhile out of your mind. You're going to go into a secure facility and be used as a test subject for all kinds of dubious experiments, unless you tell us what we want to know."

He watched the rogue struggling for words. Art felt little guilt, or shame; the rogue had decided to join a terrorist group and commit acts of terrorism. Whatever justification he thought he had was hardly important compared to the lives lost – or ruined – at Washington, let alone the economic damage the rogues had caused. And it helped that the rogue had gone to a very liberal college. He probably believed all kinds of lies about the military, including the ones about soldiers being willing to use torture at the drop of a hat and eating babies for breakfast. Art had seen too many self-assured young men come up against a hard dose of reality. He'd break.

"Leo was watching from our base," the rogue finally stammered. His entire body was shaking; Art could pick up a constant refrain of *don't hurt me* running through his mind as his mental shields began to collapse under sheer panic. "He said that he wanted to deploy the others to cause maximum havoc. He said..."

He broke off. "He knows," he added. "My God, he knows..."

Art stumbled backwards as the rogue convulsed, his entire body twisting unnaturally and then falling to the ground, stunned. It didn't take more than a tiny mental probe to realise that Leo, somehow, had reached into his former comrade's mind and scrambled it. Art cursed under his breath and looked at the other two captives, who had also collapsed. They'd all been mentally disrupted and it would be hours before they recovered, if at all.

"Damn it," he swore. "Where is the bastard?"

"You may be in luck," Alice said, through his earpiece. "One of the UAVs is tracking two figures heading away from the White House, heading downtown."

Art *knew* then, with a certainly that refused to brook any contradiction. "Keep tracking them," he ordered. "I'm going after them."

He sprinted down the streets, ignoring the policemen and Marines who had gathered at the edge of the inner perimeter. Art hadn't managed to keep up with his daily run since he'd developed telepathy, but it was still a fair bet that he was quicker than Leo, if not Alvin Greenwood. The earpiece kept whispering in his ear, telling him that the two fugitives were attempting to avoid the ring of steel that made up the outer security zone, yet they couldn't do that as long as they were being tracked. Two more telepaths popped up outside the zone, using their telepathy to spark off a riot, only to be shot down by weapons mounted on one of the UAVs. Their bodies would be picked up later for identification.

"They're ahead of you," Alice said. Art turned the corner and saw them. Leo looked desperate, thinner than he'd been the last time they'd met, but Greenwood looked...amused. A moment later, they formed a gestalt and lashed out at Art, slamming into his mental shields and sending him staggering backwards. "Art?"

Art nodded, congratulating himself on having the foresight to push the limits on practice duels after the encounter with the mind controller. Leo was powerful, all right; perhaps one of the most powerful telepaths in the country, but Art had drilled with telepaths who had originated in rival organisations. The Marine in him had refused to be beaten by a Ranger and vice versa and both of them had risked mental damage while fighting each other. Two untrained telepaths couldn't overwhelm him, even if he couldn't overwhelm them.

"Hold the drones back," he ordered, steadying himself. The two rogues had slowed their assault, perhaps realising that it wasn't going to succeed. Or, he warned himself, perhaps preparing for a more subtle assault. Art raised his voice, hoping to talk some sanity into their heads before it was too late. "You have to know that you're not getting out of here."

"And we won't let you take us in," Leo said. His voice sounded high-pitched, as if he was on the verge of panic. Art felt no sympathy. He'd looked into Leo's background and while he might have felt some sympathy for the young Leo, he felt nothing for the man who had used mundane men and women as tools and victims. Terrorists ruined their own cause when they became terrorists. "You're on the wrong side. How can you fight for a government that intends to exterminate us all?"

Art scowled at him. "There are remote drones orbiting high overhead, controlled from a remote bunker," he said. "If the two of you manage to overwhelm me, they will drop bombs on your head. No telepath ever born has been able to survive a bullet though the head, young man, so tell me – what do you think a bomb will do to you?"

"You're bluffing," Leo said, desperately. "No one would allow you to drop missiles on Washington and..."

"Read my emotions," Art said, dryly. There was nothing worse than a person who forgot what he was and besides, Art was making no attempt to conceal his inner feelings. "You can tell for yourself that I am not lying. Your mad crusade ends now. The only question is if you live long enough to stand trial, or..."

"And you will die as well," Leo said, wildly. "You'll die..."

"Occupational hazard," Art snarled, feeling genuine anger for the first time. "I knew the day that I enlisted in the Corps that I might die in the service of my country. I knew that my ass would be put in danger, I knew that enemies out there might be trying to kill me, I knew that I had sworn to put my life between my country and war's desolation...and silly fucks like you, back home in peace and prosperity, bitch and moan about what we have to do to preserve your peace and prosperity."

He allowed some of the anger to leak into his voice. "Don't you dare talk to me about death," he snapped. He pulled memories out of his head and blasted them towards the two rogues. "I saw the bodies at Washington, the bodies you left in your wake. Now give up or die. I don't have time any longer."

Greenwood moved quickly, almost as quickly as Art himself. He'd been holding a pistol within his coat pocket, an old trick. Before Art could stop him, he turned and fired – at Leo. The rogue telepath leader looked surprised as the bullet blasted through his head, a second before Art drew his own pistol and put a round through Greenwood's arm, sending his pistol clattering to the ground. Greenwood fell backwards, laughing. Art had no time for laughs.

"Why?" he demanded. A nasty thought crossed his mind, but he buried it. "Why did you...?"

Greenwood hit the ground with a gurgle. Art realised in horror that he'd cracked a dummy tooth, one that had released poison into his mouth. The rogue operative was dying right in front of him, taking his secrets to the grave.

"So you will never know," Greenwood gurgled. He was starting to foam at the mouth. "You can take your fucking feelings and..."

Art ran forwards, forgetting his safety. He pressed his hands against the dying man's temples and plunged into his mind. The poison was already sending Greenwood into an uneasy slumber from which he would never awaken, weakening his mental shields and leaving him defenceless. Even so, Art had the uneasy feeling that Greenwood's mind was shattering around him and that he couldn't stay long, or he would be dragged down into darkness with the former terrorist.

Memories flared up around him in a blinding jumble. Greenwood's life was flashing in front of his eyes. The early days at school, the decision to join the army, Ranger School, his recruitment by the CIA, his activities in Iraq, a Kurdish girl who had won his heart, the bitterness of knowing that he'd been betrayed by his own country...and that the betrayal had claimed the life of his girl. And then...a name flashed across his mind. A name that Art recognised, someone very important and dangerous...

And then Greenwood's mind shattered.

He came to several hours later, lying on a hospital bed. Alice was sitting beside him, looking down at him, her eyes bright with unshed tears. Art felt a sudden surge of love for her and reached for her hand, even though he felt too weak to do anything else.

"You idiot," Alice said, after they'd kissed. "What the hell were you thinking?"

Art shrugged, although – if the truth were to be told – he'd never been so badly scared in his life. "We had to know what he knew before he died," he said. "We had to know the truth."

He pulled himself to his feet, feeling his head spinning. "And I have to go," he said, ignoring her objections. "I have to go see a man about a dog."

Chapter Thirty-Four

The President is reported to be unharmed today after an assassination attempt was carried out by the rogue telepaths. The telepaths, who were either captured or killed by the Telepath Corps, are believed to be the last of the telepathic terrorists who fled the burning ruins of the Zeller Institute. The results of their terrorism will, unfortunately, linger on. The President is expected to address the Telepath Crisis in a speech before Congress in two days, although twelve states have already enacted anti-telepath legislation.

-AP News Report, 2015

Senator Wallis was a tall handsome man, wearing a suit that cost more than Art's annual salary and a smile that made people want to trust him. Art disliked him on sight, not least because he could tell that the smile was faked, even without telepathy. A few years of dealing with citizens who saw and heard nothing while terrorists were operating near their homes gave soldiers a strong nose for bullshit. He could see why Senator Wallis was popular, although he did wonder what his supporters would have thought if they'd realised that the anti-telepath senator had a very low-level telepathic gift himself. His mind was a closed book.

"I appreciate you seeing me on such short notice," Art said. It had been easy, if slightly unethical. He'd rung the doorbell, used a mental compulsion field to convince the senator's bodyguards that they were looking at an FBI pass and then to convince the senator's personal assistant that he needed to see the senator instantly. The senator had accepted the word of his PA, even though Art suspected that she served him in ways that weren't normally included on a job description. Her breasts, too large and shapely to be natural, revealed too much about the senator's preferences. "It is quite important."

"Not at all," Wallis said, genially. "It is always a pleasure to help a man from the FBI."

Art smiled. "And it is always a pleasure to meet an elected representative of the people," he said. "They always reflect so well upon their constituents."

Wallis narrowed his eyes, as if he suspected that he was being mocked. "You will understand, of course, that there are many demands on my time," he said, coldly. "I'm afraid that I can only spare you a few minutes without you making a proper appointment."

"Minutes are all I need," Art said. He checked the device in his pocket – an NSA-designed hacking terminal that had deactivated all of the surveillance gear in the room – and looked up at Wallis. "It's about Alvin Greenwood, and Leo Davidson, and Professor Zeller, and Senator Walker...and how they all interact."

The senator, he noted, seemed unmoved by the list of names, but his mental shields had tightened. "I'm afraid that I have little to contribute to your investigation," Wallis said, stiffly. "I know Walker professionally, of course, and I saw Professor Zeller when he addressed Congress on the subject of active civilian telepaths, but the other two are strangers to me."

"Oh, I think otherwise," Art said. He smiled inwardly at the senator's reaction. Even his tough mental shields couldn't keep a hint of fear from leaking through into the open. "You see, from the start things didn't seem to quite make sense. How could Leo, a naive student who mistook intellect for capability, manage to hide so long from us? What was Alvin Greenwood doing posing as Cyrus Valentine? How could the Church of the Rapturous Awakening obtain the illegal assault rifles and other surplus military equipment that they used to attack the Zeller Institute? And why, if Senator Walker was being blackmailed, did his blackmailer shift from demanding money to demanding political favours?"

"I am not here to be your Watson," Wallis said, calmly. "I think you had better leave now, while you still have your career."

"I think not," Art said, sharply. "We have so much more to discuss."

"Unless you want to be cleaning the director's toilets tomorrow," Wallis snapped, "I suggest that you leave..."

Art ignored him. "As long as Leo was in charge of the rogue telepaths, no explanation seemed to make sense," he said. "But if we factor in Greenwood – a former CIA operative who had gone rogue – we see the signs of an alliance that transformed Leo from a student to someone who could be very dangerous, someone with a brain and a cause. And yet, what did Leo actually accomplish? Very little, in real terms; all he really did was to convince most of the public that telepaths were dangerous and unsafe to have around. I know that terrorists are hardly the most intelligent people in the world, but it was unusually stupid.

"And even if Leo was dumb enough to believe that wanton destruction would get him what he wanted, Greenwood would know better," Art continued. "They would have to move from an insurgency force to one that actually took and held ground, except they didn't..."

"Because they were wiped out by the Telepath Corps," Wallis pointed out.

"Their actions in Washington were foolish," Art countered, smiling inwardly. Wallis was being drawn into the discussion now, rather than screaming for his bodyguards to evict the unwanted intruder. "They accomplished the exact opposite of what they were meant to accomplish. And a suspicious mind like me might start wondering what they *really* meant to accomplish.

"And then there's the question of Greenwood himself. How was he able to operate in America without being caught? Answer; someone politically powerful, with clients at all levels, was able to smooth the way for him. And Greenwood has been in the arms smuggling trade for a long time. It would be easy for him to get those weapons to the Church of the Rapturous Awakening. And, in exchange, the Church would be willing to do anything for him. He was, after all, the one bringing them the weapons they would need to resist the godless liberals when they came to burn the churches and destroy all religion."

Wallis scowled at the mockery, but said nothing.

"It must have been a real stroke of luck," Art continued, "when Greenwood developed telepathy. All of a sudden, he was able to help root out the FBI's operatives within the Church and isolate them, quite without them realising what had happened. And, a little later on, it was Greenwood who scanned Senator Walker and discovered that the Senator could be blackmailed. That was a second stroke of luck, because Walker had been appointed to the Telepath Corps Commission."

He grinned. "I traced back the payments made to the blackmailer," he added. "They were all electronic – and they were all bootstrapped through a dozen different sites and banks until they all arrived in a charity donation box. Most blackmailers want money, yet this one seemed content merely to torment the poor senator. Until, at least, the time came to demand a political favour, to insist that a certain vote went a certain way. Why would that be, I wonder?"

"I am not here to do your job for you," Wallis said, icily. Art could sense the fear underlying his words. "Why do you think it would be?"

"The blackmailer wanted a vote on telepaths to go a certain way," Art said. "Leo and his gang of rogue telepaths created all the public horror and anger anyone could need if they wanted to create new anti-telepath legislation. Most people act according to their own self-interest, but neither Leo nor Greenwood did – or did they? Who were they working for that made it so important to convince the world that telepaths weren't to be trusted?"

He leaned forward. "Who benefits, Senator? Who profits from everything that happened over the last few months? Who comes out ahead in the political struggle over telepaths and the Telepath Corps?

"You do."

Wallis stood up, so quickly that he almost knocked his chair over backwards. "Are you telling me," he demanded, "that you have come into my house with a cock and bull story about me being the only one who benefits from suppressing telepathic terrorists?"

"Sit down," Art snapped. "You want to be President. Right from the start, you have been advocating and demanding tougher laws to put telepaths under government control. You called in every favour you were owed to ensure that you got one of the coveted seats on the Telepath Corps Commission – and Senator Walker, who was your political rival, was under your thumb. That gave you two votes out of three, enough to dominate and control the Telepath Corps. And your stance on anti-telepath legislation is well known and very popular. You could look forward to becoming President, after having solved the crisis you decided to create."

"I have never heard such nonsense in my life," Wallis said. "Do you really believe that anyone will actually believe such a...*stupid* story? I would be throwing away my political career if even a *whiff* of such a dumbass stunt got out into the media. Your director will be hearing from me..."

"I think that that is unlikely," Art said. He dropped the telepathic haze he'd generated to prevent the senator from recognising him. "You see, I peeked into Greenwood's skull before he died. You met him just after the disaster in Iraq; you promised him help and support...what would you have done, I wonder, if telepaths had never come into existence?"

"And such evidence is hardly actionable," Wallis hissed. "The laws I designed myself will make it impossible to bring it before a court."

"Maybe," Art conceded. It was a telling point. "Why?"

Wallis blinked. "What do you mean – why?"

"Why did you do it?" Art asked, honestly curious. "Why did you create the crisis in the first place? Did you want power, or...what?"

Wallis scowled at him, and then clearly decided to be honest. "You must realise that the world is the way it is because of a complex interlocking of factors," he said. "If you introduce something new, for whatever reason, the world changes – and you might not like the result. Think about what might happen if the oil companies were suddenly forced out of business by the discovery of a kind of substitute oil. Millions would be forced out of work and there would be a massive economic crash.

"And telepaths are something new! The human mind is the last true refuge of privacy in the world. Until you and your kind came along, even the lowest prisoner in a foreign jail could be comforted by the privacy of his own mind. The mere introduction of telepaths reshapes the world – telepaths would start using their powers for their own advantage, while non-telepaths would fear and hate them because of what they can do. Do you understand that?

"Any new change must be controlled and guided smoothly towards integration into human society," Wallis added, sharply. "I wanted a strong governmental project to control telepaths to prevent them from tearing our society apart."

"You seem to have failed," Art observed archly. "Your stooges have wreaked vast economic and social damage..."

"The damage can be repaired," Wallis said. "This is a great country. We survived the British, the French, and the Native Americans, the Mexicans, the Germans, the Japanese and even ourselves in the Civil War. We'll survive telepaths too."

"And you wanted to be President," Art said. "I'm sure that the prospects for personal advancement suggested themselves to you."

Wallis shrugged. "What other ambition does everyone elected into power have?"

"I imagine the thought of doing your duty by your country never crossed your mind," Art observed. "You know, back when I was a kid, my teacher used to tell me that in America anyone could grow up to be a Senator. Looking at you, I'm starting to worry that the old bag was right."

Wallis flushed. "So what are you going to do now?" he demanded. "There is no way that you can prove any of this..."

Art allowed himself a smile as the trap was sprung. "Every telepath in the Telepath Corps has been watching through my eyes," he lied. Wallis stared at him in disbelief. "Do you know how many witnesses to your confession that is? Enough to convince even the most hardened judge and bribed jury that you're guilty. Not that it will get that far, I imagine, not once Senator Walker discovers who was blackmailing him and why."

Wallis cut his losses with a single sharp movement. "What do you want?"

"I'd like nothing better than for you to stand trial for what you have done," Art said. "I know that that won't happen, so...I want you to resign your office, retire back to your hometown and stay out of politics. I want you to be *completely* out of politics. You will be watched for the rest of your life and – well, let's just say that if you step back into politics, a small brown envelope will be delivered to the right journalist."

He smiled. "Do you understand me?"

"You asshole," Wallis said. Oddly, Art had the sense that it was the first completely honest thing the Senator had said. "You're undermining the Constitution with this bullshit..."

"Perhaps," Art said, tiredly. "Or perhaps I am repairing it. I doubt that the Founding Fathers ever envisaged a day when one of the country's foremost senators would commit an act of treason that would make Benedict Arnold look like a rank amateur."

He shrugged. "The choice is yours," he said. "I'll show myself out."

***

"My Fellow Americans," the President said. He was speaking to a packed Congress, but he knew that television cameras were broadcasting his speech live to the American people. He just wished that he had better news for them. "It has been a tragic few months. We have seen telepathic powers used for great evil, causing the deaths of thousands of innocents and wreaking economic havoc on the whole country. It is easy for us to take refuge in rage, to lash out at telepaths – all telepaths – in the hope that it will satisfy our desire for bloody revenge. We have seen scenes across the country where a few of our citizens, motivated by fear or rage or even bloodlust, have attempted to take matters into their own hands. We all understand, even if we don't want to admit it, where such feelings come from. We all understand the darkness that lies within the human soul.

"But telepaths were also responsible for ending the career of a telepath who believed that he and those who followed him were superior to everyone else," the President continued.

"Fifteen telepaths gave their lives to stop Leo Davidson and his rogues. Others have served their country in their own way. I have seen young men and women risk their lives to save others, to stop terrorists or to find missing or trapped children, or to plunge into the minds of traumatised patients and help bring them back to themselves. Telepaths have had many positive effects on our lives, as well as negative effects.

"I could tell you about the young medical telepath who helps doctors with children. I could tell you how hard it is to know where a child is in pain. A baby cannot explain to us, in words we can understand, where he is in pain, but a telepath can. I could tell you about the telepaths who work with the fire departments to watch for people trapped in a burning building. I could tell you about the telepaths who work in business, helping to keep the business world honest, or the telepaths who help couples to reconcile. I could tell you so many positive stories...

"And yet," he said, "all of those stories would not stop the fear. Fear corrodes; it wears away at what we are, stripping us down to base humanity. It is the fear that tells us to lash out at the telepath, be they friendly and patriotic or evil terrorists intent on bringing down the world. We fear, with good reason, the prospect of a mental police, of having our minds ransacked and used against us, or being turned into the puppets of mentally-superior people. Cold logic is no defence against such fear.

"The introduction of telepaths has caused this fear; we can only deal with it on those terms.

"The bill passed through Congress yesterday and ratified by the Senate is a step down a very dangerous path. It singles out telepaths as having been born bad, as being *inherently* wrong; as such, it is a gross offence against everything our country stands for. It should never have been proposed, or considered, let alone signed. In an ideal world, it would have been thrown out without debate, yet it passed. There was no choice, but to pass it. It is a terrible thing that we are doing, but there is no choice, not if we wish to preserve our country.

"We will make telepath testing mandatory for every person in the United States," the President said. He looked for

Senator Wallis, who had pushed for such measures from the start, but saw no sign of him. "The telepaths we discover will be given the choice between moving to Alaska or taking drugs designed to suppress telepathic ability. All telepaths who wish to work outside Alaska will be trained to follow regulations designed to prevent abuse of their talent. We will ensure that Alaska is developed; we will ensure that it is far more than a prison, but telepaths will have to live there. Violators will be treated harshly.

"I don't want to do this," he concluded. "It is a violation of everything we believe in, everything that we stand for, and yet we have no choice. Perhaps, in the future, we will come to terms with telepaths and what telepathy implies for us all, but until then..."

He shook his head. "We have no choice, but to do a terrible thing," he concluded. "The Founding Fathers would spit on us."

Epilogue

One year after the establishment of Bester Towns – the name has, alas, stuck – we can safely say that matters have cooled down in the Lower 48. There has been a marked reduction in the number of telepathic crimes, although it is believed that a small number of rogue telepaths have escaped detection and remain active. While Alaska may mourn the arrival of so many telepaths – and civil liberties campaigners may attack legislation specifically focused on telepaths – it appears that the Bester Towns have succeeded in their aim – limiting contact between telepaths and non-telepaths.

-AP News Report, 2016

"Congratulations, Director," Art said.

"Thank you," Alice said. She winked at him. "And congratulations, Mr Operations Director."

Art smiled, ruefully. After Leo and his team of rogues had been hunted down, the Telepath Corps had been reorganised. Alice had been appointed Director, which made her the youngest Director in Washington. She'd commented, in a moment of droll reflection, that she'd probably only got the job because no one actually wanted it. Art himself had been appointed Operations Director, which made him the Field Team Leader. He'd been told that he should remain behind at the office and allow someone younger and more expendable to take the lead, but he had no intention of listening to that. He wasn't an old man yet.

He shook his head. It seemed absurd to think of the Telepath Corps without wondering if they were doing the right thing. Isolating telepaths from the remainder of the general population – for some telepaths, it would help keep them sane, but for the others? He couldn't see how it could fail to breed resentment among telepaths, any more than it had failed to breed resentment among any other targeted population.

Time, he decided, would tell.

***

"I wish I knew what you were thinking," Elizabeth said, sadly. "I wish I could tell you what happened to your wonderful dream."

Professor Zeller didn't move, but then he hadn't moved since the day of the attack on the Zeller Institute. He lay on a bed, surrounded by medical instruments that were monitoring his brain patterns – or lack of them. The coma had swallowed him up and nothing anyone, even a pair of mind healers, had done had been able to free him. His breathing – light, regular patterns – filled the room, yet there was no mind inside the body. Professor Zeller was, to all intents and purposes, dead.

Elizabeth shook her head sadly. Most of the active American telepaths lived in the Bester Towns, the telepathic communities established in Alaska, an isolated region of the Nevada Desert or an island out on the coast. There were even a handful of non-telepaths, the parents of telepathic children who had chosen to follow their children to Alaska, rather than let them be drugged or put into the care of foster parents. It wasn't as if the Telepathic Corps was poor – the Corps hired out telepaths to military and business interests and used the money to fund the Bester Towns – yet there was something depressing about the accommodation. Perhaps it was the fact that, no matter what the President had said, they were prisons. The alternative was being drugged and, it was clear, the drugs sometimes had dangerous side effects.

And she was the greatest prisoner of all.

In the chaos that followed Leo's death, she had half-hoped that she would slip through the net and find a quiet life somewhere away from the rest of the world. Whatever had happened to her powers to invert them had proven impossible to fix, leaving her the only leper among the other telepaths. Elizabeth had no privacy, even among non-telepaths, and had chosen to live away from the Bester Towns. She still wasn't sure if the tolerance granted to her was a reward for turning against Leo or one final twist of the knife. The Telepath Corps regarded her as an embarrassment. The mundane population, had they known who she was, would have wanted her tried for terrorism.

"I wish I'd never met you," she told the silent Zeller. "I wish I'd never even heard about your program, even if it meant a lifetime spent flipping burgers at a fast-food chain. I wish…"

But there was no point in wishing. It never changed the world.

The Bester Towns had defused most of the anti-telepath violence in the remainder of the United States, but even Elizabeth could sense the dull resentment flickering through the telepathic community. In a town where everyone knew what everyone else was feeling – if not thinking – there was little point in trying to hide anything. The telepaths resented what had been done to them in the name of public safety, even though the President had had little choice. His successor, the one who inherited his position, would have to come up with a better solution. And yet, Elizabeth knew that there was no better solution, none that would please everyone. How could there be when there was no trust?

She took one last look at Zeller and walked away, knowing that the handful of nurses in the building would sense her depression when they saw her. By now, she was used to it, even though it felt too much like walking through town naked. It left her caught between two worlds; understanding the hatred and fear of non-telepaths, while resenting the treatment of telepaths to make non-telepaths feel safer. She was the only one of her kind.

Behind her, the machines continued their silent vigil.

The End

Elsewhen Press

an independent publisher specialising in Speculative Fiction

Visit the Elsewhen Press website at elsewhen.press for the latest information on all of our titles, authors and events; to read our blog; find out where to buy our books and ebooks; or to place an order.

The Great Game

Book II of the Royal Sorceress series

After the uprising in London, Lady Gwendolyn Crichton is settling into her new position as Royal Sorceress and fighting the prejudice against her gender and age that seeks to prevent her from fulfilling her responsibilities. But when a senior magician is murdered in a locked room and Gwen is charged with finding the culprit, her inquiries lead her into a web of intrigue that combines international politics, widespread aristocratic blackmail, gambling dens and personal vendettas... and some of her discoveries hit dangerously close to home.

Continuing on from the end of *The Royal Sorceress*, *The Great Game* follows Gwen's unfolding story as she assumes the role formerly held by Master Thomas. A satisfying blend of whodunit and magical fantasy, it is set against a backdrop of international political unrest in a believable yet simultaneously fantastic alternate history.

ISBN: 9781908168375 (epub, kindle)
ISBN: 9781908168276 (400pp, paperback)

Visit bit.ly/TheGreatGame

Necropolis

Book III of the Royal Sorceress series

The British Empire is teetering on the brink of war with France. A war that may, for the first time, see magicians in the ranks on both sides. The Royal Sorceress, Lady Gwendolyn Crichton, will be responsible for the Empire's magical resources when the time comes. Still struggling to overcome prejudice within the Royal Sorcerers Corps, she has at least earnt the gratitude of much of the aristocracy, if not their respect. Just when Gwen needs to be firmly focussed on training new sorcerers, her adopted daughter Olivia, the only known living necromancer, is kidnapped. Her abduction could signal a terrible new direction in the impending war. But Intelligence soon establishes that it was Russian agents who took Olivia, so an incognito Gwen joins a British diplomatic mission to Russia, an uncertain element in the coming conflict. Once she has arrived in St Petersburg, she discovers that the Tsar is deranged and with the help of a mad monk has a plan that threatens the entire world.

Immediately following on from 'The Great Game', 'Necropolis' sees Gwen thrust into the wider international arena as political unrest spreads throughout Europe and beyond, threatening to hasten an almighty conflict. Once again Christopher Nuttall combines exciting fantasy with believable alternate history that is almost close enough for us to touch.

ISBN: 9781908168726 (epub, kindle)
ISBN: 9781908168627 (416pp, paperback)

Visit bit.ly/RSNecropolis

Elsewhen Press

an independent publisher specialising in Speculative Fiction

Bookworm
Christopher G. Nuttall

Elaine is an orphan girl who has grown up in a world where magical ability brings power. Her limited talent was enough to ensure a magical training but she's very inexperienced and was lucky to get a position working in the Great Library. Now, the Grand Sorcerer – the most powerful magician of them all – is dying, although initially that makes little difference to Elaine; she certainly doesn't have the power to compete for higher status in the Golden City. But all that changes when she triggers a magical trap and ends up with all the knowledge from the Great Library – including forbidden magic that no one is supposed to know – stuffed inside her head. This unwanted gift doesn't give her greater power, but it does give her a better understanding of magic, allowing her to accomplish far more than ever before.

It's also terribly dangerous. If the senior wizards find out what has happened to her, they will almost certainly have her killed. The knowledge locked away in the Great Library was meant to remain permanently sealed and letting it out could mean a repeat of the catastrophic Necromantic Wars of five hundred years earlier. Elaine is forced to struggle with the terrors and temptations represented by her newfound knowledge, all the while trying to stay out of sight of those she fears, embodied by the sinister Inquisitor Dread.

But a darkly powerful figure has been drawing up a plan to take the power of the Grand Sorcerer for himself; and Elaine, unknowingly, is vital to his scheme. Unless she can unlock the mysteries behind her new knowledge, divine the unfolding plan, and discover the truth about her own origins, there is no hope for those she loves, the Golden City or her entire world.

Bookworm was Christopher's second fantasy novel to be published by Elsewhen Press, and won the Gold Award in the Adult Fiction category of the 2013 Wishing Shelf Independent Book Awards.

ISBN: 9781908168320 (epub, kindle)
ISBN: 9781908168221 (368pp, paperback)

Visit bit.ly/Bookworm-Nuttall

Elsewhen Press
an independent publisher specialising in Speculative Fiction

A Life Less Ordinary
Christopher G. Nuttall

There is magic in the world, hiding in plain sight. If you search for it, you will find it, or it will find you. Welcome to the magical world.

Having lived all her life in Edinburgh, the last thing 25-year old Dizzy expected was to see a man with a real (if tiny) dragon on his shoulder. Following him, she discovered that she had stumbled from her mundane world into a parallel magical world, an alternate reality where dragons flew through the sky and the Great Powers watched over the world. Convinced that she had nothing to lose, she became apprenticed to the man with the dragon. He turned out to be one of the most powerful magicians in all of reality.

But powerful dark forces had their eye on this young and inexperienced magician, intending to use her for the ultimate act of evil – the apocalyptic destruction of all reality. If Dizzy does not realise what is happening to her and the worlds around her, she won't be able to stop their plan. A plan that will ravage both the magical and mundane worlds, consuming everything and everyone in fire.

Christopher Nuttall has been planning sci-fi books since he learned to read. Born and raised in Edinburgh, Chris created an alternate history website and eventually graduated to writing full-sized novels. Studying history independently allowed him to develop worlds that hung together and provided a base for storytelling. After graduating from university, Chris started writing full-time. As an indie author, he has self-published a number of novels. *A Life Less Ordinary* is his third fantasy novel to be published by Elsewhen Press. Chris is currently living in Borneo with his wife, muse, and critic Aisha.

ISBN: 9781908168337 (epub, kindle)
ISBN: 9781908168238 (336pp, paperback)

visit bit.ly/ALLO-Nuttall

Elsewhen Press

an independent publisher specialising in Speculative Fiction

TimeStorm
Steve Harrison

In 1795 a convict ship leaves England for New South Wales in Australia. Nearing its destination, it encounters a savage storm but, miraculously, the battered ship stays afloat and limps into Sydney Harbour. The convicts rebel, overpower the crew and make their escape, destroying the ship in the process. Fleeing the sinking vessel with only the clothes on their backs, the survivors struggle ashore.

Among the escaped convicts, seething resentments fuel an appetite for brutal revenge against their former captors, while the crew attempts to track down and kill or recapture the escapees. However, it soon becomes apparent that both convicts and crew have more to concern them than shipwreck and a ruthless fight for survival; they have arrived in Sydney in 2017.

TimeStorm is a thrilling epic adventure story of revenge, survival and honour. In the literary footsteps of Hornblower, comes Lieutenant Christopher 'Kit' Blaney, an old-fashioned hero, a man of honour, duty and principle. But dragged into the 21st century… literally.

A great fan of the grand seafaring adventure fiction of CS Forester, Patrick O'Brien and Alexander Kent and modern action thriller writers like Lee Child, Steve Harrison combines several genres in his fast-paced debut novel as a group of desperate men from the 1700s clash in modern-day Sydney.

Steve Harrison was born in Yorkshire, England, grew up in Lancashire, migrated to New Zealand and eventually settled in Sydney, Australia, where he lives with his wife and daughter.

As he juggled careers in shipping, insurance, online gardening and the postal service, Steve wrote short stories, sports articles and a long running newspaper humour column called *HARRISCOPE: a mix of ancient wisdom and modern nonsense*. In recent years he has written a number of unproduced feature screenplays, although being unproduced was not the intention, and developed projects with producers in the US and UK. His script, *Sox*, was nominated for an Australian Writers' Guild 'Awgie' Award and he has written and produced three short films under his *Pronunciation Fillums* partnership. TimeStorm was Highly Commended in the Fellowship of Australian Writers (FAW) National Literary Awards for 2013.

ISBN: 9781908168542 (epub, kindle)
ISBN: 9781908168443 (368pp paperback)

Visit bit.ly/TimeStorm

Elsewhen Press

an independent publisher specialising in Speculative Fiction

GLASS SHORE
STEFAN JACKSON

What if 'Think Differently' was more than a campaign slogan? What if it was part of a mind control network geared towards advanced sciences, creating a vibrant, creative and competitive workforce? This is the world of *Glass Shore*, a dynamic existence featuring fierce vehicles, cruel weapons and serious body augmentation.

Manhattan, 2076. The fabled city of gold realised; a city of dazzling buildings and beautiful people; a city celebrated for converting an obsolete subway system into an adult playground. Manhattanite Nikki's life changes forever when she finds the files labelled 'Project Blue Book appendix 63-A'. The report contains a disc related to the Glass Shore, the horrendous nuclear event at Puget Sound in 2062. Disclosure of these files is not an option, so powerful people want Nikki dead. To protect her Nikki hires Apollo, her long-time friend and lover, who is magnificent at his job. He is also a clothes whore with an honest enthusiasm for life.

Nikki and Apollo are the hottest couple in Manhattan. Betrayed by friends at every turn, set upon by bounty hunters and other elements of security, law enforcement and civil protection, they utilise the best hotels, the sexy Underground and the glorious city of Manhattan as their shield.

Stefan Jackson was born in North Carolina beside the calm eddies of the Trent and Neuse rivers, but spent the latter part of his childhood in southern California. In 1994 he moved to Brooklyn looking for a change, drawn to the energetic confluence of the Hudson and East rivers of the Big Bright City. There he met a lovely woman who became his wife, and they have an enchanting daughter. And a cat.

He now lives in Queens, where he writes stories, plays drums, coaches pee-wee girl's basketball, works the cubicle life, cooks breakfast, rides the F line, laughs and rests his head in the land of jazz.

Stefan says "Cheers to the first fifty years. Hoping the next fifty are just as kind."

ISBN: 9781908168580 (epub, kindle)
ISBN: 9781908168481 (288pp paperback)

Visit bit.ly/GlassShore

Elsewhen Press

an independent publisher specialising in Speculative Fiction

BOOK 1 OF THE BLUEPRINT TRILOGY

FUTURE PERFECT

KATRINA MOUNTFORT

The *Blueprint* trilogy takes us to a future in which men and women are almost identical, and personal relationships are forbidden. Following a bio-terrorist attack, the population now lives within comfortable Citidomes. MindValues advocate acceptance and non-attachment. The BodyPerfect cult encourages a tall thin androgynous appearance, and looks are everything.

This first book, *Future Perfect*, tells the story of Caia, an intelligent and highly educated young woman. In spite of severe governmental and societal strictures, Caia finds herself becoming attracted to her co-worker, Mac, a rebel whose questioning of their so-called utopian society both adds to his allure and encourages her own questioning of the status quo. As Mac introduces her to illegal and subversive information she is drawn into a forbidden, dangerous world, becoming alienated from her other co-workers and resmates, the companions with whom she shares her residence. In a society where every thought and action are controlled, informers are everywhere; whom can she trust?

When she and Mac are sent on an outdoor research mission, Caia's life changes irreversibly.

A dark undercurrent runs through this story; the enforcement of conformity through fear, the fostering of distorted and damaging attitudes towards forbidden love, manipulation of appearance and even the definition of beauty, will appeal to both an adult and young adult audience.

Katrina Mountfort was born in Leeds. After a degree in Biochemistry and a PhD in Food Science, she started work as a scientist. Since then, she's had a varied career. Her philosophy of life is that we only regret the things we don't try, and she's been a homeopath, performed forensic science research and currently works as a freelance medical writer. She now lives in Saffron Walden with her husband and two dogs. When she hit forty, she decided it was time to fulfil her childhood dream of writing a novel. *Future Perfect* is her debut novel and is the first in the *Blueprint* trilogy.

ISBN: 9781908168559 (epub, kindle)
ISBN: 9781908168450 (288pp paperback)

Visit bit.ly/Blueprint-FuturePerfect

Elsewhen Press

an independent publisher specialising in Speculative Fiction

DANDELION TRILOGY
MIKE FRENCH

Literary surrealism, contemporary fantasy, biting satire, dystopian science fiction. The Dandelion Trilogy by Mike French is all of these and more. Starting with *The Ascent of Isaac Steward*, this is literary surrealism at its most profound. A contemporary fantasy that follows one man's journey into his own mind as he struggles to come to terms with the trauma that has reshaped his life and starts to question his own existence. Moving forward to 2034 in *Blue Friday*, this biting satire warns of a Britain where overtime for married couples is banned, there is enforced viewing of family television (much of it repeats of old shows from the sixties and seventies), monitored family meal-times and a coming of age where twenty-five year-olds are automatically assigned a spouse by the state computer if they have failed to marry. Only the Overtime Underground network resists with the illicit Avodah drug to increase productivity. Finally *Convergence* delivers us into a truly dystopian future, where a covert military/governmental project uses prisoners on death row to explore what happens to people as they die, downloading the Convergence Point formed in the brain's memory at the point of death into clones. But when combined with Avodah they inadvertently trigger what may be the end of humanity – or a new beginning.

What does it have to do with dandelions? You'll have to read it to find out...

Mike French is the owner and senior editor of the prestigious literary magazine, *The View From Here*. Mike's debut novel, *The Ascent of Isaac Steward* was published in 2011 and nominated for The Galaxy National Book Awards. He currently lives in Luton with his wife, three children and a growing number of pets.

Book 1: The Ascent of Isaac Steward
ISBN: 9781908168351 (epub, kindle)
ISBN: 9781908168252 (224pp paperback)

Book 2: Blue Friday
ISBN: 9781908168177 (epub, kindle)
ISBN: 9781908168078 (192pp paperback)

Book 3: Convergence
ISBN: 9781908168368 (epub, kindle)
ISBN: 9781908168269 (256pp paperback)

Visit bit.ly/DandelionTrilogy

Elsewhen Press
an independent publisher specialising in Speculative Fiction

The Magician in the Attic

Caspian

The first of the Curlew Chronicles

The Curlew Chronicles series opens with *The Magician in the Attic*, a story about Alexander Roebuck, a young magician coached by a mysterious recluse called Francis Curlew. Just before his fourteenth birthday, Alex first comes to the attention of the legendary Curlew and is taken under his wing.

Like any other fourteen year-old, Alex has to contend with all that family, friends, school and the local busy-bodies throw at him. If he is to realise his dream of being a renowned illusionist, he must respect the older man's seemingly strange obsession with privacy and seclusion. He wants to learn from his mentor more than anything else, but that means hours of practice, keeping secrets from his mum and his best friend, and gaining experience in (mis)directing the attention of an audience. Alex soon persuades his teachers to let him perform some illusions as part of the forthcoming school play. Is he ready for the audience… and are they ready for him?

Caspian is a thirty-something UK-based illusionist. His style of both writing and performing smacks of the classics with his own modern twist. Approaching twenty years in the magic and deception business led naturally to writing fiction with some deceptive twists and turns.

Originally from Bristol his work has taken him all over the world and he is always on the lookout for the next original idea for an illusion or a plot twist that hasn't been done before. Outside of work his passions include his faith, steampunk and other Victorianisms, pool, movies and having a near full glass in a near empty bar.

ISBN: 9781908168528 (epub, kindle)
ISBN: 9781908168429 (352pp paperback)

Visit bit.ly/MagicianInTheAttic

Elsewhen Press

an independent publisher specialising in Speculative Fiction

THE RHYMER
an Heredyssey
DOUGLAS THOMPSON

The Rhymer, an Heredyssey defies classification in any one literary genre. A satire on contemporary society, particularly the art world, it is also a comic-poetic meditation on the nature of life, death and morality.

A mysterious tramp wanders from town to town, taking a new name and identity from whoever he encounters first. Apparently amnesiac or even brain-damaged, Nadith Learmot nonetheless has other means to access the past and perhaps even the future: upon his chest a dial, down his sleeves wires that he can connect to the walls of old buildings from which he believes he can read their ghosts like imprints on tape. Haunting him constantly is the resemblance he apparently bears to his supposed brother, a successful artist called Zenir. Setting out to pursue Zenir and denounce or blackmail him out of spite, in his travels around the satellite towns and suburbs surrounding a city called Urbis, Nadith finds he is always two steps behind a figure as enigmatic and polyfaceted as himself. But through second hand snippets of news he increasingly learns of how his brother's fortunes are waning, while his own, to his surprise, are on the rise. Along the way, he encounters unexpected clues to his own true identity, how he came to lose his memory and acquire his strange 'contraption'. When Nadith finally catches up with Zenir, what will they make of each other?

Told entirely in the first person in a rhythmic stream of lyricism, Nadith's story reads like Shakespeare on acid, leaving the reader to guess at the truth that lies behind his madness. Is Nadith a mental health patient or a conman? ... Or as he himself comes to believe, the reincarnation of the thirteenth century Scottish seer True Thomas The Rhymer, a man who never lied nor died but disappeared one day to return to the realm of the faeries who had first given him his clairvoyant gifts?

Douglas Thompson's short stories have appeared in a wide range of magazines and anthologies. He won the Grolsch/Herald Question of Style Award in 1989 and second prize in the Neil Gunn Writing Competition in 2007. His first book, *Ultrameta*, published in 2009, was nominated for the Edge Hill Prize, and shortlisted for the BFS Best Newcomer Award. Since then he has published more novels, including *Entanglement* published by Elsewhen Press. *The Rhymer* is his eighth novel.

ISBN: 9781908168511 (epub, kindle)
ISBN: 9781908168412 (192pp paperback)

Visit bit.ly/TheRhymer-Heredyssey

Elsewhen Press

an independent publisher specialising in Speculative Fiction

The Janus Cycle

Tej Turner

The Janus Cycle can best be described as gritty, surreal, urban fantasy. The overarching story revolves around a nightclub called Janus, which is not merely a location but virtually a character in its own right. On the surface it appears to be a subcultural hub where the strange and disillusioned who feel alienated and oppressed by society escape to be free from convention; but underneath that façade is a surreal space in time where the very foundations of reality are twisted and distorted. But the special unique vibe of Janus is hijacked by a bandwagon of people who choose to conform to alternative lifestyles simply because it has become fashionable to be "different", and this causes many of its original occupants to feel lost and disenchanted. We see the story of Janus unfold through the eyes of seven narrators, each with their own perspective and their own personal journey. A story in which the nightclub itself goes on a journey. But throughout, one character, a strange girl, briefly appears and reappears warning the narrators that their individual journeys are going to collide in a cataclysmic event. Is she just another one of the nightclub's denizens, a cynical mischief-maker out to create havoc or a time-traveller trying to prevent an impending disaster?

Tej Turner has just begun branching out as a writer and been published in anthologies, including *Impossible Spaces* (Hic Dragones) and *The Bestiarum Vocabulum* (Western Legends). His parents moved around a bit while he was growing up so he doesn't have any particular place he calls "home", but most of his developing years were spent in the West country of England. He went on to Trinity College in Carmarthen to study Film and Creative Writing, and then later to complete an MA at The University of Wales, Lampeter, where he minored in ancient history but mostly focused on sharpening his writing skills. When not gallivanting around the world trekking jungles and exploring temples, reefs and caves, he is usually based in Cardiff where he works by day, writes by moonlight, and squeezes in the occasional trip to roam around megalithic sites and the British countryside. *The Janus Cycle* is his first published novel.

ISBN: 9781908168566 (epub, kindle)
ISBN: 9781908168467 (224pp paperback)

Visit bit.ly/JanusCycle

About the author

Christopher G. Nuttall has been planning sci-fi books since he learned to read. Born and raised in Edinburgh, Chris created an alternate history website and eventually graduated to writing full-sized novels. Studying history independently allowed him to develop worlds that hung together and provided a base for storytelling. After graduating from university, Chris started writing full-time. As an indie author he has self-published a number of novels, but this is his eight novel to be published by Elsewhen Press. Chris is currently living in Scotland with his wife, muse, and critic Aisha.

www.ingramcontent.com/pod-product-compliance
Lightning Source LLC
Chambersburg PA
CBHW062014190726
48285CB00001BA/280